W9-AZU-318

Time *and* Time Again

Time *and* Time Again

by

JAMES HILTON

An Atlantic Monthly Press Book

Little, Brown and Company · Boston

LIBRARY OF CONGRESS CATALOG CARD NO. 53-7314

ATLANTIC–LITTLE, BROWN BOOKS
ARE PUBLISHED BY
LITTLE, BROWN AND COMPANY
IN ASSOCIATION WITH
THE ATLANTIC MONTHLY PRESS

PRINTED IN THE UNITED STATES OF AMERICA

Contents

Time *and* Time Again

Paris I

TOWARD MIDNIGHT CHARLES ANDERSON FINISHED SOME notes on a talk he had had with a newspaper editor at lunch – nothing very important, but he thought he ought to keep Bingay decently informed. The hour and the completion of the task seemed to call for a drink, so he went to the bathroom for some water and then to his suitcase for the silver flask that he always carried on these junkets and tried to keep replenished. He was not much of a whisky drinker (so he would say of himself when he ordered wine), but he liked a nightcap either in bed before turning out the light or during that last half hour of dressing-gowned pottering when he would tidy up the affairs of the day both in his mind and on his desk. He was tidy by nature, and years of experience had made him save, whenever possible, some small but relaxing job for a final one, even if it were only an entry in his diary or a jotting for the book he was one day going to write.

Tonight, however, there was no doubt as to what the job should be. He had been thinking of it, off and on and with increasing satisfaction, all day; it had been a sort of protective armor at moments when he had needed it. And now, with the drink at his elbow and the sounds of the city pleasantly audible from beyond the closed and curtained windows, he took a sheet of hotel notepaper and wrote:

MY DEAR GERALD,

As you may have seen from the very small print in the

English papers, if you bother with them at all while you're on holiday, I'm with Sir Malcolm Bingay at the Conference here – a rather exacting job, one way and another, and I'll feel relieved when it's over, especially if we get any kind of agreement out of all the talk. Meanwhile there's a more cheerful event next Thursday which I expect is on your mind as well as mine. Do you remember (no, I daresay you were too young) that time at Parson's Corner when I visited you there and the fun we all had making plans for your seventeenth birthday? Anyhow, I'm enclosing a small gift in case you're still in Switzerland on the great day. I believe, though, you talked of returning to England about then, so it occurs to me, why don't you break the journey in Paris? We might see a few sights and have a civilized dinner for once, so let me know the date and time of your train if you can possibly manage it.

Your affectionate father,

Charles

That done, and the envelope addressed care of Thomas Cook's, Lucerne, Charles finished his drink in bed and went quickly to sleep. He was a good sleeper, not because he had nothing to worry about, but because as a rule he had worked hard enough to be tired and conscientiously enough to be untroubled by conscience; lately, though, he had begun to feel sometimes *too* tired. But there need not be much more of it, he consoled himself; he would soon be on pension, and with each recent year ambition had withdrawn less reluctantly from the probably unscalable cliffs and had begun to settle for the long comfortable valley just round the corner.

After a couple of days Charles received a wire sent from Interlaken:

MANY THANKS PARIS OKAY SHALL ARRIVE GARE DE L'EST SEVEN P.M. THURSDAY IF YOU CAN MAKE IT DINNER WILL BE FINE THANKS ALSO FOR SPLENDID CHECK AFFECTIONATELY GERRY

When Charles had digested this he happily made a note in

his engagement book, and then muttered, in the presence of Sir Malcolm Bingay's secretary: "I don't mind 'okay,' but '*make* it' . . . and 'c-h-e-c-k,' cheque. . . . Really . . . hasn't he got over all that yet?"

Charles was a handsome man for his age, which was fifty-two. His hair had turned austerely iron-gray, but without thinning, and since he was something of a gourmet his trim figure offered a special tribute to character and temperament. Most people liked him, including those who would have been astonished if he had ever achieved any sensational success; he never had, so in a sort of way they could like him all the more. Had he been born half a century earlier he would probably not have been nicknamed "Stuffy" by his colleagues; perhaps also in those halcyon days he could hardly have escaped becoming an ambassador or minister in one of the South American or smaller European capitals. "After you're fifty there'll be something wrong with you if you don't get a Legation," he had been told on taking up his first post, but his informant had himself been a minister, who had modestly added, in echo of Lord Melbourne: "There's no damn merit about it that I can see." But perhaps, if not merit, which Charles had possessed, there had been other things, including luck and a *Zeitgeist,* that had counted against him; at any rate, he had not been given a Legation, and for the last year or so had been sticking around at the Foreign Office. This Paris Conference was really the most considerable event that had come his way since the war period, though it was far from being world-shattering, and he surmised that Bingay had taken him along chiefly because the Balkan angle might crop up. So far it hadn't, and Charles wished it would, as a wrestler hopes for a chance to display a hold in which he has long specialized. Charles thought it possible that if the Balkan angle did crop up he might even, in a minor professional way and entirely without headlines, distinguish himself.

That he had been born during the last Victorian decade, instead of the first, was perhaps in some ways a pity, because he had just the right degree of correctness for the older-fashioned diplomat, apart from a very genuine integrity, knack with languages, suave manners, and a pretty if slightly erudite wit. He had also a taste for classical music, detective stories, and dry wines, which aptly counterbalanced his distaste for jazz, modern nondetective fiction, and sweet wines. If you thought him a snob, as some people did, you had to admit that at Schönbrunn or Tsarskoye-Selo or in a first-class compartment on the old chocolate and white London and North-Western Scotch Express (en route for Balmoral) he would have looked the real thing in times when the standards of reality, or perhaps of things, were very different. . . . Anyhow, his career had not been unworthy, and his small dinner parties in various parts of the world had even been notable – until the break in his life that occurred during the Second World War.

It was this, when it came, that had persuaded him to send Gerald, then aged five, to spend the rest of the war years in America. During such a regrettable but prudent exile, Charles had written to his son regularly every week, and once, being on a mission that had sent him across the Atlantic in the autumn of 1941, he had been able to spend a convenient week end with the Fuesslis at Parson's Corner, Connecticut.

The Fuesslis were connections of his wife's – genial people in the wholesale hardware business, comfortably off, and innocent enough to be proud of having an Englishman who was in *Who's Who* as their house guest. They made him as welcome as they had made Gerald, and Charles knew he owed them a debt he could never repay. True, the boy seemed to be acquiring a slight American accent, but perhaps this was unavoidable – he would unlearn it later when he came home, for of course the Germans would be defeated eventually; one took that for granted. For the time being, it had been and still would be undeniably reassuring to think of him safe and sound and well fed, while his father breakfasted on spam and put out incendiary bombs on Whitehall roofs.

Another thing that troubled Charles slightly during his brief visit to Parson's Corner was that the Fuesslis seemed to have odd ideas of how to treat a youngster. On the night that Charles arrived at their house it was doubtless excusable that Gerald should be allowed to stay up past his usual bedtime, but it seemed strange to Charles to have to sit at the dinner table not only with his own youngster but also with the Fuesslis' daughter Louise, aged three. He ascribed it to the kindness of his hosts and the natural good manners of both children that such an extraordinary situation passed without untoward incident.

But an even odder thing happened on the day following. It was a Sunday, and the Fuesslis could think of nothing better to do than drive a hundred miles to nowhere in particular, along roads crowded with other Americans doing the same thing. Charles and Gerald were placed together in the back seat of the Buick, and the boy, who certainly seemed happy enough, pointed out many local landmarks, such as Woodrow Wilson High, the new Sears Roebuck, and the place where a holdup man had recently been shot in a police chase. Toward evening Charles was beginning to feel hungry, the more so as lunch had been of the picnic variety, eaten in the car too hurriedly to be enjoyed. He was still thinking about a good dinner when the car turned into the parking area of what was apparently a large and popular roadside restaurant.

"I hope you like sea food," said Mr. Fuessli, as they walked their way amongst innumerable cars toward an entrance festooned with life belts.

"Sea food? . . . Er . . . fish, that is? Oh yes, I do, indeed." (Which was true enough, though this "sea food" set Charles thinking that he also enjoyed "land food," if such a term could be used to describe a really delicious *entrecôte*, or perhaps the *poulet sauté américain* which was, he supposed, the nearest approach to a national dish.)

"Then I can promise you something worth waiting for," continued Mr. Fuessli, pushing into the lobby.

It soon became clear to Charles that "waiting for" had been no idle phrase; for the place was crowded, the restaurateur did not greet them, no table had been reserved, and there were twenty or thirty patrons standing in line for the next one available.

"I guess you have to stand in line for *everything* in England," said Mrs. Fuessli.

"I believe my housekeeper does it very often," answered Charles, gently.

Not by a word or gesture did he convey his real emotions, and the only additional comment he permitted himself was at the spectacle of so many children waiting – and by no means all of them good-mannered like Gerald and Louise. "These youngsters," said Charles tentatively. "They – er – they don't . . . Their parents, I mean . . . do they – er – take them into dinner here?"

"Sure," answered Mr. Fuessli. "What else can they do with them?"

"They look a little tired – the children, I mean."

"Oh, it's just the drive. Kids love it, anyway. Besides, you can't leave 'em at home without a sitter and you can't always get a sitter, especially on Sundays."

And true enough, when at last their turn came for a table Charles observed that the dining room was quite overpopulated with children – some, like Louise, young enough to occupy high chairs supplied by the restaurant.

"So they *encourage* them to come here?" Charles mused, still grappling with his private astonishment.

"Oh, not by themselves – only with grownups," Mr. Fuessli replied. "Gosh, no – think of what this place would be like if they let the kids come in alone!"

Charles thought of it, and found the speculation indeed appalling. He noted meanwhile that there was even a special children's dinner at half price, which Gerald and Louise both ate with relish. The sea food, incidentally, proved to be excellent, and the California wine that Mr. Fuessli ordered was equal to some Charles had tasted from far more familiar bottles.

Over coffee, which they drank in a hurry because the line in the lobby was still long, Charles was anxious to dispel any impression that he had not thoroughly enjoyed himself. "You mustn't think I don't appreciate your taking Gerald with you like this. It's just that, well, I suppose one gets used to old-fashioned ideas in England — I mean, that children have their meals in the nursery and go to bed soon afterwards . . . and besides, of course, we don't have places like this, even in peacetime."

"Maybe you would have," said Mr. Fuessli, "if there was a demand for them." (He had always found this principle valid in the hardware business.)

"That's very possible," Charles agreed. "And perhaps the truth is that some of us in England are *too* old-fashioned. . . . For instance, I was twenty-one before my own father ever took me out to dinner."

The Fuesslis looked incredulous.

Charles smiled. "Of course that was overdoing it. I'll initiate Gerald much earlier."

"*Initiate* him?" Mrs. Fuessli echoed.

"In a way. After all, there's a good deal of ritual in it — how to explore a French menu, the wines that go best with various foods, clothes to wear on different occasions, what people to tip and how much — quite a lot to learn."

"Don't you think one can pick up things like that without exactly learning them?" asked Mr. Fuessli.

"Better to learn them, then you don't pick them up wrong." Charles did not intend to be either didactic or crushing, but he thought he might have sounded a little of both and it disconcerted him.

Mrs. Fuessli twinkled. "And when do you think Gerry will be ready to start learning?"

"Oh, I'd say when he's at Cambridge — maybe eighteen or nineteen." Charles added, lest he should seem to be taking the whole thing far too seriously: "I'm already looking forward to it — a grand excuse to give myself what Lord Curzon once called a *beahno*."

They did not understand the allusion, so he had to explain that "beano" was a sound, if somewhat proletarian, English word meaning "a good time" (derived from "beanfeast"), but that Lord Curzon, a man of unproletarian perspectives, had assumed from its appearance that the word was Italian, and had therefore pronounced it "bay-ah-no." Charles enjoyed dissecting the joke (for it had always had for him a flavor incommunicable perhaps to those who had not known Lord Curzon professionally); he hoped it might at least convince the Fuesslis that he had a sense of humor. But they merely smiled in a rather vague way, and after a pause Mrs. Fuessli returned to the subject of Gerald's "initiation."

"And where will you go when you first take him to dinner?" she asked. "Have you planned that too?"

"You mean the name of the restaurant? Let's see now . . . might be Michelet's. You know it? You know London? It's near the Covent Garden market. Festive but good."

"Was that where your father took you?"

"Oh no, I don't think Michelet's was in existence then. We just dined at his club and had the ordinary club dinner – nothing special, except for the novelty it was to me."

"But you'd rather have Michelet's for Gerry?"

"*I* would, yes – French cooking for me, any time – even the best London clubs aren't famous for their . . ." He realized that this was dangerous ground; the Fuesslis might think he was dissatisfied with their own table, which he certainly wasn't – after England in wartime it was wonderful. He broke off by adding: "Please don't think this is an old family tradition or anything absurd like that. It's just that as soon as Gerald's old enough there are so many things I'm looking forward to."

He had to break off again because Mrs. Fuessli was giggling and he knew it was at himself. "Oh, do make it *seventeen*–not eighteen or nineteen–when you take him to Michelet's," she pleaded. She looked very impish and provocative in such a mood. "Because he'll grow up fast in America–our boys of seventeen are almost men."

Charles thought that this might possibly be true, if by men she meant (as she doubtless did) American men; and he reflected again how charming she was, and (with a rueful glance at Mr. Fuessli, who was bald and overweight) how secure must be the position of American womanhood.

Mrs. Fuessli then turned to Gerald. "Gerry dear, wouldn't you like to have your dad take you to dinner in a big London restaurant on your seventeenth birthday?"

"Not really *big* — " Charles was murmuring, but Gerald, with his mouth full of chocolate ice cream, was already expressing some kind of inarticulate enthusiasm.

"You see he *would,* Mr. Anderson. . . . Gerry, make sure you remind him when the time comes. . . . *Seventeen,* Mr. Anderson — remember that."

Charles, basking in the thought that Mrs. Fuessli must like him at least enough to make fun of him, felt indulgent, a little puzzled by, but also warm to his hosts. "All right. Seventeen it shall be. Gerald, you and I have a date." He laughed, and hoped the Americanism did not come from him too solemnly.

Hence, in part, the letter Charles wrote to Gerald in Switzerland eleven years later. Of course he had taken the boy out to dinner countless times already, and for that matter Michelet's had gone (victim of a V-2 during the last year of the war); yet the memory of that conversation at Parson's Corner had impressed on Charles an obligation which he assumed all the more gladly because he could call to mind Mrs. Fuessli's pretty face.

Whatever else about him was in doubt, there could be none about his genuine affection for his son. It was not only his deepest emotion, it was his most difficult, and he was a man who found many of his emotions difficult. Actually, the seventeenth birthday dinner soon became far more than a pleasure to be looked forward to; it grew to be a symbol in his mind of something he hoped would eventually flourish — an adult, man-to-man friendship between father and son. During the decade that followed his visit to Parson's Corner, Charles had seen Gerald rather infrequently, even after the boy's return from America, for then had come the school years, with holidays often spent at the homes of school friends, since it was usually impossible to fit them in with Charles's periods of leave. But most of all, he was a shy man with children, and had no knack of dealing with them; he was afraid he bored them, and his unwillingness to do so made him tend to keep out of their way. All of which, in Gerald's case, was surely only temporary. Charles had pinned his faith on some change taking place quite suddenly some day – some liquefaction of his emotions, and of Gerald's, as miraculous as that of the blood of St. Januarius.

And now, in Paris, as he endured long sultry hours at the Conference, his thoughts often wandered to Switzerland, where Gerald was enjoying a walking tour with some friends of his own age, accompanied by a young schoolmaster who presumably had the knack that Charles lacked. Charles envied that schoolmaster, though he would not have changed places with him for the world.

Another man whom Charles would not have changed places with was his opposite number on the other side of the Conference table – a fellow named Palan. Palan's own chief was monolithic and taciturn; unlike Sir Malcolm Bingay he left most of the talking to his subordinate. Perhaps the monolith spoke neither French nor English, Charles could not decide. Nor could he decide whether he himself would like to measure himself in debate against this fellow Palan or not; at times he was glad that Sir Malcolm bore the brunt, but at other times he had a curious desire to justify himself in Palan's eyes – to prove that he too, though only second in command, was just as capable of performing a virtuoso job. Or *was* he just as capable? He kept studying Palan and wondering. Palan had, indeed, begun to fascinate Charles from the opening day of the Conference. He was plump and swarthy, careless of manners, certainly not the kind of person that an old-style diplomat could ever have felt at home with across any kind of table. Nor did Charles; yet he envied the man's animal vitality and impassioned voice that could carry so easily across a room (Charles knew from experience that his own gentler and more pleasing tenor was far less pervasive); he hated Palan's deplorable French accent, yet marveled at his complete lack of embarrassment in exhibiting it—a lack that almost amounted to a skill. Charles had also watched with mixed emotions Palan's habit of loosening his collar when his neck began to sweat, and the way he proudly observed the contents of his handkerchief whenever he noisily blew his nose. "*Vox, et praeterea nihil,*" muttered Charles to Sir Malcolm on one such occasion, hoping his superior would see the little joke. But Sir Malcolm was either not a Latinist or else in a bad humor; he did not even smile.

The trouble was that so far Palan seemed to have scored rather heavily. Even in his bad French he had drawn laughs from the other delegates at the expense of Sir Malcolm, and Sir Malcolm had found it possible to keep his temper in public only by losing it a little in private. Charles had had to endure this too. There were times when he would have been relieved to learn, on rejoining the Conference for another session, that Palan had been run over by a taxi during the interval. And yet . . . in a way he could not exactly analyze, he felt a quality in Palan that made him picture himself victorious, but also magnanimous, over such a foe. . . . He imagined himself saying, at some reception after a draft agreement had been signed on all the terms that Palan's side had at first violently opposed: "I trust, M'sieur Palan, there are no hard feelings between us. For myself, and speaking also on behalf of Sir Malcolm Bingay, who is unfortunately confined to his bed by a severe attack of arthritis—I can assure you, etc., etc. . . ." It would sound good in his own perfect French.

Unfortunately nothing of all this seemed likely except perhaps Sir Malcolm's arthritis, which did indeed get worse as the Conference proceeded.

Once, in the street outside the building in which the Conference was being held, a little girl of nine or ten presented Palan with a bunch of flowers. Palan picked up the child in his arms and kissed her. A few bystanders smiled. Charles, who had been a witness from a distance, turned away as shyly as if the incident had involved himself. Again he envied Palan.

How refreshing, amidst these encounters and experiences, to think of Gerald's arrival and the birthday dinner. As soon as he had received the answering wire Charles went to the Cheval Noir, a small restaurant near the Champs Élysées which was a favorite of his — not one of those famous institutions like Prunier's or Voisin's, meccas for tourists, but the sort of place he would have been disappointed to hear spoken of by any Englishman or American, and that he himself was careful never to recommend. At the Cheval Noir he talked to Henri. Of course the dinner was not to be planned in detail — it was part of Charles's anticipated pleasure that he would discuss such important matters with Gerald and (using all the tact of which he was capable) let the boy seem to be making his own decisions. But there could be no harm in considering the possibilities. Only a simple dinner — soup, fish, then flesh or fowl of the kind that Henri knew how to cook as well as any man in Europe. No cocktails beforehand, but perhaps a glass of *Vino de Pasto* — no champagne (unless Gerald seemed disappointed by its absence), but a Chablis and then one of those honest Burgundies — say a Chambertin. . . . And *crêpes Suzette* to follow, as a sporting concession to a youthful palate — Charles himself was not fond of them (just dressed-up pancakes, after all), but they did offer a spectacle in the festive mood. Then brandy — just a plain good one — and finally, if Gerald wanted to take a small chance or to show off, a very mild and thin cigar, even if he put it down after a few whiffs. . . . And during all this they would be talking, their minds released by the warmth and the wine and by the emerging phenomenon of their mutual discovery; they would talk till near midnight — father and son, aware of a new relationship. . . . They would gossip, exchange adult confidences, perhaps even a few slightly risqué stories. . . . And then last of all, if the intimacy had proceeded so far, and if Gerald felt that the evening was still young, they might take a taxi to the Place Pigalle for another kind of initiation. Charles believed that a trial crop of wild oats should be sown under experienced sponsorship – nothing extreme, of course – just a visit to one of those rather absurd places where it could do a young man no harm to get his first sight of a row of nude women cavorting so closely that one could see all their imperfections.

How pleasant to think of these things, to plan them gently in his mind while Palan bellowed his abominable French amidst the gilt-framed mirrors and Buhl cabinets that seemed, by their contrasting elegance, to focus the whole eye of the past upon the world's deplorable present.

On the day of Gerald's arrival, events at the Conference had been particularly trying. To begin with, Sir Malcolm's arthritis had forced him to quit at the lunch interval and leave affairs during the afternoon in Charles's hands, and this, which in normal circumstances would have been both a challenge and an opportunity, turned out much more like an ordeal. For Palan, under the silent surveillance of his own superior, had concentrated upon Charles with a certain grim joyousness that had been just amusing enough to keep the Conference room in the wrong kind of good humor; Charles had a feeling he was being baited, and that even a few of his colleagues were enjoying the performance. Not that Charles lacked weapons of his own. He was sound if somewhat precise in argument; he had an expert's knowledge of the matters being discussed; he was also patient, often witty, and unfailingly polite. He could not bring himself to show temper, even when he felt it rising within himself; whereas Palan, he suspected, often put on an act of temper when he felt none. Moreover, Charles had acquired a masterly technique of listening with apparent equanimity while he was being ridiculed. "M'sieur Anderson is, of course, a man of much greater diplomatic experience than I," Palan had mocked, "but I would venture to match my knowledge of the world against his, for when you have probed behind all the statistics in blue books and white papers, when you have got down to the bedrock of reality, what is it that you find? Is it merely a diplomatic game, to be played by those who have been to the right school and college like M'sieur Anderson, or is it *life?*" And all that sort of thing.

Charles had replied: "M'sieur Palan is in error if he supposes that I regard these proceedings as a game. Since I dislike games I am certainly under no temptation to adopt such an attitude." (A few titters from his neighbors.) "And as for M'sieur Palan's knowledge of the world, I have no means of computing it, but I should not readily assume it to be greater than mine, though doubtless it has been of a very different kind of world." There had been a general laugh at that, but Charles had not been quite certain at whose expense.

Throughout the afternoon they had sparred, and more and more it had seemed to Charles that Palan was regarding him as a personal adversary. By the time of the adjournment Charles could only pray that Sir Malcolm's arthritis would improve enough for him to take over the following morning. Charles felt that though he had done quite creditably as a substitute, it had worn some frayed edges on his nerves.

His spirits rose, however, as he waited on the platform at the Gare de l'Est. It was good to have a growing-up son, and he thought happily of the corner table at the Cheval Noir, which Henri was doubtless already preparing. The train came in, with the familiar place names attached to its coaches – Berne, Delle, Vesoul, Chaumont, Troyes. . . . It had been Gerald's first European trip – what magic it must have contained, and now to culminate so fittingly!

Charles was still thinking of that when his son spotted him first. "Hello, Dad. . . . I didn't really expect you to meet me – I thought you'd be too busy."

"My dear boy. . . ." They shook hands. "However busy I am, I'd take time off for this, I assure you."

The noise of the station excused him from saying more. Gerald was instructing the porter who had carried his luggage – a small suitcase – from the train. Charles was tactful enough not to correct or amplify the boy's halting French, but he did, with his own French, summon a taxi and ask the driver to put the suitcase in the cab. Gerald then tipped the porter a hundred franc note, and Charles told the driver to take them to the Crillon.

As the taxi left the station Charles said: "How times have changed – I can remember when a hundred francs was really money! But the city hasn't lost its fascination. Did you see much of it on your way out?"

"Not a thing. The train just shunted into some station in the middle of the night. I was half asleep."

"Ah, yes, the Ceinture." Charles could not repress an emotion of astonishment – that anyone who had never seen Paris before could allow himself to be taken in and out without even leaving the train for a quick look. "You were here once when you were a baby – just passing through. But this can be called your first real visit."

"Yes. I know I ought to get a thrill." The boy was peering through the window. "I must say everything looks a bit run down after Switzerland."

"Everything is. France, remember, has been through two world wars."

"And the Swiss have been sitting pretty, I know. But the mountains – the clean air – I think that's really more in my line than big cities."

"You went to the right country, then. You look very fit. And still growing – or is it my imagination?"

Gerald was a little shy of his height, which was already six foot one. He laughed. "Oh, I hope not, or I'll be a freak. I think I've stopped, though."

"I sometimes wish I had an inch or two more myself. Not that five feet nine is really short. But you can look over my head."

"It's useful in climbing," Gerald admitted.

"Did you do much of that?"

"Just Pilatus and the Faulhorn and some of the easier ones."

Charles was suddenly aware of an emotion which, in a younger man and in connection with a woman, he would have diagnosed as jealousy. "So you got along all right with that schoolmaster – I forget his name?"

"Tubby Conklin? Oh, he isn't so bad when you get to know him. Not really stuffy – just a bit of a watchdog. I suppose he felt he had to be, with all of us on his hands."

Stuffy. Charles caught the word as if it had been a hit below the belt, but immediately decided that Gerald was unlikely to have heard of the nickname – and if he had, as he must sooner or later, what did it matter? Perhaps that was one of the confessions that would develop so naturally toward midnight at the Cheval Noir. He imagined an opening. "D'you know what they call me at the Office, Gerald? *Stuffy* Anderson." (Pause for merriment.) "I suppose having any sort of nickname's a good sign – after all, they called Disraeli Dizzy, but you can't imagine Gladstone ever being called Gladdy. . . . Gladwyn Jebb, perhaps, but not Gladstone. . . . I hope, though, I'm not *too* stuffy. Now that you're old enough to judge, you must tell me if ever you think I am." Perhaps he would be able to talk like that before the evening was over.

Gerald was still staring out of the taxi window. "Where are we going, Dad?"

"The Crillon. My hotel. I thought you might like a bath before dinner. I have to change myself anyhow."

"Change? You mean – " Gerald looked round and seemed to be studying his father's attire.

"Well, I had thought of a black tie in your honor."

"I'm afraid I didn't bring – "

"Oh, then it doesn't matter. I'll wear what I have on, and if your lounge suit needs pressing the hotel people can do it in a hurry."

"I'm terribly sorry, Dad, but I'll have to wear what I have on, too. All my clothes went through in a trunk to London. This bag's only got souvenirs and things in it – "

What Gerald had on included an open-necked shirt, tweed jacket, and gray flannel trousers.

Charles smiled. "You could have something of mine, but since you've grown so tall I rather doubt . . . Well, the only real essential is a tie, which I *can* provide. I can also lend you pajamas."

"Pajamas?"

"In case you forgot to pack them. And don't worry about a room – the Crillon can fix you up in my suite."

"But I – I'm – I wasn't planning to stay overnight. I'm booked through on the boat train from St. Lazare – "

"Tonight?"

"Yes. I'm terribly sorry if – "

Charles was hurt, but did not want to hurt himself more by showing it. "You didn't say so, and I'm afraid I assumed – "

"I didn't think it mattered so long as there was time for dinner."

"Of course. Oh, of course. Though if you wished I daresay even as late as this I could have your train ticket changed – "

"Except that I – I'd – well, actually I'd planned to join up with some of the others on the boat train, some of the people I've been with – I sort of promised. . . . And then I've got dates in London tomorrow – Mallinson, for one – he has to fix a filling that came loose, so you see . . ."

"My dear boy, that's all right – don't let it bother you. I'm glad you're careful of your teeth – most important. . . . Well, here we are – the Place de la Concorde – one of the great sights of the world, and the best time to see it is about now when the lights are just coming on. Rather splendid, don't you think?"

Gerald seemed much more impressed by his father's suite when they reached it. "The British taxpayer certainly has to shell out for this," he commented, walking around.

"Only because the British Government is anxious that its representatives abroad should not appear as impoverished as they usually are."

Gerald grinned. "Are *we* impoverished?"

"We certainly should be if we had to live on my salary."

"Ah . . . so the old family fortune's standing up pretty well?"

Charles was never quite sure when Gerald was having fun with him, or what kind of fun it was. He answered, half seriously: "It isn't much of a fortune, after inflation and taxes. But you needn't worry."

"Oh, I don't. . . . You know, Dad, if I were you I'd spend every penny during the next ten years or so, then you'd be sure of enjoying yourself. Or is that a crazy idea?"

"Not at all. You'd be surprised how popular it seems to be – hence in part the present state of Europe. But don't get me on to politics or I shall say the kind of things that annoy Sir Malcolm."

"Your boss?"

"Boss, chief, or head of department."

"Like rod, pole, or perch?"

"Exactly."

"What kind of chap is he?"

"Very able. I'd have you meet him if he were staying here, but he prefers the Embassy. A fine diplomat and – so they say – an *exceedingly* fine bridge player."

"I guess all that means you don't like him much."

"Oh now, come, come," remonstrated Charles with restrained glee. "You mustn't guess anything of the sort. Sir Malcolm and I work very well in harness. But even a horse doesn't want to be in harness all the time."

Gerald laughed heartily, and Charles thought that the evening, after a somewhat inauspicious start, was proceeding well.

An hour later they were at the corner table in the Cheval Noir with Henri hovering about them like a benign and elderly angel. Charles introduced Gerald proudly. "Henri, I want you to meet my son. Quite an occasion – his first evening in Paris as well as his seventeenth birthday."

Henri bowed, but Gerald offered his hand; Charles was pleased at this – it was intelligent of the boy to realize that Henri was not just an ordinary restaurant keeper. After the exchange of civilities Charles added: "Henri is one of mankind's truest benefactors – his *huîtres Mornay* put him with Cellini and Michelangelo. Too bad they're out of season – oysters, I mean."

After Henri, beaming at the compliment, had gone off, Gerald said: "Do you really think cooking's an art, like painting, Dad?"

"A much *higher* art than some modern painting. Anyhow, it's a polite thing to say to a cook who really is an artist."

"I suppose being a diplomat you get a lot of practice saying polite things."

"I wish I got more. I sometimes feel at a disadvantage because I'm not equally proficient in saying nasty things." He was thinking of Palan.

"Why's that?"

"Perhaps because the world isn't getting any better." Charles rallied himself from the dark reflection. "Though I must admit I see it looking pretty good here and now." Henri was serving the *Vino de Pasto*. "I'm very happy to be with you tonight, Gerald. I drink an affectionate toast to your future."

Gerald grinned embarrassedly, then sipped from his glass. "Thanks, Dad. Is this sherry?"

"Yes. . . . Smoke a cigarette if you like – it's the only wine that isn't spoiled by smoking." Charles, proffering his cigarette case, thought he had conveyed his hint rather tactfully. "I hope you like it."

"It's – well, I daresay one could get used to it."

"Just about my own first reaction. That, I remember, was at a Foundation dinner at Cambridge. I mixed my drinks rather recklessly – with the inevitable result. My gyp told me afterwards I'd tried to festoon the chapel belfry with toilet paper."

Gerald laughed. "It's hard to imagine you ever getting drunk."

"That's because you think of me as I am today."

"Or else because I really don't know you properly."

The remark, so seemingly cold, was actually warm to Charles; it hinted that Gerald, too, was aware of the barrier, and that such awareness might be a first step toward their joint effort to remove it. He said agreeably: "I've often thought that's one of the biggest drawbacks of a career like mine. Chopping and changing posts, with you in England half the time when you were a baby, then the war came and you went to America, and even after that there was school and we could only meet during the holidays if I happened to be in London. The wonder is we know each other at all. But now you're getting older and I'm not likely to be abroad so much, things ought to work out better."

Charles waited for a word of encouragement, then decided that the boy's friendly face was itself one. He continued: "Besides, I'll be off duty for good in a few more years. I'd thought of buying a place in the country, if I can find something that isn't too huge or too cute. How would you like that?"

"You mean a place like Beeching, Dad?"

"Oh no, much humbler . . . but I'm sure you don't remember Beeching."

"I do — because I remember Grandfather there."

"Really?"

"There was a big white fireplace and once a hot coal fell out on the rug and Grandfather squirted soda water over it. I think that's really the first thing I remember about anything."

"I don't recall the incident, but there was certainly a big white marble fireplace in the hall, so perhaps you're right. . . . Much *too* big — the fireplaces and everything else — we used to consume fifty tons of coal a year and still the rooms were chilly in the winter. Think of trying to get fifty tons of coal nowadays to heat a private house. . . . No, the place I might look for would be small and modern — just to settle down in after I've retired. Not too far out of London, but quiet."

"You might be lonely. You're so used to London."

"Don't forget there's the book I'll be writing."

"You're really going to do it?"

Charles smiled; the book was almost a joke because it had been talked about for so long. Whenever Charles said anything witty at a dinner party, which was fairly often, people were always apt to exclaim: "You know, Charles" (or "Stuffy," if the occasion were intimate or ribald enough), "you really ought to write a book someday," to which Charles would answer either thoughtfully "Yes, I suppose I might" or confidently "That's exactly what I intend to do." But nobody really believed he would, whatever he said; somehow he dined out too often and lived too elegantly to seem capable of such sustained effort. So one day the book would astonish everyone by actually appearing – published by Macmillan, he hoped, and at not more than twenty-five shillings, if the price of things didn't go up any more. But it would offer a further surprise by being the kind of book few would expect from him – a really serious and authoritative piece of work, in fact, that of a man *who ought to have been made an ambassador*. Charles could even extract wry satisfaction from the thought that this lesson would be learned too late, for he was fairly certain now that it *would* be too late. He was disappointed, but realized that the character he had built up for himself would not allow him to show it.

Anyhow, it was his secret intention that the book should reveal rather startlingly that behind the façade he really did know his job, and it pleased him in rueful moods to invent comments he would most like his friends to make – not to him but among themselves. "Really, you know, I've read worse. Well documented – almost scholarly in spots. Didn't think Stuffy had it in him. The *Observer* gives it the big article – calls it 'a footnote to history.' " The phrase suited Charles's humility at the shrine of Clio, and also his own experience, derived from Gibbon, that footnotes were apt to be more interesting than the larger print. Not, of course, that there would be much of that sort of thing in it – just a few titbits here and there. . . . Mostly it would deal with the Balkan and Greco-Turkish problems, would record matters of which he had been both witness and student, such as that delineation of the Macedonian frontier that had made him (for what it was worth, and it appeared nowadays to be worth nothing) the greatest living authority on the ethnographic history of the Sanjak of Belar-Novo. (Which was the only unique distinction he ever claimed for himself, and often, like so much else that he said, it raised a laugh.)

So he replied to Gerald, thinking of all this and trying not to seem portentous: "I really ought to tackle the damn thing, Gerald. My career, though far from outstanding, hasn't been entirely uneventful. . . . Rome – Bucharest – Athens – I happened to be there at interesting times. And other places. Someday I'll tell you about them."

"I'm looking forward to the book."

"Oh yes, that would probably be easier for both of us. You could skip when you were bored."

Gerald gave his father an appraising glance which he turned into a smile. "You know, Dad, you're a bit prickly, aren't you?"

"Prickly?" Now came the perfect cue. "I've been called *stuffy* in my time, but *prickly*. . . . Well. . . ."

But Gerald passed over "stuffy" without interest. "I mean, you put up your defenses even when nobody's attacking."

"Do I? Maybe a conditioned reflex after so many years in the Service. I'll try to unlearn it when I'm just a retired old has-been writing a few pages a day in that terrible handwriting of mine – or perhaps I ought to learn to type and spare the eyesight of some unfortunate secretary."

"How long do you think it will take you?"

"Two or three years, maybe more. I won't mind."

"Sort of a labor of love?"

"Well, certainly not of profit. As I said, my career hasn't been outstanding enough to send the public scurrying to the bookshops."

"Still feeling prickly? I don't know what's eating you, but I'd say you haven't done so badly. Whatever sort of life you've had, you're fifty-three and you don't look anything like it."

Charles beamed; from his own son, on his own son's seventeenth birthday, and at such a moment, there could have come no more timely reassurance. "Fifty-*two*," he corrected. "Not fifty-*three*. I was born at the turn of the century, on July 28, 1900."

"That's a fine beginning. *The Story of My Life, by Charles Anderson. Chapter One. Early Years.*"

"Good heavens no, not that sort of thing at all. It's my *work* I shall deal with – I'll begin when I took up my first post."

"Why? What's wrong about the early years? Didn't you have a good time then?"

"Of course." Charles seemed slightly embarrassed. "Nothing to complain of. That's why there wouldn't be much to write about."

"Nothing to Complain Of"

CHARLES HAD JUST FINISHED PREP SCHOOL IN THE summer of 1914; he started at Brookfield while those tremendous opening battles of the First World War were ending an age. The Somme, Jutland, and Paschendaele came to him later as headlines in the daily papers that reached Brookfield about mid-morning, at which time the school butler clamped them to the stands in the reading room. Not till the lunch hour did the boys get a hasty glimpse over the shoulders of other boys, and usually after they had satisfied a much greater eagerness to discover who was on the list for the afternoon's compulsory games. There was neither stupidity nor callousness in this – merely the knack (so often necessary in life) of putting first things second. Many of them had brothers and some fathers in the war; all knew that if it lasted long enough they would be in it themselves. Charles had joined the school cadet corps, and with more effort than zeal was picking up the rudiments of being a soldier, drilling twice a week under a ferocious sergeant, who taught him exactly where to lunge into an enemy's body with a bayonet. He did not think he would be very good at it, and was comforted to learn from Old Boys on leave from the front that most fighting was done with other weapons. In the evenings, when drills and games and lessons were over for the day, he relaxed in his School House study talking to friends and drinking coffee – sometimes, when he was on his own, reading poetry. He even wrote some, which was duly published in the *Brookfeldian* under the pseudonym "Vincio." It had no special merit.

The school was then in charge of old "Chips," who had been summoned from retirement to plug a hole in the wartime shortage of masters. Chips ran things with a benignity that made Brookfield more than tolerable to several boys who might otherwise have found it unpleasant. Charles was among them – by no means a misfit, but temperamentally not what many people would have called a typical public schoolboy. Since Chips doubted that such an animal existed Charles got along with him very well indeed, and it was Chips who made him a prefect despite warnings that boys who were bad at games were rarely good in authority. Charles, however, proved excellent – somewhat on the lenient side, but wise in his decisions and a steady handler of crises. One of his duties was to keep order in the junior dormitories during the hour before lights-out, and he found this easiest to do by being friendly and chatty. The youngsters liked him and called him "Andy," a nickname that spread throughout the school. On Sunday nights he would read aloud a chapter from some favorite bloodcurdler; he read well and enjoyed reading, and once, during a tense moment in *Dracula,* a listener fainted – an event which gave Charles singular and lasting renown.

Considering that he was bad at games (which he pretended to enjoy, nevertheless, but which he actually detested), Charles was quite popular at Brookfield and fairly, though not enormously, happy there. He made a few close friends who stayed friends in later years, and besides Chips there was another master who influenced him – a young Frenchman named Brunon, who visited the school once a week to give art lessons to a few eccentrics. Art at Brookfield was an alternative to chemistry; on reaching the fifth form one could choose, and as the laboratory promised better fun than the studio, it was favored by most. But Charles liked M. Brunon and was encouraged by him to develop an aptitude for painting, so that he whiled away many a pleasant hour in the school grounds, producing small watercolor landscapes so quickly that he would often give them away to onlookers and thus conciliate those who might otherwise have scoffed at such a hobby. One such painting by Charles hangs in the head's study at Brookfield today; it shows the school roofs beyond the trees in winter when clouds are rolling up for a storm. It is not as mediocre as the poetry he wrote (indeed, for his age, it shows distinct promise), but its chief interest perhaps is that a schoolboy should have wanted to go out in such weather for such a purpose. You can almost see that the clouds on the horizon will bring snow, not rain.

Like most male members of his family, Charles was intended for Cambridge when the time should come, and it was Chips again who suggested his entering for a history scholarship, despite an absence of encouragement from home. Charles did not win the scholarship, but came so near to it that he was awarded an exhibition entitling him to enter the University in the following September — that is, if the army did not claim him first, which it probably would.

His last term at Brookfield was in the summer of 1918, when the war, despite a heartening turn of the tide, still looked desperately far from a finish. He was now of military age, but found that by joining the Cambridge University O.T.C. he could, for a short time at least, combine the profession of arms with actual residence at a college. It seemed a miraculous device for getting a little pleasure before being killed, for at that stage of the war second lieutenants on the Western Front did not live long. To Charles the war was something he would face, like compulsory games, when he had to, but he had no romantic illusions, and the poetry he wrote, if it ever touched on the subject, was more in the spirit of Siegfried Sassoon than of Rupert Brooke.

During that autumn of final battles that few could guess were final, Charles formed fours on the cobbled quadrangles and night-maneuvered on the fenlands along the Ely road. He wore a uniform that looked like an officer's, and sometimes on dark days he was mistakenly saluted by noncommissioned men on leave from France. When this happened he felt he wanted to run after them and apologize, but of course that would have been absurd;

so he either saluted back, which seemed presumptuous and was certainly incorrect, or else ignored them, which made him feel churlish. (The problem, with its absence of any completely satisfying solution, was a sample of many that plagued him in later affairs.) In the main, though, life was pleasant and not too military – the O.T.C. adjutant, for instance, was a history professor who could lecture on the machine gun as gently as on the Holy Roman Empire.

Charles was given college rooms that dated from the early seventeenth century, and when he returned to them after a route march old Debden, who was his gyp, always had a hip bath and a can of warm water waiting in front of the sitting-room fire. (The college had not yet installed any other kind of baths.) After rinsing himself in this meager but traditional fashion Charles would dress, drink a cup of tea, and sally forth into the twilit town. The buildings in the narrow streets had an air of stooping over him protectively as he walked; he liked to push open the side door of Heffer's bookshop in Petty Cury and spend an hour or so reading what he could not afford to buy. Then back to college in time for dinner in Hall, where he would drink his pint of beer under the portraits of old collegians who had been in their time the kings and counselors of England.

Charles loved Cambridge with an ache because separation hovered so close and perhaps so tragically. Then all at once the war ended. Along with millions of other youths throughout the world he was reprieved – catapulted without warning into the idea of a future. After the initial thrill there was a curious feeling of anticlimax. He got drunk several times and took part in a riot with which the armed forces stationed in the town and district celebrated the end of the slaughter. The change was so abrupt that emptiness rather than happiness followed the withdrawal of other sensations, and as day after day passed by, each one so full of events abroad that even the palate of a historian must be jaded, Charles sought peace of his own by a process of wishful reasoning. England had won, and as a young Englishman he might well concede the timeliness of having been born in that birth-year of the century, so that he was old enough to have been ready, yet too young to have been called upon. He had been luckier than his best friend at Brookfield, killed in Mesopotamia, or than his brother Lindsay, stuck in a German prison camp awaiting repatriation. Perhaps these were reasons why he lacked the completely festive spirit, though he knew his own good fortune was to be alive. And also to be English. For with half Europe starving and another half in revolution, England, after the long ordeal, was still recognizably herself, and Cambridge was beginning to breathe again to an ancient rhythm of its own. The long Latin grace, which had been discontinued when there were so few undergraduates to read it, was resumed in Hall before dinner; professors brushed up their old lectures (Bury on Rome, Quiller-Couch on English Literature, Coulton on the Middle Ages), and for a victory banquet the gold plate of the Tudor founders was taken out of bank vaults and laid reverently along the high table. Meanwhile in some vague way the O.T.C. disbanded or dispersed or seemed merely to vanish, and there was nothing left for Charles to do with his khaki uniform except pay an exorbitant tailor's bill for it and have the overcoat dyed chocolate brown for civilian use.

Then term ended, and he went home to Beeching to spend that first Christmas of the new era that people would call post-war till the word became far too sadly confusing.

Beeching is gone, and there are hardly traces of it except on old maps and in the memories of a later generation of combatants, who will soon themselves be no longer young. For during the Second World War an airfield was laid out almost at its front door, and the house itself, for some time derelict, was patched up and made into an R.A.F. club. One night in 1943 a bomber taking off for Germany crashed into the roof and exploded; there was nothing much left when the fire had burned out. Because of censorship no mention of the disaster appeared in the papers. Charles, who was then at the Foreign Office, did not hear of it for several days, and then, of the house itself, he spoke whimsically rather than sadly, for the moment was not one for sentiment over bricks and mortar. "It was a decent house, and a great many people must have had fun in it. They were having it, too, up to the end." He recalled also that his father had always had a premonition that the place would someday be destroyed by fire. "It bothered him whenever he thought about it. He had a sort of canvas chute made to let down from the top-floor windows and at least once during every school holiday when I was young we had a fire drill with everybody sliding down to the front lawn and getting sore bottoms."

There is a photograph in an old Gloucestershire guidebook that shows Beeching with a landau waiting in the drive outside, and this may well have been the vehicle that preceded Sir Havelock Anderson's first car, which he bought when Lindsay and Charles were children. In the photograph the house looks imposing, with its three floors grouped around and above the much-enlarged portico — a merging of inherited elegance and Victorian solidity that somewhat spoiled the proportions, but not at the expense of character. The house and surrounding glebe lands had been with the Andersons since about 1700. Before then the family had lived in Yorkshire and Scotland, and there was an Anderson who had fought under Sir Philip Sidney at Zutphen in 1586.

At the side of the house a small square breakfast room overlooked the terraced gardens; it was in this room that Charles, whenever he recollected or dreamed about him, could most often see the father he had known as a small child — the tall, already silver-haired figure, not stout but plain big, staring out of the window with his back to the door through which Cobb bustled in and out with cutlery and crockery, and through which, about eight o'clock, Charles himself would cautiously enter — cautiously, not because he was in any fear, but from an unwillingness to face an ordeal of contact which he instinctively felt was mutual. Charles was five years younger than Lindsay, so that his feeling for him was one of hero worship rather than partnership; it had always seemed to him that his brother lived with his father in a world of grownups. The other meals of the day Charles took in the schoolroom with a governess, Miss Simmons, but breakfast was the immovable family feast, and for this reason marked inexorably the passage of early years – winter mornings when the lamps were lit and dawn paled on the frosted panes, and Cobb would hold each page of *The Times* before the fresh-lit fire to dry out the dampness . . . smells of coffee and bacon and kedgeree along with those of warmed paper and the methylated spirit flickering under sideboard dishes; summer mornings when sunlight moved in slow slabs over the carpet and wasps buzzed in for the marmalade . . . chatter about plans for the day, in none of which he was ever included . . . the handful of mail which Cobb brought in with a wastepaper basket . . . Aunt Hetty's glance across the table as envelopes were slit one by one and their contents amiably destroyed or grimly noted or merely stuffed into one of the huge poacher's pockets that his father's tweed coats always had . . . his aunt's look of relief when a familiar crunch sounded on the gravel outside, this being the signal that Havelock had ordered the car and was going to be away for at least the morning.

Charles's mother had died when he was born, and as soon as the boy was old enough to understand the situation he began to wonder if his father hated him for being alive at such a cost. There was also a story, which he heard later from Lindsay, that his parents had quarreled a good deal and that for a time his mother had actually left Beeching and gone to live with relatives in London. Then she had returned, and Charles, it would seem, was the result of the reconciliation. If that were so, then perhaps his father had reason to love him as well as hate him. It was hard to figure out, or rather, it was easy to figure out either way, and Charles as a boy could never make up his mind.

This was the same matter that came to an adult and rather frightening issue during that first postwar Christmas at Beeching.

When he reached there from Cambridge Charles found the house full of "family" — aunts and uncles, with children of various ages — all assembled for what might well seem the occasion of a lifetime, the coming of peace on earth, though certainly not of good will toward all men. Aunt Hetty, who had kept house at Beeching since Charles was a baby, made everyone welcome, and Havelock, seeming to enjoy the noise and bustle of it all, strode in and out of the crowded rooms with something of the air of a field marshal at ease among his staff. The general election took place about this time, giving Lloyd George's Coalition government a tremendous majority, and this momentarily cast a shadow, for Havelock had never forgiven Lloyd George his prewar demagoguery. But a much worse blow fell on Christmas Eve. Charles happened to be crossing the hall when he noticed his father reading a telegram that had just arrived; though he could not see his face, there was a sudden slumping of the massive shoulders that made him hasten up in dismay. His father then turned, gave him a dazed stare, and handed him the telegram. It was from the War Office, regretting that Captain Lindsay Anderson had died of influenza in a German prison camp on December 10. Only a few days later he would have begun the journey home. Something in the sheer wantonness of this — that a son should survive the battlefield and then succumb to a civilian illness in the defeated country weeks after the war had ended — drove Havelock to a frenzy in which he flung at Charles an entirely unfounded assertion that the Cambridge O.T.C. had been a funk hole for shirkers, and that if Charles hadn't been smart enough to get himself enrolled in it he too might have died.

This was so unfair that Charles was stung to the retort: "Do you wish I had?" But his father by that time was beyond argument, and Charles, fighting hurt as well as grief, left him mouthing and muttering unintelligibly. Charles then took a long walk in the rain and did not return till after dusk, when he slipped into the house by the back stairs and went up to his room to change. Somehow or other he must face the ordeal of the family dinner, but he wondered how he would be able to meet his father after what had been said between them. During his walk over muddy farmlands he had even searched for a cross-grain of truth in the accusation – Was it possible that by joining the O.T.C. he *had* secured a few weeks' delay in the then inevitable destiny of being sent into battle, and that those few weeks, by the timing of history, had meant life for him instead of death? But even if this were so, it could not justify even remotely his father's attitude.

While he was putting on dinner clothes the bedroom door opened and Havelock entered. He was still in the rough tweeds of everyday wear, but he looked already years older.

"We aren't dressing tonight," he said quite calmly. "Didn't Cobb tell you?"

"No, I've only just got back. I took a long walk."

"Well . . . I tried to read a little . . . everyone has to get over these things their own way. I don't really remember what it was I said to you – probably something foolish."

Charles answered: "Oh, that's all right, Father – it was nothing." He was too deeply moved to say more. Havelock then left and Charles changed his clothes again. It struck him as odd that, because of his brother's death, he was actually taking *off* a black tie, though of course he put on another one of a different kind.

Charles looked forward to the end of the vacation. Not only was the news about Lindsay a devastating grief, but its coming at a time of family gathering and sentimental association made it trebly hard to endure. And there was a new kind of unease between himself and his father, as if the sounding and exploration of a rift were all the time in progress even though both had agreed to bridge it. After the new year the house rapidly emptied, leaving Charles alone with his father and aunt during the last week before term began.

Sir Havelock Anderson was a remarkable man by any standards, and it was unfortunate (as somebody once said when this remark was made) that any standards had not been good enough in his chosen profession. In his thirties, a barrister beginning to be talked about, he would have been forecast for a brilliant career, with a likely outcome in parliament or as one of the law officers of the Crown; in his middle forties he seemed at the point of achievement, having already taken silk and received a knighthood. He had many attributes of the successful advocate – good looks, a fine presence, quick wits, commanding eloquence, and an enormously persuasive manner. He could demolish or inveigle a witness with a technique that amounted to genius. The one thing he lacked was a certain responsibility of judgment at moments of intense pressure; as his career advanced and he gained in opinion of himself, he would sometimes overstep the limits of propriety, attacking the other side in ways that drew rebukes from judges, then turning on the latter with less than traditional respect. Since he seemed increasingly unable to handle a difficult case without this sort of thing, solicitors came to regard him as a doubtful asset; after one sensational court "scene" he narrowly escaped disbarment. Though he apologized and all seemed forgiven, he had done himself harm which he knew had put him back to the bottom of the ladder, and it was perhaps again unfortunate that a private income enabled him to settle into embittered retirement rather than begin the climb afresh or seek a new career in some other field. Everything was unhappy and inglorious when, about this time, he inherited Beeching. For years thereafter he lacked interest in the property, his chief consolation being Lindsay, in whom he could well take pride. For the boy, who was very like him in looks, developed fast and promisingly – excellent at games as well as studies – destined, Havelock might have hoped, to become as remarkable as himself but without the flaw.

When Lindsay went to school Havelock had to find things to do, even at Beeching, and gradually established himself as the kind of chartered eccentric that English society permits and tolerates – which really means that none of his neighbors, whether they liked him or not (and most of them didn't), thought it *very* odd that he should be a *little* odd. Though he was never now in the headlines, he often appeared in print — writing letters to *The Times* about his hobbies, which included bird watching, collecting snuffboxes, and visits to country churchyards, where he liked to rummage among old tombstones and discover neglected graves of minor celebrities of the past; he was something of an expert on lapidary inscriptions. Strong in physique and passionate by nature, he was also a magnet to women, but here again the flaw presently showed itself — a scandal involving the suicide of the daughter of one of his neighbors, a girl in her twenties. This was when Havelock was in his fifties and a widower.

One quality he had to which both friends and enemies gave the same name, but with differing inflections — *charm.* His friends had in mind the urbane host and the delightful talker, but his enemies said that this charm was something he could turn on and off at will, and always on when he wanted anything — an old courtroom trick put to nonprofessional use.

Before Charles left for the station to catch the London train en route for Cambridge, he had a talk with his father in which the charm, turned on or not, was as antique as the snuffboxes. Havelock began by discussing the Anderson name and his own pride in it — one of those great families of commoners, he said, that in a sort of way constituted an English aristocracy of their own. In such company a mere knighthood was not so much a painting of the lily as a defacement. "Who can wish to rub the eager shoulders of provincial mayors and successful shopkeepers? Of course if I'd stayed at the Bar I should have climbed much higher — but today, as things are, I'm probably stuck where I am, and you must reconcile yourself to having Sir Havelock Anderson for a father instead of plain mister or esquire."

All of which seemed to Charles either obtuse or a snobbery of extra-special vintage. He said: "Oh, it doesn't make much difference at Cambridge. I don't think many of my friends even know about the title."

"You have my full authority to conceal it from them. Anyhow, your own affairs and what you intend to do in life are more important. Have you thought of a profession?"

Charles hadn't, especially. So they ran through the possibilities, some of which were impossibilities, such as the armed services and medicine, for which Charles had neither desire nor aptitude. Havelock himself ruled out the law; he did not think Charles was suited, which was a politer way of saying he did not think he had the brains. Charles knew, though his father didn't mention it, that Lindsay was then on his mind; Lindsay was to have entered the law, for which a brilliant Cambridge career had already prepared him just before war came. It was as if Havelock did not want Charles's career to trespass, even had it been possible, on the hallowed might-have-been territory that Lindsay would always occupy in his mind.

What about the Church? Charles shook his own head at that, and Havelock smiled in part concurrence. The City? Selling stocks wasn't much of a job, but undeniably there were youths of decent family who nowadays went into brokers' offices and made money there. Charles said innocently that he didn't think he would ever know what stocks to buy, which made Havelock smile again and remark that his own broker didn't seem to, either.

Thus, having arrived at a fairly cordial impasse, father and son could only concede that the matter was in no way urgent and that the first step was for Charles to do well at Cambridge, taking an Honors degree. Charles said this would be expected of him, since he was an exhibitioner. To which Havelock replied: "Oh yes, of course. I really didn't congratulate you enough about that. But at the time, you see . . ."

Charles knew what he meant; Lindsay had been alive at the time, and Charles's achievements and future hadn't then mattered. Now they did matter, but only in a pale shadow of the way Lindsay's had mattered.

Havelock continued: "Well, you've made a beginning. You must have studied quite hard. Somehow I never thought you did much in your spare time except paint little pictures. Or have you given that up?"

"No, I still like to do it. A pleasant hobby that gets one into the open air."

"So long as you don't take it too seriously. No man should take his hobbies seriously till he has succeeded – or failed, for that matter – in his profession." (He might well have been speaking of himself.) "And by the way, there's one profession we forgot. Diplomacy. Not bad if you have manners and like travel. Dressy fellows – useful too, so they'd have us believe. They didn't prevent the last war and they won't prevent the next, but at least it's work that doesn't soil the hands."

Charles then responded to his father's irony with a remark that he recalled, long afterwards, with a certain irony of his own. "Oh, I really don't think we need worry about another war in your lifetime or mine, Father."

"No? I wonder. There's France. There's Japan. There's Russia. There's America. Even Germany again if we're fools enough – and we shall be."

Evidently nothing less than the total destruction of the entire rest of the world would give Havelock any confidence in a lasting peace; and there were times in later life when Charles was almost driven to think his father might have had a point, though surely not an acceptable one.

Charles worked steadily at Cambridge. Except for a little beer drinking that sometimes ended up as a private spree among friends, he lived and studied quietly in rooms that overlooked the College Backs and the river; to his gyp he was "a reading gentleman," and among the dons he earned the kind of modest reputation that tempted nobody to prophesy anything remarkable. In his father's letters the suggestion of a diplomatic career was renewed, and with this in mind Charles mentioned the matter to his tutors. It seemed to be looking rather high and far for a first-year undergraduate, but they steered his studies slightly in the required direction, emphasizing modern languages and political science. He found he had a knack for languages, and during that first year something happened that was specially fortunate — André Brunon, who had been the arts master at Brookfield, took a post at a school in Cambridge, so that Charles and he were able to continue their earlier friendship. Not only did Brunon reawaken and stimulate Charles's interest in painting, but by their agreement to talk always in French Charles was given an opportunity which he used to the full. He and Brunon would spend many an afternoon together in and around the town, finding old buildings or street scenes that offered material for sketches; sometimes they went further afield to Grantchester and Madingley and Ely, cycling with painting gear strapped to their machines. Charles had always thought he would stick to water colors, but Brunon introduced him to the art of oil painting, and thus a new world was opened. The extra satisfaction of it all was that he need never regard time with Brunon as a self-indulgence, since they chattered all the while; and Charles knew he was acquiring not only conversational ease, but the beginnings of an ability to *think* in French. "And you have also an ear for accent," Brunon told him. "This is important in French as it is in English. Either you must speak French like an Englishman, which is bad but permissible, or you must speak it like the right kind of Frenchman. I myself am not the right kind of Frenchman, so it will be advisable for us soon, Charles, to stop talking French and revert to English."

Charles asked what Brunon had meant by saying he was not the right kind of Frenchman.

"I am from the Midi. Any Parisian hearing me speak would know that."

"Does it matter?"

"A little. Nothing to hinder you from passing examinations here, but still, the accent is not socially correct, and you will soon be copying it so well that you would cause raised eyebrows at the Quai d'Orsay. It would be like a French Ambassador arriving in London and paying his respects to your Foreign Minister in perfect grammatical English but with a set of Cockney vowel sounds."

"Rather amusing to think of."

"Yes, but you would wonder where on earth he could have picked them up – and then in your mind there would just be the faintest beginnings of doubt about him. Whereas if he spoke with a slight Scottish burr or a slight Irish lilt, all you would think would be, how charming, he must have had a Scottish or an Irish governess as a child. . . . There is no logic about these matters, but it *is* rather odd that the native accent of your capital city is so out of favor. . . . Personally I *like* Cockney, it has a real music of its own, but then I also like a made-up bow tie, which saves me trouble, though I was once told that no English gentleman would ever wear one."

"Oh, really? I didn't know that."

"Do you wear one yourself?"

"No, I tie my own, but it certainly never occurred to me that . . ." Charles laughed and added: "Oh well, André, you listen for danger and give me the signal when we'd better start talking English again."

In the summer of 1920 Charles took Part One of the History Tripos, getting a Second in it. He had hoped for a First, but his tutor congratulated him so warmly that the inference might have been drawn that only brilliant people got Firsts. Charles, however, still hoped to do better in Part Two, which he would take a year later. It was a more specialized examination that included the submission of a thesis, and he had already thought of a subject – "The Influence of the Arabian Caliphate on the Seljuk Turks during the Reign of Toghrul Beg." Why he chose this he was never quite sure, apart from his general interest in the period. Perhaps a deciding factor was that, so far as he could discover, nobody had ever written a Tripos thesis about the Seljuk Turks before. To his tutor, who approved the idea, there also occurred the comforting thought that a researcher on such a subject would soon reach a point at which he knew more than the examiners.

Those years at Cambridge immediately after the Armistice were unique, though doubtless if one had said so some don would have brought up conditions after the Napoleonic Wars or the Great Rebellion or the Dissolution of the Monasteries. There was always this flavor in the Cambridge spirit – a willingness to accept the new because it was not really new at all, or at least not as new as an outsider might think. Perhaps it was easier, in this spirit, to welcome the older generation of undergraduates who crowded the colleges in 1919 – married men and fathers, strange men, maimed men, and mystery men whose normal lives would not have included Cambridge at all, but whom the war had used and spared and had finally enriched with this unlooked-for experience. Many were from the Dominions – rangy six-footers to whom even the mildest collegiate discipline was irksome, and who were apt to find snobbery rather than enchantment in all tradition. And along with them, of course, was the usual crop of youngsters fresh from the schools, the handful of Harvard-exchanged Americans, and that winnowing of dark-skinned empire-built plutocracy which university regulations so tactfully referred to as "natives of Asia or Africa not of European parentage." The mixture was never quite as before, and sometimes did not mix, nor did the spell always work; but Cambridge, where the spell was everything unless Cambridge was nothing, could only do its best.

(Those were the days when Kolchak marshaled cavalry against the masters of the Kremlin; those were also the days when, hardly more than a stone's throw from Charles's college, Rutherford was plotting the split of the atom. But nobody threw that stone.)

Charles spent all his vacations (except part of one) at Beeching. The exception was a week in Normandy with Brunon during the August of 1920. They landed at Dieppe and hired an old Citroën; then they drove to Yvetot and Jumièges, loitering and painting wherever they saw what they wanted. The whole week was full of wonderful weather, warm and sunny but not cloudless, ideal for obtaining a variety of light and color. Charles had never in his life been so happy, not only because he liked Brunon but because for the first time he was beginning to sense a relationship with paint which could be called control, though it was far from anything that could be called mastery. "It is just possible," said Brunon, "that you might be fairly good someday. Probably not *very* good, but at any rate better than I am. But of course I am not really good at all. After all, I just amuse myself."

Charles returned to Beeching bronzed from the sun, and with a new confidence in himself that expanded far outside the realms of art into the traffic of everyday life. Havelock was quick to recognize it and asked many questions about Brunon. "He sounds a decent sort of fellow," he remarked. "To admit that he's not a good painter and that he has a bad French accent – a rather surprising modesty in one who has so much influence over you."

"It isn't exactly an influence," Charles said. "We just like each other and have similar interests."

"And no doubt similar opinions."

"On some things, yes. We exchange opinions a great deal because it helps my French."

"Naturally." Havelock mused a moment. "Which reminds me. . . . Charnock will be here next week. I told him the portrait of your mother seems to be fading a little – he wants to see it and tell me what to do. Perhaps you'll be equally interested in *his* opinions."

"Why, of course. I'll enjoy meeting him."

Charnock had been one of the fashionable portraitists of an earlier day; he had painted Charles's mother soon after her marriage, and the full-length canvas hung over the hall mantelpiece at Beeching in deserved pride of place, for there was no other picture in the house of any value. It showed her standing on the terrace holding in leash the two Airedales who were ancestors of the animals they now had (there was an Airedale tradition at Beeching). Charles had often admired the portrait, not only with his eyes but with his fingers touching the brushwork.

Charnock was old now, in his seventies, and nobody took much notice of what he still regularly sent to the Academy, but he was sometimes asked for his views of younger exhibitors, and these were often pungent enough to make good copy in the newspapers. His own style was somewhat after Millais and the pre-Raphaelites, paying much attention to dress. Nobody could, or would, paint a fold of velvet to look more like a fold of velvet.

Charles had no intention whatever of showing Charnock his work, any more than an amateur pianist meeting Schnabel at dinner would ask him to sit by the piano afterwards to hear a Beethoven sonata. Besides which, Charles rarely painted at Beeching, feeling the place curiously out of bounds for doing so with any pleasure. Many of his canvases, including several he liked, were stored in his rooms at Cambridge; others were in a studio in St. John's Wood that Brunon rented during school vacations. Brunon had promised to find frames for some of the recent Normandy paintings and had kept them for this purpose. Not only therefore was Charles surprised when Charnock after dinner asked to see some of his work, but there wasn't much to show him. He went to his room, nevertheless, and found a few samples – water colors of Cambridge scenes, a head of an old man dozing in a café at Lillebonne – sketched and then painted from part-memory; a still life improvised on a wet day in his college rooms; a landscape in oils of the fens near Waterbeach. He showed these to Charnock with embarrassment, partly because he hated to impose on a guest, but also because it was the first time his father could have seen most if not all of them.

Charnock kept silence for a long interval when the display was over and while Charles thankfully stacked the pictures against the wall. Presently the old man cleared his throat and commented: "Well, my boy, you certainly must have had a lot of fun."

"Yes," agreed Charles. "I wouldn't have done them if I hadn't."

Havelock smiled a slow smile. "I'm afraid the great painters had more serious motives . . . wouldn't you say so, Charnock?"

"Oh yes, but fun's all right too." Charnock grinned. "I never found it did any harm to a painting to enjoy painting it. . . . But I suppose what you really want me to tell you, my boy, is whether you ought to take it up for a living."

Charles hadn't wanted this at all; he had no intention of trying to become a professional painter, and if this were the assumption he felt himself to be falsely a suppliant for Charnock's opinion. Evidently his father had caused the misunderstanding and there was no way now of clearing it up without being rude to a man whose work Charles admired and respected. So he just smiled back and said nothing.

"And you want me to be frank?" Charnock continued.

"Well yes, of course, sir."

Charnock nodded and shrugged. He slowly lit the cigar that Havelock offered; it was as if Havelock were gently prompting him to exploit the fullest possible drama of the occasion. Then Charnock began, puffing between the words: "In that case, my boy, the answer is fortunately simple. You have nothing but a talent. A nice talent, and one that may continue to give yourself and others pleasure, but beyond that . . ." He shrugged again.

Havelock turned to Charles. "I hope it isn't a big disappointment, Charles, but I think you'll agree it's far better to have it now than nourish an impossible hope."

"I never had such a hope, so there isn't any disappointment," Charles answered.

Which was true, and yet in a way not entirely true. For there was always the hope that one admitted to be preposterous – like wondering what one would do with the money if one's sweepstake ticket won the first prize. Charles, had he ever been asked, would have told anybody (and sincerely) that he doubted if he had more than talent; but he did not enjoy being assured of it by a man whose opinion he valued but hadn't sought, and in front of his father, who (he was now convinced) had planned the whole thing as some kind of personal humiliation. Later he began to wonder if it might be simply revenge for the week he had spent away from Beeching with Brunon.

One day in the spring of 1921 Charles left Cambridge by an early train to spend the day in London. His researches into the Seljuk Turks had reached a point where Cambridge libraries had nothing more to offer, but there were several sources at the British Museum that he thought might yield something. The morning was wet and he was glad to exchange the chill of London streets for the leathery warmth of the great Reading Room under the dome. After he had searched the catalogue and filled in slips he found a desk and read the paper while he waited; there was nothing much in the news – riots in Vienna, famine in Russia, Anglo-French squabbling about German reparations, a murder at Golder's Green – just an average cross section of daily mishap. It was really more satisfying to stare about and observe the familiar types – students planning success in examinations, as he was; droll characters probing crannies of knowledge for the strangest morsels; tired-looking gleaners who Charles imagined might be free-lance journalists gathering material for the kind of article they would never sell. Once the Museum official who brought his books had leaned over to whisper: "Know who used to sit at your desk, young man? *Karl Marx.* . . . And you know where Lenin first met Trotsky? . . . In the street – in the middle of the night – just round the corner from here."

Charles had been interested, though Marx, Lenin, and Trotsky were no particular heroes of his. But he was young enough to find a thrill in feeling so close to the kind of history that seemed alive in newspapers, rather than dead in books.

The books arrived, and Charles busily made notes till one o'clock, when he stacked his material where he could return to it later and strolled along the corridor to the Museum restaurant. It looked full, so he reclaimed his hat and coat and scampered down the long Grecian flight into the open air. He was in a mood for scampering. The rain had stopped and a watery sun was pushing aside the edges of cloud and trying to dry the streets.

He felt happy. He could have painted those clouds. He had done a good morning's work and he would do more during the afternoon, and then catch the 7:15 back to Cambridge, eating dinner on the train. That would give him plenty of time to be in college before midnight; and the next day he could sort out his notes and fit them into the thesis where they best belonged. It seemed a shadowless program as he entered the stream of hurrying Londoners outside the Museum. There was a Lyons teashop nearby, but this too was crowded and the only vacant chair he could see was at a table already in use. It was better than waiting, though, and as he only wanted a sandwich and a cup of coffee he threaded his way across the room. Suddenly he saw that the other occupant was a girl; or rather, the girl whom he saw to be the other occupant gave him a sudden emotion. There was no special reason for it; she was not prettier than average, and in her rather shabby mackintosh and with wisps of rain-wet hair a little disarranged over her forehead she must be aware, if she were giving it a thought, of not looking her best. Clearly she was not giving it a thought. She was reading a book and seemed engrossed; when Charles sat down she did not look up, and this gave him a chance to observe her more carefully. All the time the emotion he had had on first seeing her persisted, and meanwhile something else happened that he would not have noticed except at a moment of heightened intensity — the sun broke the edge of another cloud and a single ray pierced the interior of the teashop. He saw the scene then as he would always remember it — the slopped tables and muddied floor, the clothes rack hung with coats and dripping umbrellas, the sign pasted on a mirror that read: BAKED BEANS ON TOAST NOW REDUCED TO FIVEPENCE. He also saw that the book she was reading was a novel by Compton Mackenzie called *Guy and Pauline*. She was rather pale, and though her eyes were on the book he guessed they were large; the small finger that turned the pages had a dark stain on the tip. He felt like a detective when he decided that this was not merely from ink but from typewriter-ribbon ink.

He gave his order to the waitress, and continued the diagnosis till the sandwich and cup of coffee arrived. Then he ate and drank slowly, and throughout all this time she had not once looked up. The book, he thought, must be surpassingly readable. But he was glad, in a way, because it enabled him to continue his detective role. She had had a cup of tea, he noted, and a bath bun. That was not much of a midday meal for an office girl – perhaps it was all she could afford. But then he imagined the same deduction being made about himself, from similar evidence on the table; and he wished it were she who would look up and be interested enough to make the mistake. She didn't. Presently, though, she glanced at the clock on the wall behind, put a marker at the page she had reached, grabbed her bill, and hurried to the cash desk.

Charles stayed for a few minutes, then picked up his own bill and left. "Just like April," said the cashier as she gave him change. He was puzzled for a moment till he saw that the sun had gone in and another shower was beginning. He had to walk through it back to the Museum.

All afternoon, and during the train journey to Cambridge, and on and off during the days of work that followed, Charles found himself thinking of the girl in the Lyons teashop. Indeed, he had never thought so persistently of any girl before. Amorous adventure had so far in his life been of a kind to make him think its pleasures exaggerated, or at least overcompensated for by regrets and confusions; and the girls he met fairly often were mostly the daughters of Beeching neighbors, horsy or hockey-playing. They thought him shy, which he was, and dull, which he was not; he had sometimes hoped that one of them might discover this. As for the Newnham and Girton girls who attended the university lectures, he hardly knew any of them except by sight, and the sight was rarely blood-tingling. Perhaps, he feared, he was impossibly hard to please, since he did not seem to care for either the bluestocking or the sportswoman type.

One thing he did with a promptness that startled him; he

bought *Guy and Pauline* at Heffer's and read it at a sitting. It was charmingly written, but he thought Guy was a bit of a prig, and an Oxford prig at that – which put him at odds with the entire idyll. His surviving interest, when he came to the last page, was with the girl in the teashop – why had she found the story so absorbing? Of course it was quite possible she hadn't. Maybe she merely preferred a novel – any novel – to reading a newspaper or chatting with the girls she worked with all day. And maybe she always read like that – with an air of having surrendered totally to a spell.

The following week, term ended for the Easter vacation and Charles decided to put in another hour or so at the Museum on his way home. He planned to catch an afternoon train from Paddington to Stow Magna, which was the station for Beeching; but while he was making his notes, with one eye on the clock, it occurred to him that he needn't hurry unless he wanted to, since there were later trains and it was of small consequence when he arrived. Relaxing, he then forgot the time till he began to feel hungry. Of course he had known all along he would revisit the Lyons teashop.

He found a table near the one he had had before, but he could not see the girl anywhere, and while he watched the entrance the whole thing seemed to become both fantastic and of increasing importance. How absurd, he reflected; but *what* was absurd? Was it not his own folly, if it mattered to him so much, in not speaking to her when he had had the chance? The thought made him decide not to repeat the absurdity if ever he were granted a second chance. An hour passed. The appetite he had felt at the Museum had deserted him; he could hardly finish his coffee and sandwich. He told himself he would leave at a quarter past two and that would be the end of it. Quarter past two came and he still stayed. She walked in five minutes later.

The shop was half empty by then, and of course she went to another table, but not far away. She had a book which she began to read as before. The waitress knew her and they exchanged a friendly greeting. Her smile was somehow what he had expected, except for a little gap between one upper tooth and the next one, at the left side; this was pure caprice, unimaginable beforehand in any mind's eye. When the waitress had gone he left his table and went over to hers, with a deliberation he knew would be hard to explain when she looked up, as she must; and almost in panic he realized he had no explanation at all, except the truth which could not be spoken. For the truth was simply that he loved her, if ever the word had, or had had, or would have, any complete meaning for him. She looked up. He blushed, pulled a chair, and said with stammering inspiration: "I wondered if you were still reading *Guy and Pauline*. . . . Why yes, so you are."

She stared for a few seconds, then glanced round as if to verify, without displeasure, all the vacant tables. "Are you Ethel's friend?" she asked.

"Ethel?"

"Oh, then . . ." She looked apologetic, as if it were she and not he who had precipitated the encounter. "You see Ethel's friend lent it to her, and then she lent it to me – Ethel's *my* friend – and I liked it so much she told him. He said he'd like to meet me and talk about it, so she said I was always here for lunch – well, nearly always. That's why I thought – but of course – if you're not . . ."

He said: "No, no. I just happened to be here the other day and noticed what you were reading. You didn't see me. I was interested because – well . . ." He struck out for a reason like a swimmer for the shore. "Well, I'd read the book myself and was interested."

Her eyes widened, and he had been right about them too – they were large. They were also a deep violet in color.

"Oh yes, it's a lovely story, isn't it? Even my dad liked it. He said it was so good about gardens."

Charles did not know what to say to this, but it was time to come to terms with her voice, which was not quite what he had expected. Or rather, perhaps, he had simply not used his brains about what to expect — for he had already deduced her as an office girl with not too good a job. If one didn't know English, he reflected whimsically, one would have found her voice as delightful as her eyes — soft and warm and altogether pleasing; but since one did know the language, one had to admit that her voice was also rather Cockney, and Charles wished it wasn't, a few seconds before he asked himself why it mattered. For he had been brought up with that crucial consciousness of accent which is so much in the air of English public schools that a boy with the wrong kind would feel outcast till, by conscious mimicry or slow absorption, he could conform to pattern. And the pattern, of course, was the clipped unregional utterance associated by name with Oxford rather than Cambridge, an utterance based on upper-class standardizations achieved over a period long enough to acquire tradition.

She went on, smiling now with complete friendliness: "I've nearly finished it. Don't tell me how it ends."

"It's a sad ending."

"I don't mind sad endings if they're real. I mean, I don't like a happy ending to be dragged in."

"Mackenzie wouldn't do that — he's too good a writer. But I don't think *Guy and Pauline* is his best book. You ought to read *Carnival.*"

"*Carnival?* I'll remember that. . . . Are *you* a writer?"

"Oh no." But then he recollected what he was in London for. "Not of novels, but at present I'm working on a thesis." It was clear she didn't know what a thesis was, and he didn't hold it against her. "Something I have to do at Cambridge."

Her eyes widened again. "Cambridge? You're at Cambridge College?"

The question hadn't been put to him before in that form, and because he didn't want to make her seem ignorant or himself pedantic, he answered: "I'm a student at the University, but I come to London sometimes to look up things at the British Museum. . . . Now it's your turn. Tell me what you do."

There was no check on the conversation from then on. She

said she was a typist at a firm of importers with offices in Kingsway. She had a boss named Mr. Graybar. She was eighteen. She lived with her parents at Linstead, and Linstead, she explained, was near Chilford. (Charles had heard of both, but could only place them vaguely as northern London suburbs.) Her father was a superintendent of local parks. (She spoke the word "superintendent" with pride.) She had two sisters and a brother. Another brother had been killed in the war.

That led him to tell her, with no reticence at all, about Lindsay. "He was five years older than I. He was going to have a wonderful career — everybody was sure of that — he'd already taken a brilliant degree. He was good at everything — games as well. He could ride beautifully — some of those big fellows that I was always scared of — "

"Where do you live?" she interrupted.

"In the country. Cheltenham's the nearest town."

"What's your dad?" she then asked.

The question closed and barred the door that Lindsay had opened wide, for the thought of his father made Charles suddenly cautious. To discuss his family and Beeching might set a distance between them, and he could not take such a risk at this early stage of their relationship (for he knew already there must be later stages). He said guardedly: "You mean his job? He doesn't actually have one, except . . ." And then he floundered because the words seemed ill-chosen — would she think he was telling her that his father was out of work? He went on, trying to correct the wrong impression, if any, without conveying the right one: "We have a bit of land and he looks after it most of the time."

"Oh, I think it's wonderful he sent you to college. My dad let Bert stay on at the grammar school till he was sixteen."

So she *had* misunderstood? Charles couldn't be sure. Anyhow, it was as if she were pridefully seeking to match either her own father's financial sacrifices or his devotion to learning with anyone else's in the world, and this drew his hand across the table to hers in a warmth that made their first physical contact something to remember like all the other first things. He saw the color spring to her cheeks, and she glanced at the clock while his hand was still on hers. "Oh dear, I must run – Mr. Graybar will make such a fuss. It's our busy day with the Japanese mail going out."

"Japanese mail?"

"Yes, we do a lot of business with Japan. *And* China."

"Are your hours long?"

"Nine till six."

"Work hard?"

"Not so bad. It comes in rushes. That's why I'm so late today. I have to go, really. It's been awfully nice talking to you."

"You say you always come here to lunch?"

"Well. sometimes I go to the A.B.C. in Holborn. But mostly here. It's nearer." She picked up the bill.

"No, no, let *me* . . ."

"Oh, I couldn't. . . . No, really. . . ."

The bill was only a few pence, and he thought it too unimportant to argue about, the more so as he didn't know whether she had protested conventionally or because he had said his father had no job. So he said, testing the matter from another angle: "All right, *this* time – but I must see you again. Will you have lunch with me next week – one day?"

"I'll be here, yes. Every day."

He followed her to the cash desk, paying his own bill. He still stayed with her when they reached the street. A clock outside was either five minutes fast or else the one in the teashop had been slow. She noticed it with alarm. "Oh look, I'm terribly late."

So they scampered together, half running and half walking, along a zigzag of side streets to Kingsway, making plans meanwhile. When they reached the office doorway another clock, confirming the one in the teashop, seemed to give them a moment miraculously their own. He said: "You won't be late – not now – and why don't I meet you *here* next week, instead of at the Lyons? We don't really have to go there at all, do we?"

"All right."

"Here, then, next Wednesday, at one?"

"Yes." She gave him a bright breathless smile. "And I'll try not to be late, Charlie, but if I am, you'll know it's Mr. Graybar."

She ran inside and he stood on the pavement, watching the swinging doors till they were still. She had called him Charlie, so promptly and easily, and no one else ever had – neither family nor friends. At Brookfield most boys used last names, except intimates, and those had called him "Andy" – a nickname that had then been transplanted to his circle of Cambridge friends because one of them had also known him at Brookfield.

She had told him her name was Lily – Lily Mansfield, but he had not used it yet, aloud.

On the train from Paddington he could hardly find perspective in a world so changed. He ate the Great Western dinner, his appetite now briskly restored, and staring through the window was almost glad there was a full week before he would see her again – a full week to taste the new dimension of events. Toward the latter part of the journey night fell, and then he got out his notes and found to his relief that he could concentrate magnificently. She cozily made room for the Seljuk Turks in his mind.

At Stow Magna he took a taxi to Beeching. As the cab swung past the lodge gates into the half mile of carriage drive, he saw a tall figure pacing in circles on the front lawn at a rate that, with its lack of purpose, suggested frenzy rather than exercise. Charles knew it must be his father in one of his "moods," though what kind of mood was not yet apparent. Maybe deep depression, or maybe a high excursion on the crest of a mind wave; "plunging" and "vaulting" were the adjectives which, for want of anything more scientific, Charles gave to the two extremes. The difference between them and the quickened intervals of their recurrence had already become as obvious as the fact that Havelock's eccentricities were increasing as he grew older and as the years denied him more than they offered. It was as if the slowing tempo of a powerful physicality had liberated him for forays, while it barred the grand offensives of earlier days.

Havelock stopped his pacing when he saw Charles arrive. The first words of greeting as they entered the house together revealed that the mood was "vaulting" this time, which was certainly, of the two, more cheerful to live with. But not always more tranquil. During what was left of the evening Charles discovered the nature of the latest foray. Havelock, it seemed, had just contributed to *The Times* a letter that was not about birds or tombstones, but ventured into new territory – political. Beginning with a reference to "my son, who is at Cambridge," it had gone on to mention an honorary degree recently conferred there on a leading politician (named) and the list of this man's virtues, as enumerated in the usual Latin speech delivered on such occasions in the Senate House. Havelock's contention was that the Latin had not been well translated, and after quoting it he supplied his own "better" version as follows: "Sagacity, Willpower, Integrity, Nobility, Experience." All of which could have been called a piece of harmless pedantry till Havelock had gleefully pointed out (to friends, neighbors, and fellow members of his London club) that the initials of the enumerated qualities spelled the word "swine," and that *The Times* editor had thus been magnificently duped. Havelock now expounded this *crème de la crème* of the jest to Charles in the real or assumed expectation that he would derive equal enjoyment.

Of course Charles thought the whole thing preposterous and a disturbing symptom of his father's heightened irresponsibility. He could not decide on the motive; whether Havelock by the completely unnecessary reference to "my son" had sought deliberately to involve him in unpleasantness; or whether he had merely surrendered to some euphoria in which his mind (not for the first time) operated without judgment. Charles told him frankly that if the story got around it couldn't exactly help a budding diplomatic or any other kind of career. "The fellow you called a swine may be the one I'll be having to ask for a job one of these days."

Suddenly deflated, Havelock then claimed that this had never occurred to him, and that in any case the risk of real harm was trivial. Perhaps it was, Charles admitted; only time would show. When later the whole incident seemed without result of any kind, Charles could only conclude that the letter had attracted absolutely no attention, and that people to whom his father had talked had merely disregarded him as a crank. Full relief came later still, when *The Times* proved its unawareness by printing Havelock's next letter, which was innocuously concerned with the migratory behavior of the green sandpiper.

But for the time, during that first week of the Easter vacation, it was only behind a curtain of exasperation that Charles could savor his own private happiness – the thought of the Wednesday ahead, the Wednesday he had chosen as just a random day for meeting Lily again, but which already he wished had been Monday or Tuesday.

As soon as he saw her pushing through the swing-doors of the Kingsway office he knew she had dressed up, and though she would have looked just as well to him in what she had worn at their first meeting, he was touched. Naturally, as a man, but still more as a man of his class, he had not thought to do anything similar. There were certain things one wore in the country and slightly different fashions at Oxford or Cambridge, and a third set of rules for London – none of them more difficult than the the task of choosing a good tailor and paying his bills. Charles had indeed been in a state of high excitement as he dressed at Beeching that morning, but so far as clothes were concerned, he was just going up to town for the day, and anyone who saw him waiting on the platform at Stow Magna would have known exactly that.

They shook hands and for a moment were both of them nervous and almost speechless till he raised his arm to halt a passing taxi. "We'll decide where we'll go while we're going," he said gaily. And then to the driver: "Trafalgar Square, to begin with."

But he found she had very few ideas about lunch. It seemed that on certain gala occasions she had been to the Strand Palace and the Regent Palace, which she had thought very splendid; but they were not his style, and since he could not afford Claridge's or the Ritz, he wondered if she would be disappointed with the kind of restaurant that suited both his tastes and his pocket pretty well. There was one he and Brunon had discovered, called Le Beau Soleil, in Soho – a small foreign place with no marble and gilt about it, just a few tables in a plain room, rather grubby menus, and a good cuisine for the price. So he said, taking her arm in the taxi: "Let's go somewhere I once went to – nothing much, but at least it's quiet and we can talk." It wasn't even quiet; what he meant was that there was no six-piece orchestra booming out popular tunes to drown conversation or to fill the gap of silence between people who had nothing to say.

It troubled him to think that Le Beau Soleil might disappoint her; but soon he realized how willing she was, at all times beginning with that first one, to go where he took her and to be actively, not merely passively, happy about it. There was a sense, indeed, in which everything that ever happened to her was a gala occasion, needing no particular background to make her enjoy it to the full.

They had the *plat du jour,* and she refused wine but drank several cups of coffee. The room was downstairs from the street level, in a sort of semibasement whose windows looked up beyond a railed area to the pavement. One saw the legs of people passing continuously, but no more of them than that without craning one's neck. Sometimes a pair of legs would stop – perhaps to rest, or during the lighting of a cigarette, or for no special reason at all – and then proceed again. Sometimes a pair of legs would stop close to another pair of legs – a meeting. It was amusing to guess, and then to lean sideways to verify. Once a man stooped and stared, presumably to see if the restaurant was full; it was the only outside face they saw, and behind the railings it looked like that of some strange crouching animal in a cage.

"But *he* sees *us* through the bars," she said. "Maybe to him it looks as if *we're* in the cage."

"I've often had the same thought at the Zoo. . . . You like the Zoo?"

"I've never been," she answered.

That seemed to him quite amazing. "You've never been to the Zoo?"

"I've never been anywhere much – except round about where I live."

He found, by closer questioning, that this was true – she had visited hardly any of London's famous sights; all she really knew of the city was the daily route by bus or tube from the station to the office, plus a few jaunts to cinemas and theaters. She had never been to the British Museum, though it was only a short stroll from where she usually had lunch. But she had been to Madame Tussaud's, and Charles hadn't. "Reg took me. He wanted to see the Chamber of Horrors." She didn't explain who Reg was, and Charles didn't ask; but the mere existence of a Reg stirred in him a desire to be the first to take her to all the places that Reg had so far neglected.

He got an impression that she had lived a very sheltered life at home – and of course there had been the war years during which sight-seeing wasn't easy or always possible. She said she had reached the top class at Linstead High School for Girls, and had gone straight to an office job on leaving. "We learned French at school," she said proudly, "but I don't remember much now." This came out when the proprietor greeted them at their table and Charles addressed him in fluent French, resulting in the discovery that Le Beau Soleil was owned and managed by a Greek, and Charles did not know any modern Greek. He realized then, from his dismay, how much he had been wanting to show off in that particular fashion.

Suddenly, over a third cup of coffee, she noticed the clock.

"Oh, my goodness — a quarter to three. I'll have to run. Mr. Graybar . . ."

"May I say damn Mr. Graybar?"

She giggled. "I've said that many a time. . . . It's all right, though — we're not so busy today and I'll work late tonight to make up for it. . . . But whatever could we have been talking about all this time?"

And that was a question hard to answer. For they had talked unceasingly, yet not about anything important. Just their own everyday affairs, which interested each other the more they were revealed, though Charles was still reluctant to be as frank as she was. It was strange; he did not mind impressing her with news of Cambridge, and the work he was doing, and his fluent French, but he did not want her to know much about Beeching. Yet perhaps he had been less reticent than he supposed, or else she had intuition about it, for in the taxi on the way back to Kingsway she said: "Your family are rather well off, aren't they?"

"Oh no, not really. You can be poor nowadays if you own land. My father often has trouble paying his bills."

"Do you own a lot of land?"

"Just farmland. All of it wouldn't be worth as much as a few square feet round here." That was an exaggeration, but he wanted to minimize certain differences between them. Other differences he didn't mind — some even amused him. Her naïveté, for instance, and her lack of the pseudosophistication that most girls had — a lack which he knew had nothing to do with primness or being strait-laced. He noticed this when she declined a cigarette. "You don't smoke or drink, Lily?"

"Well, I've tried them both, but Dad doesn't like me to, till I'm older. And it costs money."

"How much do you earn — if it isn't something I oughtn't to ask?"

"Why not? . . . Two pounds fifteen a week." Charles was shocked; he had no idea that wages in offices were so low. But she seemed to think she was well paid. "I'll say that for Mr. Graybar, he's not mean if you can do your job. He gave me the extra five shillings last New Year without even being asked. Of course I live at home, that makes it easy. I give my mum thirty shillings – she won't take any more. She's awfully good to me."

He was beginning to realize already that Lily found most people "awfully good" and therefore easy to excuse, forgive, appreciate, and love. And if love were too strong a word, surely any other would not have been strong enough for the emotion that radiated from her in all human directions. She loved her mother and father, her sisters and brother, the girls she worked with at the office; she even loved, in a sort of way, the redoubtable Mr. Graybar. And she had a bright cloudless mind that threaded the love into the pattern of all her behavior. He could tell that from an incident when the cab waited in a traffic block at the corner of Aldwych. A queue was lined up for the gallery of a theater and the usual buskers were doing their turns at the curbside. One of them, singing in a cracked voice almost inaudible above street noises, turned to the cab and thrust his cap through the open window. The manner of the appeal was impertinent and the driver gestured him off, as Charles would have also had he not seen Lily fishing in her handbag.

"No, no, let *me*. . . ." He managed to find a shilling in his pocket and dropped it in the man's cap.

"You shouldn't have done that," she said, when the cab moved away.

"Why not? *You* were going to."

"But a *shilling!*" she protested. "They don't expect that much. Goodness, nobody could afford to, if it had to be a shilling."

"So you always give to them?"

"If I'm passing I sometimes do. Some of them are really good singers, and if they aren't you feel sorry for them. . . . Only a few coppers, of course."

"I'll bet that fellow didn't need money as much as you do. I'll bet he makes more in a day than you earn in a week."

"But if people always thought like that they'd never give anything to anybody." The cab was making the turn into Kingsway.

"Oh Charlie, I've had such a wonderful time. I can't remember when I've talked so much. Next time I'll try not to."

He took her hand in an uprush of exultation that gave his voice a tremor. "Well, when shall it be – *next time? Tonight?* What time do you leave the office?"

"Oh no, I'll be working late, and besides, they'll expect me at home."

"You could telephone."

"We don't have a telephone at home – "

"How can you work late then, if they expect you – ?"

"Just an hour or so late doesn't matter – they're used to that. But if I went out for the evening – "

"That's what we'll do, the next time. The whole evening. The next time I come to the Museum. That'll be soon." (But how soon? Not before the term began again? Could he endure such a delay?) "What about the week after next? Wednesday again? We'll have dinner."

They fixed a time and a place. There wasn't a whiff of coquetry in the way she agreed to what she was so willing and happy to do, and, for that matter, both "the next time" and "the evening" had been her words before his. It was also comforting, up to a point, to think that she probably loved him no less – and perhaps more already – than some of the other inhabitants of her world.

He did not overwork at the Museum that afternoon, and at Beeching, during the ensuing fortnight, he began to assemble the thesis into final shape. There was much more to be done for the Tripos examination than just that, but he would have all the following term for the rest of it once the thesis was out of the way. He found it hard to work at Beeching, and several times after breakfast he walked the dogs or rode his bicycle a few miles to some hill with a view or a tree-shaded riverbank where he could concentrate on a book till distractions came – rain, or a chill wind, or his own thoughts tempting him to dream.

One morning he received a wire from Brunon suggesting a

meeting somewhere immediately, since Brunon had accepted a post in France and would soon be leaving England. Charles had the idea to invite him to Beeching, and it was arranged that he should come to lunch and dinner and stay overnight. Brunon duly arrived and met Havelock, who turned on the charm and proved an entirely delightful host. There were such times as this when Charles felt, not so much that he loved his father, as that the emotion of loving a father would have been a satisfying one, if he could ever have been given long enough to develop it.

During the drive to the station the next morning Brunon hinted at another holiday in France during the coming summer. "We might go to the Cévennes and see those towns built on the tops of hills. I think you would find things to paint there."

Charles answered vaguely, not because the idea did not attract but because his thoughts of Lily made the future hard to delimit. Brunon noticed this and continued: "Well, let me know if you can manage it. . . . Or perhaps you have lost a little of your interest in painting since our Normandy excursion?"

"Not a bit. It's just that I'm working so hard and don't have as much time."

"But you have scarcely mentioned painting while I have been here."

"I don't often talk about it in front of my father. He isn't very interested." Then Charles told Brunon about Charnock's visit and the opinion of Charles's work he had expressed.

Brunon snorted. "That old *pompier!* What could you have expected? Pretty ladies on chocolate box lids – it is all he is good enough for."

"He did a portrait of my mother. I don't know if you noticed it – over the mantelpiece in the hall."

"I did, but I did not know it was your mother. A very beautiful woman – though not, in my opinion, a very notable painting. Just competent and commercial. And who am I, you may ask, to despise either quality? You are right: I am nobody, and my opinion, as I have often told you, is of no value whatever."

Charles smiled. "I have a feeling it is, if only because you've never told me *I* have any genius."

"Genius is a foolish word. It is not a label to be pinned on like a medal. Most likely you do not have it, whatever it is – that I will readily admit. Maybe I would not recognize it even if you did have it. I can only say that one of your paintings – the one of the ruins at Jumièges on that day when the white clouds were so big, you remember? – I showed that to a friend in Paris." He mentioned the name of a well-known dealer who had made a fortune by commissioning and marketing the work of the newer school of postimpressionists.

Charles forced a mask of nonchalance over his excitement. "And did he say I had any genius?"

"No."

"Did he even offer you a price for the picture?"

"No. But he said something he would not have said if he had been quite sure you had only talent. He said you should go on painting for ten years, and then, if he was still alive, let him see something else."

Charles laughed and took Brunon's arm affectionately. "Ten years, André . . . that's quite a time to wait, isn't it? Not that I'd mind a bit."

Wednesday came and he went to London and took Lily to dinner at Le Beau Soleil. They talked till he had to leave to catch the last train that would get him back to Beeching that night (or rather, early the next morning); and this decided him that next time he would stay overnight at a hotel. He did so the following week, but then there was *her* train home to consider; it left Liverpool Street at five minutes past midnight. "Oh no, it isn't the last one, Charlie. Trains go to Chilford every hour all night – that's the station after Linstead – but Dad doesn't like me to miss the twelve-five." Of course he suggested seeing her home, which she wouldn't hear of at first – she said there was really no need, she was used to the journey alone and her parents'

house was only a few minutes' walk from Linstead Station. But it wasn't merely politeness, he explained; he really wanted that extra time with her, and since she also wanted it with him she soon relented. So it came about that at one o'clock on a spring morning, full of the scents of trees just breaking into bud, Charles saw Linstead for the first time.

Linstead is one of those huge dormitory suburbs of London that have spread till they touch other suburbs on all sides, like adjacent blobs of ink on blotting paper. You never know when you have entered or left Linstead unless you notice the slightly different ornamentation on the lamp posts or a faint change in the texture of the road surfaces. The town has a core of history at its center — a few old cottages in the widened High Road and a parish church rebuilt on the site of an earlier one; but for the most part (say 99 per cent) Linstead is recent without being modern. Streets of small two-story houses were pushed into a then open countryside by the speculative builder during the first decade of the century, their names sufficiently dating them — Kitchener, Roberts, Mafeking, Ladysmith. Lily lived in Ladysmith Road — Number 214, which was exactly like Numbers 212 and 216, to which it was physically joined, sharing the walls of both. For that matter it was exactly like every other house in Ladysmith Road, beginning on one side with Number 2 and going up to 278, and on the other side from 1 to 277.

Charles had never explored a suburb of this kind, never before having known anybody who lived in one, but he knew something of what they were like because every railway out of London in every direction ran through miles of them. The backs of the joined houses passed before the train traveler's eye in long successions, with gardens reaching to within a few feet of the tracks. Nobody could visit London frequently without sometimes, in sheer idleness, observing these back gardens, for they showed all the evidence of individuality that the houses so totally withheld. A paradise of flowers could succeed a littered wasteland in a second of train time; and on fine days the occupants were all so differently busy — boys mending bicycles, men digging, women chattering to neighbors across fences or hanging up clothes. Even an animal population throve variously – cats and dogs, rabbits in hutches, birds in cages; and once Charles had seen a monkey in a red jacket strutting along a garden path with its proud owner.

But at the front of the houses, facing the street, all was uniform and characterless. The gardens there were small, with no more than a privet hedge to shield the bay windows from stares of passers-by – though for added protection the windows themselves were veiled with thick lace curtains. In Ladysmith Road the bay windows stretched for half a mile without a break, and because the road was so respectable there was not so much as a damaged fence or a house turned into a shop to break the monotony. Charles, however, came upon it first at night, when the municipal lamps made a golden lane between structural perspectives that might have been Versailles for all he could see of them.

What he noticed most, during that first walk home with Lily from Linstead Station, was that she seemed so thoroughly satisfied with the place. She pointed to the new cinema just opened in the High Road; she showed him the Carnegie Library and the secondary school and the shopping area which for some things, she claimed, was almost as good as the West End and much cheaper. But what stirred her to real boasting were the trees. Every road in Linstead, she said (and in Linstead the streets were all called roads), had trees planted on each side at intervals of a few yards, so that as they grew they would make long leafy avenues the like of which were not (she assured him) to be seen in any other suburb. And who did he think was largely responsible for this? "My dad . . . he's in the Parks Department – it was his idea, and at first the Council wouldn't agree because of the cost, but after a while they tried it in a few of the roads and it looked so nice they did it in all of them. My dad chooses the trees for the different roads – for Ladysmith Road he chose laburnum. This is Ladysmith Road. It'll look lovely in a few weeks."

"I think it does now." Which only meant that he was with her still, treasuring the last few moments before he must walk back to the station alone, but not knowing when exactly that last moment would come, since she hadn't told him the number of the house. It might be the next one, and too late. So there and then, a few laburnum trees away from Number 214, he stopped and pulled her into an embrace. He was shy and a little clumsy about it, but she yielded so utterly that he found confidence as well as ecstasy. "Lily . . . are you surprised? You know I love you? . . . Do you?"

"Darling, yes. All along I have. But I didn't know if you . . . and now I'm so happy. . . ."

He knew she had answered the question he hadn't yet asked, and how like her not to waste time, to let her mind race with her heart. They stood together for a long moment, exchanging words that fell away into speechlessness. Suddenly a large ginger cat sprang from a nearby garden and squirmed against them. She laughed herself out of his arms and stooped to caress the animal. "Midge, Midge. . . . This is Mrs. Carroway's cat – she lives next door. . . . Midge, it's time I was home, isn't it? . . . Oh, Charlie, I won't sleep tonight and the South African mail goes out tomorrow, we'll be terribly busy at the office. . . . Charlie, darling, I'm so happy . . . good night. . . . Midge, Midge, Midge. . . ."

She ran away, waving to him, the cat following her.

A week later Charles returned to Cambridge. On the way across London he met Lily for lunch and it was agreed that he must work hard and without time off till the examination. She not only consented, she insisted on it. Whatever happened, he must not neglect his work, though if she could help him by typing his notes . . . wasn't there anything like that she could do? "Charlie, I know how important the examination is. That's why I don't mind not seeing you. We can write, of course, but send your letters to the office because the post comes at home after I leave in the morning."

Within a week he had written that he must see her sooner, he couldn't wait till the end of term, he would take a day off the following week and come to London – he would work all the better afterward, he was certain. She wrote back a firm No, but after a second letter in which he said her refusal had made it hard for him to work at all, she gave in. Then, when they did meet, it was as if the last barrier had broken down and they could no longer think of their relationship as limitable either by times or places.

So thereafter, and throughout the term, meetings were every other week in London–on Saturdays, as a rule, since she finished work at one and they could spend the afternoon and evening together. Sundays, of course, she was entirely free, but that wouldn't have served, because she was expected to be at home most of the day unless she said where she was going and with whom. Without ever discussing exactly why, they both felt they had better keep their relationship as private as possible; all Charles's instincts were against letting his father know about her, though it was less clear why Lily had told her own parents so little about him. "Of course they know there *is* somebody, Charlie – and they know you're at Cambridge College. . . . But my dad – well, he's a bit old-fashioned about some things."

On those Saturdays they went to all kinds of places – parks, museums, art galleries, the Zoo, the river up to Richmond and as far down as Woolwich. Sometimes they would take a bus at random and travel "all the way," wherever it might lead and even in pouring rain; and then in some corner of a café, in an unknown suburb, find shelter and privacy. The hours sped by, no matter where they went. Usually he saw her home before beginning his own return journey, for he had to be back in college by midnight, and this meant catching the last train from Liverpool Street and a wild rush through Cambridge streets – scampering and running if the train were punctual, taking a cab if not. He managed to get in before the gates closed on every occasion except one, when there was thick fog; but this enabled him to clamber over the ancient college wall unobserved, following a tradition that was itself quite ancient. He barked his shins and ruined a pair of trousers and felt very adventurous. Those were happy days.

Once he took her to the Alhambra where they saw a pale and polite resuscitation of the old-fashioned music hall. But Little Tich was on the program, and though far past his prime, was still incomparable. It was a twice-nightly show and they went again to the second "house," staying just to see Little Tich. "My mum and dad used to see him when they were young," she said, enraptured. "That was at the old Collins in Islington. They lived in Islington then. My dad was born there, and my granddad was born in a house that was pulled down to build St. Pancras Station. We're real Cockneys – on my dad's side. Mum comes from Norfolk. She was a cook in a big house and Dad traveled for a firm that put water pipes in greenhouses. That's how they met. He gave her a rose and she gave him a meat pie. They often laugh about it now. Funny, isn't it, to think of your parents just before they see each other for the first time, not knowing what's ahead – "

"*We're* ahead," said Charles. "That's why it's funny." But he was thinking that he didn't know where or how his own parents had met, and to change the subject, even in his mind, he added: "So they got married and came to London and lived happily ever after?"

"Oh yes. They have tiffs sometimes, of course. Dad bringing in mud from the garden and things like that. Nothing serious. They both like a quiet life. Most years they go to the seaside for a week. Mum always liked Margate – that's where they had their honeymoon – but Dad's a bit of a roamer."

"So they roam?"

"They generally go to Margate. Or Broadstairs."

Another time, on one of those Saturday excursions, he took a sketchbook with him. In a few minutes, while she watched, he roughed out an impression of the Serpentine on a May afternoon – children paddling and couples on the grass and riders close by along the Row. It was not very good because he had been showing off a little, anxious also not to spend much of their limited time on something he would do just as well on his own. If only their meetings could be oftener and longer; if only he could take a holiday with her as he had with Brunon, driving an old car from village to village with no need to worry about missing trains or getting home late. . . .

She was captivated by the sketch and begged it from him. "It's nothing," he said, which was almost the truth. "I've always liked trying to put what I see on paper. I paint a little too, when I have time." He was deliberately casual about it. He wanted her to ask to see his paintings and was slightly disappointed when she didn't, though it would have been hard to arrange if she had. Then he realized that such reticence was part of her entire attitude; despite willing gossip about her own and her family's affairs, she was equally willing not to know the things he did not choose to disclose. Likewise she accepted all his suggestions for places to visit, neither in subservience nor indifference, but from a simple pleasure she took in doing whatever he wanted.

She was small, physically, and all his own preferences were permanently set by it — her height was the right height, the crook of her arm in his had the cozy curve and pressure, beauty to him was in the angle of her upward glance as they walked along. And she was *loving* — in a curious way that warmed the blood, yet cooled the fever of it. Many times he waited for her at street corners and on railway platforms, and always, at the revelation that it was she and none of the hundreds of others that had passed or were passing, something in his mind clicked into certainty, like a key turning in a lock.

One evening as he was taking her home they met the Superintendent of Parks enjoying his evening stroll along Ladysmith Road. Naturally she made the introductions, and Charles noticed that after the first instant of surprise she showed little nervousness or embarrassment, but was clearly moved by an affection for both of them that made the whole encounter cordial. Mr. Mansfield was plump and slow-moving; the pursuit of horticulture under a municipal employer seemed to have given him a special serenity compounded of having a job he both enjoyed and could not lose. His high-pitched squeaky voice and Cockney accent (much more noticeable than Lily's) were odd but not inharmonious with his solid frame and deliberate movements.

"So you're the chap Lily's bin seein' so much of litely?" He pumped Charles's hand up and down. "Pleased to meet you, Mr. Anderson, I'm shore. And 'ow d'you like our part of the world?"

"I think it's very nice," said Charles tactfully, "especially the trees in all the streets."

"I'll warrant that's what she put you up to say." He was pleased, though. "Not that you ain't right about the trees. Mike all the difference, don't they? . . . You know Linstead?"

"I'm afraid not, sir. This is my first visit."

Mr. Mansfield chuckled as he relit his pipe. "You don't 'ave to call me 'sir.' What d'you think I am – a schoolteacher? Any'ow, 'ave Lily bring you round some Sunday for dinner. Can promise you a nice bit of roast beef, if you fancy it."

"Thank you very much."

Mr. Mansfield passed on his way with a nod. When he was out of earshot Charles gripped Lily's arm with extra warmth. "Well, aren't you glad? The best things sometimes happen by accident. Now he's met me he won't mind you being out late so often. Or at least I hope he won't. Nice old boy. . . . Why . . . Lily . . . what's the matter?"

"You *really* like him, Charlie? You really *do?*"

"Of course. And remember what he said – you've got to ask me to dinner at your house."

"On a *Sunday?*"

"Yes, I can take a Sunday off instead of a Saturday. When shall we fix it?"

"Any Sunday – if they know in time. You really want to come? You'll like my mum, too, that's certain, but I'm not so sure about Bert and Reg."

"Who's Reg?" At last he had been forced to ask.

"He's Bert's pal. Reg Robinson. He always has dinner with us on Sundays."

On Sundays in summer Ladysmith Road was rarely at its best. The air was apt to be hot and impregnated with smells from a hundred households in which the ceremonial meal of the week was being prepared, and of this meal, though the ingredients were many and various and wholesome, the predominant smell was usually that of boiling cabbage. Ladysmith Road was far higher in the social scale than would have allowed noisy children to play in the gutter or dance to a hurdy-gurdy; indeed it was higher in the social scale than would have allowed street music on any day of the week; so instead, on Sundays, there was this vast and cabbagy calm, broken only by the murmur of someone's piano or the distant grind of trams along the High Road. At one P.M. the pubs opened and the Sunday schools closed, but the nearest pub and Sunday school were round several corners, so that their traffic was straggling and intermittent by the time it reached the laburnums. Nor was there on Sundays any of the movement which, like systole and diastole, drew the inhabitants to and from Linstead Station and gave Ladysmith Road, between certain hours on weekdays, the appearance of being actually on the way to somewhere.

Charles's visit to Number 214 was not an entire success, though he didn't think it was either his own fault entirely or that of the Mansfields. Their hospitality was friendly and their roast beef excellent. Charles had seen the outside of the house so often that its interior hardly surprised him; if at all, it did so by being cozier and more comfortable than he had expected. On the whole he blamed Reg Robinson for the fact that he failed to get over his initial shyness. He was always inclined to be shy with a group of strangers, at Beeching or Cambridge or anywhere else, but at Ladysmith Road it seemed to stay with him more obstinately because all the time he was afraid the Mansfields were thinking him stuck-up.

Dinner was delayed (he could gather) by some minor mishap in the kitchen, so that they were not at the table till after three o'clock, by which time Reg had fully established himself as the life of the party. He banged the piano with slapdash facility, he sang (in tune but thunderously), he played gramophone records of comic songs he had brought with him, cueing the laughter in which he expected everyone to join. Charles, after deploring a first painful handshake, was ready to admit his good intentions, but soon found even this effort hard to sustain; while Reg, it seemed, saw in Charles the kind of dull fellow whom it was his social duty to wake up at all costs. To assist him he had the natural equipment of a loud voice and a set of verbal clichés and stale witticisms which he unloaded at every chance, evoking shrieks of laughter from Bert and from Lily's two sisters, Evelyn and Maud. Charles was troubled to notice that Lily also laughed, though perhaps only from politeness; it soon became clear, though, that Reg was much attracted by Lily and was on jocularly affectionate terms with her. "Nice bit o' stuff, ain't she, Charlie?" he commented, nudging Charles in the ribs, and Charles could only mumble an affirmative.

After dinner they sat in a small glassed-in annex to the dining room while Mrs. Mansfield and the girls cleared the table. Beyond the windows was the garden, neat and pretty as might have been expected, with tall hollyhocks affording a token privacy from neighbors on either side. After an ample meal and in a comfortable chair Charles was ready to relax; he could have done so, and by now would almost certainly have lost his shyness, but for Reg. Reg was indefatigable, and his range of facetiousness limitless. It seemed he possessed a motorcycle and had driven to Cambridge on it with Bert. He gave a vivid description of the undergraduates with their caps and gowns; indeed he had a snapshot which he produced there and then for general inspection. "You mean the boys have to wear them in the street?" Maud queried, and when Reg answered: "Well look, stupid, that's in the street, ain't it?" — Maud turned to Charles with an incredulous: "Do *you* have to, Mr. Anderson?"

"Don't call him Mr. Anderson, he's Charlie," said Reg. "Of course he does, don't you, Charlie? Looks like a dog's dinner in 'em, too, I'll bet. . . . Wonder how I'd look if I wore 'em up the Mount?"

This caused roars of merriment, during which Charles asked Lily, who was next to him, what the Mount was. "It's where Reg works," she whispered, but did not explain further.

Maud did, whispering in his other ear. "It's a cemetery. Reg works for an undertaker."

Charles smiled. At last he saw an opening and claimed his audience by the way he spoke up. "I can understand, then, why Reg has such a sense of humor. What work exactly do you do, Reg?"

"I'm in the office," Reg answered, not quite comfortably.

"You don't do any – er – spadework, then?"

"*Spadework?*" Reg was at first genuinely puzzled, and puzzlement made him look sullen. After a pause he said truculently: "I ain't a blasted gravedigger if that's what you mean."

Charles was still smiling. "No? I just thought that some of your jokes sounded a bit as if they'd been . . . disinterred."

At Cambridge or Beeching it would have raised a laugh, but not at Ladysmith Road. Evidently Reg's jokes were funny and Charles's weren't. Indeed a somewhat chilly silence supervened till Mrs. Mansfield broke it by a gentle rebuke to all: "Really, I don't think we ought to laugh about things like that." (But they *had* laughed, when Reg had first brought up the subject by mentioning the Mount!) Charles was bewildered, even more than disconcerted, and from then on made no further attempts to challenge Reg in the field of humor. It was perhaps some consolation that Reg also seemed put out, and presently left to take a walk with Bert.

Conversation was easier after that, and Charles gladly accepted an invitation from Mr. Mansfield to tour the garden. It could not have been more than a hundred feet long and twenty across, but it took Mr. Mansfield half an hour to name and explain the various plants and flowers. He hadn't spoken much at all inside the house, but the garden made him garrulous. Charles, who loved gardens, warmed to the man's obvious pride and quiet satisfactions. Presently Mr. Mansfield pulled out an old-fashioned watch and checked the time. "Dunno 'ow you feel, Mr. Anderson," he said hesitantly, "but round about now I usually 'ave a little stroll. Just ourselves, mind you – I don't 'old with takin' ladies along, not on Sundays, anyway."

Charles was very willing to escape, and Lily looked equally pleased to see him on such good terms with her father. The two left the house and walked half a mile to the end of Ladysmith Road, then right along Mafeking Road to Roberts Road, then left as far as the Prince Rupert, a modern sham-timbered but decent-looking pub.

"Dunno why they call it the Prince Rupert," commented Mr. Mansfield, as they pushed through the doors. "I never 'eard of no prince named Rupert."

Charles had, but he did not want to seem learned. "Looks a nice place," was all he said.

"Not too bad – and quiet, mostly. It's what you might call the local round 'ere, for those that ain't teetotallers. . . . What's yours, Mr. Anderson?"

"Thanks, I'll have a bitter," said Charles, beginning to feel more at home than for hours. "But I wish you wouldn't call me Mr. Anderson."

"I know . . . the others kept callin' you Charlie. . . . Ah, good evenin', Milly, two bitters for me and this gentleman. . . . Some'ow, though, I thought they wasn't treatin' you quite respectful."

"*Respectful?* . . . Nonsense – why should they? I'm no older than any of them, except Lily."

"Well, yes, that's true, but after all you was a stranger, and that Reg – 'e shouldn't rightly 'ave carried on the way 'e did. . . . Mind you, 'e soon calmed down afterwards – you got your own back all right, only I think you 'urt 'is feelin's."

"I hope not. I certainly didn't intend to."

" 'E's a nice smart young feller," Mr. Mansfield continued.

"Always ready with a joke, and—like you said, only you was bein' sarcastic—he ain't in a job where there's much fun, in a manner of speakin'."

"I'm really sorry if I did hurt his feelings," Charles repeated.

"Oh, 'e'll get over it. Lily'll tell 'im you didn't mean no 'arm."

The two bitters arrived, and Mr. Mansfield raised his glass to Charles. "Well, Charlie . . ." He paused to let the name achieve significance, then added: " 'Ere's to us and our dear ones. . . ."

Lily walked with him to Linstead Station later, and on the way they had their first slight tiff. It was about Reg, whose discomfiture after Charles's single crack at his expense seemed to have aroused her sympathy. Like her father, she thought Reg's feelings had been hurt, but Charles felt in no mood to apologize again as he had done once already at the pub. "Look," he said, "here's a fellow digs at me all afternoon and I take it—bad jokes included. Then I make one joke about him and he goes off in a huff."

"Not *bad* jokes," she objected. "Reg has his faults, but he never says anything blue in front of ladies."

"*Blue?*"

"I mean the sort of jokes men tell to each other. Reg tells them to Dad, but only when they're on their own."

"I see. I didn't know that's what 'blue' meant. And you didn't know what I meant by 'bad.' I meant silly jokes, not blue necessarily, just jokes that aren't amusing."

"Almost as if we didn't speak the same language," she said gaily. "Anyhow, Charlie, they made everybody laugh."

Charles had to admit that they had, and that his own joke hadn't, and that any further development of that issue might bog down in a philosophical impasse. Was laughter a valid empirical test of humor? If there were no one to see it, could a joke ever be said to exist at all? It was a bit like the nominalist-versus-realist arguments of the medieval scholars. But all that he could hardly go into with Lily, and by this time the fact that they were at odds was beginning to trouble him, as also her suggestion (shrewd or naïve, he wasn't sure which) that they didn't speak the same language.

"Oh Lily," he exclaimed, taking her arm (they were on the platform and the train was due and he couldn't endure the thought of separating from her on clouded terms) — "we're not going to quarrel about it, are we?"

"Of course not." And of course they were not. "But I can't help being sorry you were bored."

"I wasn't bored at all." He had to get back into the argument. "It's just that a fellow of Reg's type always makes me shut up in company. I just can't compete with them."

"I know. He *is* a bit noisy sometimes. Poor old Reg — he'd like to have had your advantages, going to Cambridge College to study. He's really clever, everybody says, but he had to leave school at fourteen. If only he'd been properly educated it would make all the difference."

"I don't believe it would," Charles could not help replying. "I've met fellows like Reg at Cambridge and I can't get along with them there either. You mustn't think education changes what people are like."

"Then what does it do?" she asked, again either naïvely or shrewdly, and he had no time to speculate, for the train was coming in. He pressed her hand. "Even if I knew an answer it would take me all night to give it to you." He found a compartment and leaned out of the window to kiss her. "Maybe you'd better come up to Cambridge and see for yourself. . . . Yes, why not? That's a wonderful idea. Come the week end after my examinations, then I'll be free and won't have anything on my mind. Leave on the Saturday and I'll get you a room at the Lion or somewhere — there's a good train back on Sunday evening. . . . Will you, Lily?"

"I don't know if Dad would let me."

"But it's only fair — for you to come and see me once after all the times I've come to see you."

"Yes, I know. . . . Oh, I'd love to, Charlie, but I'll have to ask Dad first."

"Fine. Ask him. I don't think he'll mind. He and I got along all right."

"Yes, you did, didn't you?" At last they had found something to agree and be glad about, and on this happier note could time their separation. "I knew it when he took you to the Prince Rupert. He only does that with people he likes." The train was beginning to move.

At Cambridge, Charles was thereafter sustained a good deal by thoughts of Lily's visit. Those were the days just before the examination that (with the Diplomatic in mind) might make or mar his career; and he had better not think it absurd, while he girded himself for last-minute cramming, that what he would be doing thirty years hence might depend on a few thousand facts so chancily selected and forcibly absorbed. The days entered a tunnel of eventlessness, but once the actual examination started the tunnel became dreamlike, streamlike, a silent aqueduct of time. Every evening, after the six-hour ordeal, an entire section of knowledge was banished from his mind, as if it had no longer any business there, so that concentration on the remainder could become more intense. His tutor had warned him not to overdo the cramming, but Charles found he could not sleep even if he went to bed, and it was no harder to read than to lie awake. By the end of the third of the five crucial days he could roughly estimate how he was faring, and he did not think too well. Many questions he had been unable to answer confidently, and there had been few he would have chosen for a display of what he knew. One afternoon he half collapsed over the desk; the day was hot and the examination hall airless – all that, plus lack of sleep, probably accounted for it. An invigilator went out with him for a spell in the open, and Charles found it a strange effort to make conversation, knowing they must avoid mention of anything remotely connected with the questions. There was one about the

Amphictyonic Council that Charles had been answering at the moment he slumped forward. He was afraid he had leaked his fountain pen all over the page, and he wondered if, in the circumstances, this would matter – whether, for instance, he should asterisk the smear with a note of apology: "Here I fainted owing to the heat."

"If there is any relief you wish for, please suggest it," said the invigilator, after they had walked twice round a small quadrangle. Charles did not guess what he meant till he added: "Though I am unfortunately compelled to accompany you, even to the humblest abode." He was a lean elderly professor whom Charles had never seen before and whose name he did not know.

"Oh no, thanks – I'm all right now. I think I can go back."

"I hope so, Anderson. When I mark your paper I shall try not to be unduly influenced by sympathy."

Charles smiled, wondering what made university dons grow up like that. Yet he was aware of genuine friendliness behind the man's tee-heeish manner.

Back in the hall he found the ink smear already dry and the atmosphere sultrier than ever, but he managed to endure it without further mishap. He had lost half an hour, though, and didn't have time to finish all the questions.

One evening, as by some gorgeous miracle of light and air, it was all over, and he returned to his rooms after the last paper had been consigned to whatever fate might be in store for it and for him. He felt somewhat as he had done when the war ended – a sense of anticlimax following hard on the heels of relief. But the emptiness soon filled with thoughts of Lily's visit, which was by now a definite arrangement. Mr. Mansfield had given permission, and even Mr. Graybar had been persuaded to let her leave the office an hour earlier to catch a better train. In a recent note to Charles confirming all these matters, both handwriting and spelling had betrayed her excitement.

Saturday (almost to his unbelief) was the day following, and he spent half the night sleepless for thinking of it, but quite pleasantly awake for the same reason. In the morning, which was warm and fine, he rose early and bought armfuls of fresh-cut flowers at the stalls in the Market Square. Then he made plans with the college kitchen for special meals to be sent to his rooms. He had planned a small dinner party for that evening, inviting his two best friends – a man named Weigall, whose rooms were on the same staircase across the landing, and another man from Sidney Sussex, whom he had got to know at history lectures. Since the cost of this party would come on the college bill at the end of the term he could indulge himself without any immediate financial problem, and with all the examinations over he felt he had earned the right to do so. His allowance from his father was not inadequate, but it had been stretched pretty far of late by all the traveling back and forth to London and the dinners and lunches and excursions there; he was beginning to look forward to his next birthday (his twenty-first) if only because he would then come into some money of his own. He had already borrowed a little from his Cambridge tailor (a wealthy and knowing tradesman) on the strength of this.

He felt very proud of her as they rode in an open taxi from Cambridge Station to the Lion Hotel. Other students had been meeting girls on the same train, and he could not avoid the comparison; Lily was not so well dressed as many, nor so strikingly pretty as a few, but she had poise and grace and some quality for him of sheer radiance. It was so personal that he was often relieved when he saw others – and not only men – aware of it; this seemed to prove he was no victim of love's illusion, though it also showed that the radiance was not for him alone. Anyhow, her own extreme of pleasure now cast a special halo round it, and he felt doubly exultant. "You're really here – at last!" he kept saying in the cab, as if the distance to Linstead and London were reckonable in thousands of miles.

"Charlie, I always wanted to come here to see you."

"Then why didn't you suggest it? Or why didn't I – sooner? It's so obvious – and yet wonderful."

"I thought perhaps you didn't want me mixed up with your work."

"You already are mixed up. I see you on every page of Stubbs and Maitland."

She laughed gaily. "And I see you on every page of Mr. Graybar's dictation."

"Forget Mr. Graybar – for two whole days." He squeezed her arm, and thought that possibly in his own room, sometime during her stay, they would enjoy the privacy they had sought till then in streets that happened to be dark or train compartments that happened to be empty between stations; he knew this Cambridge visit was bound to mark a stage in their relationship.

He began to point out the colleges. "That's the first one, Downing – I mean the first on the way from the station. The next is Emmanuel. . . . They're all separate and together they make up the University. So you see why you can't say Cambridge College – there isn't such a thing – if you talk of a college you have to use its own special name, like Downing or Emmanuel." He had always wanted to explain that to her.

"How many colleges are there?"

"Over a dozen, I should think – yes, at least a dozen."

"Don't you know exactly?"

"I don't believe I do, unless I counted them on my fingers. . . . This is Christ's – John Milton's college. We'll look round some of them later. . . . Here's Petty Cury – this narrow street, where your hotel is. I think you'll be comfortable."

He had engaged a room, even going so far as to inspect it before approval; it overlooked Petty Cury and might be noisy till late at night, but she wouldn't be using it till then. While she took her bag to it he waited in the glass-roofed lounge. Then she came down, spruced and tidied, and his heart melted to see her against this new background, but at the same time he felt tense, as if the full significance of her visit was only just dawning on him. He also hoped he could sleep better during the coming night; it was a need, like others he was beginning to be aware of, that went deeper than a desire. Suddenly he wondered what on earth had made him ask Tony Weigall and Bill Peters that evening — how much cozier just to have dinner on their own, with no strangers intruding when once Debden had cleared away and said good night.

They crossed the center of the town to his college, which he was anxious to show her first, as a sample, though it was not the oldest or one of those most visited by sight-seers. She was much impressed by the salute the porter gave him as they passed into the First Court, and surprised by the narrow staircase they had to climb and the double doors he had to open to get to his top-floor rooms, and entranced by the rooms themselves — so much larger and grander than she had imagined. He then took her to the chapel and the library and the hall, where he showed her the ancient tables and the Holbein and the piece of wood, shaped like a hand mirror, that had printed on it the college grace which he had taken his turn to read aloud until, with no particular effort of memory, he had come to know the long Latin paragraph by heart. Then they strolled along the Backs and looked into King's Chapel till it was time to return to his rooms, when it was revealed to her (by the most plausible of circumstances) that seventeenth-century college rooms lacked some of the basic conveniences of the modern house. She was surprised again, but agreeably unshy about such things and therefore amused. Perhaps because of this he decided to conquer his own shyness about something very different, but in its own way just as intimate; he got out some of his paintings. He was always reluctant to do this — too often he had read in the eyes of people looking at other people's paintings neither enthusiasm nor distaste, but merely a desperate struggle to think of something to say that was clever or at least flattering. It was a test, therefore, that he shrank from putting his friends to, because he shrank from putting himself to it. But now with Lily, acting on impulse, he took the risk. He fixed the easel and placed the canvases on it one by one, saying nothing about any of them, while she sat curled in the window seat viewing them equally without word or gesture.

When she had seen the lot and he had put them away again he poured himself a glass of sherry. She still didn't speak, and he began to approve of her silence in a miserable sort of way. At least she wasn't dealing out insincere and meaningless compliments. Presently she said: "Charlie, I'm so glad you let me see the pictures. It's no good my trying to tell you what I think of them because I don't know. I liked some better than others. I liked the one of the windy day."

"Which one was that?"

"The third, I think, or the fourth."

He knew the one she meant; it was a fenland scene, mainly clouds — a windy day, to be sure (the canvas had been blown down by one of the gusts), but there were no obvious clues like bending trees or drifting smoke. What he had tried to do, but did not think he had succeeded in doing, was to get the wind into his lighting of the sky, into the whole surface texture of the picture. And now she was telling him he had succeeded.

Never had he felt such a moment of utter and blissful reassurance. He went over to her and put his arm round her in full view of anyone who might be passing across the court, and in a curious way he hoped he might be seen, as the finder of a new truth wants to proclaim it.

"Lily, my little one — my darling. . . ."

"Did I say the wrong thing about the pictures? Oh, I'm sorry, Charlie."

"Nothing you say is ever the wrong thing. It's I who *do* the wrong things. Tonight, for instance, we ought to have been alone."

"But you asked some friends of yours, didn't you?"

"Yes, I did, and I — but no, it's all right, you'll like them. They're good fellows."

"Of course I'll like them."

The college clock began to strike the hour, followed by other clocks all over the town. The miscellaneous near and distant chiming lasted for some time, many of the clocks being minutes fast or slow, and he told her it would all begin again, for the quarter, after about a ten-minute interval. "They'll probably keep you awake all night."

"I won't mind. I'm so excited to be here. Charlie, d'you know this is the first time I've ever been away from home by myself?"

"You're not by yourself."

"I mean at night . . . without a friend."

"What friend? I didn't know you had any other particular friend."

"Of course I have. I mean girls. There's Ethel at the office—we always go away on our holidays together. And there's Phillis Baxter I used to go with at school. You haven't met them because every time you're free I'd much rather be with you."

"A good answer."

"Don't you believe me?"

"I do. And it *was* a windy day in that picture. It was, indeed."

In the mood he was in, torn between exultation and regret, between the wish that they were alone and the hope that his friends would like her, and over it all the tensions that had not been eased by sleep, he could hardly understand himself, much less expect her to understand him.

"Charlie, what's the matter? You sound so sharp, as if you were nervous about something."

It was because he had heard Weigall and Peters coming up the stairs.

Within a few minutes he was relieved at least on one count. Weigall had draped his long legs from the far end of the couch and Peters was at the nearer end, and in between, laughing and chatting as if she had known them for years, was Lily. It came out that Weigall's family were from Norfolk and that Lily too had relatives there; they talked about Norwich and Sandringham, and other places they both knew. With Peters, who was a historian, Lily found less in common at first; but soon they discovered a shared interest in films, Peters being something of a highbrow while Lily was just an ordinary regular patron of whatever the Linstead cinema offered. Peters seemed to find her comments both amusing and delightful; and when Debden announced that soup was served Peters insisted on sitting next to Lily, although Charles had planned to have Weigall there. But with only four persons at a small table it really didn't much matter how they sat. What did matter, as Charles began to notice it, was that Peters was bringing Lily to a kind of life Charles had never seen in her before. Charles even wondered whether he had ever been jealous before, for the glum and spiritually disabling sensation he felt was new in his experience.

Lily was telling Peters about a dog they had had at Ladysmith Road when she was a child, and it appeared that Peters also liked dogs and that his family had had one of the same breed. "There's nothing like a dog," Peters assured her.

"Except a cat," said Lily. "We have a lovely cat."

"But a cat isn't really like a dog," said Peters.

Weigall winked at Charles. "Too intellectual for me – this conversation," he commented.

"We have two Airedales at Beeching," said Charles, suddenly desperate to assert himself.

Peters laughed. "You see, Lily, we can't win! *Two* Airedales! Think of that . . . and how many horses, cows, housemaids, butlers, grooms, and other domestic pets? I don't suppose Andy knows – he's never bothered to count."

"He didn't even know how many colleges there are in Cambridge," said Lily, extending the joke. "Did you, Charlie? And you never told me they called you Andy, either."

Charles was concerned lest she should gain an exaggerated impression of Beeching from Peter's nonsense, but he was also astonished – and perhaps dismayed – that Lily seemed to be impressed so little. It was the "Andy" she had picked up. "It's just a nickname I had at school," he explained, adding rather foolishly: "From Anderson."

"Really?" Weigall gave himself an ironic poise. "I think we can accept that as a hypothesis." He intoned in imitation of some professor. "And as for how many colleges there are, does *anybody* know?"

This kind of thing was lost on Lily. "Well," she said, "when I was at school we were told how many counties there are in England."

"What a depressing school it must have been!"

"It was not! It was better-looking than some of these old colleges."

Weigall assumed his most languid air. "*Better*-looking, Lily?"

"Newer. More modern. I tell you, Linstead's an up-to-date place. You should see some of the parks we have. My dad's the superintendent of them."

Peters abruptly seized Lily's hand across the table. "Lily . . . ignore these other two and listen to me. First, I congratulate you. To have a father who superintends parks is magnificent. My own father, God bless him, is a coal miner. Lived in the same cottage for thirty years – a cottage in a town where there are no parks and consequently no superintendent of parks. My father began work in the pits when he was eleven, and he still works in the pits. But by sheer grit and ability his son, whom you see here in a preliminary stage of intoxication . . . by sheer . . . whatever it was I just said . . . plus, of course, an army grant and a scholarship and sundry other assistances . . . has been admitted to this ancient seat of learning to study, ape, and acquire the manners and customs of his betters . . . while still retaining, Lily – and this is important – that innate sympathy with the working classes that makes him salute you, as he does now, in profound adoration!"

Charles contrived a smile, but Lily was blushing through the beginnings of tears. "Oh, go on with you," she murmured, but she did not withdraw her hand. "I'm not crying because I believe a word you say – it's the way you make me feel. . . . Charlie, does he often talk like that?"

Charles would have had to admit that Bill Peters often did, after a few drinks; but there wasn't time to answer at all before

Peters raised his glass and demanded a toast. "To the Labor Party and the working classes, Lily!"

"Oh, that's a lot of nonsense!" she retorted. "My dad votes Conservative!"

She wouldn't drink, but she turned to them all with a rosy smile, finally settling it on Charles. "Darling, it's such fun being here. . . . I didn't know clever people could be so silly."

The rest of the evening passed for Charles in a fog of sensations, one of which was amazement at the new dimension of personality Lily was revealing. It pleased him up to the point where it began to hurt. He had feared that Weigall and Peters might not like her, or that she might be too nervous to talk to them, and though he was glad he was wrong he was not quite at ease enough to be happy.

But he was beginning to be sleepy and that was something. The party could not last much longer, for by midnight according to university rules Lily would have to be out of college and Peters back at his lodgings across the town. When half past eleven struck and Peters did not make a move, it was Lily who picked up the signal. "Ought I to go, Charlie? You tell me when."

Peters said: "Don't fidget, Andy – she doesn't have to leave till a few minutes to twelve."

"But I have to get back here before they shut the gates," Charles said.

"You don't have to go at all. I can drop her at the Lion – it's right on my way and I'm in rooms – my landlady never says a thing if I'm a few minutes late."

Charles felt himself challenged by some test of fair-mindedness, logic, magnanimity, reasonableness, and other qualities which he admired. He didn't exactly consent to the arrangement, but somehow he let it fix itself without further argument, and about five minutes to twelve Peters left with Lily. She was evidently thrilled that he was wearing a cap and gown and would thus escort her, and it was just Charles's bad luck not to have given her this pleasure himself, for academic costume in the streets was at all times permissible, though not compulsory till after dark.

While the departing footsteps were echoing down the staircase and across the court to the gateway, Weigall lit another cigarette. He, being of the same college, could stay as long as he liked. "Good company," he commented.

"You think so?"

"For her age . . . must be very young. You know, Andy, when you first mentioned a girl coming up to see you, I thought she was a friend of the family or something."

"What do you mean?"

"Well – er – isn't there some girl that your family hopes you'll marry someday? There generally is, with most families. Some dreadful creature quite often, with huge front teeth and lots of money. Thank God your little Lily isn't like that."

"No," said Charles, "she isn't like that."

Weigall went on: "She's charming, and she has a bright eager mind that's a joy to make contact with. I think I could ring most of my change on her counter – when she's a little older. What puzzles me is where you could possibly have picked her up?"

"Why is it such a puzzle?"

"Because . . . I suppose I somehow didn't think of you as a picker-up – not in that sense."

"What sense?"

"Oh, come now, Andy, have a heart! Don't you want me to talk frankly? I've told you I like her, and that's the truth, but unless she's destined to be your future wife do I have to pretend you were introduced by the vicar of Beeching?"

Charles said in a clipped staccato voice: "I met her in a Lyons teashop in London. Her father, as she told you, works for the local council in a suburb. They live in a small house in one of those terribly long streets – not a slum – just dreary and respectable. She's got a Cockney accent, which you heard. Socially I suppose you'd call her lower middle class – "

"Good God," Weigall interrupted, "who cares about class nowadays except smart fellows like Bill Peters? He's a snob in reverse — one of these days he's going to make that miner's cottage business pay off like a bonanza. Whereas you and I, Andy, are stuck in between — we weren't born at Blenheim or Chatsworth on the one hand, and on the other hand we didn't starve in tenements or pick crusts out of gutters. . . . We just come from country homes with bits of land and families that go back a few centuries without having collected any titles or riches on the way. . . . Well, that's not quite true in your case, your father has a knighthood, but I gather he earned it, which is bad. . . . I tell you, Andy, in the world I see coming our background — yours and mine — is going to be a pretty fair handicap. We'll be the excluded middle — if you'll pardon a logician's term. So prepare to defend yourself, not Lily. She's all right. She'll sleep well tonight — she hasn't our worries. You look worn out, by the way. Why don't you get to bed?"

"Yes, I think I will. Thanks, Tony."

"Thanks for what? I haven't given you any advice. . . . Good night."

But again Charles could not sleep and heard the quarters maddeningly till nearly dawn. Then he got up and crossed the courts to the new bathhouse (built as a postwar innovation in collegiate life); a hot bath made him feel better and fresher. He had promised to have breakfast with Lily at the Lion at half past ten, but after eight, when the college began to come to life, time passed most slowly of all. Debden, who was doubtless curious about Lily, chattered with his usual amiable inquisitiveness as he tidied up the room, venturing to observe that it would be "a lovely day for taking the young lady on the river."

Charles agreed. "Yes, I might do that." And so he might. He had not made definite plans, hoping that Lily might care to spend part of the day quietly in his rooms.

She was a few minutes late coming down to meet him at the

Lion, and while he waited in the lounge he wondered about Peters and her the previous night. Had they talked till much later, at the hotel, and was this why she was late? Peters had said his landlady would let him in after midnight without making a fuss. . . . Was it possible, then, that . . . but no, it was not only impossible, it was absurd . . . and anyhow, here she was.

"Charlie, I'm sorry. Been waiting long?"

"No, I only just got here. Did you sleep well?"

"Wonderfully. The clocks didn't bother me at all. . . . Oh, what a lovely time I had last night."

"You did? I'm glad. I had an idea you'd like Weigall and Peters."

"Oh yes, they're nice."

"Peters especially. Did he talk to you much on the way?"

"All the time. He does talk all the time, doesn't he? But of course it was only a few minutes. It's really a small town to walk across."

"Compared with Linstead – and when you're in amusing company."

"Oh, you can't compare it with Linstead. And I'd much rather have been with you – only, as you said, it would have meant leaving earlier."

"I think it was Peters, actually, who made the arrangement."

"Was it?"

"It doesn't matter." He seized her arm clumsily. "Lily, you must forgive me – I'm being foolish. One good night's sleep and I'll see everything straighter. . . . Don't take me seriously now. Let's have breakfast."

During the meal he felt happier, relaxing in her company and in her obvious pleasure to be with him. But she was troubled about his earlier mood. "Charlie, what's wrong? Why can't you sleep?"

"Overwork, I suppose, these last few weeks. Nothing to worry about."

"And taking all those days off to see me. You shouldn't have done that."

"On the contrary, they kept me going." He laughed uncertainly. "I probably can't live without you, Lily."

"Anybody ever say you had to?" she laughed back. It was one of the few times she had touched, even as lightly as that, on the notion of a future.

"They'd better not."

She caught the grimmer note in his voice. "Don't be cross about something that hasn't happened."

"I'm not cross about anything, really. Not when I'm with you."

"Maybe you'll sleep better tonight."

"After you've gone? I wonder."

"If those chimes keep people awake at nights I don't know why they have them."

"Probably because they've had them for years and years and years. In Cambridge that's a good reason."

"Never mind, you'll be on your holidays soon. It's country where you go home to, isn't it? That's one thing about the country – nice and quiet."

"Not always nice and sometimes *too* quiet. What will I do there now I haven't got an examination to work for?"

"Aren't there some more examinations sometime?"

"That's a cheerful idea."

"Well, I thought if you *wanted* something to do. . . . But if I were you I'd just take a rest. Bill told me you'd been working too hard."

"Bill Peters? He wouldn't know – he's in another college. Besides, nothing's hard work to him. I mean, he takes everything in his stride – examinations, sports, debates, even acting at the Footlights. Just like my brother Lindsay who died. One of those all-round fellows. Sure to have a career. A First for certain and probably a Blue and President of the Union – the whole bag of tricks. Nothing can stop him . . . and I like him enormously. I'm lucky to have him for a friend. He's very popular."

"Why are you talking so much about him?"

"Aren't you interested? You seemed so last night – and he liked you too, that was obvious."

She shook her head, but in dismay more than denial. "Oh Charlie, it doesn't seem to work well, does it, either when you meet my friends or I meet yours?"

"*Please*. . . ." He struggled with some inward fret that centered round the pit of his stomach. "Please forgive me again. The same old foolishness. The truth is, I wish I could have more time alone with you. Other people somehow seem to get in the way."

"All right then, let's be alone."

"For the rest of the day? That isn't much."

"It's all we have. I wish it were more too."

Then he heard his longings framing themselves into words that desperately came close and yet fought shy of what they really meant. "Lily, you're supposed to go back by the 9:12 – what if you didn't? Suppose I borrow a car – I think I could – and we'll go off somewhere on our own – now – this morning . . . and have all the time we can together – at some quiet place in the country. . . . And tomorrow I'll drive you right to the door of your office – not too late for Mr. Graybar, I promise. . . . Could you? *Would* you?"

She answered immediately and simply: "Yes, if you want. But I must send Dad a wire."

"Tell him you're staying here another night."

"I won't say 'here,' I'll just say 'staying.' Then it won't be a lie. I'd hate to tell my dad a lie."

It took him till midafternoon to fix all the details of the sudden change of plan. He had to rent a car (not as easy on a Sunday as he had thought), and secure an overnight exeat from the college authorities (easy now that examinations were finished), and think of something plausible to tell Debden. The truth seemed most plausible of all – that he was just driving his guest back to London and would return the next day.

Meanwhile she sent the wire to her father.

They drove out of Cambridge southward over the Gog Magog

hills, toward those rolling Essex uplands that are never high but give every half mile a changing contour. Presently they stopped at a small country town. It had a church with a crocheted spire that Charles would have sketched if he had been less tired, but they were satisfied to look around and then have tea in a nearby cottage. They didn't know where they would drive on to next; Charles hadn't even a map. It was the kind of wandering he had often dreamed of having again, after that week in Normandy with Brunon, and here it was, with her, a reality, yet still enclosed in a dream. As they explored the narrow streets the dream reached to the sky, as if actual sleep, like a great bird, were already wheeling and swooping over his head. The town was almost deserted, full of Sunday stillness till they reached a central square, where a Salvation Army band oompahed in the sun without any audience. There was an ancient timbered building which they crossed the square to inspect; it was a fifteenth-century cloth hall, still in use as a municipal office. They passed close to the band on the way back, and as they did so there came over the trombones and tambourines a sound so startling in an Essex town that they stared incredulously. A Salvation Army man approaching with a collection plate grinned at their astonishment and supplied the explanation. "The circus just came in. Starts tomorrow for the fair week."

"Fair week?" Charles echoed, fishing in his pocket.

"Oh yes, we have a real big fair once a year – thank you, sir – people come from miles around. Just up the road." He proudly jerked a thumb. "Turn to the right over there by the bank. That's where you heard them lions." He seemed to be generously recommending a better entertainment than his own.

In a mood to see what was to be seen, they took the indicated direction and soon found why the center of the town was so empty. A crowd that looked like the entire population was watching the unloading of a long line of circus vans into an open field. Everything was lively and noisy and smelly; the lions roared again in their cages, men yelled to each other as they hoisted the big tent, whips were cracked, ponies trotted, men in top hats and riding boots gave what was halfway a free show. In a field next to the circus there was to be the fair itself; here men in shirt sleeves were putting up stalls and coconut shies, and unpacking hideous china that would doubtless be given away as prizes. Soon the street lamps gleamed over the scene of such unusual Sunday activity; naphtha flares were hung on the stalls, and a searchlight began to test itself against the sky. The noise and smells and brilliance increased as the job proceeded; but sometimes in the midst of a lull the Salvation Army band could be heard still playing cheerfully on and on.

During one of those lulls Charles said: "I think all this must be a bit like Nizhni Novgorod."

"What?"

"Somewhere you've never been and neither have I. It has a fair too — every year — or rather it did, before the Revolution. Perhaps still does. It's a place in Russia. I must have read about it somewhere."

"And it's like this?"

"Might be. I don't really know why I think so. But a fair's a fair — everywhere."

"Yes, you're tired," she agreed, as if that was what he had told her. "You can't drive any more. Let's stay here."

"All right. If Nizhni Novgorod has a decent pub."

The Swan was full, but recommended a cottage round the corner, the hotel being available for meals and garaging the car. A Mrs. Renshaw. "Tell her the Swan sent you." They told her the Swan had sent them, and the room she offered was under the thatched eaves, small and low-roofed and crammed with mahogany. The cottage was probably three hundred years old, but nobody had bothered much about that and all the walls had florid paper covering the uneven plaster. On the modern mantelpiece there were shells from some seashore and photographs of (presumably) Mrs. Renshaw's relatives. They were a glum collection and Charles was beguiled by their stares of disapproval. Lily was sympathetic, wondering from their faces if they had ever been happy.

"Of course they were," Charles said. "It's just the way people used to pose for photographs. Now the man tells you to smile — in those days he must have said, 'Look serious.' That was the fashion. Did Gladstone ever grin? Was Queen Victoria ever amused? . . . Well, yes, she was — a friend of my father's told him he was once at the Sutherland estate at Dunrobin when the Queen was being shown over, and in one of the rooms they looked into — by mistake, I suppose — they found a very fat policeman in bed with his clothes on. . . . The Queen nearly collapsed with laughter."

"A friend of your father's knew the Queen?"

"Oh, he didn't really know her — he was just there when it happened. Fat people in bed can be funny . . . thin people, too."

"There's a lot of fun in just being a person — anywhere."

"So that's your view of life?"

"Don't you like it?"

"My little one . . . my darling . . . you know . . . you can't possibly know . . . how much it makes me love you."

"Love is fun too."

"Nizhni Novgorod is fun."

"I'm glad we came here. Is that what you'll always call it?"

"I don't think the people who live there call it that any more. I mean, in the real Nizhni Novgorod. They've got some new name. I don't know what. I only know the old name because I read about the fair in a book. They used to have a fair there. A big fair there. . . ."

"Darling, you're so tired. I'm glad we came. Fancy, we both keep saying the same things again and again."

"Yes, fancy. . . . I had an aunt who said 'fancy' to everything. 'Fancy' or 'Just fancy' or 'Fancy that.' Fancy this. Just fancy us being here. . . ."

Later he said: "I've done rather badly in the examination. I know I have, but I don't mind about it now — that's why I can tell you. I couldn't even finish one of the papers — I fainted or something in the middle — the heat it was — I can't think why they chose a hall that had such poor ventilation. . . . Anyhow, I probably won't scrape through with more than a third, which isn't good enough for what I was supposed to be aiming for — the Diplomatic. . . . So there you are — cards all on the table."

"I oughtn't to have taken up so much of your time."

"Oh no. Never think that. I couldn't have worked much harder than I did, anyhow."

"You could have rested instead of making all those trips to London."

"No, I shouldn't have rested — I should have tried to put in extra work and then broken down completely. Maybe you saved my life. . . . Lily, I'm not like Peters. I can't take things in my stride. I'm not first-rate in his way, or the way my brother Lindsay was. That's why it's just as well to have a real failure now, at the beginning — then I'm definitely out of the race that I know I can't win. I'm not disappointed. My father may be, but not me. Or else he'll be disgusted . . . or perhaps in a queer sort of way glad that I've come such a cropper."

"*Glad*, Charlie? I don't understand that."

"Never mind. . . ."

"But how . . . how . . . could he . . . ?"

"Darling, all I mean is that this thing isn't a tragedy. I was never terribly keen on the Diplomatic — from what I've gathered it can be pretty dull and stuffy, and they send you to a lot of places you can't possibly enjoy. . . . It was just one way of getting started."

"Away from home?"

"Oh yes, of course. I couldn't want to stay at Beeching."

"You don't really like it there, do you? You've never told me much about it."

"That's not the reason. I didn't tell you much at first because I thought you'd imagine me too far out of your world, and I didn't want to be . . . and then I went on not telling you because I just hadn't before. There's nothing special about Beeching. Might impress you till you tried it, then you'd discover it had bad drains and no damp course and wasn't really very comfortable to live in."

"But your home — that's more than the house — that's really what you want to get away from."

"How do you know? . . . Well, in a way, you might be right. There are reasons I couldn't go into — "

"Charlie, can I ask one more question?"

"All right."

"What was your mother like?"

"We have a big portrait of her and if she was like that she was wonderful. Of course I don't remember her."

"So you couldn't love her. And you don't love your father."

"Why do you say that? . . . Well, I'll admit I don't love people as you do. You love everybody. Which really means anybody. . . . Oh no, that's an unfair thing to say. I'm sorry, Lily. All I mean is that it must make it hard for you to *fall* in love when you — "

"I did with you — the first time we met."

"No, the second. The first time you didn't even look at me. That was when *I* did — while you weren't looking. I think we ought to get married quickly — before you look at somebody else. . . . Lily, I mean that."

"Do you?"

"Yes. . . . Oh God, yes. More than I've ever meant anything."

"Are you *sure* it's what you want, Charlie?"

"Don't you want it?"

"Yes, if you do . . . and if Dad consents. I can't without that, because of my age. You can't either, till you're twenty-one."

"I'll be that in a month. We might live abroad. It's cheap in France these days, on account of the exchange. And another thing — I could do some painting there. . . . Yes, even after a third. You never guessed I was serious about it, did you? You thought it was just a hobby?"

"I thought it was a serious hobby — like Dad's gardening."

"Well, why not? Oh Lily, we shall get along fine. The things I really want in life are simple if only I stick to them – and stick to wanting them . . . that's the trouble, I'm not one of those vital characters. I'm not power-driven, like Bill Peters. . . . But a serious hobby I *do* have – thank you for that description, I love you for it. So it's all settled – we'll live in France and I'll paint. How about it?"

She said thoughtfully: "Mr. Graybar does a lot of business with French exporters – I know their names and addresses – I've typed hundreds of letters to them – "

He was thinking how delightfully irrelevant this was till she added: "I'm sure I could find a job with one of them." Shock and amazement were then added, so that he gasped out: "Good God, you didn't suppose that was in my mind, did you?"

"But you mightn't earn enough at first, Charlie. Not everybody buys paintings."

He didn't know then whether to laugh or cry – the intensely practical naïveté of it reminded him of plunging into an ice-cold crystal stream in the sunshine. "Look, darling . . . please understand . . . there's no question of you having to find a job, whether my paintings sell or not. As soon as I'm twenty-one I come into some money from my mother's estate – not much, but enough to live on in France. . . . About three hundred a year. . . ."

"Three hundred pounds a year without working at all?"

It occurred to him that he had never heard the central issue of modern economics stated so eloquently as by her own incredulity. It made him feel he had something to brazen out. "Well, yes . . . so you see how it is – I can *afford* my serious hobby – *and* you." He began to laugh. "I'm laughing at myself for ever having worried about the future. Aren't *you* looking forward to it, Lily? There are beautiful places in France – "

"And I could come home sometimes, couldn't I?"

"Home?"

"To Linstead. I'd like to see Mum and Dad now and again."

"Of course, as often as you want. France isn't the South Sea Islands."

"That would be fun too. Like that French painter who went there and lived with a native girl."

"*What?*" He was amazed again. "You mean Gauguin? I didn't know you knew anything about painters. . . ."

"I read a book about him once. I do read, Charlie – you ought to know that – I was reading when you first saw me. I'm not really so silly – "

He found this utterly adorable. It was, he supposed, the effect of Cambridge – of seeing colleges and libraries, of meeting Weigall and Peters, who had also found her adorable. The whole idea of marrying her and going to France to paint gained on him so fast that he felt an intoxication in being alive; the darkness of the little room glowed into deep colors, the touch of her body next to him was an easing of every strain. She was so small and unshy and gay, and she had another quality the word for which had been pale in his mind for years – ever since he had first heard it in church as a child; but now it sprang to warmth and meaning. *Loving-kindness.* She was loving-kind.

They talked over all the details of the future till dawn showed at the sides of the window curtains. Now and then, in the distance, a lion roared.

A few hours later they began to journey to London, having slept till it was too late for breakfast. As they approached the inner suburbs the sky darkened and rain began, so that the final miles of tram-lined roads were slow and slippery. Charles had hoped to keep his word by delivering her at Kingsway in time for the normal office opening, but he was nearly an hour late. She said it didn't matter – and it would have been absurd, of course, if it had. When he stopped the car at the curb and before he could get out, she kissed him quickly and scampered through the rain to the swing doors with an alacrity that seemed more absent-minded than apprehensive.

He had a cup of tea at a café in Holborn, then drove back to Cambridge with the windshield wipers marking slow time to his thoughts. It was two o'clock when he reached his rooms. He lay on the couch while Debden prepared a late lunch, but fell asleep and Debden did not wake him. He slept all afternoon and most of the evening and night. He had no more engagements; it was merely a matter of putting in days at the college till term was over and he could leave Cambridge for good. This was hard to realize – that it was his last term and his university career would soon be ended. He had no particular plans for a vacation and was in no present mood to think of any. Presumably he would go to Beeching, at any rate for a while, and he had arranged to meet Lily on his way there across London. That would be on the following Friday – five days hence.

Afterwards when he looked back on that curious interval it seemed to him that most of the hours had been of sleep. For the first time in weeks the clock chimes did not trouble him, and he would often doze on the couch and wake to find Debden offering some odd-looking meal on a tray. Debden was an understanding fellow and had seen many a reading gentleman overwork himself for an examination and then half collapse in this fashion. "Sleep's the thing, sir. Can't do you any 'arm no matter 'ow much of it you get – and that's more than you can say of most things in life. . . . There was a man I 'ad 'ere once who didn't sleep a wink for weeks. . . ." This, thought Charles, was an unlikely story, but he listened quite contentedly to many such excerpts from the lifelong saga.

On Friday morning Charles went to early chapel. He was not a regular attender, but at the beginnings and ends of term he had made it a custom, and this morning, the last one of all, seemed an extra-special occasion. He remembered how emotional he had felt about Cambridge during his first term and that last year of the war, but of course the atmosphere then had been charged with the *mystique* of youth facing death. Three years later, amidst dubious peace and economic depression, the mood was far different, and Charles, at almost twenty-one, was different with it. He would have liked to let that final chapel service soak into him sentimentally, but he couldn't relax enough; the thought of meeting Lily for lunch in London made him look at his watch too often.

Crossing the quadrangle afterward he met Debden outside his staircase. He had tipped him well, and the man's mood was confidential and extracurricular, as if Charles had already passed into the saga. "Gentleman to see you, sir. Wouldn't give 'is name, but said 'e'd wait. He was the kind I knew it was all right, sir, to let 'im into your rooms."

He had never seen Havelock looking so well since the days before Lindsay's death; that was a first impression. It was not merely that he was in one of the vaulting moods – there was a hint of something else that must have happened to generate such an air of authority. Charles fancied he was seeing his father as had many a judge and jury during those early years of triumph, and the spectacle was notable – even in some ways intimidating.

"Well. . . . This *is* a surprise, Father!"

"Yes, I'm sure it is. How are you, Charles? I'm glad I've caught you before you took the train, because I have the car here. I thought we'd travel back together. Nice day for a drive across country. Farrow's with me."

Farrow was the chauffeur, which meant that the car would be the big Daimler, which Charles never liked as much as the small open car he drove himself. This detail cast its minor shadow; the larger and darker one was that his father's unexpected visit meant canceling the arrangement to meet Lily in London. There was no alternative, though of course he could make a special trip to see her some other day, and soon. The disappointment hit him all the more acutely because their last meeting had left, as it was bound to, so many afterthoughts and afteremotions.

He said, seeking to disguise how he felt: "That would be nice. . . . Have you had breakfast? Debden will get you some coffee . . . and, in the meantime, I must send a wire."

"A wire?"

"Just to cancel an engagement. I'd planned to meet someone in London, but now that I can't manage it I must let them know."

"I see." And then, when Charles had reached the door: "Is it, by any chance, a girl?"

Charles flushed and tried to laugh. "Supposing it is – what then?"

"If the girl's name is Lily Mansfield you needn't send it."

Charles recrossed the room, the warmth in his face draining to pallor as he approached his father. "What makes you say that?"

"She's not there – to receive it."

"Not where?"

"Anywhere you would have sent it." Havelock's eyes were shining. "Now sit down. I've something to tell you. . . . And no coffee – Close your outer door – sport your oak – do they still use that phrase? . . . We don't want to be interrupted."

Charles was now possessed by a single fear. "Father, what's happened? For God's sake don't make a drama of it. Is she all right? Is she well? Has anything – ?"

"She's perfectly well – I didn't mean to alarm you. Now will you close that door?"

After Charles had done so he heard a simple story of coincidence. Reg Robinson, it seemed, had been motorcycling on the previous Sunday evening and had found himself thirsty just outside the Swan in the little market town. From the saloon bar he could see into the dining room where Lily and Charles were at one of the tables. Quelling an impulse to intrude, he had decided more shrewdly to watch and wait; presently he had seen them walk down the lane to a cottage. The possible significance of this grew on him slowly, but was soon (Havelock suggested) reinforced by personal jealousy and a strong surge of class-conscious virtue. He had made a few inquiries, taken down names and details, and then jumped on his motorcycle with the news. It was the following evening, however, before he passed it on. "An interesting delay," Havelock commented. "Did he want time to think things over? Or was he enjoying a sense of power? He could have called before Mansfield went to work in the morning — but no, he waited till evening. Perhaps he was teased with the thought of talking to the girl beforehand, which he did — He telephoned her at her office during the day — just an innocent chat between friends, no disclosures on either side, yet both with a secret that must have been infinitely preoccupying. He asked her, perhaps, if she had had a pleasant week end, and one may imagine her answer — casual enough, yet bringing a flush to her cheeks that no one observed. . . ."

Havelock was soaring into an empyrean of his own, so far unclouded by blame or moral censure. The voice, lyric in quality, flowed on effortlessly from sentence to sentence, developing a theme, building to some sort of climax. "The temptations of youth, Charles, are not beyond comprehension to any man of mature age who remembers his own. I don't know what kind of youth you think I had myself, but I assure you it was far from flawless, far from the patterns of pulpit and schoolroom. . . ."

But by this time Charles was impatient; there was so much still that he did not know. He interrupted: "Suppose we don't go into all that now, Father. Just tell me a few more facts. . . . Do you mind?"

"Of course not. Talk it over as much as you like. The whole matter's cleared up — there's no urgency. I'm telling you that in advance, because I don't want to scare you again. I'm sorry that at the outset you misunderstood me — it was my own fault for a somewhat clumsy opening — "

"Please, Father — just the facts. Tell me — "

"You've had them all — all that are important. Your little escapade — as I said — was discovered and reported, and I'm bound to say it was sheer bad luck — this fellow cruising about on his motorcycle — "

"But what do you mean by saying it's all cleared up?"

Then a curious transformation came over Havelock's face. It changed almost in texture as well as expression — from smooth and bland to rough and tough. It occurred to Charles, still under the influence of his first impression, that this was the sort of thing that must have happened when his father had cross-examined witnesses — first the sweet mellifluous questions, the artless probings, the seeming sympathy, the words, words, words to soften and disarm; then, all at once, the rapier thrust.

"Just this," Havelock snapped. "You were in a damned mess and I've got you out of it. This girl and her parents could have ruined your life. They had you in their power. I'm not exaggerating. It would have been easier to handle them if they'd been blackmailers, or if the girl had been some cheap little tart. But they're decent people. Keep away from decent people when you're in the mood for mischief of this kind. That's sound advice from a lawyer. I've known cases like this before and seen men jailed for them. Luring a minor from home for an immoral purpose — Criminal Law Amendment Act of 1885 — abduction — how do you like the sound of it? But that's what I could convict you of, you fool, if I were prosecuting and you were in the dock!"

Charles didn't like the sound of it at all. He was sheerly appalled and there wasn't a word he could reply. He felt he had heard a story about someone else whose behavior couldn't be likened to any that had ever been his own.

Then Havelock's face relaxed somewhat. Beguilement began again, the sentences became less staccato, even the words seemed drawn from a different vocabulary. "As I said, the Mansfields are decent people. That, at the outset, was an obstacle. But in the end — and due largely, if you must know the truth, to a certain skill I have always had in presenting a point of view — they agreed to behave magnanimously. They will not prosecute. You have nothing to worry about. And — incidentally — the girl isn't pregnant."

All Charles could then say was a muttered, "Oh God" — which he was glad his father did not hear because it represented a personal emotion which he did not want to explain or even to analyze. He then went to the window and stared out; men were still loitering in the court on their way from chapel. What a wonderful last morning of one's college career! he thought bitterly. He swung round and broke the silence that his father had made intolerable by his merely watching presence. "Where is she? Where is she now?"

"They've sent her to stay with some relatives in the country."

"I *must* see her."

"I don't think you can."

"But . . . dammit . . . as you yourself said, she's not a cheap little tart. I'd have married her. . . . I *want* to marry her. Don't you realize that?"

"I'm sure you feel the Mansfields ought to jump at such a thing, but believe me, they don't. It speaks well for them, Charles. Many a respectable family would have regarded that as quite legitimate blackmail."

"I'm not concerned with what they regard. It's what I want – and what Lily wants."

"What a girl of seventeen wants isn't – "

"*Seventeen?*"

"Oh? Didn't she tell you that?"

Charles replied absently, as if the matter were already unimportant: "She said eighteen."

"In court I should point out that we have only your word for that. But of course I believe you, and I've no doubt the girl herself would confirm the deception."

"Good God, it isn't much of a deception. It's nothing. A year."

Havelock laughed in a way which, Charles reflected, would give a fine impression beyond the double doors that the two of them were having a very jolly time together. "You know why I find that funny, Charles? Because you said a year is nothing. A year is just about what I could have got you off with!"

So it *was* funny, maybe. But hardly jolly. Charles felt ill, and of all things in the world the one he least desired was to travel in a car with his father across several counties and finally arrive at Beeching. Yet that, quite clearly, was all he could do. So he went to his bedroom and began packing the last few things in a suitcase.

They didn't talk much during the journey, but Havelock remained in excellent humor. Not only must there be pleasure in having saved a son from ruin, but fatherly intervention had awakened old techniques, had unsheathed rusty swords from mildewed scabbards. They stopped for lunch at Banbury, and Havelock then mentioned Charles's approaching twenty-first birthday. He could not have chosen a worse time for evoking any warm response, and this may have been why he chose it, for he brought up the matter of the big party for tenants that landowners traditionally gave when their sons came of age. Havelock had done this for Lindsay, but now it was clear he didn't want to do it for Charles. Charles didn't mind a bit (he would have found such festivities irksome at the best of times), but he could only marvel at his father's astuteness in breaking the news just then. He said: "Really, Father, it suits me not to have the thing. So far as I'm concerned everybody can forget the birthday."

"Oh dear no, not at all. I had thought of a jaunt to town, perhaps – just the two of us. We never have had that, have we? Dinner at my club and then perhaps a theater."

"Oh, let's decide later."

"I thought I'd mention it, though, to stake out my claim before you plan anything else."

"I'm not planning. I can't make plans. I don't know what I'm going to do. Everything seems uncertain. How can it be otherwise just now?"

"You mean that your future depends a great deal on the results of the Tripos Examination?"

"God, no, I wasn't even thinking of that – but of course it's true. And I may as well tell you, I haven't done well. In fact I've done damn badly. Maybe I haven't even passed – and I don't care. I want some happiness in life. I don't see why it all has to be broken. I don't see — I can't — I — "

He became speechless and incoherent, breaking down a little, and his father summoned an old and rather decrepit waiter who presided over the hotel dining room. "My son is ill," he said. "Would you kindly help me to take him to my car?"

Charles soon pulled himself together at that. "I don't need any help," he said roughly. "I'm all right. I can walk — there's nothing the matter with me." But the old waiter had taken his arm by that time and Charles did not want to push him aside and perhaps off his feet, so before he properly knew what was happening he was taking part in a spectacle that moved slowly through the dining room and across the hotel lobby and down the steps to the car, in front of the curious stares of a score or more onlookers. Probably they thought he was drunk. He reflected afterward that his father must have staged it suddenly and for a mere whim before such an utterly random audience, since nobody in Banbury knew them and they were unlikely to stop there again.

Charles was ill at Beeching for several weeks, of no ailment that the local doctor could diagnose, and with no particular symptoms except a high temperature. But it was easy for Dr. Somerville to ascribe the trouble to recent overstudy, and to recommend rest and a holiday as the only but a very certain cure. Havelock was sympathetic and talked of a European trip, if Charles would enjoy it later in the summer. Or perhaps he would rather stay at Beeching and do nothing except paint whenever he had the mood. But to Charles the thought of painting was a signal for despair, and the first day he got up after being in bed he collected all his paraphernalia — easel, brushes, paints, and finished canvases — and packed them in an old trunk in the loft over the stables.

Only one positive decision had emerged from the confusion of notions and emotions that had sent his temperature to fever height, and that was to visit Ladysmith Road. He had sent several letters there, addressed to Lily, and had not been surprised when they were unanswered. He knew that a personal visit might be just as fruitless, the Mansfields might refuse to admit him or discuss anything, there might be an unpleasant scene, they might even call the police (though knowing their respectabilities he did not really think there was much risk of this); but whatever happened or did not happen, some points would be elucidated, or at least removed from the sphere of total doubt. One of these questions was how far, if at all, his father's story was untrue or exaggerated. He did not expect to find much discrepancy; nevertheless the visit to Ladysmith Road became somehow obligatory in his mind, a *scène à faire* that had to be acted out.

One day he went up to London without telling his father, leaving merely a message with Cobb that he might be back late that evening or the next day. On arrival at Paddington he made a routine test by telephoning the Kingsway office; a girl's voice answered that Miss Mansfield was no longer working there. This again was no astonishment. He next called in person and asked to see somebody named Ethel. Ethel, it seemed, had gone to lunch at the Lyons teashop near the British Museum, where he had first set eyes on Lily. He was told to ask the girl at the cashier's desk to point out Ethel to him, and all this procedure, which normally he would have found devious and embarrassing, he went through in somber misery that was aware of nothing but itself. Ethel was hostile; she would tell him nothing (perhaps she did not know much), but it was clear she held him responsible for at least the interruption of a friendship. After a few moments Charles left her and wandered vaguely through the streets till he found himself in Lincoln's Inn Fields. He sat down on a bench and tried to think of a way to get the afternoon over. He did not think he could concentrate on a film, still less on a revisiting of any of the places he had been to with Lily (and these had included practically everything in the guidebook); so he took an early train to Linstead and spent the intervening hours in that suburb. He knew it was no use calling on Mr. Mansfield before seven, by which time he would have finished his evening meal. Oddly perhaps, Charles had seen little of Linstead with Lily. Except for the walk from the station to Ladysmith Road, less than half a mile and by an unchanging route, they had never made it a background of adventure or experience; they had always been hurrying somewhere else or home again afterward. Yet Charles knew that Lily liked the place, and had shown pride in it on that first occasion he had gone there with her; but, as was her nature, she had let the matter drop when she found in him no special response. So now he walked about Linstead streets, as if by so doing he could commune with something that had shared with him Lily's affections. It did not work out very well. He still found Linstead dull and featureless, its long roads of bay-windowed houses infinitely depressing. And yet, he realized, there were streets of Regency houses in the better parts of London almost as long and as uniform, and those houses too had been put up by speculative builders at a time of boom and with no aim but profit. So where, then, lay the difference that made the one style so much less deplorable than the other? The answer, which was only the beginning of other questions, gave his mind a focus for a while; but soon he was in dim perspectives again, wondering if and how he could trace a thin line of happiness for himself on the blind face of the future. Toward evening he entered a restaurant in the High Road near the station. He wasn't hungry but he wanted a cup of coffee. A first-floor window offered a view of trains that arrived every few minutes from London; he saw the countless doors open before the trains came to a halt and the crowd spill out like burst liquid, then shape into a stream, thickening and congesting as it reached the station exit; but once beyond this bottleneck the mass suddenly unliquefied – human beings with separate aims dispersing in every direction. Charles watched till after six; then he picked up his bill and left. On the way out to the cash desk he passed a big mirror and saw himself, like any other fellow walking across a restaurant with his hand in his pocket feeling for change; he wondered what he would think of himself as a stranger met thus for the first time. Medium height, brown hair and eyes, no distinguishing marks — the passport specifications came easily. Or would it be no marks of distinction? Just a tired look and a worried face. But not even that; he did not think the stranger in the mirror looked more than averagely bothered about anything. A man he passed in the street outside had an air of far greater harassment, and Charles watched him for a few seconds, saw him buy an evening paper and turn to the stop-press column that gave the racing results. Charles smiled to himself; the incident was calming. People, it would seem, were apt to be neither as happy nor as unhappy as they looked; and he was one of them. The anonymity of being anybody nudged his mind with the first touch of philosophic comfort he had been able to muster. The world's end was a long way off, further even than Ladysmith Road. But then, thinking this, there came to him an echo from a forgotten source — something he had read somewhere, he wished he could remember where — "It is not many miles to Mantua, no further than the end of this mad world."

He reached Number 214 about a quarter past seven and rang the doorbell. He was not very nervous. The afternoon in Linstead, walking about and thinking things over, had been helpful. He saw the familiar lace curtains in the bay window and noticed the center one draped to enshroud a plant that was new there — an exotic fleshy-leaved thing, bigger than the much derided aspidistra. Probably Mr. Mansfield's latest pride. Somehow this evidence, if it were such, that Mr. Mansfield was still functioning in his beloved world of horticulture gave Charles another nudge of comfort. A nice job, being a parkkeeper — and if one wanted to make a play on words rather than realities, what had generations of Andersons been if not parkkeepers, since Beeching was called Beeching Park on old maps? The idea beguiled him — Havelock and Mr. Mansfield in a park together. But it was thus with so many words — *love,* for instance, a perfect catchall of meaning, since one could use it about anything from God to goulash; and yet so clinchingly compared with *like,* because one never spoke of "falling in liking" with anybody, and also because one often said one "rather liked" somebody, whereas nobody ever "rather loved." For instance, he rather liked Mr. Mansfield. . . . And so his thoughts rambled on till he heard footsteps approaching along the hall. He knew then he was in luck—not only because someone was at home, but the footsteps were surely those of the one he rather liked. The door opened. Yes, indeed. Mr. Mansfield was in gardening boots and an old jacket, and carried a large earthenware flowerpot which he had apparently been too absent-minded to set down anywhere. Naturally he was more taken aback than Charles, though the latter had to scrap all his rehearsed conversational openings when Mr. Mansfield suddenly dropped the flowerpot. It shattered on the floor of the lobby. Charles had prefigured just about every possibility but this. He crossed the threshold without invitation and stooped to gather the fragments into a heap.

"Butterfingers!" exclaimed Mr. Mansfield, gasping a word that Charles had never expected to be the first one spoken between them. "But you give me a turn, Charlie, that's wot you did—you really give me a turn. You was the larst person I'd 'ave thought—"

"I'm terribly sorry," Charles interrupted. "Perhaps I should have let you know, but—here, let me tidy this up."

"No, it's all right." Mr. Mansfield was fast recovering, and with recovery came a mounting resentment. "Look 'ere now, I dunno wot you've come for—Lily ain't 'ere now, your dad must 'ave told you that. I really dunno wot you want, unless it's to mike trouble, and I tell you, I ain't goin' to 'ave no trouble. See?"

But having delivered that, his protest and his credo, he was clearly at a loss to continue. He let Charles open the door of the parlor and followed him meekly inside. Then with his own big hands, but carefully wiping the garden dirt off them before he touched the knob, he closed the door. He looked incongruous with his old clothes and gardening boots in this small spotless room packed with furniture and ornaments. But at least, Charles reflected, he seemed already to have exhausted his anger.

Charles said, breathlessly improvising: "Mr. Mansfield, I've not come here to make trouble at all. I don't want it any more than you do. My father, as you say, told me more or less what happened, but I felt I had to see you for confirmation before I could take all of it in. . . ."

"It ain't a bit of good," Mr. Mansfield interposed. "She ain't 'ere and you ain't goin' to see 'er. I give my word and I mean it."

"You mean you give me your word now or you gave it to my father?"

"I give my word, that's all. I just give my word." And then abruptly: "I believe that front door's left open. Mind if I see?"

And so it was, the front door left wide open, as people never left their front doors open in Ladysmith Road; amidst the excitement of their meeting and the smashed flowerpot neither of them had thought to close it. Mr. Mansfield went out to the lobby and did so, while Charles was aware of a quality he knew and loved in Lily, a gentleness, a humility, an almost foolish sweetness that would make Mr. Mansfield ask an unwelcome visitor if he might close the door of his own house.

When Mr. Mansfield returned to the parlor Charles abandoned all his mentally rehearsed speeches to resume eagerly: "Let me tell you this before we go any further. I love Lily and I want to marry her. And if I'd known there'd be all this upset I'd never have — " But then he stopped. What would he never have done? Did he mean merely that had he known Reg Robinson would be motorcycling anywhere near the Swan, he would have found another town and another hotel? This, even if true, was hardly worth saying; but was it the whole truth anyhow? Could there not be regrets that did not imply apology or confession — regrets for the grinding of memory into the sawdust of shabby outcome? But Charles could not hope to explain this question, still less expect an answer; and therefore he did not know how to finish his sentence. He broke off simply, without floundering, content with the silence that followed. Then, as if it had been the most natural inquiry of a friend, he said: "She's all right, I suppose?"

Mr. Mansfield replied in the same key and seemed relieved to do so. "She's with the wife in the country. I give my word I wouldn't say where, but it's a nice place. She'll stay there awhile. She ain't come to no 'arm, in a manner of speakin'. Oh, she's all right — right as rain — she's at the 'ouse of the wife's sister and 'er 'usband. 'Er 'olidays was due, anyway. Bert and Maud are on their 'olidays too."

"Leaving you all by yourself?"

Mr. Mansfield nodded, a crease of humor rounding the edge of his nostrils. "To tell the truth I ain't sorry. Gives me a chance to do a bit extra in the garden."

"I was admiring this plant as I came in. New, isn't it?"

"*Ficus elastica.* From Brazil. Fancy you noticin' it. Grows out-of-doors as a rule, but I brought it 'ome to see wot 'appened. Sometimes they like a change. Bin a good year for most things. I got a fine show of roses out in the back." He paused, as if meditating an invitation and then thinking better of it. "I was just goin' out to water 'em when you come."

"I'm interrupting you, I'm afraid."

"Oh, they can wait. Matter of fact, if you don't mind, I'll take off these old boots. Dunno wot the wife would say if she saw me in 'ere with 'em on. . . . Be back in a minute."

Mr. Mansfield then went out and Charles heard him climb the stairs to the floor above — the room above also, for after a few seconds the ceiling shook to heavy footfalls and some glass beads in the lampshade began to tinkle. Charles had nothing to do but look about him, remembering the only time he had been in the room before and Reg's terrific handshake received over by the piano. Pictures and photographs crowded the walls; there was an old-fashioned overmantel above the fireplace, and a center table covered what would otherwise have been the only completely visible square yard of carpet. Pride of place was given to a modern radio-gramophone of exactly the same model as the one at Beeching. Sir Havelock had not been keen enough on music to equip his house with anything de luxe; whereas the Mansfields must have made sacrifices to buy such a relatively expensive machine. So the two families could meet, as it were, on the social level of mass-produced entertainment. And for that matter, Charles reflected, if one were to go round with the eye of an artist there was just as much junk in the Beeching drawing room.

Presently footsteps descended the stairs and Mr. Mansfield re-entered. He had changed not only his boots but his clothes, and Charles thought he must also have brushed his hair and given himself a general spruce-up.

"Well, I wasn't long, was I? . . . Dunno 'ow you feel, but it seems to me — if you ain't in a 'urry . . . always quiet there this time of an evenin'. . . ."

"Why yes," said Charles. "A good idea."

They talked mostly about gardening as they walked the short distance to the Prince Rupert, and Charles did not press the conversation to any more serious issue. He could bide his time, and he judged that after a drink or so Mr. Mansfield might be more communicative. Charles had learned very little so far, except that Lily's father had given a promise to his; he felt he must know more about this, where and how it had happened; it was the atmosphere he wanted to explore almost more than the territory.

Then, during that first moment at the bar of the Prince Rupert, something happened that told him so much of everything that all else was merely a filling in of detail. Charles had been the first to say, "What's yours, Mr. Mansfield?" and Mr. Mansfield had replied: "Bitter for me, Charlie." There was nobody else in the bar, not even the barmaid; soon, however, a buxom woman who was evidently the landlady came up and greeted Mr. Mansfield as an old and favorite customer. "Two bitters," said Charles, but before she could serve them Mr. Mansfield cleared his throat to proclaim with great solemnity: "Mrs. Webber, I want you to meet Mr. Anderson." Mrs. Webber smiled and Charles shook hands with her across the counter. She had the air of being a great lady. Mr. Mansfield continued: "This Mr. Anderson's the son of Sir 'Avelock Anderson who was with me 'ere the other evenin' – you remember Sir 'Avelock, Mrs. Webber?"

"My goodness, I should say I do! We were so glad to meet Sir Havelock." And then to Charles: "What a wonderful man your father is! The stories he told! I really do believe he enjoyed himself here, don't you, Mr. Mansfield?"

Charles could believe it also. Over their drinks Mr. Mansfield was not in the least unwilling to talk of an event that had evidently added so much to his local prestige. Havelock, it seemed, had in the first place received a letter from Mr. Mansfield. "Mind you, it was Reg that wrote it – Reg said your dad ought to know. And then your dad came to see us as soon as 'e got the letter. We was 'avin' supper but 'e'd 'ad 'is so the wife made 'im a cup of tea and we all talked it over."

"*All?*"

"Well, not Bert and Maud – they was away on their 'olidays, like I said. But Reg was there."

"And Lily?"

"She come in during the middle of it. She'd just bin round the corner to get some needles."

"Some *what?*"

"Needles. For the gramophone. Reg brought over a lot of new records and we was all goin' to 'ear 'em after supper." Mr. Mansfield took in Charles's glance and slowly interpreted it. "Oh, we was all on good terms by then – we'd 'ad it out with 'er. No good 'angin' on to trouble, I always says, or it'll 'ang on to you. . . . Besides, we couldn't blame it all on the girl. She didn't orter 'ave done what she did, but 'oos fault was it really?"

Charles shook his head, not in either reluctance or inability to answer the question, but because his mind was boggling at the picture of his father sitting at the table in the living room at Ladysmith Road, drinking a cup of tea and "talking it over" with the Mansfields and Reg, then Lily entering the domestic circle with a supply of gramophone needles. . . .

Mr. Mansfield took advantage of the silence to catch Mrs. Webber's eye and signal for two more bitters. He continued:

"I'll tell you, Charlie — and once said we won't say no more — it was *your* fault, because you wasn't a gentleman. I thought you was, and I was wrong. I didn't know *'oo* you was, mind you, but I did think you was a gentleman. That time after we first met in the street I said to Lily when she got 'ome . . . Lily, I said, 'e's a gentleman. Because I did think you was."

Charles could only pick up a single point of this indictment. He said weakly: "I don't quite know what you mean when you say you didn't know *who* I was. . . . Lily introduced us."

"Wot I mean is, you never told Lily about your dad bein' a Sir. It was Reg found that out. You never told nobody."

Charles agreed that he hadn't. "I didn't think of it — or maybe when I did I thought it would sound boastful. Anyhow, to get back to what happened, my father came to see you and had a talk with you all, and then . . . then what?"

"That's all. We just talked and I brought 'im 'ere and 'im and me 'ad another talk, man to man. A real gentleman, your dad is, that I will say."

"What did Lily think of him?"

"She liked 'im. Who could 'elp it? Of course 'e was upset, but then afterward 'e got friendly same as if 'e'd known us all for years."

"He was upset?"

"An' why shouldn't 'e be? 'E 'adn't bin told any more than we 'ad. 'E didn't even know you knew Lily. It was a shock to 'im, the way it would be to any father. 'E 'as 'is 'opes on you, Charlie. An' all the time 'e thought you was studyin' at college you was carryin' on with a gel 'e never knew about. Natchrally 'e was upset. . . . Mind you, that was at first, at the 'ouse. Afterward when 'im and me came 'ere we 'ad quite a lively time, like Mrs. Webber was sayin'."

"Tell me — tell me just this — did you ever, during the talk you had — threaten — or say anything to him — about bringing a charge against me?"

"A *charge?*"

Mr. Mansfield's stare was so bewildered that Charles knew it was the completest possible answer in itself. But he felt driven to continue: "A charge in a police court – a charge of . . ." But he somehow could not bring himself to speak the word "abduction."

"Gawd, no, I never said nothin' about that," Mr. Mansfield answered glumly, as if it were a mystery that must remain one or spoil his evening. Charles was devoutly glad that an interruption enabled them both to drop the matter at exactly that moment. For the door of the bar had opened and a voice was shouting: "Wotcher, Freddy – and 'ow's Freddy?"

Mr. Mansfield swung around, happily diverted. "Well, if it ain't old 'Arry! . . . 'Arry, this is Mr. Anderson – you remember Sir 'Avelock Anderson 'oo I came 'ere with the other night? This is Sir 'Avelock's son. . . . Charlie. . . . Mr. Byfield."

Harry Byfield, an excited little tub of a man with waxed mustaches, gripped Charles's hand and held it while he bestowed a beam of overacted recognition. "My goodness, and don't 'e look like 'is dad too! Same eyes, same nose. . . . Charlie, what're you 'avin? . . . Three bitters, Mrs. Webber, and 'ow's Mrs. Webber?"

Charles, who had never thought he looked much like his father at all, found this rather disconcerting. But it was a sample of what went on all the evening, with customer after customer. What an audience his father must have had, he reflected, and after so many bitters and in spite of his own personal troubles, he could not help feeling slightly amused.

The bar filled up as the evening progressed, and the very crowding of it enabled Charles occasionally to get Mr. Mansfield alone. Then he put questions that seemed all the more urgent because he had either to shout them at normal speaking range or else whisper them loudly in Mr. Mansfield's ear. Whenever possible he did the latter. Nobody was listening or trying to, and there could not perhaps have been any place safer for the discussion of utterly private matters.

"Tell me about Lily," he kept saying more insistently as the drinks affected him. "Tell me about her. You say she's all right – but is she happy?"

"Well now, you know Lily," Mr. Mansfield temporized. "She ain't wot you might call an un'appy gel by nature. She was upset, like we all was, but you don't 'ave to worry. She'll get over it."

Charles was more worried that she might than that she mightn't. And then, through the undulating lens of alcohol, he saw Lily as incomparably fair and lovely, beckoning to him from some distant land where she would be happy anyway, with him if he joined her or without him if he didn't. Yes, he knew Lily. She liked people. She *loved* people. She loved *everybody*. She loved her father and mother and Bert and Evelyn and Maud. She loved Reg. She loved Mr. Graybar and Ethel and the busker outside the theater who had stuck his collecting bag through the taxi window. She loved Weigall and Peters. She even loved his father. It was easy for her to do all she could to please all these people because she loved them all. And for the same reason it had been easy for her to do anything she could to please him, Charles. Why, she even loved places, too. She loved Linstead. She loved Cambridge. And she would doubtless love that nice place in the country whose whereabouts Mr. Mansfield would not disclose.

"But surely we can write to each other," Charles pleaded. "If I send a letter won't you forward it?"

"I give my word I wouldn't, Charlie."

"But what if she writes to me? Can't I answer? You can't stop her from writing."

"Well now, Charlie, we was all 'opin' you'd understand."

"I'm damned if I do. I don't think you do either. Because – don't you realize – I want to marry her. I asked her and she said she would if you consented. I'm twenty-one next month, so I don't need my father's consent after that."

Mr. Mansfield stroked his chin and was about to reply when someone pushed through the crowd and clapped him violently on the shoulder. There followed the inevitable greetings and introductions and respectful references to Sir 'Avelock and another round of bitters; it was half an hour before Charles had a chance to repeat what he had said, though somewhat less coherently.

So Mr. Mansfield stroked his chin again. "Charlie, wot you say does you credit. Maybe you wasn't a gentleman that once, but you tike after your dad, like 'Arry Byfield said, and your dad's a gentleman if ever there was one. That's why I give 'im my word. It's right wot 'e said, too. Lily's a nice gel, as nice a gel as a father could wish to 'ave, but she wouldn't be a 'elp to you, Charlie, not in your kind of life. Man to man, and speakin' as men of the world, your dad and I agreed about that. Not that I ain't just as proud of my own family, mind you – my great granddad was in the Battle of Waterloo – we got a 'istory too, the Mansfields 'ave. Only, as your dad said, with all your ejucation and the position you'll 'ave later on – "

"Oh, for God's sake," Charles interrupted, "will you let me tell you the plain truth? I'm not going to have the kind of future my father's planning for me. I've done so badly in my examinations I couldn't have it even if I wanted it."

"That's wot Lily said, and it upset 'er, thinkin' she was part responsible."

"Let me finish. There's no reason for anybody to be upset. When I'm twenty-one I shall have enough money and I'm going to live abroad and if Lily will marry me we can both be happy. Now then, will you consent?"

"Charlie, it ain't a bit o' good you carryin' on about it. I give my word to your dad. You're too 'eadstrong, that's wot's the matter with you. But I tike back wot I said when I said you wasn't a gentleman. . . ." Mr. Mansfield also was beginning to feel the effects of six or seven bitters. It was almost ten o'clock; the barman was already blinking lights and calling for the last reorders; Mrs. Webber and Milly were rolling up their sleeves for a final crescendo of service. "Gawlummy, look at the time! Charlie, boy – one more, just to show there's no ill feelin'. And call me Fred. . . . Easy now, mind them glarsses. . . . Goo' night, 'Arry. . . . Goo' night, Mr. Wilkinson. . . . Two more please, Mrs. Webber, when you've a minute. . . . But wot I was sayin', Charlie, you're too 'eadstrong. She's only a gel yet, but like I said to the wife, a gel of sixteen can go around with an older feller, provided 'e's a gentleman, and that's wot I thought you was, Charlie." Mr. Mansfield seemed to have some vague awareness that he had said that before and the memory troubled him in a wispy sort of way. His eyes were red and wet, but probably due to the smoke.

The bitters came. Charles raised his glass and saw past the brown liquid to something on the opposite wall that brought him to a jerk of attention – the picture of a pretty girl holding up a glass of beer, just as he was, and the girl reminded him of Lily, and Lily reminded him of a word that Mr. Mansfield had just spoken about her.

"Sixteen," Charles muttered. "You said *sixteen*. . . ."

"Sixteen *then* – when you was first seein' 'er. . . . Goo' night, Mr. Beale – remember me to Mrs. Beale. . . . Goo' night, Scotty. . . . Seventeen now – seventeen a week ago larst Sunday."

"She never told me."

"You never told 'er things neither. But I tike back wot I said, remember that." Mr. Mansfield raised his own glass and for the first time that evening offered a toast. "Well, Charlie . . . 'ere's to us and our dear ones. . . ."

Charles did not remember much of what happened during the next few hours. He had an impression that they left the Prince Rupert together, but their conversation, if any, did not stay in his mind. Later he woke up in darkness with a terrific headache and an enormous confrontation of difficulties – physical difficulty in finding a light switch and, when he had found one and pressed it, mental difficulty in recognizing the scene, and visual difficulty in facing any kind of illumination. At length he decided he had been asleep on the couch in the parlor at Ladysmith Road. He was fully dressed except for jacket and shoes, which were beside him.

Feeling parched, he fumbled his way to the kitchen sink. Along the lobby he could hear loud snores from upstairs. He drank several glasses of water and returned to the parlor to put on his shoes, but this was too much of an undertaking, so he leaned back on the couch. Doubtless more time passed, because when he looked again there was light beyond the *Ficus elastica* as well as dangling from the ceiling. He remembered then that Lily had said there were trains every hour throughout the night between Linstead and London. So it really didn't matter what time it was. This seemed an enormous boon as he laced his shoes and put on his coat. In the pocket he found a pencil and his Cambridge tailor's bill that had arrived at Beeching the previous morning; he hadn't opened it, but he did so now, merely to use the envelope. On the back of this he wrote: *Dear Mr. Mansfield, Thanks, I'm all right. Best wishes, C.* He left the note on the top of the radio-gramophone.

As he went to the front door he could still hear snores from upstairs. They reminded him of something that sent him back to the parlor and the radio-gramophone. He crossed out "Mr. Mansfield" and wrote "Fred."

In the street the cool air, which he had hoped might be refreshing, merely invited a fuller onslaught of nausea. He had been drunk a few times before, but never like this. His last act in Ladysmith Road was to vomit, monumentally, into the gutter a few yards from the corner of the High Road. Then, with some relief, he was able to catch the 4:23 at Linstead Station. From Liverpool Street, where he felt worse again after the train journey, he took a taxi to an all-night Turkish bath in a street near the Haymarket. But even after every ministration it could offer, including a long doze in the steam room, he still felt far from himself when he left it around noon. Or rather, he speculated, perhaps he did feel himself, and what he had felt before had never been himself at all. A rather grim change, as if he had grown out of something, but not yet into something else.

During the next few days at Beeching Charles was able to confirm that the change existed, though less grimly and no longer by any possibility the result of a hangover. For the first time he found himself meeting his father on territory where boundaries were recognized. He made no disclosures of his recent trip to Linstead and Havelock put no questions. Charles walked about the Beeching gardens feeling somehow adult and hard-bitten, and in a perverse kind of way relishing it. He wrote, for instance, to Brunon, who had a teaching job at Clermont-Ferrand; he asked what sort of place that was to live in. What he must wait for, of course, was his twenty-first birthday – the first step; but he gave his father no inkling of any special urgency. That would be revealed on the day he was of age for acts as well as words. Not that his planning was sensational – merely to step down finally from the educational ladder, without trying for any higher rung, and live abroad on his private income. It might not be heroic – private incomes rarely were – but he had no wish to be heroic. As for Lily in his scheme of things, he was, he knew, handicapped by her age; perhaps he would have to wait awhile, but surely not till she also was of age – that would be unthinkable. The whole matter was one he must explore, legally to begin with, then he would know where he stood. So far he had behaved like a youth; from now on he must do things with a man's determination and responsibility.

Havelock was immensely genial during this period. After dinner father and son would usually sit in the library drinking port for an hour or so – a pose of eighteenth-century comeliness that well matched the house. But each was secretly measuring the other and aware of a trigonometry of distance between them. Often the conversation turned to Havelock's early triumphs in the law – he liked to recollect them and how he had outwitted this or that witness or an opposing counsel. Charles could picture his father wigged and gowned and pointing a playful finger over the courtroom – Prospero casting his spell till, suddenly, the mask withdrawn, everything dissolved in Caliban fury. Charles had seen this happen in his dreams, but now, because he was no longer afraid, he did not banish it from his waking thoughts — he even welcomed it, with a slight burlesque of being impressed. He knew his father reveled in the high drama, but his own enjoyment was to snap the tensions by some light remark that Havelock could not relish, though it was never anything to which he could object. "I'll bet you put on a show," was the sort of thing Charles would comment, in half-derisive admiration. For Havelock was still putting on a show.

The darkest moment came when he asked why Charles didn't paint any more — had he given it up after Charnock's verdict? Charles shrugged in answer, then said obscurely: "You're the one to worry about verdicts, not me." The truth was, he couldn't endure just then even the thought of painting, much less a discussion of it with his father. It belonged somehow to the part of him that was hurt, the part that could not be bitten hard enough to become hard-bitten.

Sometimes comedy came unsought as when, for instance, Charles asked if there had ever been any reply to that letter Havelock had written to *The Times* about the honorary degree.

Havelock seemed to have to ransack his memory for any recollection of the incident (he always found it easy to forget the foolish things he had done), but at length he replied: "Oh yes, just one — but only from some crazy fellow." Amiably he went to the bureau where he kept his papers and began a search. "Some parson — if I can find it. Addressed to me personally, of course — he must have known it wouldn't do for *The Times*. . . . Here it is."

Scribbled on embossed notepaper from a Yorkshire vicarage, it pointed out that the initial letters of "Sagacity, Willpower, Integrity, Nobility, Experience" (which Havelock had offered as his own better translation of the Latin) could well supply a motto for the entire Coalition administration in its choice of appointees to government positions — a choice naturally dictated by such a leader as Lloyd George. The motto the parson suggested was: "Scottish, Welsh, Irish, Never English."

"Now who would have thought of that?" Havelock mused. "Of course the fellow must be off his head."

Charles began to laugh, and soon was laughing almost hysterically. The whole incident seemed to find its perfect end in a joke that was all the better because his father did not see it.

The twenty-first birthday fell on a Friday, so Charles and his father went to London that morning, having planned a week end that would include dinner at Havelock's club and an evening at the London Pavilion, where there was a good revue. They would stay a couple of nights at Claridge's and return on Sunday morning. On the Sunday evening a few local guests would come to dinner at Beeching.

Havelock's club was among the more exclusive, and it was hard for a young man just of age not to feel that admittance to it, as his father's honored guest, symbolized something not to be lightly disregarded in the world's scheme of things. The fact that Charles was about to disregard it, and not lightly at all, made him feel rather serious as he sat in the deep library chair before dinner and drank an almost sacramental sherry. The superbly proportioned room with its high ceilings and near-great portraits and vistas of wine-red carpet — all were alchemy to the soul; it was a very wonderful life, doubtless, for those who were rich and important and well content to be both. A far cry from Ladysmith Road, and nearly as far from living at Clermont-Ferrand on three hundred a year (for Brunon had already replied that this was possible if one were content with a modest *ménage*). It only remained now for Charles to make the announcement, and because he would rather spoil an evening's entertainment than a good dinner he had decided to bring the matter up while they were drinking coffee in the library afterward. There would only be a short time then before having to leave for the theater, but Charles did not see why the announcement should take long.

The dinner was indeed good, though Havelock assured him it was just the ordinary club meal. "But I'm glad I brought you here, Charles. I hope to put you up for membership one of these days, so it's appropriate we should choose it for our celebration. Incidentally, I believe this is the first time we've ever dined out together." It was, not counting train dinners and times when they had both been guests of neighbors around Beeching. "You may not realize it, Charles, but a father finds it hard to get to know his son, and therefore easy to postpone the effort. I hope we shall make that effort jointly – from now on." He waited for some response, but Charles could not think of any. "I'd like this to be the beginning of confidence between us. Don't think I shall be unsympathetic – even about Lily."

Charles flushed, resenting Havelock's use of the first name, as if there were in it some intolerable assertion of intimacy. Yet he could not help probing the matter by answering: "Yes, you met her, didn't you?"

"I did, and thought her charming – though of course utterly unsuited to you, apart from her age."

"You mean her Cockney accent – all that?"

"Well, it would be no help, though she might manage to unlearn it – others have. Much more important is a lack in her of something you need, Charles – you especially. Even at her age one can tell she hasn't got it – a drive, a dynamism – you need a woman who will push you ahead, not just freewheel along in any mood you set for her."

Charles was surprised by his father's assessment of Lily; he had expected the class angle to count much more. He said: "How about being happy? Doesn't that come into the scheme of what you think I need?"

"No one should put happiness first, Charles. One doesn't die without it. From my own experience I can assure you of that."

"But wouldn't you have *preferred* to be happy?"

"Yes, if it could have come from achievement – from triumph. But not from mere *being*. Not just bliss. The Orientals believe in bliss – and look at them. Whereas, to take an opposite example, the Americans *pursue* happiness – it's the pursuit they stress, not the happiness itself. The phrase is even written into their Declaration of Independence — and look at *them.* They count."

"Because they've pursued happiness without finding it?"

"Yes — rather than finding it and languishing with it."

"I don't much care for pursuing things. I suppose that's why I'm no good at games."

"But you haven't the blood in you to languish. Or if you have, I don't know where it comes from."

"From my mother, perhaps. I hope so."

"You mean you wish you were not my son?"

"I don't think that follows . . . but haven't you wished it too — sometimes?"

They faced each other, as near to the core of some central issue as they had ever been, and aware of it. At that moment, if the message in Havelock's eyes had persisted, Charles might have decided to leave Beeching and his father and never see either again. But it changed, and Havelock further eased the tension by a slow smile. "I don't see any reason to bicker, Charles. I just wanted you to know I liked Lily."

"That's fine. I liked her too. In fact I still like her. And if I had the chance, now that I'm of age, I'd marry her. But you've seen to it that I don't have the chance."

"You can still have it if you want it enough."

"What do you mean?"

"Didn't Mansfield tell you *anything?*"

"He said nothing about . . ." Then Charles saw he had fallen into the oldest trap in the cross-examiner's repertoire. "Oh, well," he added, transferring some of his anger to himself, "you evidently know it all, so what's the difference? Mansfield told me nothing except that he'd given you his word, he'd given you his word — he repeated that like a litany."

"Then he kept his word too. Quite a fellow." Havelock paused. "Share another bottle of claret? . . . No? . . . Just the ordinary claret they have here, but not bad, I think. . . . Sure you won't? . . . Charles, let me be frank about all this. No father nowadays can put a final veto on a son's marriage — and that's as it should be. But when the girl's still so young – younger than you ever thought she was, younger than she told you she was – surely there's a case for delay . . . or at least no need for any special hurry? Mansfield and I agreed that if, at the end of a year, you and Lily both wished, you could begin meeting again. . . . And later still – say in eighteen months or two years – and she'd only be nineteen then, remember – "

"And in the meantime?"

"No meetings – no letters, communications of any kind – for a year – on either side."

"And what did *she* say to that?"

"Very little, as I remember. She didn't make a scene, though. Bless her."

"But she agreed to the separation?"

"In all fairness, Charles, I must point out there was nothing else she could do. After all, a father does have some control over a seventeen-year-old – "

"Did she know it was only to be for a year?"

"We didn't go into that with her. I didn't intend to with you, either, but I was tempted just now – I wanted to make your birthday a more cheerful one. Don't be distressed. If, after a year, as I said – "

"I know what *you* said – what I want to know is what *she* said. What were the words she used? How did she take it? I can't believe – "

"As I told you before, she was perfectly charming – both to her father and me. Other girls might have been sulky or hysterical or hostile – instead of which – well, I couldn't help admiring her attitude. And perhaps in her heart she felt the reasonableness of ours."

"Damn the reasonableness."

"A year isn't much, Charles. You once said that yourself."

Charles remembered and it made him bitter. "Yes, I suppose as a test of true love it's romantic as well as reasonable."

"I've weakened it, though, by letting you know it exists. I've given you that much advantage."

"Like throwing a dog a small bone."

"No . . . like revising — slightly — the handicap in a race."

"To make it more exciting for the spectator."

Havelock chuckled. "Your brain works rather well when you're excited."

"I'm not excited — not in the way you are, anyhow. And whether it's a week or a month or a year, as far as I'm concerned, I promise nothing, I've agreed to nothing. Let's end the argument on that."

"Yes — gladly. I was equally glad to end my argument with Mansfield, in which — I think you tend to overlook this — I really succeeded in getting you out of serious trouble. . . . Tell me, incidentally — this isn't arguing, I'm just curious — what would be your rating of Mansfield?"

"Rating? I don't know that I rate people at all. I thought him decent and honest, simple and — and — in a sort of way — sweet. Like a good apple. I'd trust him. He'd keep his word — even if he ought never to have given it."

"So it puzzles you a little — why he did give it?"

"Not when I think of you in action against him. You have a persuasive manner."

"And you think that was all? I'm really flattered, Charles." Havelock poured himself more claret and again Charles saw, as in his dreams, the pose of one about to strike, even at the risk of unwisdom; grim glee infesting the eyes, a euphoria that ran riot in the bloodstream, so that the cheeks reddened and shone with what, in an athlete, would have suited the moment of passing the tape or vaulting the bar. "Charles, my experience in the courts taught me many things. One of them is the meaning of the word 'corruptible.' It means 'more corruptible than the person using the word.' Take plain bribery, for instance. With some people — those we call honest — a bribe has first to be explained as something else, something reasonable and fair and legitimate. Then cupidity must be aroused — a universal attribute — after which the payment offered must be large enough to administer a slight shock, so that the honest payee will wonder if it *is* a bribe, and — out of a mixture of doubt and guilt and gratitude — will wish to treat the payer with the utmost fidelity. It's a very interesting process." He paused, aware that he was losing Charles's attention, then retrieved it by a fast grab. "How do the Mansfields come into all this? I'll tell you. They're quite hard pressed financially — buying their house through a building society and a radio-gramophone on the installment plan, all that sort of thing. He has steady employment, but poorly paid — only about five pounds a week, so the three girls and the boy have to help to support the family from their own small earnings. Clearly then, Lily couldn't give up her job and live in the country for a year at their expense . . . so the fair thing to do was quite obvious. But — and this really *is* the point at last — how much do you think it costs a girl to live with her relatives in the country for a year?"

Havelock took out his wallet and pushed a folded paper across the table to Charles. It was a canceled check made out to and endorsed by Frederick Mansfield for two thousand pounds.

Charles felt rather sick. "All right . . . so you pulled it off. You've been clever, I admit that. It's an odd thing to prove to me on the day I'm supposed to become a man — that life's full of wormholes and that you know how to find them . . . never mind, though, I'll admit that also. But now I've got a disillusionment for you. This career of mine you talk of — this career — this — this . . ."

His eyes were riveted by something else on the table before him. It was a telegram, addressed to Charles at Beeching, from his college tutor.

> HEARTIEST CONGRATULATIONS ON OBTAINING NOT ONLY FIRST IN TRIPOS BUT YOUR THESIS ALSO CONSIDERED SO GOOD STRONGLY RECOMMEND SUBMISSION FOR THE COURTENAY PRIZE. . . .

"It came yesterday," said Havelock. "I took the liberty of holding it back for our celebration tonight. . . . *Now* will you have a little more claret? We shall be late for the theater, but who cares?"

Paris II

THIRTY-ONE YEARS LATER CHARLES COULD SUM UP HIS early life as "nothing to complain of" without really wondering whether it had been or hadn't. He was much too pleased by his son's remark that he didn't look anything like his age; and for a second he glanced in a mirror on the wall of the Cheval Noir that showed him trim and *distingué* in his dinner jacket. "Do you really think, Gerald," he asked, fishing for another compliment, "I could safely allow a photograph of the author to be used as a frontispiece for my book?" He laughed, of course, so that his son should know it was partly a joke.

"You bet you could," Gerald answered, loyally. "You're really very handsome. You look a bit like Ronald Colman."

"And *who* is Ronald Colman?"

"Oh come now, Dad, you must know that."

"I will admit I do, but I find that a great impression can be made nowadays by claiming never to have heard of somebody."

Gerald grinned. "You're pretty smart too."

"Am I — away from dinner parties and agreeable company? Sometimes lately I've begun to doubt it." At a remark like that Palan stepped into Charles's mind like an unwanted guest who finds the door left open, and because he would otherwise have had to quell an almost unconquerable preoccupation Charles began to talk about Palan to Gerald, though of course without mentioning the name. "You know, Gerald, this job I have isn't the kind of thing it used to be. You may think me snobbish — it's so easy to be thought that nowadays — but when I first started in diplomacy one could always assume that whatever the sort of fellow one was up against there'd be at least some things in common – a professional training, for instance, and a minimum code of manners. Your opponent might trick you, he might be dishonest or corrupt – my father used to say that everyone was corrupt to some extent – but you could count on him not yelling across the room like an auctioneer or belching after a heavy lunch. . . . But I mustn't bore you – here's Henri, wondering what we're going to eat. Anything special you fancy, my boy? This is an occasion, remember."

Henri presented the menu, which Gerald studied for a moment before replying: "My French isn't equal to it – maybe you'd better do the choosing."

Charles smiled. He had been prepared for this. "How about soup to begin with? May I suggest *tortue claire?*"

"Fine, whatever it is."

"Just turtle soup. And then perhaps *sole Véronique* – that's sole cooked in wine and served with a very delicate cream sauce and fresh grapes. And after that I can recommend Henri's way with a small chicken – *poulet en casserole à la maison* – "

Gerald put down the menu and tried to catch Henri's eye with a knowing wink, but of course Henri did not respond. "I wonder if I could just have a good thick steak after the soup."

"Certainly, m'sieu'."

Charles continued to smile; he had been prepared for this too. All he said was: "One thing you never have to specify here, Gerald – everything always *is* good. . . . I think then a *tournedos garni* for Gerald, Henri, with those little potatoes and *champignons*. I'll have the sole."

Henri bowed. After he had left them Gerald said, still looking amused: "What first made you so interested in food, Dad?"

"To that question, Gerald, I had better quote an answer made by a titled Englishwoman to the Duchess of Marlborough – who, as perhaps you know, was a titled American. The Duchess was informed that considering it is the only pleasure one can count on having three times a day every day of one's life, a well-ordered meal is of prime importance . . . *ben trovato,* possibly." Henri had approached with the wine list. "A Chablis, Henri. . . . Try a small glass, Gerald, after the soup."

"Okay."

"It's a very simple wine."

"I thought one ordered wines by the year."

Charles smiled again; it was a matter he liked to have brought up. "Your millionaire junk merchant *always* does – he learns a few words and dates like Liebfraumilch Forty-seven and thinks it makes him a connoisseur. I myself would *generally* know the best years for a Burgundy or a champagne or a claret, but with a Chablis I leave everything to Henri, who was born quite close to the town of Chablis. . . . Isn't that so, Henri?"

"At Auxerre, m'sieu'," said Henri beaming.

"Oh yes?" Gerald suddenly spoke up. "I think I know of it." He was evidently at pains to demonstrate that he wasn't an ignoramus in every field of knowledge. "Didn't Clovis capture Auxerre from the Romans in the fifth century?"

"I haven't the slightest idea," answered Charles with keen delight, "and I don't suppose Henri has either. So you put us both in our place. I took my degree in history, and I've never regretted doing so, though I expect I've forgotten 90 per cent of all I ever learned. One does, you know. But the other 10 per cent, if well cared for, can stand one in pretty good stead. . . . Thank you, Henri. Oh yes – and a small *salade gauloise.*" Henri bowed and left them again. "I'm glad you're interested in history, Gerald. Perhaps it'll win you a Cambridge scholarship next year."

"I think I shall take economics."

"Well, that includes a lot of history – and vice versa. I remember when I was at Cambridge I used to go to Pigou and Keynes – that was at the end of the war which we now call the *First* World War, though it was Colonel Repington back in 1919 who originated the phrase and was well trounced for it."

"Did you enjoy Cambridge?"

"Very much indeed. Of course I'm fortunate to have it associated in my mind with pleasant things – such as a First in the

Tripos and the Courtenay Prize. I didn't like games and I was too shy in those days to take part in Union debates, but I think I can say that Cambridge gave me, if nothing else, a sense of kinship with tradition — of being privileged, if the metaphor isn't too fanciful, to touch the pulse of five centuries with the tip of one's little finger. I remember what a thrill I got when I found that a previous occupant of my college rooms had introduced the turnip from Holland in the late seventeenth century — thus becoming a benefactor of English agriculture, though certainly not of the English dinner table. . . . Strange, though, when one looks back on early life, how it's the little incidents that stay in the mind. I remember once, while I was researching at the British Museum, being told that the desk I was working at had been used by Karl Marx when he was writing *Das Kapital*. . . . I mentioned that to Palan the other day, by way of making conversation — "

"Who's Palan?"

Charles had spoken the name without thinking, though now he had done so he felt it did not matter. "One of my opponents at the Conference. A disciple of Marx, of course."

"I think I've seen pictures of him in the papers. Rather a jolly-looking fellow."

"He would certainly never forget to smile when being photographed."

"What did he say when you told him about the desk at the British Museum?"

"Nothing. He just stopped picking his nose."

Gerald laughed. "You've certainly got your knife into him all right."

"On the contrary, he has his into me. Mine's quite incapable of piercing such a hide. And yet, in an odd sort of way, I don't absolutely *dis*like the fellow. It's hard to say why not. I have every reason to — personal, professional, and political. The other evening I was reading Montesquieu and I came across . . ." Charles stopped; he saw that Gerald had glanced covertly beneath the rim of the table at his wrist watch. The fact that the movement had been so carefully shielded, that the boy was clearly anxious not to hurt a father's feelings, gave Charles a needlelike twinge in the center of his stomach. Was it possible that he was *boring* Gerald? He continued hastily: "But don't let me run on like this. Tell me more about your adventures in Switzerland."

"Yes, I'd like to, before I – I mean, while there's still time. I mustn't forget my train."

"When did you say it was?"

"Er . . . ten-thirty. . . ."

"And from the Gare St. Lazare, I think you said. Leave here by ten and you'll be all right. . . . You were telling me earlier that you did some climbing."

"Oh yes – and golf and tennis too. At Mürren they were having tournaments at the hotel and I entered – just to get a game actually – never thought I had a chance, but I won the mixed doubles – my partner was awfully good. It's a silver cup – I've got it in my bag – like me to show you?"

Even had Charles been interested in games he would not have cared to interrupt a dinner in such a way. He smiled tolerantly and answered: "Oh, don't bother now – I'll see it when we're at home. But I'm very glad you were able to get the kind of holiday you enjoy. So many people – diplomats, for instance – have to enjoy the kind they get. When I think of all the time I've spent at horrible little resorts that happened to be the only places where the Legation staff could go to escape the heat, or dysentery, or some national holiday that was sure to be marked by anti-British demonstrations in the capital – "

"You can put all *that* into your book, anyway."

"Oh certainly. And I shall. There was a place near Constanza, on the Black Sea . . ."

At ten minutes to ten he called for the bill and excused himself, ostensibly to make a telephone call. The only telephone at the Cheval Noir was in Henri's little office at the rear; but Charles did not actually use the instrument. Presently he returned to find Gerald ready to leave and a little fidgety.

"Dad, it's been a wonderful dinner – I've had a grand time."

"My pleasure too, Gerald. I only wish we could have seen more of Paris together."

"Yes, so do I."

"Maybe we'll have some other chance."

"You bet we will. . . . And Dad, why don't you stay here and finish your coffee? I hate to rush you out like this – no need for you to see me off at the train, we'll be meeting again in London so soon."

"Very thoughtful of you, Gerald. In that case I'll just put you into a cab."

Charles noted the relief on Gerald's face. It hurt him again, but less so because he was now making plans of his own. He took the boy to the curb and summoned a taxi from the line of them in the middle of the street. Then he shook hands with his son and gave the driver instructions in very rapid French.

" 'By, Dad. Thanks again."

"Good-by, my boy. *Bon voyage.*"

Charles returned to his table and asked Henri to bring him another *fine*. He felt chastened and also a little unworthy. For the thing he had done instead of telephoning was to look up the timetable and confirm that there was no such thing as a ten-thirty boat train from St. Lazare. And what he had told the driver in rapid French was to return to the restaurant and tell him where he had taken the young man.

Half an hour later Charles was in the same taxi, having ordered the driver rather testily: "Just take me there – you don't need to describe the place." Feeling, as he did, somewhat contaminated by the thought that he was about to spy on his own son, he certainly did not want to cement the treachery by any sort of gossip in advance. Naturally after such a rebuff the driver navigated the streets with added recklessness – the route led along the Boulevard des Capucines, then the Boulevard des Italiens toward the Place de la République. . . . And with every mile Charles wondered what he was going to do when he got to wherever it was, or if he could even do anything at all. For there were circumstances in which Paris was a wonderful city to be fatherless in . . . and at such a speculation Charles had nothing to aid him but certain recollections of his own.

It would probably (he remembered) be one of those dingy buildings with a mansard roof and peeling stucco and an advertisement for Byrrh facing from across the street in huge letters. . . . And to think of Gerald at seventeen . . . Why, in his own case, he had been twenty-two when he . . . when he spent those six months with the Décharays to polish up his accent. Professor Décharay used to take him and the other students to the Louvre and the museums during the day; but sometimes in the evenings, after dinner, on the pretext of a lecture a few of them would go off on their own. . . . He had often wondered if the good professor had guessed where they went, for he twirled his mustache rather waggishly when they greeted him the next morning at breakfast. . . .

And somehow now those adventures, though Charles shrank from the translation of them into the life and times of his son, nevertheless did not give him any equal distaste when they were recalled. Rather the contrary. Too bad one mustn't put that sort of thing into a book – not that he would dream of doing so, even if he could. He wasn't that sort of writer, though he must confess he could sometimes enjoy himself as that sort of reader. Fashions were changing, standards were crumbling, people talked at dinner tables more freely, one might suppose (though one could hardly be sure), than eminent Victorians in bedrooms; chats on the radio and faces in television were taking the place of spellbinding oratory and the front line of the chorus. . . . Perhaps he might devote a chapter in his book to the changing world he had seen – or no, there could be nothing new to say, he had better stick to what was important. The big thing in his career had undoubtedly been the Macedonian Boundary Commission; he must concentrate on that. It was his only title to fame, if any; the rest was just run of the mill. . . .

"*Run of the Mill*"

CHARLES AND BRUNON WERE AMONG THE NEW YEAR'S revelers welcoming 1922 at a Rhineland hotel. It was not a good time for painting, but Brunon had a short vacation from school and Charles, after Christmas at Beeching, had been glad to return to the Continent to meet his friend. During a succession of cold and sunny days they walked along the west bank of the Rhine, southward from Bonn. Brunon had visited this fabled territory before and knew of a small village called Assmannshausen, near Bingen, that would be pleasant to stay at; so they had arranged to have mail sent there *poste restante*. Assmannshausen was reached toward twilight, after a flurry of snow from the hills, and Brunon went to the post office while Charles sat in a café reading German papers. There was not much news. More snow was forecast. Francs and marks had fallen further. The Washington Armaments Conference was still in progress. Charles felt drowsy in the warmth after the icy air outside. He also felt very fit and reasonably content. It had been a good idea, taking a walking tour in January. Eccentric but invigorating. Brunon came in with a batch of letters and sorted them out on the scrubbed table top. There was a sprinkling of fresh snow on his coat and his face was pink from the wind. None of Charles's letters looked important, and he was putting them aside to read later when one slipped to the floor. As he picked it up he did not recognize the handwriting under Cobb's heavy crossing out, but the postmark "Linstead" caught his eye.

After a moment Brunon said: "Not bad news, I hope?"

"Not tragic, anyway. . . . A girl I know got engaged to somebody else."

Charles was pretending to reread, but actually looking for a miracle to make it all untrue. There was no miracle, and presently Brunon asked: "Is it going to bother you much?"

"I don't know – quite – yet – but I don't think so."

It was true that at the first moment of shock he didn't know. He hadn't thought of Lily a great deal, consciously, during the trip. Nor during Christmas at Beeching, nor during previous weeks in Berlin, where he had been fraternizing pleasantly with the German language and with the family of Professor Stapff. The separation, so hard to endure at first, had become something he was austerely used to, something he could almost fold to himself for perverse comfort; and the anticipation of seeing her again, which had been all there was to live on during summer and early autumn, had fallen into place along a quiet horizon of the future. But now, with her letter in his hand, the horizon darkened and a sense of loss brought such misery that he could hardly force himself to think, much less to talk rationally to Brunon about any other matter. A snowstorm began that evening, practically marooning them for several days at a small inn. There was nothing to do, and because he was utterly wretched Charles told Brunon the opposite of what he felt in the hope that by having to suit his behavior to it he might achieve some degree of self-discipline.

"Matter of fact, André, it's probably just as well." Even while he spoke the words he felt a betrayer, though what could he now betray?

"Were you engaged?"

"Not exactly. She was sixteen when we first met and that was less than a year ago. Absurdly young. Sweet though. A typist in an office."

"Anything wrong with being a typist in an office?"

"Of course not. I didn't intend to suggest – "

"But since you volunteer the information, is it not implied that the match would not be in all ways a suitable one?"

"I daresay the snobbish view might be that – for what it's worth. But otherwise – "

"And in your chosen profession it is worth a great deal. So you are perhaps fortunate to have been given such an easy escape."

"You think so? . . . Oh hell, let's have a bottle of wine – I'll bet the local stuff's good here."

"It is excellent. But tell me, Charles – and then we will not speak of her again unless you wish – I suppose it is because I paint that I like to visualize . . . was she *beautiful?*"

"*Was* she? You mean, *is* she – she's not dead just because someone else has her. . . . No, not specially beautiful, but . . . You want a description? Let me see . . . she has large violet eyes and a wide forehead and dark brown hair, complexion rather pale and a straight nose that seems somehow long because it isn't big. . . . And there's a gap between one upper tooth and the next, on the left side – a tiny gap that looks better than if it weren't there – it shows when she smiles and she smiles a lot because she's generally happy. . . . And she has small hands and feet–in fact, she's little altogether–incredibly little–practically no figure to speak of–"

"But at sixteen, my friend . . ."

Charles stamped angrily from his chair, then turned the anger against himself and the movement into a stretch and a yawn. He began to laugh in a ribald way. It seemed the final Judas touch, but having accomplished it he felt better able to compose, as he would have to, the necessary letter of congratulation. . . . hoping she and Reg would be happy. He hadn't much doubt about it.

Decades later, when he began to think he would one day write a book, 1922 was the year at which he decided to start the story of his life, because it was the year in which his career opened with quite a spurt of success. After spending six months in Europe polishing his languages, he did very well in the Foreign

Office examination; and when, about the same time, he won the Courtenay Prize for History it seemed possible that he was one of those young men for whom all ways are to be made smooth. His first chief, Sir Lionel Treves, at whose Legation in one of the smaller European capitals he presently became an attaché, thought highly of him, and Lady Treves liked his looks and was considerably intrigued by his manner. Neither had known him before, so they were unaware of how much he had changed. They thought he was far too quiet, but such a fault promised well in a youth whose appearance and ability were both beyond reproach.

Life at the Legation was tranquil, and the work so simple for a junior staff member that, except for further language study, Charles was able to give his brain a long and satisfying rest. He had little responsibility, and was amused to discover that after all his abstruse cramming most of the tasks that fell to him (such as deciphering and copying dispatches) were not beyond the resources of a reasonably intelligent sixth-former. He spent the mornings in the Chancery, often with long intervals of leisure during which he could read French and German novels; he got to know his colleagues, and the entire atmosphere, with its air of a cheerful enclave whose chance chosen inmates might as well make the best of each other, reminded him a little of the Brookfield Sanatorium in which, as a boy with some slight ailment, he had found a haven from the rigors of the outside world. Sir Lionel was a comfortable chief and did not count the hours his staff put in provided the job was done. Charles naturally took the menial duties, if that adjective could be applied to any of them; again it was rather like being a new boy at school. He began to make friends, most of them among the resident English — it was surprising how few, or at any rate how slowly, relationships developed with the people of the city. After leaving cards at the other Legations he was asked out to dinners, and found many pleasant acquaintances among his opposite numbers. Most afternoons, though, he spent alone from choice, exploring the city or attending some lecture or concert.

After that he would return to the Legation in case anything had been left for him to do; even if so it rarely made him late for dinner. Sometimes there was a rush of business when a bag came in, and once a royal visit threw everybody into a well-controlled commotion that lasted several weeks; but as a rule one could watch the European world through a delightful window on the edge of it – for the country had been neutral during the war and was consequently quite spotless and a little smug.

Charles shared a flat with the Second Secretary, a man named Snowden, who was unmarried; the First Secretary had a Swedish wife who sang Schubert and Hugo Wolf songs exquisitely. There was also a very handsome Military Attaché who drifted in and out of the Chancery with gossip about parties he had been to the night before; so far as Charles could judge, his functions were almost entirely decorative, and most of all at requiem masses whenever it was obligatory for the *corps diplomatique* to attend them. At these affairs the Military Attaché looked as if he had stepped right out of the pages of Ouida.

(Later in life, when some of Charles's moments were more arduous, and those who shared them with him pictured whimsically or ironically the kind of heaven they would choose for themselves, Charles would say: "Ah, you should have been *en poste* at —— during the twenties – those were the days!" But once, when he so expressed himself, a very old and distinguished-looking gentleman in a dressing gown replied, as urbanely as was possible within the confines of an air-raid shelter: "My boy, they were only the pale shadow of the life before you were born! Those were the real days – to be a youth of good family sixty years ago, when you could get into the Diplomatic without all this modern fuss about firsts and degrees – when all you needed was a private income and a father or uncle or somebody in high places to take care of you. It was simply the best club that ever existed – founded by the Congress of Vienna, developed by the wealth and conveniences of the industrial revolution, and not yet affected by all the political and social changes that have finally upset the applecart; a club of charming people living a gay life in every capital from Lisbon to what was then St. Petersburg — a few thousand families supplying the personnel, so that wherever you went you met people who knew the people you knew — a truly international set in a world full of international settings and social counterparts in every country — Ascot and Chantilly, Sandhurst and St. Cyr, Osborne and Ischl, the Quai d'Orsay and the Wilhelmstrasse and the Ballplatz, all the Bristol Hotels, and the *Compagnie Internationale des Grands Express Européens*. . . . The very words are remembered music that even guns and bombs cannot shatter! Ah, what a lovely world if you were born into the golden ranks of the inheritors!" And then the old man ended startlingly: "But I wasn't, and I hated its guts." Charles never saw him again or found out his name.)

Though in retrospect they acquired an austere and compensating glamour, Charles's first professional years contained many misgivings and a great deal of boredom. Occasionally also he was visited by a lost look that Lady Treves noticed and took to be some mysterious kind of reserve. It usually lifted among a crowd, and once or twice at some dinner party a few drinks released him into a mood in which he was apt to talk wittily enough for her to comment afterward to her husband: "Charles was quite amusing, wasn't he? Madame Papadoulos was much taken with him — asked me where he was from — I didn't know a great deal, I'm afraid."

"He comes of a very decent family, my dear. Sir Havelock Anderson was a successful K.C. till he made a fool of himself — they say he still does." Sir Lionel searched still further in the card index of his mind. "The mother was a Calthorpe, one of the Irish Calthorpes — she's been dead a long time. I think there was another son killed in the war. Not too much money. Charles will inherit what there is. . . . I met the father once — bit of a character — rather like a crazy old viking. Young Anderson's a more normal type, thank goodness."

"He has an interesting face. Is he going to do well?"

"I wouldn't be surprised. Fairly good school — and Cambridge. He did well there. Oh yes, he might have his own Legation sometime. The other day I had to tell him that."

"You *had* to tell him?"

"He suggested a brilliant idea for completely reorganizing the Register. So damned brilliant the Foreign Office would have had a fit. I told him that by the time he had his own Legation it would probably be adopted, but that for the present he'd better hide it as he would an affair with the mistress of one of the Russians. . . . I think I managed not to hurt his feelings."

"I hope so. He's really one of the nicest men we've had."

"If only he'd write a bit larger — or else I'll have to get some new spectacles. I think he could put the Lord's Prayer on a threepenny-bit if he tried hard."

"Did you know he paints?"

"Snowden mentioned it, but he's never offered to show me anything."

"I caught him at it once. He was doing the view of the square from the big window on a Sunday afternoon when he thought no one was around."

"Any good?"

"I wondered. But I couldn't very well ask him, could I? Anyhow, I could see he wasn't bad."

⁂

During his leaves, Charles sometimes spent short holidays with Brunon and for the rest of the time rented a service flat in London. He rarely visited Beeching for longer than a week at a stretch because, he told himself, the country bored him — which was easier, if less truthful, than to admit that he found his father's company a strain. It was not that they quarreled or failed to get along; indeed their relationship seemed more cordial than it had formerly been. Yet there was still an unease about it . . . a feeling that made Charles, if ever he heard his father going downstairs after they had gone to bed for the night, tiptoe to the landing with a curiosity he could hardly define — because he would never have acted thus with Snowden or Brunon, though in the morning he would probably have asked them what they had been roaming about the house for. But with his father he never put such a question.

Havelock, now approaching his seventies, had retained much of his fine physique and all his capacity for charming those he wanted to charm. Nor could it be said that he had become more eccentric, since he had already reached a limit beyond which the word would seem inadequate. What had happened was a sort of leveling off along a high plateau of singular behavior, in which the singularities were often so trifling that the mean average distance from normal could easily be overlooked. Much of his life was outwardly like those of his neighbors, and his pastimes, though odd, were no more so than those of many another man of his age and income. The porter at his club could doubtless have capped any queer story about him with other queer stories about other club members. Letters to *The Times* continued without further complications, for there were still old tombstones to be discovered and written about. All this was acceptable. So were parties at Beeching at which he could be a delightful host. It was just that sometimes in his company one could feel, by a heightened awareness, that one was in the presence . . . of a presence. Once Charles came upon him in the library pasting a typed poem inside a copy of the *Oxford Book of English Verse*. Here again, a normal curiosity would have made Charles approach and look over his father's shoulder, but he felt unable to do this; later, however, he found the book and inspected it. To his astonishment there were many of these pasted inserts, and most were obscene parodies of well-known poems. A few were rather clever. Charles was no prude, and quite unshockable by words, but what he did find depressing was the thought of so many busy hours devoted to some of the loveliest things in literature with only such a purpose in mind. He never mentioned the matter.

More discussable were Havelock's political views, which had become increasingly bitter and at odds with almost every charted orbit. He had hated the Coalition Government, but he hated the Labor Party just as much, and he despised the Liberals. If anything he was a Conservative, but of such an extreme variety that only a few men in parliament ever said anything he approved of, and these often belonged to other parties. He sometimes found things he agreed with in the unlikeliest quarters — a remark, for instance, by D. H. Lawrence: "Let there be a parliament of men and women for the careful and gradual unmaking of laws."

A book that impressed him a great deal was Spengler's *Decline of the West,* which was having an enormous vogue just then throughout Europe. Charles had been less impressed — partly, he admitted, because he had talked to so many professors who found innumerable technical errors in those parts of the book that concerned their own fields.

"But of course they would," Havelock retorted. "Ever watched a schoolteacher marking an exercise? The giggles of glee when he spots a mistake?" Havelock took a silver paper knife and scarred deeply into the mahogany desk top, as if crossing out a wrong answer. "That's how professors read Spengler — missing the point because they're waiting for their own pounce."

Charles thought there was some truth in this, but he was also puzzled by his father's vehemence and physical violence. After a pause Havelock said: "I suppose you're thinking I've spoiled that desk?"

"Well, you haven't improved it, have you?"

"It's not an antique. Came from a priest's house in Maynooth — my father-in-law bought it. Just a Victorian piece."

"But rather nice."

"So you really do care about these things — furniture, heirlooms, silver, all the stuff there is here?"

"I didn't say I really cared *for* them, but I'd do my share of taking care *of* them. There's a bit of difference, I think."

"Do you ever wonder what will happen to it all?"

"Well . . . what do *you* think?"

"One of these days it will burn."

"You mean catch fire? I hope not — but a great many country

houses do. The wiring's bad – Cobb tried an electric toaster the other day and nearly set the kitchen alight."

A moment later Charles was sorry he had mentioned this matter, for it made Havelock remember that they hadn't had a fire drill for over a year. So they had to have one – and immediately, since (as Havelock said) the essence of a fire drill is that you don't plan for it in advance. They fixed the canvas chute, with the guide ropes inside, that led down to the lawn from one of the top-floor windows. Havelock rang the big brass hand bell, whose only other function was to summon guests to the tea tent at garden parties. Since the servants slept in their own quarters away from the main house block, there was little reason for them to take part in the demonstration, but it was geared to Havelock's enjoyment of the whole thing that they should, especially the housemaids, whose nervousness and disordered skirts made him feel quite blithe. Aunt Hetty and Cobb were excused on account of age, but Havelock himself, older than either, sometimes made the descent twice, emerging at the bottom like some excited thrill-seeker at an amusement park. Charles did not much care for the experience, for he usually slid down too fast and got scratched, but he realized that since his own bedroom was on the top floor there was some point in it. His chief doubt was whether, if a fire ever started in the middle of the night, anyone would wake up in time to unroll the thing out of the window.

One June afternoon during his leave Charles had just made such a descent when a young woman came cycling up the drive. Without any introduction or preamble she exclaimed, amidst her own astonished laughter: "What on earth are you doing? You came shooting out as if it were the Tunnel of Love or something. . . . Have you hurt your arm?"

"No," said Charles, "but I've torn my trousers, that's why I'm keeping my hand there. . . . Is there – er – anything I can do for you?"

"I'm your new neighbor – Jane Coppermill – we've just moved into Burton Bridgwater. I thought I'd pay a call."

"Delighted. I'm Charles Anderson. My father's in the house somewhere. This is a fire drill we have once a year or so. . . . Those top rooms, as you can see — a regular trap. I believe the insurance company recommended this contrivance." He felt he had to offer some plausible reason for it all. "Excuse me and I'll go in and change, if you don't mind hanging around till I come back."

"Can't I go in and meet your father?"

"Why, er — certainly, if you want."

She leaned her bicycle against the portico and entered the house with him. As they crossed the hall she whispered: "Tell me first, though — is it true he's a little mad?"

Charles answered: "Yes, we all are. The Mad Andersons. Didn't you know that? We're the talk of the county." How else could one deal with such a question? He would rather have snubbed her, but he could not think of a snub in time, so the badinage would have to do, and if she caught behind it a reproof, so much the better. Meanwhile, without helping her to search for Havelock, he left her standing in the hall and went upstairs. When he came down she had apparently gone without seeing Havelock, but Havelock had seen her through the window and asked who she was. Charles explained.

"Yes, I heard somebody had bought Burton Bridgwater," he mused. "Coppermill — *Coppermill.* If it's the newspaper Coppermills they're rich."

They were indeed, and Jane was their youngest child. Not so much of a child, though. She was thirty-one, unmarried, and completely unafraid — even of remaining a spinster. She went through life armored by personality, so that she could be herself, whatever behavior that involved, and more often than not she got away with it because it was all over, clearly well meant and forgivable, before anyone could stop her. She was not pretty, but she was healthy and vigorous and lively, and there were times when one examined her features separately and wondered why the total did not add up to real beauty, but the very fact of wondering made the discrepancy less. She had clear blue eyes and a downright look. She would talk to a butcher boy, if she met him in the course of her day's affairs, as abruptly and frankly as she would to the Third Secretary of a Legation (Charles had recently been so promoted). This was not because she felt herself to be consciously democratic, but simply because a natural inclination to follow her impulses had been reinforced by long experience that she could always afford the luxury.

During this particular leave Charles did not see her again, but a few months later when he was back at work he was called to the Legation telephone; it was Jane Coppermill, just ashore from a cruise liner. She would be staying in the city for three days and wondered if they could meet. Charles was mildly pleased, for he suddenly thought of the Tunnel of Love and realized that his life in the neutral capital, though increasingly agreeable, was still somewhat lacking in fun. Unfortunately all three evenings were taken up with official engagements he could not get out of – one of them a rather big reception which all the *corps diplomatique* would attend. After he had explained this she said: "Oh, tell your boss I'm here – he'll probably invite me." Afterward Charles thought it would have been more correct for her to announce her own arrival, if she knew the Treveses, but it was too late then to suggest it. When Treves came in later that afternoon Charles mentioned that Jane Coppermill had called. Treves immediately remembered her. "Anyone would who was at Berne in those days."

Charles looked his interest and Treves continued: "She must have been in her late teens then – at some finishing school – just before the war. The Minister was away and I was in charge, which made it all the worse – for me."

"What happened?" Charles asked.

"She fell into the bear pit among the bears. It's a well-known show place at Berne. Goodness knows how it happened. She poked at the bears with an umbrella to hold them off till she was rescued, but the keeper broke a leg doing it and the Swiss said it was all her fault. There was an inquiry and letters in the Berne papers – then London got to hear of it – oh, quite a set-to.

In the end I believe her father had to pay the man a very handsome amount. . . . The Bernese, you know, really love those bears. I think if she'd poked one in the eye even in self-defense we should have had a real international incident. . . . She's probably less of a hoyden now. Why don't you ask her to the reception if she's going to be here tomorrow?"

Charles said he would be glad to.

When he met her he was startled by her appearance. Naturally he had expected her to look very different in evening clothes from the only recollection he had of her — leaning on a bicycle in rough country tweeds; but he had not realized the strikingness of her. She was a woman one would look at twice and wonder who she was, whether or not one afterward decided that it mattered. Moreover her personality had an air of challenging without breaking the rather stiff protocol which marked the opening proceedings of a reception of this kind. Afterward, of course, formalities could be relaxed, though it was still a wise precaution not to forget them altogether.

Charles had already discovered that in the small world of a diplomatic corps there were always white sheep whom one personally liked and could treat as friends, and black sheep whom one didn't like or who represented countries suspect by one's own government; but to all, of course, one must behave with correctness. So much was elementary, but a problem could arise when someone personally liked fell into the black category. This had recently happened in Charles's world to a foreign attaché named Davanrog, who had been very popular till his country did something unpopular, after which everyone was so sorry for Davanrog that he was in some danger of becoming more popular than ever. However, the cautionary word was slipped by Treves to his staff, with a resulting cancellation of several projected hunting and fishing trips. And Davanrog, who must have known there was nothing personal in it, probably did not take it too much to heart.

He was a fine-looking fellow, and when Charles saw Jane Coppermill greet him at the reception like an old friend, he wondered if his own instant feeling could have any personal jealousy in it; but he decided not — after all, Jane was nothing to him, just a country neighbor he had met once and hadn't bothered to meet again till she herself made the effort. They had met for this second time with cordiality, but no more — not as much, it would seem, as there was between her and Davanrog. Charles wished, though, he had had a chance to tell her that Davanrog, for purely political reasons, was somewhat out of favor with the British; noticing that Treves also had his eye on her, he hoped his chief would not feel he was to blame. It was not clear how he could be, but the niceties of diplomatic behavior were apt to carry such vague and indefinable responsibilities. Anyhow, Charles was relieved when he saw her leave Davanrog and allow herself to be taken to supper by one of the Dutchmen, with whom she also seemed extremely cordial; but Charles was troubled again when, after a minimum of polite circulation among the throng, Davanrog made his excuses to the Treveses and left early. It was a perfectly proper thing to do, but it left glaringly obvious the fact that the man's only fun at the party had been with Jane.

Later in the evening Charles danced with her. She was a good dancer; he was just average. He did not much like dancing anyway, but it was a social accomplishment he could not disdain as he did golf and tennis. "So you know Davanrog?" he asked casually.

"I met him once before — in Copenhagen."

With such a cue, and knowing so little about her, Charles was quick to comment: "You travel about a good deal, don't you?"

"I enjoy seeing new places."

"But do you go alone?"

"Unless I can find the right companion. I like a lot of people but I don't like everybody a lot."

"That sounds reasonable. You don't have to."

"No. I'm more or less free to do as I choose. I know I'm lucky. Luckier than you. You probably have to do plenty of things you don't care about – dancing, for instance. Why don't we sit down somewhere?"

"Well. . . ." he exclaimed. He was amused and not ungrateful. They found a corner in a conservatory that overlooked the lights of the city. "Getting settled in at Burton Bridgwater by now?" he said, unable to think of anything else.

"Oh yes, the family is. I don't think I'm a very good settler anywhere. You know what I like to do most?"

"Am I going to be horrified?"

"Probably. I like to climb mountains."

"Well, that's just where you're wrong. I like it too."

"But I mean *real* climbing."

"Try me someday."

"Clogwyn Du'r-arrdu?"

"I've done it."

"The North Wall of the Grandes Jorasses?"

"No, and neither have you."

She laughed. "You evidently know something. To tell you the truth, I'm good–quite good–but not as good as that. I've done most of the standard Alpine climbs, and I was with Melrose and Linmayer in Corsica last year. That's some sort of testimonial, maybe."

"I should think it is."

"What I'd like now is to go further afield–say the Caucasus."

"Not by yourself, surely?"

"Oh no, it would have to be a real expedition. But I know Melrose and some of his friends would come if it could be arranged. Unfortunately you need all kinds of permits even to get near the place. I was talking to Davanrog about that."

"Could he help you?"

"That's what I had in mind. But he wasn't very encouraging. I pressed him for a reason – I'm the sort of person who expects a reason for things – but all I could get out of him was some mumble about possible trouble in that direction during the summer. That old Turkish-Armenian business, I suppose."

"He mentioned that?"

"What he actually said was '*les querelles intérieures du pays Turco-Arménien.*'"

"Well, well. . . ." It was part of Charles's training that when he was told anything important he did not betray that it was. In this case he did not know whether it was important or not. But when the party was over and the hired waiters were clearing up in the banqueting hall he wandered into the office and found his chief there, whisky and soda in hand, going over some cables that had arrived. "Nothing much," he remarked, passing them to Charles. "A good party, I thought."

Charles said he thought so too.

"That Jane Coppermill of yours certainly has changed."

Charles didn't altogether approve the "of yours"; after the bear-pit story he would have considered her just as much Sir Lionel's. (He had mentioned that incident to Jane and she had told him how it had happened—she had been trying to retrieve an umbrella which had slipped through the railings while she was watching the animals, and with which she afterwards defended herself. "But it was nothing – they were a mangy lot. I only had to prod them to keep them off.")

Charles said to Treves: "Yes, and for the better, I should say."

"She seemed quite friendly with Davanrog."

"They met in Copenhagen once, she said." Charles then told Treves what Jane had told him about Davanrog's discouragement of a climbing expedition in the Caucasus that summer.

It was part of Sir Lionel's training that when he was told anything important he did not betray that it was. In this case he thought it was probably not important at all, but to be on the safe side he might send a memo to London about it.

So he said, sipping his drink good-humoredly: "What does she think she is, that young lady? International spy or something?

Did you happen to notice a bundle of stolen treaties tucked away in her corsage?"

What Charles had noticed in her corsage — while they were dancing, in fact — had been more tempting than stolen treaties. Thinking of this made him smile as he answered: "She's reliable, I should say. I'll bet she's good to climb with."

Later still that evening, or rather early the next morning, Treves conducted the usual bedroom post-mortem with his wife. They were a very devoted couple, behind the façade of being *chef* and *chéfesse.*

"That Coppermill girl heard an interesting thing from Davanrog." He gave the details.

Lady Treves said: "I don't suppose she got it out of him deliberately."

"Oh no, she'd never have managed it if she'd tried. What *was* smart of her, though, was to pass it on to Anderson."

"I wonder if that was accidental too."

"Anderson said he thought she knew it was something we'd be interested to hear."

"Does Charles know her well?"

"They're neighbors. Some place in Gloucestershire. She's one of the Coppermills that bought the *Record* when Derry sold out."

"Plenty of money?"

"Far more than you and I will ever have, my dear."

"I rather like her, what I saw of her, and if she's so smart and has money — might not be a bad thing for Charles — "

"Oh, I don't think there's anything like that in contemplation."

"Well, you never know. He's attractive, and she looks to me the sort of girl who gets what she wants."

Six months later Jane Coppermill got what she wanted. They were married in Salzburg, where Charles had gone for the Festival and she for some climbing in the Dolomites. Since each had known that the other would be there at the same time, it was always a matter of argument afterward whether they had planned it, consciously or subconsciously; the fact that Jane, who did not particularly care for music, went to several concerts with Charles was reckonable against the fact that Charles, who enjoyed climbing, allowed himself to be considerably seduced from Mozart to the mountains. After a few weeks of this sort of thing the decision was made. They did not tell anybody, but somehow the announcement got into the English papers (and here again there could have been an interesting argument—was it Jane's or Charles's minor importance that made them worth a three-line wire?). Charles then wrote to his father and received an elegant letter of congratulation and an invitation to bring Jane to stay at Beeching as soon as they returned to England. Charles, of course, was to be similarly welcomed at Burton Bridgwater by Jane's family, and as the houses were less than a mile apart it was easy to combine the two invitations. Havelock also seemed to like Jane personally, the more so when she took up from the outset a no-nonsense attitude toward him which cleared away many difficulties. "I heard rumors you were mad and now I'm convinced you are," she told him sportively before she had been a guest at Beeching a full day. It was because of something he had said—not too outrageous, for him. But Jane could match him in outrageousness, both of speech and action. "You're just a wicked old man," she told him at a party in front of a crowd. "And it's not just weakness with you, it's strength, isn't it?" Havelock's eyes flashed back a response in which there was an amused awareness that Jane was a person to be reckoned with.

Both Charles and Jane, however, were glad to leave England at the end of the extended leave, especially as Charles had been appointed Second Secretary in a city much nearer to the crossroads of world affairs than his previous post. It could be regarded as a speedy promotion, and though he wondered if Jane, through her various family connections, had pulled any strings to get it for him, he felt confident of being able to justify himself. He was very happy indeed as they crossed the Channel from Croydon to Le Bourget. It was for both of them a first trip by air.

Jane soon showed her qualifications not only as a wife, but as a Second Secretary's wife. She tackled the job with a respect for it that muted the strings of her personality without putting any of them out of tune. The Ambassador, Sir Richard Thornton ("Papa"), was a senior diplomat who (someone once said) possessed many merits developed to a marked degree of averageness; he had married late, and for the second time, and it was his wife who set the key and pace of the Embassy. Older than he was, sharp-tongued and domineering, of an aristocratic family and twice widowed by men who had won high distinction in the Foreign Service, she had an air of making comparisons that must always be unsatisfactory. Perhaps Sir Richard guessed this. He was completely under her thumb, and therefore astute enough to pretend not to like Jane as much as he did; while Jane, sizing up the situation, knew that sooner or later Lady Thornton would have to be tackled.

The clash came over Jane's behavior at a reception given by a foreign Embassy to a visiting royalty. The entire diplomatic corps was present and protocol reigned heavily. Somebody, however, must have spilled the bear-pit story, for when Jane was presented to His Majesty he mentioned it, and the result was a rather long and jovial *tête-à-tête* later in the evening, which nobody failed to observe. Jane happened to have lived for a time in His Majesty's country and to have a smattering of the language, all of which helped. When the affair was over she thought she had done quite well to give royalty such a chance to unbend, but the next day Lady Thornton made a point of snubbing her for it in Charles's presence. "I suppose," she remarked, "he was your first king and he went to your head?"

Since Jane was not one to take rebukes of this sort easily, Charles jumped in with excuses for her before she could reply. But then Lady Thornton turned her guns on him, interrupting: "When you've had more experience, Mr. Anderson, you'll perhaps be less ready to contradict me."

"He wasn't contradicting you," Jane retorted, prompt now to

defend Charles. "He just can't think what I did wrong, and neither can I."

"Exactly," Charles agreed. "After all, it was the King who started it — I daresay he felt in the mood for a joke. Those fellows must get awfully bored with formalities — it seems rather hard if they can't ever be allowed to relax like anybody else."

"Nonsense," Lady Thornton snapped back. "It's no harder for them than it is for us. They *expect* to be bored. They're usually on guard about their rank, and if you forget for a moment who they are — no matter how much they've seemed to encourage you — they're apt to see a slight. Of course there are exceptions, but when you've met as many kings as I have, Mr. and Mrs. Anderson, you'll know it's much safer to bore them than to try to amuse them."

"I never like doing things that are too safe," Jane said, but she caught Charles's eye and could see that he too was somewhat disarmed as well as astonished by Lady Thornton's frankness.

"Then you'll run grave risks of damaging your husband's career. And believe me, that warning is well-meant."

Afterward Charles exchanged a glance with Jane and burst out laughing. "Well, well . . . we're still alive, that's something. But what a crushing old battle-ax!"

Jane said, more seriously: "I wonder if she's right — about kings. I don't suppose we shall meet as many as she has, anyhow."

"There aren't as many."

"Darling, that's far more crushing than anything *she* said."

The odd thing was that after this incident they both got along much better with Lady Thornton — indeed, it could almost be said that she showed signs of liking them. She was a remarkable woman and doubtless much could be learned from her example. The atmosphere at her parties was far too disciplined, but they were socially efficient and set a standard. She worked hard. She devoted herself to local charities. She bullied the American Minister (a poker-playing millionaire politician) into serving on committees for the care of refugee children and the restoration of ancient cathedrals. Duty was her watchword, and attention to duty her prime requirement in others. In her opinion all diplomats under forty were ill-trained and bad-mannered, frivolous and deplorably slack. She considered Charles to be most of these things to an extent made worse by his pleasant disposition, and she conveyed her misgivings to Jane with the implied suggestion that Jane and she were sisters under the skin, steel-ribbed in contrast to the invertebrates all around them. Jane was amused. "She really thinks that," she told Charles. "And I'm afraid to disillusion her."

"I don't think you're afraid of anything, and I don't think she could be disillusioned about anything," Charles answered, baiting Jane affectionately. "And maybe you *are* a bit like her. She's not a bad sort."

"Poor Papa."

"How do we know?"

"She puts him in his place all the time."

"Perhaps that's just exactly where he likes to be."

One thing was certain: the rigidities of Embassy functions under Lady Thornton pointed up the fact that Jane's parties, which she gave often and unostentatiously and with a clever mingling of seniors and juniors, became noted among the diplomatic crowd for their sparkle and general enjoyability. Nor did they lack moments at which things were said and discussed of some importance. Afterward Jane and Charles would hold their own intimate post-mortems.

"I thought the new Bulgarian was sweet."

"Battle-ax won't approve of him. Especially that long cigarette holder."

"It suits him, though. Did you talk to Madame Lesinsky?"

"Not much. Did you?"

"She said Delafours told her the outlook for the new German loan isn't promising. . . . By the way, I must teach Héloïse to make ice cream properly or else get it sent in next time. Cintara poured his wine into his. Did you notice?"

"Maybe an old Portuguese custom. . . . I wonder where Rampagni's wife got those earrings?"

"Either an heirloom or very bad taste. . . . What did you think of Beatrice Kindersley?"

"Perfectly delightful."

"She told von Ahndorf the reason her father plays poker so well is because he learned it at his mother's knee and other joints."

"I've heard that gag before, but it sounds good about Kindersley. I rather like the old boy. Must be a headache to his staff, but he's refreshingly out of place among all the career men. Wherever he goes there'll be some corner of a foreign field that's forever Texas."

"That's not a bad gag either."

"Grandison's was the best. He said Kindersley always made him think that perhaps a tired salesman in a china shop must sometimes just *long* for a bull."

Those were the gay years, the gayest perhaps for centuries, perhaps also for centuries to come. The First World War had become something one did not bring up unless one had to; personal recollections of it were nearly always a bore or the mark of one. How ironical to recall, if one could, the recruiting poster that had pictured a father being asked by his son; "What did you do in the Great War?" Charles hadn't a son, but if he had, he couldn't imagine the question, much less the answer. The only time the matter had point was if one became friendly with individual Germans. . . . "Were you on the Somme?" "Why, yes, so was I" — and then leave it at that, with some sort of freemasonry established. But Charles's experience did not yield any such item. Once, however, he met a German who said he came from Ingolstadt, and Charles was able to reply: "Indeed? My brother died there — in a prison camp just after the war ended. The flu epidemic." Just the casual common denominator of a past that one hoped was on the way to oblivion.

But it was this curious interval, during which the first war was not quite forgotten and the next one not yet feared, that made for a sudden short-lived fashion of remembrance. Remarque's *Im Westen Nichts Neues* swept the world; so did Sherriff's *Journey's End.* Charles and Jane made up a party to see this play when it came to their city, performed in the language of the country; and afterward, at a restaurant, memories were unleashed by guests of half a dozen nationalities. For once, it seemed, and perhaps never again, Europeans could unite in a single emotion if not in a common cause; the only faint division line, indeed, was between the ex-warriors and the neutrals who had missed the ordeal. "Would you fight again?" was asked, and the answers of the diplomats were both undiplomatic and unnecessary, for surely they would never have to face the problem. Even an enemy would whisk them safely home across frontiers with full honors.

Charles said to Jane on the way back to their house: "I wonder what all our Foreign Offices would say if they got a verbatim report of that conversation. Give us all the boot, maybe."

"And then there wouldn't be any younger generation to take over from people like Papa."

But Sir Richard also saw the play and discussed it later in an equally undiplomatic way, though privately in his office. "Were you in the war, Anderson?"

"No, sir, I was just too young."

"I'd say you were damned lucky then. My son was killed. Makes you wonder – almost – how human beings could be forced to endure such things. . . . I mean if they'd all packed up suddenly and run home – both sides – who could have stopped them?" This was surely a naïve thought for an ambassador to utter, and perhaps he realized it, for he continued hastily: "Funny the effect a play can have. You ever met this fellow Sherriff?"

"No, sir."

"If I ever do, I'll tell him how much I was impressed."

"I'm sure he'd be very glad if you wrote to him and said so."

"All right. Draft me a letter. . . . I was in London during one of the Zeppelin raids. Happened to be at Liverpool Street Station – you know Liverpool Street Station?"

"Yes."

"It's got a very high glass roof. . . . I was in a train just about to leave when a bomb fell. Killed about twenty people in another train coming in across the platform. Hope I never see anything like that again – people on their way to business from the suburbs – lots of girls. . . . I pulled some of them out of the mess – the glass did the worst. . . . I'll never forget those office girls – cut to ribbons, some of them. . . . Well, well, must work. Fetch me Herstlett, I want to look up something. . . . Oh, and – er – don't bother about a letter to that writer fellow – might lead to a lot of useless correspondence. . . ."

The years passed, and Charles was transferred again. Already he was beyond the stage at which his work was mostly simple and routine; it began to present problems, and these he thought he tackled rather more than adequately. There were times when he was bored and fancied he would have been happier in some other job, but with later detachment he usually decided that he wouldn't – he didn't really envy the lawyers, politicians, and businessmen whom he frequently had to meet. The ones he did occasionally envy were shy engineers on their way to some project, or a few stray writers globe-trotting for local color and showing off their freedom at all the parties they could pick up en route. There were times also when Charles thought of the millions living around him whom he would never encounter unless they figured personally as servants or tradespeople or impersonally as statistics in books of reference – people who might, by some movement of force beyond the reach of protocol, become suddenly "allies" or "enemies." Like all the great professions, diplomacy seemed to him a marvelous conspiracy that never did, in the long run, quite succeed in either achieving or defeating the ends of something bigger than itself.

He was at a South American post in 1929 when Wall Street crashed and he received a lugubrious letter from Havelock bemoaning the way the London market had dropped in sympathy.

Since Charles had American friends whose plight was almost desperate, he did not waste much concern on his father's financial position, but he was sorry to learn from Cobb that Aunt Hetty was ill. His father had not mentioned it. A few months later Aunt Hetty died, and Havelock did mention the matter then, listing it as another of the crosses he had to bear. But the next letter was reassuring—it enclosed a clipping from *The Times,* to which Havelock seemed to have contributed the blithest letter of his career. It narrated how, in the churchyard of Pumphrey Basset, Berks., he had discovered the resting place of a forgotten female dwarf, judging from the inscription on the eighteenth-century tombstone, which read: "Aged 42 Years, Height 35 inches, *'Parva sed apta Domino.'"* Havelock made a good story of it, and Charles pictured him kneeling and feeling on the grassy grave, for (as he remembered from having taken part as a boy in several of these expeditions) the stone was apt to be so flaky and moss-covered that it chipped away if one tried to clean it, and in such cases the sensitive fingertip was often a safer reader than the eye.

Charles was still in South America five years later when the sudden death of Jane's father summoned her to England. Charles would have asked for leave to accompany her, but he was First Secretary now and it was possible that his chief might also be taking a leave in the near future, so he said he had better stay. Jane agreed with him. What they both meant was that he mustn't miss the chance of being Chargé for a time. It was only a small Legation, but to have full authority and responsibility at his age, even temporarily, could be a stroke of luck in his career. So little ever happened to stir the placid relations between His Majesty's Government and that particular country that Jane and Charles tried to cheer themselves, the night before she sailed, by imagining some incident that would give him scope to show his capabilities.

"If Argentina were to grab the Falkland Islands," was Charles's choice.

"An earthquake," Jane countered. "You plunge into the wreckage and save some red boxes."

They agreed that both these suggestions would involve unnecessary disaster. It was the Commercial Attaché who joined them then and, being admitted to the game, scored easily by his vision of an airman making a forced landing near the top of the Andes. "First of all, no one can climb to rescue him but Charles. And then it turns out the fellow hasn't any passport or visa — a man without a country. But he carries a secret formula that will revolutionize the art of warfare — "

"In that case," interrupted Charles, "I'd leave him there."

"Which would spoil my point — so I'll change the formula. It's for something beneficial to humanity — a cure for bubonic plague or pellagra or foot and mouth disease. Anyhow, because of this you promptly confer on him honorary British citizenship."

"Having just then decided to invent such a thing," Charles interjected.

"That's where I get to my point — you take a chance. The Nelson touch — so rare among chargés d'affaires."

This attaché, Claud Severing, was a young man whom they had come to like and had taken with them on several climbing expeditions. Jane was glad she was leaving Charles with a real friend, and Charles, though he was sorry to see her go, felt that three months of bachelorhood might yield austere pleasures. It would be agreeable, anyhow, to spend so much time with Severing, with a few trips into the mountains if they could be arranged.

Yet after Jane had gone Charles made a discovery that surprised him; he not only missed her, but he missed something in himself that seemed to vanish when she left. Perhaps it was the way she managed things in the house, her decisions about parties and party-giving, her advice on small matters of etiquette or behavior, even her actual help in his work, for she liked to spend time in the Chancery odd-jobbing in a way that would have been impossible in a larger and more systematized Legation. So now his extra work was quite often a symbol of her absence even when he was thinking of other things. When he most acutely missed her was late in the evening after a party, when they would have held their post-mortem on the guests and conversation. Because they were both popular, Charles received a rush of invitations well meant to appease his loneliness, but somehow accepting them only seemed to increase it; he missed the flash of Jane's eye across the dinner table, signaling in secret what her partner was like; or the quizzical look which conveyed that she had overheard him say something witty at his end. Without her, indeed, he found it twice as hard to be only half as amusing, and since he had the reputation for being amusing he wondered if his hosts were thinking him bad company or merely realizing what a good wife for him Jane was. He thought so too, but he wished he need not prove it quite so negatively. Partly from this somewhat obscure motivation he began a small flirtation with Madame Salcinet, the wife of the French Minister. She was pert and youngish and apparently ready for the diversion, since the place bored her and her elderly husband was tetchy enough to regard his post as the Quai d'Orsay's equivalent of Devil's Island. "Of course Edouard will retire after this," she confided. "There is really nothing for me to do but count the days – and even more depressingly, the nights."

"Where will you retire to?" Charles asked.

"I shall live in Paris and he will live at Limoges. That is where he comes from. Nothing on earth would induce me to spend the rest of my life at Limoges."

"It's not a bad place," Charles said. "I have a French friend who paints – we once made Limoges a center for a very pleasant holiday. We found many beautiful scenes."

"You paint also?"

"Not as much as I used to. I don't get the time."

"You spend so much of your time climbing mountains."

"Well, that's true. I enjoy it."

"I think you enjoy it because your wife enjoys it. She does not enjoy painting so you do not paint. If she enjoyed snake hunting I think you would hunt snakes."

Charles laughed. "You're absolutely right. It's the recipe for a perfect marriage."

"You think your own marriage proves that?"

Lightly and without much thought behind the merely verbal dialectic Charles countered: "Does yours *dis*prove it?"

Whereupon Madame Salcinet became suddenly indignant and with a touch of hysteria. "You have no right to say such a thing to me! You take an unpardonable liberty! I shall certainly inform Sir Bancroft – it was a most insulting and improper remark to make to the wife of one of your Minister's colleagues!"

Charles, astonished at her vehemence, apologized and said no more. It was during the interval at an afternoon concert, where they had met by accident. He believed the outburst had not attracted attention, since they had spoken in French, but he sat rather unhappily through the rest of the music; and walking back to the Legation afterward he could not help thinking: Oh God, if only Jane were here. . . . It was not that he had been dangerously indiscreet with Madame Salcinet, or that the remark she had taken exception to had been in worse taste than several of hers to him. Nor did he think that anything she said to Banky could do him much harm, and Banky would certainly take his word against hers if there were any disputed accusations. But the whole thing was just one of those incidents that Jane would have handled so capably – or rather, it was the kind that wouldn't have happened at all if she had been on the spot.

The Germans were giving a small party the following week for chiefs and their wives only. As the time for it approached, Charles had slight qualms, not quite of apprehension but of a somewhat glum curiosity as to whether Madame Salcinet still planned her complaint. Nor was this curiosity ever resolved, for several days before the party it became known that she had been removed to a private institution. "Completely off her rocker, so I heard," Banky said. "I must write a note of sympathy to Salcinet. . . . Anderson, didn't you meet her at the Brahms the other day? Somebody said he saw you talking to her. What was she like then?"

"Just charming as always," Charles answered. "And Toscanini was wonderful as always."

He was really becoming a diplomat.

Banky didn't take leave after all, so Charles was denied his spell as Chargé. Then Jane returned, tanned and refreshed after the long sea trip. Her stay in England had been full of legal business and sad visits to relatives; she was glad to be back. Her father had left her some money – it was not yet clear how much, but of course the bulk went to her brothers. The family would probably get rid of Burton Bridgwater if they could find a buyer. It would be easier to sell than most such houses (Beeching, for instance), since it had been ruinously modernized and provided with more bathrooms than anybody could use. Perhaps some American would want it. Jane chattered on thus during the taxi ride from the docks to their house near the Legation; not till they were alone in its cool Spanish style interior did she turn to him in a personal way. "Well, Charles, have you been missing me?"

"You bet I have. I don't suppose you've missed me, though."

"Oh yes, I have."

"Not as much, anyhow."

"Much more, I'm sure."

"Impossible."

"This is a childish conversation. . . . Come here, Andy."

She called him Andy at moments when they were closest, and presently at such a moment somebody opened the door and hastily backed out. They thought it must be Severing, but when Severing came later he denied this so stoutly that they were quite certain – and rather relieved – it had been only he. Of course it didn't really matter. They drank champagne and were very merry. After Severing left, Jane said that someone she had met in London had told her that Charles was highly thought of at the Foreign Office and could expect a transfer to Europe before long.

She had also seen his father once or twice. He seemed to keep very well for his age. "He's taken up kindness to animals."

"Good . . . not that he was ever *un*kind to them, I must say."

"But he won't have traps that kill mice any more — he has a kind that click down and imprison them in a sort of cage, and in the morning he goes round the kitchens collecting the cages. Then he sets the mice free in the middle of the lawn and they all run back to the kitchens."

"I wonder how the servants like that."

"The housemaids are in a state. They're scared enough even of dead mice in traps. But that's part of his fun. . . . Now tell me what kind of fun you've been having. . . ."

"Nothing nearly so exciting. . . . The Wohlmanns gave a big party when the German cruiser came in. . . . Lallieni's ill and Borignano's in charge. . . . That Mrs. Gervase came over from Rio — seems to have more money than ever. . . . There's a nice American you must meet — some job with the railways . . . the kind we like. . . . The De Volvas have had a baby. . . . Carucas did well in the local elections — they talk of him as the coming man — I hope not, because he's a crook. . . . Mary Deakins now takes ballet lessons from a real Russian, if you please. . . . I think that's about all."

"What about the Greiffenburgs?"

"They're still here."

"And the Salcinets?"

"They went home. A rather sad thing. . . . She went a bit out of her mind."

"I'm not too surprised. She always hated *him*. I meant to warn you to be careful about her, but I'm sure you were."

"Were you careful about everybody?"

"Yes — except that man in London who told me how much they thought of you. He said you were bound to get a Legation eventually. Fifty per cent seniority, he reckoned it, 30 per cent luck and 10 per cent merit. He was a cynical old devil."

"It only adds up to ninety. What's the rest?"

"I hoped you'd ask that. *Me.* The diplomat's wife. That's why I flirted with him. He's in the Government and could be quite useful." She mentioned his name.

Charles snorted. "Good God, *that* fellow?"

"Darling, you can't be particular these days. And really, I think I handled him rather well."

"I'm sure you did – you're a good man-handler. Remember the line in the Henry the Eighth film – Charles Laughton saying, 'The things I have done for England'?"

"All right, Andy, you can do them for England – I'll do them for you. I don't really know whether you love me or not, but I know you get along with me pretty well, both in and out of bed, and from what I've seen of other people's marriages, that's as good as love – and rarer, too."

"Perhaps it is love, if you have it long enough."

"And if you've never had any other kind. . . . But 'man-handler' – I rather like that. It's a compliment."

Charles was happy. People observed it and said indulgently: "He's got his Jane back, and now just look at him. And look at her too." It made them both more popular than ever, so that when a few months later they let it be known there was going to be a baby, everyone felt sentimental and wondered if it meant they had tried before without success or had recently for the first time been trying.

Severing said to Charles: "I suppose you'll go home."

"Jane will and I know she'd like me to go with her this time."

"I'm sure Banky will understand. Too bad this isn't Washington – then you could both stay. I mean, because of the dual citizenship. Nice thing for a kid to start off with. . . ."

The Coppermills had moved out of Burton Bridgwater by the

time Jane and Charles arrived in England. Jane thought she would prefer the country to London, so they rented a house near High Wycombe and paid several short visits to Beeching. Havelock greeted them hospitably and seemed excited at the prospect of becoming a grandfather. At seventy-five he was still upright and active, able to walk miles without tiring, and no less vigorous in some of his opinions. Politically he was now so far to the right that one wondered where he would or could emerge, for he had lost favor with most local Tories when he expounded the unfashionable argument that Mussolini had as much right to conquer Ethiopia as England had had to defeat the Boers. He called the League of Nations a hypocrisy and Anthony Eden a Pecksniffian Galahad. Normally this sort of extremism would not have mattered much in a country addicted to almost unlimited free speech; but the barometer of English opinion, as of European and world opinion, was rather rapidly moving to stormy. Only for this reason Charles was concerned. His father's political views, whatever they were, seemed far less important than the fact that friendships and the tolerance of neighbors were being put to strain.

One June Friday about two months before the birth was expected, Charles and Jane set out from High Wycombe intending to spend a week end at Beeching. Charles was enjoying himself with a new car, and they stopped for lunch in Oxford and walked a little around the colleges. With every discount as a Cambridge man, he still thought Oxford had been ruined as well as enriched by its automobile industry; always sensitive to noise, he wondered how an undergraduate of Queen's or Magdalen could ever work if his rooms faced that once tranquil curve of the High, along which traffic now passed in roaring procession. Jane said the place had given her a headache; but by the time they were on their way again and approaching the Cotswolds, it was clear she was suffering from much more than that. At Beeching she felt worse, and during the night suffered severe pain. By mid-morning Dr. Somerville had diagnosed possible appendicitis and ordered her immediate removal to a hospital. Charles accompanied her in the ambulance, realizing as he watched her (she was already under sedatives) how unimaginable would be any disaster that separated them. Presently he learned that an operation was necessary and that there was some risk of losing the baby. A recommended London surgeon named Blainey was telephoned; he said he could arrive that evening by train.

As the day progressed, Charles grew increasingly anxious and was almost glad he did not have to put on an act in front of Jane – though if even half conscious she would doubtless have seen through it. Yet he felt she could not possibly know what store he had set on fatherhood. People thought they had planned it, and he did not mind anyone thinking so; actually it had been accidental, not even consciously desired, yet afterward a cause of such encompassing joy that they both wondered why they had ever considered their lives too roving and unsettled for such an event. Somehow the baby, even unborn, had already turned wherever they lived into a home.

Charles met Blainey – *Mr.* Blainey, since he was a very distinguished surgeon and not a physician – at Stow Magna Station and drove him to Beeching. Charles was favorably impressed by a first look at him – fiftyish, red-haired, slight in build, curtly polite. They did not talk much on the way and hardly at all about Jane. Charles had the professional man's reluctance to intrude on another professional man's field; he had suffered too often from the naïveté of dinner partners who had discussed international affairs. At the hospital he waited while Somerville took Blainey to see Jane. Blainey was reticent afterward; he merely confirmed the doctor's tentative diagnosis and said he had arranged for surgery at seven in the morning.

"Seven?"

"Yes. Everything ready by then. You think that's terribly early?"

"Oh no – on the contrary. I mean – if it's so urgent – " What he really meant was that he was already beginning to fret about the overnight delay, but Blainey went on, smiling: "Don't worry – we surgeons are used to it. We don't keep civil service hours, you know."

Charles was puzzled for a second; then he realized it was not only Blainey's idea of a joke, but Blainey's idea of the time for a joke. Oh, well . . . so he smiled back. Even the implication that he could properly be described as a civil servant hadn't its normal power to irritate him. He then had the sudden idea that Blainey should come to Beeching for a meal and a bed—much quieter and more comfortable than the nearest good hotel, and only a mile or two farther. He made the suggestion, which the surgeon accepted nonchalantly; then he telephoned Cobb to prepare a room. It was eight o'clock before they were on the road, exchanging few remarks during the journey. But when they reached the lodge and had to slow down past the opened gates, Blainey remarked, peering out: "Quite a place for your son to inherit."

"My . . . my *son* . . ." echoed Charles, gathering his wits. "You mean . . ." In exultation over what might be Blainey's oblique way of conveying reassurance, he nearly steered the car off the gravel. "Sure it'll be a son?" he added, forcing a smile before he found it need not be forced.

"Try again if it isn't. Plenty of time."

Charles warmed further to the remark, though he hadn't much of the ancestral feeling for Beeching that Blainey was taking for granted. But he needed comfort and Blainey had given it. "Too bad it's dark," Charles said, ready to meet the wrong but hopeful assumption halfway. "There's quite a view of the house from here."

"Any special reason why it's called Beeching? Is there a river where boats used to beach?"

"Oh, it isn't *that* beaching—it's b-double-e-c-h. Beech trees, I suppose. My father once talked about changing its name to suit his profession—he said he'd call it Loopholes. . . . He being a lawyer." (I, too, can joke at a time like this, was in his mind.)

"Ha, ha. . . . So if I ever live in one of these places I ought to call it Gallstones, eh?"

They both laughed more than the humor deserved, and Charles felt quite cheerful when, a few minutes later, he led the surgeon into the dining room and introduced him to Havelock, who had apparently delayed his own evening meal to give the welcome its fullest possible scope. Charles was also a little touched by evidences that during his absence the old man had been busy – a bottle of rather special claret and the table set more elaborately than Cobb would have done it without particular orders. They all drank sherry standing by the mantelpiece, then sat down to the soup. Charles was glad to let his father steer conversation, which he did fluently and with tact, avoiding strictly medical territory yet touching near enough to bridge the interesting gulf between medicine and the law. It was quite fascinating, an interplay of really first-class minds; yet suddenly, between one sentence and another, Charles ceased to be fascinated and could only itch for the meal to finish so that Blainey could get to bed for a full night's sleep. With shock he realized it was already midnight. From then on what was left of the meal seemed to progress so slowly that Charles thought there might have been some upset in the kitchen till he verified that every minute was crawling like an hour. Finally Cobb entered with coffee.

Blainey shook his head when Havelock passed the decanter of brandy.

"It's good stuff, Blainey – very gentle. . . . I wish you'd try it."

"Oh, all right." Havelock filled liqueur glasses and had Cobb take them round.

"As I was saying," Havelock went on, "the medical aspects of poisoning cases are so technical that the accused is often in danger of being tried by expert witnesses rather than by the court. Take the Marsh test for arsenic, for instance. How can a juryman possibly give the benefit of a doubt when a fellow like Spilsbury comes along and says there isn't any doubt? And yet, as every toxicologist knows, there are doubts – small ones, maybe, but doubts all the same – margins for error and admitted incalculables in every chemical test known to science."

"That's true, but on the other hand what would happen if

Spilsbury were to give these doubts the place they would certainly have if he were lecturing to scientists instead of offering an opinion to a group of laymen? You'd simply never get a conviction — the jury, unused to the philosophic assessment of probabilities, would just acquit one poisoner after another."

"They might acquit a few more of the innocent."

"Oh come now, I can't believe that many innocent victims go to the gallows."

"Can't you? Let me tell you of a case I had once — before your time — an insurance agent in Manchester . . ."

Five more minutes of that. Charles did not want to seem either fidgety or ungracious, but he could not help saying, when a suitable pause occurred: "I expect Mr. Blainey would like to get to bed. . . ."

Havelock nodded. "Of course, of course. Any time he likes. . . . But what about a nightcap, then we'll all turn in? . . . Busy day tomorrow. . . . Cobb, we won't adjourn anywhere tonight — just leave the decanters on the table."

Charles hoped the surgeon would refuse any more drinks, but he did not do so, and his signal, though prompt, was not in time to stay Havelock's generous hand. "I must lend you a book, Blainey — take it up with you when you go . . . case histories somewhat on the lines of the one we were talking about. . . . Charles, fetch Winfield's *Problems of Medico-Legal Practice* — it's on the top shelf in the window alcove in the library."

Charles did not move, but forced a smile. "I really don't think Mr. Blainey will want to read much tonight."

Blainey smiled also. "And I know the book quite well, so don't bother."

"Then you'll remember," Havelock continued, "how Winfield attacks the medical evidence in the Seddon trial. There's no doubt that if Seddon hadn't given such a callous impression in court he'd have had a good chance of acquittal."

"What you mean, then," answered Blainey, "is that his counsel should have given him better advice as to how to behave. Blame the lawyers too."

"Oh, certainly. But I've cross-examined too many doctors not to know that a skilled opposing counsel can usually twist them any way he wants. Why not, after all? It isn't a doctor's job to learn the art of being cross-examined – which in my opinion is a much rarer art than that of cross-examining. That, of course, is where Spilsbury excels – and where he's most dangerous. He's the cleverest cross-examinee in the business."

"I'm afraid we're arguing in circles. First you say a doctor can be twisted any way a counsel wants – then you attack Spilsbury because he can't be – "

"I said an *average* doctor – "

"But surely the fault lies again with the lawyers. If their aim is to establish truth and not merely to win a case, why do they try to twist a doctor at all – he's generally an honest man who has no ax to grind – "

" – or, in the case of a surgeon, no knife to sharpen, eh?" Havelock's eyes lit with a vivid excitement. "I suppose the professional difference is even more jealously regarded than that between barrister and solicitor? . . . Try that whisky – it's practically a liqueur – if you're a connoisseur I think you'll like it. . . . But to come back to this question of cross-examining the expert witness. . . ."

Charles leaned forward across the table. He did not know whether he was pale or flushed, but he knew that something had happened to his face – it was moving in a way he could not control, like a small tic. "Look," he muttered, and found his voice so weak that he had to project it as before an audience: "Look, Mr. Blainey ought to sleep. Let me take him upstairs."

Blainey made a slightly staying gesture with his hand. "It's all right – I'm in no great hurry. I had a nap on the train. . . . What were you saying, Sir Havelock?" He sipped the Scotch and soda.

Havelock's face was wholly animated. "You must forgive my concern with the subject – perhaps it stems from an experience I once had in Wales. In those days the circuit judges . . ."

Another ten minutes. The story ended and before Blainey could comment Havelock began another. Charles could endure it no longer. Stumbling to his feet he made his way round the table and stood above his father. His hands shook, he swayed, he had to press his words through an impairment of breath and lip-movement that made him hardly coherent. "For God's sake, *can't you shut up?* Let the man go to bed. Don't you know what he's got to do tomorrow morning?" Then he broke off to lean against the table, straining for control and mumbling "I beg your pardon, I beg your pardon" to nobody in particular.

"My son is distraught," said Havelock urbanely. "I'm sure you'll excuse him. But it *is* perhaps time to retire. . . . I'll show you up to your room, Blainey — take your drink with you. . . . Good night, Charles. Perfectly understandable. Get a good night's sleep yourself."

Blainey also said "Good night" as he left with Havelock. Charles heard them climbing the stairs, still arguing. He did not want to see his father again if he should come down later, so he crossed the hall to the garden door and went outside. The open air seemed to calm him. He walked to a place where he could watch the windows of Blainey's room. They remained lighted for nearly an hour. Charles waited all this time, patiently but with determination; then he re-entered the house and went to his own room. He knew he had made a considerable fool of himself, but that was a small worry compared with the other one. He did not think he could sleep, but in case he did he set the alarm for five. He intended then to get up and see that Blainey had coffee and that Farrow was ready with the car. But none of this happened. He lay sleepless till nearly dawn, then slept so heavily that he failed to hear the alarm, and when he woke it was nine o'clock. Dressing hurriedly he drove to the hospital, but the operation was over by then.

Charles insisted on driving Blainey back to the station at Stow Magna. When they had left the hospital grounds the surgeon said: "You really shouldn't be doing this — you look very tired. Somerville gave you the news, I daresay. The operation was quite successful and there's no reason why either your wife or child should be any the worse for it. . . . Now take it easy – I'm nervous of other people's driving."

"I'm sorry," Charles said, out of a deep dream of happiness. "And I must also apologize for last night."

"Last night? What do you mean?"

"Losing my head – or my temper – or something. . . . What a way for a diplomat to behave – God, how Jane would laugh. I don't think I'll ever tell her what happened."

"Are you sure you *remember* what happened?"

"I know, I must have been distraught, as my father said. All those stories of his – they lasted so long. . . . He talks very well and I suppose he enjoys himself so much that even at a time like that he could forget – or seem to forget – more easily than I could."

Blainey said quietly: "May I ask a very personal question?"

"Yes, of course."

"Are you protecting him, or are you really in ignorance?"

"I don't quite know what you mean."

"You were distraught last night because you were afraid I should stay up too late and perhaps drink too much – "

"I assure you I never – "

"Why not be frank about it? You thought your father was to blame for keeping me there, talking and drinking – and of course he was. But you also thought – or at least the thought crossed your mind, didn't it? – that he was *deliberately* doing all that?"

"I – I don't know that I ever – actually – or if I did it was – "

"All right, have it the way you want. It's what *I* thought, anyhow."

"That he – was – doing it – *deliberately*?"

"Yes. I've seen people in his condition before. It's a sort of dementia. Didn't you notice his arguments? For all their fluency, there was no logic in them – they just went round and round – his mind racing like a slipping clutch. If the brain had a temperature his would have been at fever heat."

"But I still don't see – "

"Well, never mind. You're a diplomat, as you said—you're trained not to see what you don't want to see—or else to pretend not to see what you do see."

Charles said heavily, after a pause: "Yes, it's that. I'm sorry I wasn't frank. I've known he was like it for a long time. Is there anything one can do?"

"Not much, I should think, at his age. Though I'm no expert in that field. . . . Well, here's the station."

They talked of other matters on the platform and just before the train left Charles thanked him again, but rather sadly. He had learned nothing new about Havelock, but to hear it in words, clinically and for the first time, was a blow. When he got back to the house his mingled emotions, which included intense relief and a resurgence of happiness, also included a deeper sympathy with his father than he could remember. He did not quite know why that was. He found Havelock at his desk in the library pasting another insert into the *Oxford Book of English Verse.*

"Hullo, Charles. Splendid news about Jane, I hear. Great fellow Blainey—how wise you were to have him!" He swung round, book in hand. "Listen to this—a parody on the well-known poem by Landor. . . .

> I strove with none, not even with my wife,
> You never saw me drunk or heard me swear;
> I never could get near the fire of life,
> So if it sinks or not, why should I care?

Not bad, eh? I amuse myself with this sort of thing when I feel in the mood. Of course some of them come out a bit naughtier than that. . . . But—er—well, I didn't *feel* naughty this morning. I was too anxious about Jane."

Jane's baby, a boy, was born in a London nursing home, and as Blainey had forecast, all went well. Charles was ecstatic, and about the same time (as if to cap his good fortune) he was offered a European post so situated that it was natural for him to serve on one of those intermittent Balkan boundary commissions that never settles anything more than a few years before a major war unsettles everything. Charles had made himself an expert on this particular locality, and it was easy for him to consider the work he did on the commission the most valuable he had yet performed, as well as a likely steppingstone to further promotion.

Jane had agreed that after he settled down to Legation work again she would join him with the baby, and this she did, for it was a pleasant city and healthy except at the height of summer.

Those were the years when (as Blainey might have said) a diplomat's training not to see what he did not want to see came in handy, for they were the years between Ethiopia and Munich.

Charles and Jane were now experienced in the diplomatic world. They could begin "When we were at So-and-So"—to match anyone else's stories with one of their own, and they had known several First Secretaries who had since become Ministers, and many Second Secretaries who had since become First Secretaries, and thus down the ladder. They were learned in the personal mythology behind the names in the Foreign Office List, and since they knew exactly how to behave to everybody (including visiting monarchs, local Foreign Ministers, and distinguished travelers) they could take quite a load off a minister's or an ambassador's shoulders, especially if he were old or slack, and Charles's new chief, Sir Morley Considine, was inclined to be both. The *doyen* of the corps, he was a charming relic of the old school whose gallantries were famous and sometimes a little foolish. There was a yarn that he had once had a Third Secretary transferred because he did not spring quickly enough to open the door when the ladies left the table at a dinner party; a footman should have been there to do it, but his negligence was no excuse for a Secretary's lapse. Sir Morley was, however, comparatively lenient with another Secretary who left the keys of the Chancery on a park bench where, by a remarkable coincidence (as Sir Morley always said), they were found by a distant relative of Sigmund Freud (though Sir Morley never explained just in what the coincidence consisted).

They named the boy Gerald, after a Gerald Anderson in the seventeenth century who had become governor of a West Indian island (perhaps the most officially illustrious of all the Anderson ancestors); and Gerald spent most of his first two years in this foreign capital where he was admired and petted by women of all nationalities and nursed by a Frenchwoman who many an afternoon pushed him in a pram along a mile of tree-shaded boulevard to a kiosk where an old Italian sold *citronade*. The old Italian would also touch and admire him, the swarthy mustachioed face beaming down so much more notably than his mother's or his father's or his nurse's that quite possibly it made a faint smudge on the first blank page of the child's memory.

After Munich even diplomats could see ahead; they knew at least that war would come, and might come suddenly. For this reason Charles, who had sent Jane and Gerald back to England during the September crisis, was not anxious that Gerald should return, though Jane flew back and forth several times, leaving the child with her sister in Cheshire. It was a cluttered family arrangement, but the year that succeeded Munich was a cluttered year. Toward the end of it (in July 1939) Charles took leave, and was in London when war broke out.

Paris III

THIRTEEN YEARS LATER CHARLES SAT IN A PARIS TAXI on Gerald's seventeenth birthday, and he no more knew where the taxi was going than where the world was going, but he supposed to the devil in one form or another. He could only indulge a mild hope that, if the taxi took him to where Gerald was, the form of the devil would be found agreeable, even if deplorable. For Charles had long since discovered that he was not really a moral man, in the too strict sense of the word, and that most of his qualms were no more than shrinkings of taste or expediency.

The taxi squealed to a halt so suddenly that he thought at first it must be to avoid some accident. But, no; the driver was merely pointing to a destination. "Rocher's!" he snapped. "*Voilà!*"

Charles, catapulted from reverie, bestowed the fare and a handsome tip (a certain lavishness in this case being justifiable), while he blinked to the varicolored neon lights with which Rocher's, whatever it was, announced itself both to the passer-by and to the approacher from a distance. Rocher's. . . . Certainly no place that he could remember. . . . "Rocher's," he muttered, sizing up the neighborhood. There was nothing particularly wrong with the neighborhood, or right either; it was just a part of Paris he did not think he recognized. "You saw him go in *there?*"

The driver was emphatic about it.

"With his suitcase?"

"I carried it in for him, m'sieur."

"H'm . . . very well."

As he drove off the driver shouted raffishly: "*Restaurant sanitaire! Cuisine américaine!*"

Charles walked toward the entrance of Rocher's as into the lens of an unwelcome searchlight. It was certainly new since his day — in fact, there had never to his knowledge been anything in Paris quite like it. With a dazzling frontage on two streets it offered no privacy to its patrons, and its air of intense hygiene was equally un-Parisian. Tiled walls, marble floors, white-uniformed waitresses, all added up to something that made Charles wince. Then he realized it was ice cream that was the specialty. *Cuisine américaine* indeed. And it was for this that Gerald had been eager to leave the Cheval Noir.

Charles was peeved. He had been fully prepared to discover the boy in some haunt of depravity, or even to rescue him if the need should arise — he could have faced that sort of thing with resolution, and afterward with a sense of humor — indeed, during the taxi journey he had already composed sentences of tolerant rebuke, ending in a confession that he, Charles, had been shrewd enough to suspect something of the sort all along. . . . But *this* place — what *could* he say? He pushed his way through the swing doors. The interior was hot, noisy, spotless, dazzling — and all of these things he hated except the spotlessness, which he thought was an excellent quality deserving of more decent concealment. His eyes and ears cringed to the assault of a nightmarish jukebox that hurled the loudest kind of jazz over innumerable conversations which, because of it, had to be shouted at close range. Prices were placarded on the walls, and Charles, who liked most things in life to be either expensive or economical, formed the opinion that Rocher's was neither. Waitresses as antiseptic as hospital nurses scurried among the tables; bartenders as proficient as pharmacists mixed their highly colored concoctions in front of mirrors with an air of performing some cleansing rite. The whole establishment was about as obtrusive — and, to Charles, as appetizing — as a barium meal he had once had to take when he thought he was developing an ulcer.

Then he saw that Gerald was sitting at a table next to a huge uncurtained plate-glass window that faced the side street. A girl was with him. This did not startle or shock Charles at all — indeed, it confirmed his guess and relieved a little of his hurt. Both of them, anyhow, were sipping through straws out of tall glasses, their heads bent together in an absorption at least physical. Charles drew back sharply, aware of his own dubious position, for it was one thing to spy on his son with the moral advantage all on his side, but quite another to have trailed him to this den of gaudy innocence. Unfortunately he had already come too close; Gerald looked up.

"*Dad!*" he exclaimed, flushing deeply.

Charles was glad to observe the flush. It reminded him that the boy had, after all, told several deliberate untruths. So he smiled, as across a conference table. "Well, Gerald . . . quite a surprise! So *this* is what tempted you to miss the boat train!"

Gerald gathered his wits with a dexterity which, even at such a moment, Charles had to concede. "Dad, I want you to meet Miss Raynor. . . . She and I played tennis together in Switzerland — she's leaving for America tonight. That's why we had to meet in a bit of a hurry. . . . You see how it was?"

Charles saw how it was, for he was looking at the girl, and it was actually her beauty that peeved him afresh, for he thought: Good God, if he's only got so little time with her, and in Paris of all cities, why does he want to spend it in a place like this? For Charles knew of so many other places. . . .

The girl was offering her hand. "I'm so glad to meet you, Mr. Anderson. Do sit down. Gerry's told me a lot about you."

Charles had an opening to reply that this was all the more remarkable since Gerald had told him nothing about her, but he forbore to make the point at this stage, though undoubtedly it must come later. He was enjoying her voice — it was well modulated and pleasing. Moreover, her blonde hair delightfully matched her tanned face. She looked rather older than Gerald, in fact he was sure she was — in her early twenties, perhaps. Had she been of any other nationality than American he would have been certain, from her clothes and air, that she was rich.

"So you're the one who helped him win the cup?" he said, admiring her.

"He told you then?" Her laugh was pleasant also.

Charles went on smiling. One thing the best part of a lifetime had taught him was to use a smile as an all-purpose stopgap when he didn't know what to say, but wanted to look wise, or when he hadn't decided what attitude to take, but wanted to look as if he had an entire campaign of behavior mapped out in his mind. And of course he was not unaware that he had a rather engaging smile. So he protracted it now, deliberately allowing the conversation to lapse till he knew that Gerald would interpret his silence as a sign of reproof. Then he said, looking at the table: "What's that you're both eating?"

"Raspberry frappé," the girl answered. "Will you have one?"

"I don't think you'd care for it, Dad," Gerald interposed, asking forgiveness through his solicitude.

Charles declined the hint. "Oh, but I might – you never can tell. Maybe it's like you with the sherry at dinner – something I could get used to." He turned to the girl confidentially. "I don't know if Gerald mentioned it, but he dined with me earlier this evening. I'd have asked him to bring you along had I been given the slightest hint that he was going to meet you later." The reproof was still being roguishly administered.

"That's very kind of you, Mr. Anderson. Why don't you try the frappé?"

Charles gave the order, specifying that he wanted as few trimmings as possible. He made some little joke about this that sent the waitress away laughing. That relieved him too; they really were Parisiennes, under their extremely clinical disguise.

"I wish I spoke French as well as that," Miss Raynor commented.

"But you don't have to," said Gerald. "They all speak English – or at least they understand it. Mostly English and Americans come here."

Charles could well believe it. "So you're off for home tonight?" he said, turning to the girl.

"Yes, our trains leave almost together – Gerry's and mine."

"A pity you couldn't stay longer."

"Yes, isn't it? Gerry told me why *you're* here. He's very proud."

"*Proud?*" echoed Charles. He honestly could not, for the moment, think of anything in his being in Paris that should make Gerald proud.

"He thinks it's wonderful," the girl continued, "that you should be representing England."

Charles was torn between acute pleasure that his son had been boasting about him, and equally acute embarrassment at the phrasing of it. "Representing England," forsooth – as if he were taking part in some international Olympiad! Then it occurred to him that Gerald perhaps did think of it like that, and that since the boy enjoyed games, the athletic image was from him the sincerest compliment. Could it be that? He hoped so, but it brought him back to his abiding handicap; that he did not really understand Gerald. He knew the boy was no fool; he was doing well at Brookfield. But what was Gerald beginning to learn about *life?* Or rather, what sort of life was it that Gerald was beginning to learn about? By that Charles sadly meant: How much – or how little – have I and my son in common? It was hard to attempt an answer. For he, Charles, was what could be called a man of the world, but a man of a world that had already died or was dying; no boy of Gerald's generation could grow up to be a man of such a world. . . . What other world, then, was Gerald's, and was it, or would it ever be – occasionally – as enchanting? Gerald certainly seemed to be having a good time in it, but that was not quite the same as feeling sure that times were good in it. There had been moments in Charles's life when he had had this feeling. He was still pondering on the problem when the tall glass with its pink contents was set before him. He discovered then how correct had been Gerald's forecast. He would be unable to manage more than a small portion of the stuff, though — to be frank — it was better than some of the desserts he had tasted at diplomatic receptions.

But he had conquered his peevishness and was now no more than quietly at odds with life — a sensation so familiar that he had learned every technique of coming to terms with it. He said, in a friendly way: "So you've been enjoying Switzerland, Miss Raynor?"

"Yes, very much. It was my first visit since I was at school in Berne."

"Ah, Berne . . . a charming city."

"You know it?"

"Very well. I was *en poste* there for a couple of years. Perhaps the world's luckiest capital, unless you vote for Stockholm."

"What about Washington?"

"It didn't quite miss two world wars."

"But no air raids — one doesn't see all the bombed ruins."

"Nor does one in Paris, or Rome, or Vienna, or Moscow."

"But in London."

"London, I grant you."

"Were you in London during any of them?"

"Raids? . . . Oh yes."

"Were they very bad? I suppose that's a naïve question — "

"They were quite bad enough, though not nearly the kind of thing the German cities got toward the end of the war. Dresden, for instance."

She said musingly: "How much easier it is to feel pity for cities than for countries."

He nodded. "That's because cities seem like people — lovable and helpless and innocent. Whereas countries stand for governments — cold and strong and always a bit guilty. Of course the whole notion's false, but it suits the mythology of the times."

"That's a rather calm and detached way of looking at it."

He was suddenly aware that they were talking beyond the scope of mere acquaintance and that Gerald had relapsed into a rather prolonged silence. Charles had so often in his own youth been the victim of such a situation that he was specially anxious for it not to happen to Gerald, so he looked for a chance to bring him back into the conversation. Fortunately Miss Raynor gave it when she added: "Were you as calm and detached during the raids?"

He answered: "*Calm?* My dear Miss Raynor, there's only one word for what I was. I was *scared.* So scared I packed Gerald off to some friends in Connecticut immediately." He smiled and looked to Gerald for confirmation. "Didn't I?"

"Yes, but you stayed in London, Dad."

Charles caught a note in Gerald's voice that gave him an instant bewildering satisfaction. So the boy *was* proud of him, however absurdly? That was something. Something to build on. Something that would perhaps help to unsnarl the father-son relationship. It helped him now to answer cheerfully: "What else could I do? My job was there. Otherwise I'd have been off like a shot." He half turned to the girl again. "But actually it wasn't as bad as some Americans may have pictured it. I think perhaps we overdid the publicity on your side." Yes, he liked her. She was charming and intelligent. "You see, we wanted you to feel sorry for us because we hadn't time to be sorry for ourselves. We were so damned busy we didn't know what we'd been through till it was all over."

"*Till It Was All Over*"

THE AUTUMN OF 1939 BROUGHT THE PHONY WAR and the song that so dismally suited it — the one about hanging out the washing on the Siegfried line. As a visible symbol of the same period there was the portable boxlike gas mask, never used, insignia of false preparedness as well as a preposterous nuisance.

Charles had sent Jane and Gerald to the country (Jane's sister's house on the outskirts of a small Cheshire town) as soon as war was declared. He joined her at week ends, but preferred to spend the other days in London, meeting people and trying to learn what was really happening. It was a time when being officially on leave meant little; one looked around for some emergency use for oneself. Charles found none. Many men of his age and of equal status were similarly preoccupied. No older than the century, he was clearly young enough for most kinds of service, and though he did not imagine he could be usefully employed against the Siegfried line, he would go anywhere and do anything if anybody in authority suggested it. Of course nobody did. At the Foreign Office it was assumed there would be plans for him by the time his leave was finished, but the Office was in a polite chaos owing to the return of so many personnel from enemy territory. Charles spent long lunchtimes at his club talking to other men equally stranded and restive.

One day, toward the end of his leave, he was summoned by a Private Secretary named Gosford. It was a dark morning; a yellowish fog totally obscured the trees of St. James's Park and

Gosford himself seemed electrically bright behind the desk as he swiveled round to shake Charles's hand. He had had a career of such sensational brilliance that though he was Charles's junior by several years, the pages of *Who's Who* supplied an accurate measure of comparison – almost half a column as against barely an inch. Yet, of course, in an Etonish All Souls' fashion he was friendly enough, if that be considered friendly at all. Charles knew, respected, and only slightly disliked the type.

"How are you, Anderson. . . . Sit down. . . . Smoke? . . . God, what a day. Don't you wish you were basking on Copacabana Beach?"

Charles's South American post had not been Rio, but he did not think it worth while to make the correction. He smiled, took the proffered cigarette, and murmured congratulation on Gosford's recent K.C.M.G. Gosford replied deprecatingly: "Oh, well. . . . " and then, to add tartness to the flavor: "I suppose they just had to after Pelham-Frobisher got one." Charles knew Pelham-Frobisher as an official in the Treasury, but that was all; he supposed the joke lay in some interoffice politics of which his absence had made him ignorant.

Presently Gosford lit a cigarette himself and studied Charles through the smoke. "You're living in London now, Anderson?"

"At my club for the time being. My wife's in Cheshire with the baby."

"Ah, very sensible. . . . You don't go to your family place then – let me see, isn't it Beeching?"

Charles wondered how Gosford had known or why he had bothered to find out. "Yes, I go fairly often."

"Your father live there still?"

"Yes."

Gosford swiveled another twenty degrees till his face was cut into layers of light and shadow by the green-shaded desk lamp at eye level. "I'd like to ask you a few questions about Sir Havelock, if you don't mind. Rather personal questions."

"Certainly. What's he been up to now?" This slipped out, as

perhaps it should not have done from a trained diplomat, yet it was useful sometimes to give rein to the functions of an equally trained subconscious, and Charles, as soon as he had spoken the words, was not wholly regretful.

Gosford picked up the cue as Charles had known he would. "Oh? Does he often – er – misbehave?"

"He can be rather naughty – at times."

They were both fencing with these words of innocence.

"What *are* some of the things he's been up to?"

Charles thought a moment. "I think the last was a mousetrap that didn't kill the mice but kept them imprisoned so that he could release them afterward. . . . He had to drop it – the servant problem was quite hard enough at Beeching."

Gosford smiled faintly. "Are you on good terms with him?"

"Personally, yes. Of course I don't see eye to eye with all his opinions and enthusiasms."

"Has he visited Germany recently?"

Charles was startled by the question, but also puzzled. "I don't know that he ever has. For the last ten years he hasn't been anywhere out of England, that I'm certain of."

"What does he do with his life – at Beeching – so far as you know?"

"He has hobbies. Some of them a bit eccentric, but not all. Old tombstones. Latin inscriptions. Ornithology. Writes to *The Times*."

"He likes letter writing?"

"I'd say he must."

"Well, he's in real trouble about it now. He's been sending letters to Hitler and Goebbels."

After all the preliminaries the gist of the thing came out like that, in a simple sentence, for Gosford had a technique of his own. Charles countered it by underplaying his reaction. "Oh dear," he said, in the manner of an old lady who has dropped her knitting. Then he added, establishing a small line of resistance: "I deplore his taste, but surely until September that was no crime?"

"He's been trying to communicate since, through a known German spy in Bucharest."

Charles was shocked and silent.

Gosford watched him for a moment, then continued: "Of course our Intelligence has been intercepting it all – they're not *quite* such fools. . . . Does all this surprise you – or doesn't it?"

Charles answered carefully: "Nothing about my father surprises me very much, but he's an old man, almost eighty, and I know him well enough to feel sure that any correspondence he's been having with Hitler and Goebbels is a waste of time . . . and I mean *their* time."

Gosford opened a desk drawer and took out a file. "Care to look at some of the letters?"

Charles spent the next ten minutes reading them and pretending to be still reading when actually he was thinking. They were photostatic copies. Those from Havelock were in his undisguised handwriting and on Beeching notepaper. In brief – and considering the magnitude of the subject they *were* brief – they told the Germans what to do to clean up the world. They also assured their addressees of Havelock's personal admiration, and that they could count on him as a supporter of any English movement similar to theirs. The English government was denounced as effete and the English people as ripe for dictatorship if a strong man should arise, and there was a definite hint that in default of any other suitable candidate Havelock would not consider himself too old for the job.

The return letters were fewer and shorter. Neither Goebbels nor Hitler had sent any, but those of underlings were noncommittally flattering and one of them mentioned a source that would supply the names of other Germanophile Englishmen with whom Havelock might care to make contact. It looked as if the Nazis had been only mildly impressed by Havelock as an Englishman of title and substance who might just conceivably be worth cultivating – a small possible cog in the machinery of the master plan.

Charles handed back the letters with a close concealment of his concern. "I still say he's wasting their time."

Gosford put the letters back in the drawer. Then he contemplated the yellow windows that were getting yellower. Already the fog had percolated into the room so that one could hardly see the full-length portrait of some eighteenth-century statesman above the marble mantelpiece.

"You know, Anderson, we English have missed the tremendous test of armed invasion for a couple of centuries or so, and this immunity has led us to indulge in the most comforting and therefore the most dangerous illusion – that we're fundamentally different from other people. I don't believe we are. I don't believe an Englishman can jump off a cliff without falling. I don't believe that a hostile army, if strong enough, couldn't land here, or that if it did, it would find no Englishman ready to co-operate. . . . So you see how interesting these letters are – especially the one that mentions a source from which certain other names can be obtained."

"Yes. I see that."

"Of course we know that source and we have those names."

"*Important* names?"

"I'm sure it would surprise you if I told you."

Charles did not ask for an elucidation, because he guessed that so donnish a speaker as Gosford would not be equivocal except deliberately. Gosford suddenly got up and paced across the room. "You see where this leads us, Anderson? If the government has to start making arrests, it might be difficult not to include Sir Havelock."

"I see that too. Though perhaps on account of his age – "

"A point certainly. Of course it's all outside my province except so far as it concerns your own immediate future. It would be a pity if you were in a position to be embarrassed by anything unpleasant that might occur."

Charles nodded, and out of the bitterness of his heart answered: "Yes, it would be embarrassing to be at a reception in a neutral capital when the B.B.C. announces the arrest of one's father for high treason."

Gosford gestured slightly against this dramatization. "Please understand I'm not forecasting any such thing. When does your leave expire?"

"The twenty-fifth."

Gosford made a note on his desk pad. "I ought to be able to tell you more before then. Don't do anything yet."

"What *can* I do? Seems to me I'm pretty helpless. . . . Perhaps, though, I ought to tackle my father – find out at least if he realizes how serious it is. Any objection?"

"*I* have none. And I don't see why – " Gosford stopped pacing and put an arm on Charles's shoulder. He became human and the humanity made him sixth-formish. "Look, Anderson, this is the damnedest situation. Your father's probably being watched, and there's nowhere he can run to even if he tried, so what harm can it do to talk to him all you want? He may have done nothing at all but just write letters. On the other hand, these are incalculable times and there are circumstances that might arise . . . a parachute landing, for instance. What would he do in such a case? Do *you* know? Does anybody know? That's the sort of problem the authorities are up against."

Charles suddenly thought of the Tunnel of Love, with his father popping out of the canvas chute on to the lawn. The thought gave him ease to meet Gosford's greater cordiality with his own as he answered: "You mean what would he do if German parachutists came down on his land at Beeching? Well, he might shoot them if he had a gun and they didn't shoot him first. Or he might ask them in the house and offer them brandies and soda. Or he might recite them a poem he'd just composed. . . . That's the sort of problem *I'm* up against."

Charles found his father in quite a rollicking mood; wartime excited him, and local hostility (for he had made no secret of his political views) did not make him unhappy. His whole life, since the age of forty, had been a training to accept the penalties of disfavor, and this was only the climax of it, all the more endurable because at such an age many things become easier, to compensate for many others that become harder.

When Charles began, without much preamble: "I'm afraid, Father, you've got yourself in a considerable mess" – something flicked across his memory; it was Havelock, two decades before, making almost the same remark, though in sharper accents, on that last day of Charles's last term at Cambridge. "*You were in a damned mess and I got you out of it.*" Perhaps if Charles could have added the second half of the sentence he might also have copied the sharper accents; as it was he could give no such assurance and therefore spoke quietly. He just told Havelock what had happened, without elaboration or drama.

Even after long experience there was never any certainty how his father would take things. This time Charles had been prepared for an outburst, some tremendous diatribe against England, the government, democracy, and all they stood for; but instead Havelock merely shrugged and poured himself more port. "All right then. They can jail me. I've jailed plenty in my time. One thing, though, I won't need counsel. I'll defend myself." It was clear from his eyes that he was already composing a great speech from the dock. Charles was ready to deflate this mood. In fact for some time deflation had been his familiar weapon in dealing with his father's ebullitions; it had proved better than indignation or censure, and was specially suited to Charles's own temperament. He had long ago ceased to hope that his father could be reformed or would ever become much different; the problem, therefore, was to come to terms with an insolubility. Charles had often found himself in a similar position in regard to some professional issue, but if one accepted from the outset the philosophic idea that certain problems in life (as in mathematics) *might* be insoluble, it was easier to tackle them, to shirk them, to pretend they did not exist, or by starving them of attention to find one day that they had solved themselves. Charles, therefore, tried to regard his father as something like the Macedonian Problem to those who lived in Macedonia; and it was comforting then to reflect that many people living in Macedonia were doubtless completely unaware that there was such a thing.

So he said now, pricking the bubble as he saw it expand: "I wouldn't count on them letting you make any speech. If you've done nothing but write a few stupid letters they'll probably never even bring you to trial. You're just the small fish that gets into the net with the big fish, but they can't let you out till they've hauled in the catch."

Havelock didn't like that. "I don't know that I'm such a small fish."

"Oh come now, it's a bit late in life for you to make history – even as a traitor. Don't imagine you're a Colonel Lynch or a Roger Casement."

"That's not very civil, Charles."

"What do you expect from me – congratulations?"

"Of course I know you don't agree with my views."

"I not only don't agree with them, but if I knew any real evidence that you were seriously mixed up with the Germans I'd hand you over to the authorities myself. But of course I know you're relatively harmless."

"Charles, that's not a nice thing to say."

"Well, aren't you?" And with a sort of impish derision Charles continued: "For instance, there's all this talk of Germans landing by parachute. Supposing one of them did, on your front lawn, what would you do? Not what would you say – or write – but what would you *do*?"

Havelock pondered a moment, then his eyes lit feverishly. "You know what? I think I'd telephone the police and have them send old Daggett. That fellow's been so officious lately about blackout curtains it would teach him a lesson. I'll bet he'd run if he even *saw* a German!"

Charles was handicapped by his sense of humor at a moment like this, however serious he knew the matter to be; but he forced himself to clear up one detail that still puzzled. "How was it," he asked, "that you had the name and address of a German spy in Romania?"

"Professor Fontanescu? I didn't know he was a German spy. I just asked him to forward a letter through the German Legation there. Mere courtesy, after all. He was the man you asked me to write to about the red-necked phalarope. Don't you remember?"

Charles remembered. He had met the professor once at a Bucharest reception, and learning he was an ornithologist had thought it might interest his father to be put in touch with a brother enthusiast. That was all.

"You know, Charles," Havelock continued reproachfully, "if this fellow was a German spy, you really ought to have warned me. You were on the spot out there. . . . Isn't it the sort of thing you diplomatic people should have been aware of?"

It certainly was; but they hadn't.

Charles went to see Gosford the next day and reported the conversation, adding lamely: "You may find it hard to believe, especially about Professor Fontanescu and the red-necked phalarope, and I daresay there's not likely to be any corroboration except from my father himself — and even he might not be in a mood to give it."

Gosford was cool. "This isn't much of a time for having moods."

"I know that very well."

"Or even for believing things that are hard to believe. Sir Havelock, after all, had a legal training — he must have known that to communicate with the enemy in wartime by *any* method would constitute an offense."

"I agree that he must have known."

"Yet what you tell me now seems — almost — as if you were trying to establish some degree of innocence?"

Charles paused unhappily, then nodded. "Yes, that's so. Some degree of innocence. It's curious you should have used the phrase.

Some degree of wickedness, but also some degree of innocence. That's my father all over."

"I don't think it can really affect the situation much."

"Probably not. Which is why I've written a letter of resignation. Here it is . . . for use if and when." Charles placed it on the desk. It was in an unsealed envelope and he paused in case Gosford wanted to read it. When there was no move to do so, Charles continued: "That's about all, except one thing – the result of some thought during a rather sleepless night. . . . It seems to me my father oughtn't to be at a place like Beeching nowadays. Not only because of parachutists. He's talked as well as written foolish things – there's quite a bit of local feeling against him. I think he'd be better off in or near London where he can be, not exactly under my surveillance – because I suppose I'll have some kind of work to do somewhere – but at least where I can keep a more frequent eye on him than in the country. . . . I don't know how far it can help matters, but it might . . . and perhaps, if I'm lucky, it will. . . ."

Charles spoke the last words with difficulty. He had been hoping the letter of resignation would be refused, but Gosford had already put it in his pocket without reading it. Now Gosford got up as if to signify that there was nothing else to be discussed, no promise he could ask for or give, nothing more to do but let events take their course. All he said was: "I assure you, Anderson, there are times when I feel tempted to resign myself."

Charles did not think the remark either sincere or sensible, but a few days later when Gosford died suddenly of a heart attack, he remembered it. By that time the letter of resignation must have been passed to higher levels – unless, through deliberation or neglect, Gosford had kept it in his desk. In the latter event it would be there for his successor to handle. Yet his successor, when in due course he met and talked with Charles, did not mention it; so Charles didn't either. And in the meantime there came for him an official transfer to the Foreign Office.

Charles stayed in London, waiting for something he thought might happen at any time. It was like picking steps across a snow slope under cliffs that at any moment could dislodge an avalanche. The simile pleased him with its memories of happier days and its assurance of belonging still to at least one kind of an élite. He found a flat in Kensington, not far from his own in Chelsea, and established his father there with Cobb to look after him. None of the other Beeching servants wanted to come to London and Charles did not blame them. But Cobb was devoted to the old man, and Havelock undoubtedly returned an emotion of some sort. Since he was apt to treat his friends with far less consideration than most of them would a butler, it could well be said that he treated Cobb like a friend.

Charles told his father the reason for the move, and met with no objections. The fact that the government could think of him as a potential threat to national security seemed only to gratify Havelock's ego, and much as he disliked the attitude, Charles was glad of it as an aid to making the transition easier.

Meanwhile Jane and Gerald stayed in Cheshire, where Charles joined them whenever he could, but this was not very often or regularly. There was pressure of business at the Office, and most evenings he worked late.

Early in the new year, 1940, Havelock was approached by a man who wanted to buy Beeching. Charles took him for a businessman of some kind, and assumed that the rather high price he offered was either folly or the measure of his anxiety to move his family out of the likely area of air raids. Neither Havelock nor Charles would entertain the idea at first; then, all at once, it began to seem attractive. Beeching was run down; it needed extensive repairs that could not be made till the war was over; the upkeep was wasteful; war work and enlistments had taken most of the staff; and there were tax considerations that made a sale more advantageous than it might ever be again. So Havelock sold Beeching. A few months later Charles learned that government engineers were laying out a huge airfield that took in most of the land, with the house left standing but derelict just beyond the end of a runway; but he could never discover exactly how much profit had been made on the resale.

In the drawing room of his sister-in-law's house Charles would exchange news with Jane when he arrived there for a few days. The style of conversation was the same, but how different the items from those of earlier years. A First Secretary in a foreign capital in peacetime had been in some sort of swim; a minor Foreign Office official visiting his wife and child in an English country town during the phony war was in a backwater almost as stagnant as the war itself. Only family affection could compensate for the tedious train journey; but Charles was always thus compensated.

"Gerald looks well, Jane – I swear he's an inch taller than when I saw him last."

"Probably. He's found a new playmate – the Grandison girl who lives at the stone house past the bridge."

"Grandison?"

"They're a leading family here – own the local picture theater among other things, so Gerald gets in free whenever he wants."

"Fine. I'm glad he's so happy. . . . Grandison, did you say?"

"I know – you're thinking of the Grandison who used to be our pet attaché. I don't believe he's any relative."

"Wonder what happened to him? I'll look up the List when I get back. . . . How are Birdie and Tom?" (Jane's sister and her husband.)

"Tom thinks he'll be sent to India. Birdie's worrying about it."

"Not a bad place to miss the war in."

"We're missing it so far here."

"Till it starts."

"But for Gerald I'd rather live in London whatever happens."

"I get more comfort thinking of you here."

"How's Havelock?"

"In great shape. He did an amusing thing the other day – he left the flat in the morning and took the first on the right and then the first on the left and so on till the middle of the afternoon. By that time he was somewhere round Muswell Hill – at least that's what he said. Then he came back by bus."

"Why is it so amusing?"

"Because of the idea of anyone following him – if he still is being followed. They'd probably put some old chap on the job – after all, keeping an eye on a man of eighty wouldn't seem much – and then he does a seven mile walk all across London to nowhere! Just struck me as a bit funny. . . . But he probably isn't being followed."

"You think they won't do any more about the letters?"

"They haven't done anything yet."

"Except upset your career."

"You mean the transfer to the F.O.?" (He hadn't told her about his letter of resignation – time enough to worry her if and when it had to be used.) "That might have happened anyway."

"I don't think it would in your case – at least not for long. You were so high up on the List, and I'm sure they had something good for you."

"Perhaps they still have."

"Not till this business about the letters blows over."

"Well, it will . . . let's hope."

"Providing he doesn't send any more."

"I think I can guarantee that. Cobb watches him – it's more feasible, in the small flat. I see him too for a short time most evenings."

"As if you hadn't enough to do nowadays."

"He's often quite good company."

"You're very tolerant, Charles."

"Well, I look at it this way – quite apart from his being my father – I sometimes think when he's at his best – not being too eccentric, that is – suppose we'd met him at some big party – as a stranger. . . . We'd both come home afterwards and talk about him – We'd say, Who *was* that man? – not just his name, but *who?* He's a *who* . . . and you can't say that of everybody."

"Not even of everybody you like."

"No."

"And you *can* say it — sometimes — of people you don't like."

Charles accepted the implication, then answered: "I don't blame you, Jane. I daresay you feel that but for him we'd be having a much pleasanter time somewhere else." An obscure desire to take her side in the argument made him continue: "Yes . . . think of Viña del Mar in February — the Cavalhos giving a party at that Chinese restaurant overlooking the sea. Not that I was ever terribly keen on the Cavalhos . . . or on Chinese food either."

"Andy . . . tell me something, will you?"

"Yes, of course."

"What happened at Beeching the night before I had the operation?"

Charles's face acquired the sudden protective blandness which he was afraid she knew only too well.

"What happened? Why, nothing. . . . What do you mean?"

"During dinner."

"Dinner. Let's see, I don't think we had dinner — it was more a sort of supper, very late. Blainey was there — I'd met him at the station. . . ." He was stalling for time, of course. Since only three persons could have told her anything (Havelock, Blainey, and Cobb) he did not think she could possibly know the whole story; but she clearly knew something, and he wanted to find out how much before he gave his own answer. It was a familiar situation in diplomacy, though Jane, being equally familiar with it, unfortunately knew all its tricks. He waited for her to speak while she too waited for him. Presently he said: "If you tell me what's on your mind, I could better try to remember, perhaps. . . ."

"I just wondered what had happened."

"But why should you think anything had happened?"

"When I saw Blainey weeks afterward, just before Gerald was born, he asked me how I liked Havelock. I don't think he would have, in the way he did, unless he'd formed an odd impression himself, and as he'd only seen him that one time at dinner, I wondered what had happened."

Jane always told the truth, though she did not always tell all the truth, and Charles felt reasonably certain now that she knew nothing definite, but had merely been made shrewdly suspicious by a question that Blainey had put rather naïvely. So he answered, with confidence: "Oh, I wouldn't doubt that Blainey got an odd impression — did anyone meeting my father ever get anything else? All I remember is that we talked a lot — nervous tension, on my part, anyhow. Matter of fact Havelock would have kept Blainey up all night if I'd let him — got in one of his reminiscent moods about law cases — You know how he is at those times. . . . I think the tension affected us all." Charles had often found that to tell the truth, casually and unimportantly, is a very effective substitute for a lie, with the additional advantage that it never requires retraction afterwards. Having told the truth in this way, he put in a little further probing of his own. "A pity surgeons are always so busy. I'd like to see Blainey again. Did he say what *he* thought of Havelock?"

"He said: 'You've got a rum fellow for a father-in-law.' "

"That all? I'd call it a mild diagnosis. . . . And then what did *you* say?"

"I said I knew I had."

Charles laughed. "If this damned war ever gets over, let's ask Blainey to dinner. . . . God, it would be something to live a civilized life again, wouldn't it? Not that it's too bad in London — putting on a tin hat once a week and having drinks in pubs. Our friends abroad should see me. I often wonder whether some of the German Secretaries and Attachés we used to meet are doing the same in Berlin. . . . Talk about rum fellows — it's a rum world altogether. . . ."

Six months later the word "rum" was hardly one that an Englishman would have chosen — with Scandinavia, the Low Countries, and France already fallen, German armies just across the

Channel, and the first air raids on London beginning. Charles did his duty *on* as well as beneath the roofs of Whitehall, and of the many exciting moments that came to him a few were fairly unpleasant.

Early one dark morning, as he was leaving his fire-watching post after the all clear sounded, he learned of an emergency summons for extra helpers in a certain street in Notting Hill where a large bomb had fallen. With others, he responded. When he got there he found that several five-story houses had collapsed into rubble, under which were buried numerous victims, some of whom might still be alive. Rescue squads were already at work, boring and digging and passing out baskets of brick and plaster. Charles took a place in the line, and presently volunteered when a call was made for someone thin enough to crawl beneath a beam toward an elderly man who was pinned down under a mass of debris. Charles reflected, as he did so, that he wasn't really so thin; it was the other fellows who just happened to be stouter. He worked for perhaps an hour, scrabbling bricks out of the mess and passing them behind him. He was getting closer to the man, but still not close enough to do anything for him. Not having had experience of this sort of thing before, he kept thinking he was slower than anyone else would have been, and this spurred him to extra exertion. From sounds outside he judged that the raiders had returned and were dropping more heavy stuff in the neighborhood. The man who was pinned down groaned quietly from time to time; presently the groaning stopped. By the time Charles finally reached him he was dead. There was no point then in continuing to work at that particular place, so Charles withdrew from the hole and went to help somewhere else. This kept on till past dawn. He worked in a vacuum of sensation, not feeling any of the expectable emotions — neither fear of the still-falling bombs, nor pity for the dead and injured, nor anger or indignation at anybody or anything in particular. His most conscious thought, almost amounting to a worry, was that he wouldn't be much good for some rather important work at his office later in the day.

About eight o'clock the all clear sounded again and Charles, with a local warden, left the scene of what was so genteelly called an "incident." The street was close to where Havelock lived, and Charles was not utterly astonished to find his father standing at the corner, fully dressed and looking quite spruce. They exchanged a greeting, but no more; Charles felt now his own exhaustion and wanted nothing so much as to get to his flat and have a bath. His companion, a sturdy rough-spoken friendly fellow, commented: "That old bloke your dad?"

"Yes," said Charles. "He lives just round the corner."

"Don't you want to take 'im 'ome, then – make sure 'e's all right?"

"Oh, he's all right. I'll see him later."

"Bin a narsty one, though, tonight – some of the old folks need a bit of cheerin' up after it."

"My father doesn't. He enjoys it all."

"*What?*"

"It excites him. All the bombs falling and the fires and everything."

"Go on – I don't believe it!"

"It's a fact. I wanted him to go away when the raids started, but he wouldn't. He likes it here."

"Wot's the matter with 'im then? Is he loony?"

"Yes," said Charles.

But he did not often lose his nerve enough to speak with such nerveless detachment.

It was true, though, that Havelock was in London from choice. After the opening nights of the heavy September raiding Charles had seen no reason why his father should stay, since he could just as well live with Cobb on the coast or in some inland town. The affair of the letters seemed to have blown over, at least for the time, and Charles had heard no more from anyone about his own letter of resignation. Even if Havelock were still on any secret list of suspects, he could be watched as easily in one place as another. But the old man himself declined to move. It was perhaps too much or at least too simple to say that he enjoyed the raids, but they certainly fascinated him; in some obscure way they offered a challenge and a reassurance of destiny, as if every bomb were aimed at him personally, so that every raid he survived represented a personal victory.

Toward the end of the year there came a lull in air attacks, and Jane (using this as an excuse) joined Charles at the Chelsea flat, leaving Gerald in Cheshire. But when the lull ended Jane also refused to leave. Charles could not convince her that he worried about her safety even more than he took pleasure in her company. But *did* he? He often asked himself the question afterward, speculating how much had been in his power, even had he chosen to exercise it.

Besides a desire to be with Charles, she soon had other reasons for staying where trouble was. She found a job with the local authority, arranging shelter for bombed-out families; in this she became an instant success and (to Charles's dismay) quite invaluable. Sometimes when they both returned to the flat, she from the Town Hall and he from his varied duties in Whitehall, it was long past midnight. Then if there was no raid they could have a meal of sorts and a few hours' sleep before morning took them to work again. It was hard, amidst these compulsions, to remember that they were financially well off – hard, and also, as a rule, irrelevant. Money was still the lubricant, but it was not the driving power of this new kind of life; it conferred a few small privileges, but no large immunities. To Charles these months in London during the blitz reminded him more of his schooldays than of anything else – the physical austerities, the extraordinary way one enjoyed any small pleasure that came unexpectedly, the regular almost taken-for-granted ordeals (now the raids, at school compulsory games), and over it all a sense of time passing that must, if one were lucky, bring some eventual finality – the end of term, or the end of the war. Toward Christmas, so Havelock assured Charles, Hitler missed a terrific psychological opening wedge into the Londoner's heart. He should have announced, with all possible propaganda fanfare, that raids would be totally suspended during the festive season, that London could put on its lights, enjoy social engagements, and sleep the good sleep for a whole week. The British authorities, naturally, would then have warned that Hitler was not to be trusted and would have insisted (rightly) on continuing every precaution; after which Hitler should very simply have kept his word. The curious psychological effect of this would have been to make Londoners feel almost grateful for not being killed, and irritated with their own rulers for being overzealous. At least that was the way Havelock worked it out; but since to make Hitler popular was neither Charles's desire nor within his power, the argument remained purely academic.

Charles was an averagely good citizen, performing his duties by day and night no better or worse than tens of thousands of other Londoners — that is to say, without any special heroism, but with a good deal of conscientiousness. The time he crawled under the ruins of the house to try to free the trapped old man was the nearest he ever came to a personal exploit; there were other ticklish moments, some of them even more unpleasant, but none that put him so close to the center of any stage. He did not want such a position, anyhow, and if chance had decreed it for him he knew his friends and colleagues would have responded with far more badinage than applause.

Charles's happiest moments at this period of his life (and they had a piercing intensity while they lasted) were the rare ones when he and Jane found themselves at home with nothing much to do in some small pocket of the immediate future that seemed to have miraculously detached itself from the rest. The flat was near the river, and on raidless nights they would stroll along the Chelsea Embankment before going to bed, watching the tugs horn their way under the Albert Bridge and wishing they had a dog. But of course this was no time for having dogs in London. Or wives either, Charles sometimes thought during raids. The safe moments with Jane were precious because of the fears that at other times beset him. He had never felt so alone with her, dependent on her, worried about her – and, perhaps because of it all, so close to her.

And there were other moments, weirdly and painfully happy, when he had checked after raids to find that all was well with Jane and he could then unclench the muscles of his stomach and join a group of tired men clustering round a mobile canteen to drink tea. It was the least palatable liquid he had ever tasted – sticky and oversweetened and pale with condensed milk; yet he found in it a flavor that again reminded him of schooldays – of horrible concoctions prepared and enjoyed in his study after a football game that he had particularly loathed.

Jane, however, was much more than an averagely good citizen. In no time at all she seemed to have acquired a position of authority at the Town Hall, distributing chits for this and that, fixing homeless families in temporary quarters, smoothing out countless difficulties and bringing order out of chaos wherever she turned. All the qualities that had made her hoydenish as a girl and excellent as a diplomat's wife made her now superb. She knew how to talk to poor people without condescension and to officials without subservience. She knew exactly when to insist and when to cajole, when to rebuke and when to flatter. And she seemed to have no physical fear. This, to Charles, who had, was the most remarkable thing of all.

Due partly to an early fresh-air upbringing and partly also to much experience of savage injuries caused by broken glass, she developed what Charles jokingly called a "window neurosis." As soon as she entered a room she would rush up to closed windows and open them, thus lessening the danger of blast, but also (as Charles pointed out) destroying the effect of indoor heating on cold days. Charles, in his office overlooking the Horse Guards Parade, was one of those who found the government heat ration hopelessly inadequate unless he worked in his overcoat and trusted to drafts for ventilation. Once Jane visited him and went straight to the windows, opening them wide and exclaiming: "Charles, you're stuffy in here." A man named Etheridge, who happened to be with Charles at the time, gave the statement a prolonged joy ride. "Of course he's stuffy in here. Isn't he stuffy when he's with you too? Why, that's what we call him — Stuffy Anderson."

They hadn't, until then. But afterward those who knew him well enough and liked him sometimes did. Others picked up the nickname without the story of its origin, and thinking of him as Stuffy found stuffiness in some of his behavior. His minute handwriting helped, and perhaps also a certain fussiness over details that did not, just then, seem to everybody worth the attention he gave them. He could not have explained, and perhaps he did not know, that he clung to the importance of these trivia as to a symbol of what could not be blown to bits or buried under rubble. The verbal correctness of dispatches, for instance. He abhorred jargon, the diplomatic as much as any, and would frown on any junior who talked or wrote of "implementing a decision" or "activating a policy." For certain words his dislike amounted to prejudice — "rededicate" was one; "underprivileged" was another. To the surprise of some in his department, he had no objection to "okay." He was not a pedant. Now that the immediate threat of a German invasion looked to be over, there were often arguments about the value and quality of Churchill's oratory — that speech, for example, about fighting on the beaches and in the fields and the streets and the hills. How far could it have weighed in the hairline balance that had so recently existed? It was often conceded that further fighting would have been hopeless if ever an enemy had seized the airfields, the railways and roads into London, and the Channel ports, nor was it certain that all this could have been prevented if enough German lives had been staked. Yet the romantic view, the heroic attitude, however false or illogical — what a weapon it had been, and especially in the almost total absence of other weapons! Charles, whose service to his country was at no time romantic, nor did he ever think it was, could share nevertheless the sense of glory that sometimes touched London's tired morning faces like an extra color on a painter's palette that came from no known mixture of other colors. It would have been hard to make a memorandum about this, but it was clearly the stuff that dreams were made of, and English dreams at that. Charles was a great admirer of Churchill and of the fighting-on-the-beaches speech. But of the other famous one, about having nothing to offer but blood, toil, tears and sweat, he would only comment: "It always *was* good – even when Garibaldi and Lord Byron and John Donne thought so."

Charles alternated with Jane, as a rule, in visiting Gerald at week ends; it rarely happened that they could go together. But Gerald meanwhile was happy enough with Aunt Birdie, and had made friends of his own age in the small Cheshire town. Charles told Jane he sometimes doubted whether the boy really enjoyed his visits or was just polite enough to give him a civil welcome.

"Of course he likes to see you, Charles. But he's as shy of you as you are of him."

"I don't mind. My time will come later. What I'm really looking forward to is when he's about seventeen or eighteen and we can start being companions. Climbing, for instance – I'd like to take him up Scafell."

"I'll be getting on for sixty when Gerald's eighteen."

Charles's vision of Scafell had included only himself and Gerald, but he replied gallantly: "Why all the mathematics? People have climbed the Matterhorn at sixty."

She shook her head. She was in one of the somber moods that had come rather frequently of late – the strain of the raids, he surmised. He wished she would go back to Cheshire and rest for a few weeks.

Abruptly she came over to his chair and sat on the arm. "Charles, do you remember those little islands near Stockholm that we always said were so fascinating though we never found time to land on them?"

"Yes?"

"Well, that's the point. We never found time. And it would only have taken a day."

"That's so. But what made you think of them?"

"I've been thinking of a lot of places lately. For relief, I suppose. You have to think of *other* things when you're doing *some* things. . . . Places where we've lived, or just visited, or passed in a train or boat, and memory put a red star in the corner like pictures in a gallery that get sold. . . ."

"That's a pretty comparison."

". . . the Danube at Giurgiu, do you remember, and the old man who came on board festooned with green peppers and pomegranates? And St.-Rémy-de-Provence on the night they had the wine festival? And Kandersteg, where you said you'd like to paint, but I wanted to climb, so we climbed. . . . I'm sorry about that now. I should have let you paint more."

"We couldn't climb and paint at the same time, and I always enjoyed climbing."

"Charles, if you ever marry again, pick a young girl who doesn't like climbing, because you're getting to the age when painting is so much better for your heart."

Charles laughed, yet was increasingly puzzled by her mood. He said lightly: "My heart's all right, Jane, as you know better than anybody."

"That's pretty too. Reminds me of old times. Compliments and champagne under the chandeliers. Our lives have had so much of that, haven't they? You remember François Pichel? He once told me you could pay a compliment as well as any Frenchman."

"Which was a nice way of paying himself one."

"He also liked your paintings. Where are they all now?"

"Goodness knows. Brunon had a lot, and where's he? Still at Clermont-Ferrand, I hope – it's pretty safe there. . . . Some others were at Beeching, and when the place was sold they got mixed up with the stuff that went to auction. I have a few here, probably ruined by dust and dampness. . . . Why this sudden interest in them?"

"Because . . . oh, Andy, paint some more sometime, will you? Would there be anything to paint on one of those islands?"

"Why, yes, I daresay, but – "

"Could we ever go there and see?"

"After the war, of course. . . . But Jane, what's the matter? You're not — specially — *upset* about anything, are you?"

As soon as he had spoken it the question seemed absurd. There they were, huddled in a cold room after a makeshift meal, weary from a day of effort and nervous tension, waiting for the night which, if it followed a familiar pattern, would bring them more of the same.

"I'm all right," she answered. At that moment the sirens began, and from then on it was the plain truth; she *was* all right. And though Charles wasn't, altogether (his stomach never could get used to the sound), it was easier to brace himself for the performance of certain known duties than to prowl wistfully among the memories. "No champagne under the chandeliers tonight," he said grimly, reaching for his equipment. It was his turn for fire watching, and with a raid in prospect he must start at once.

He often felt that he endured these occasions only by having to go out and do things instead of staying at home to wait for things to happen.

One morning in April there was an "incident" in a street called Marlow Terrace, where bombs had fallen during the night. The usual after-raid work was in progress — digging into ruins to discover if anyone trapped were still alive, and an evacuation of families from nearby houses that had been declared unsafe. The sun shone like a red globe through the dust, the air was warm with a touch of spring, and a canteen served tea to anyone who wanted it — officials, rescue workers, and residents alike. All the routine of behavior that had by now become so dreadfully normal was operating smoothly, and there was nothing in Marlow Terrace that made it different from scores of other London streets that morning. Suddenly a delayed-action bomb exploded from the front garden of a house where evacuation had just been ordered. It was an enormous explosion heard miles away. The walls of all the adjacent houses caved in and made a mountain of rubble from pavement to pavement. A roaring fire broke out almost immediately from escaping gas. The whole street had been so busy, just before, that survivors were unable to say exactly who had been there and who elsewhere; only a roll call, undertaken later, gave a list which could be no more than tentative. A few persons were just not seen again, and nothing was ever found of them, or guessed about them unless someone came along to say that so-and-so was missing and might have been or must have been in Marlow Terrace about that time.

Charles was caught up in an unexpected flurry of office work that day, and toward late afternoon telephoned his flat that he would have to miss dinner and (since it was his night for fire watching) would not be home till next morning. He left this message with the woman who came in to clean and tidy up; she said Jane had been out all day and had not telephoned. This was fairly unusual, but there were a dozen possible reasons; the whole fabric of wartime life was interwoven with such unusualness. Charles thought little of it, ate a sandwich at his desk, and worked throughout the evening. Toward eight o'clock he telephoned again, just to say hello, but there was no answer. This was on the way to being unusually unusual, since even if Jane had gone out again for the evening, after receiving his message, she would hardly do so without giving him a ring. He therefore telephoned again just before nine, which was his hour for beginning watch and ward; still no answer. It was an eight-hour spell, and after it of course he could go home, but generally he finished the night on the army cot that the government had austerely installed in his office. Etheridge was sharing duty with him. He did not tell Etheridge why or where he kept dialing fruitlessly every hour or so. Etheridge was sleepy and dozed part of the time on his own cot; Charles was ready to wake him in any emergency. But there was no raid that night. About four o'clock Charles decided that as soon as he was free he would go to his flat immediately. He was already disturbed enough to wonder at what time a call to the police would cease to seem panicky. After half an hour of wondering he didn't even care, and a few minutes later he felt he could wait no longer. He telephoned the police from the office. They put him on to some young woman whose job seemed to be nothing but dealing with that kind of problem, and after he had given all the details he fancied he caught in her answering voice an implied rebuke for his premature anxiety. Actually this comforted him a good deal during the hour or so before the same voice spoke to him again.

He was then alone in his office, preparing to leave. He could not at first accept what he heard, but soon it fell into a perspective of credibility, being no more unlikely than much else one heard about every day. He sat at the desk for a moment, his hand still on the telephone. Then Etheridge came in. Etheridge did not apparently notice anything wrong, or perhaps he was too tired to observe Charles closely. Presently Charles said: "Etheridge, I've just had . . . what may be bad news . . . about my wife. . . . It seems . . . they say . . . by the way, where's Marlow Terrace? Isn't it near Sloane Square?"

Etheridge came over and gripped his arm. Charles then turned to him with a stricken face and a remark that sounded foolishly like the kind he might have made at a cocktail party: "You met my wife once, I think?"

Etheridge accompanied him to Marlow Terrace, but there was nothing to see or do and hardly any more to learn. The rather remarkable circumstance, even for those times, was that there was just the slightest possibility that Jane might still turn up from somewhere else if one could think of any plausible reason for her continued absence from home. Charles, as the hours passed, could think of fewer and fewer such reasons. That she had had business in Marlow Terrace on the previous morning was verifiable, and that she had actually gone there was verifiable, but many had been killed who might have been with or near her at the time, and a postman delivering letters further along the street had already said he had seen someone roughly answering her description, just about where it happened and before he was blown unconscious. He had noticed her particularly, he said, because she had been doing her job so briskly and cheerfully, handling a group of evacuees as if (in his own words) she were "running a school treat or something."

The hairline of doubt, the ten-thousand-to-one chance, preoccupied Charles for weeks and drove him near what he himself felt to be a dangerous edge of mental balance. Perhaps he was saved because he thus felt it, and could therefore exert the necessary controls. But there were times when control was uncertain. It was surprising how many people, seen at a distance or passingly for a few seconds, looked like Jane; and how plausible then became the theory that Jane might have walked away from all the commotion unnoticed and unhurt except for complete loss of memory. There were stories about things like that. One afternoon he was on top of a bus along the Strand when he saw Jane (his recognition was quite positive) standing outside a cinema. He started up like a madman, ran down the steps and dodged traffic at the risk of his life, but too late to intercept her before she entered. His excitement at the box office and subsequent explanations of why he was wandering up and down the aisles to peer along rows of dim faces, did not satisfy the ushers, who ordered him out and threatened to call the police if he didn't clear off. He went on explaining, so they called the police, who listened more tolerantly and advised him to go home. He did not go home, but waited three hours till the show was over, watching the main entrance from as close as he dared. But there was a side-street exit that he could not also watch.

Again he saw Jane in the Burlington Arcade leading a Pomeranian. That was strange, because she had always preferred big dogs. He hurried up to her. "Jane. . . . *Jane!* . . ." She smiled a professional smile and took his arm, but the little dog yapped and snapped at his heels. From the way she scolded the animal he knew she could not be Jane at all. He apologized. "What's the matter with you?" the woman jibed. She called after him as he walked away: "Nuts, that's what you are!" Odd, he reflected, suddenly sane inside his normal self, how American slang was driving out English slang — though "nuts" was certainly a good word, as good as a good monosyllable can be.

This sort of thing disturbed Charles so much that he thought he might do well to see a doctor or a psychiatrist, but he shrank from the ordeal of discussing his affairs with a stranger. Then he remembered somebody who was not a stranger. On impulse he called on Blainey in Welbeck Street, catching the surgeon just about to leave for his hospital. They talked for a short while. Blainey was sympathetic, but had to insist he was unqualified to give more than the most general advice. He could, however, recommend a colleague – Heming Wentworth, just across the street. . . .

Charles said: "I suppose the real reason I came to you is because you were a witness that time of my father's somewhat – er – peculiar behavior, and I thought – I wondered if – by any chance – things like that . . . father to son, you know . . . not necessarily the *same* kind of peculiarity, but. . . . But you're probably reluctant to give an opinion?"

"I couldn't as an expert, Anderson, but for what it's worth I'd say your father's trouble is entirely his own affair – nothing to do with yours, which sounds to me like a very understandable result of what you've recently been through. . . . You need rest, probably that's all. And mental rest. Haven't they found any trace – some piece of jewelry or something you can identify and then feel sure about it?"

"There was part of a wrist watch that might have been hers."

"What do you mean – *might have been*?"

"It was the same type. But I went to the shop and made inquiries – they said it was manufactured in thousands before the war."

"So you still feel . . . but that *is* the trouble, isn't it?"

"I know. It's foolish. Like going back to the front door to try the lock when you know it's closed."

"You don't really *believe* she's still alive?"

"No, not at all. Well, hardly at all. Except when I see her – *think* I see her, that is. I'm a . . . temperamentally, I mean . . . I'm a bit of a sceptic. But perhaps a credulous one."

"A credulous sceptic, eh? What sort of animal is that?"

"Well . . . if I saw a man walking on the water, I don't think I'd conclude he was the son of God, but I'd probably say: Look, there's a fellow seems to be able to walk on water. . . . Because so many strange things happen today. One must cling to one's doubts, but it's just nonsense to disbelieve everything on principle. . . . I won't take up more of your time, though. You're right about my needing rest – I'll try to get it. I wish I could join the army and get away somewhere. Sort of *requiescat* in khaki. But I'll be all right. You've given me the answer I wanted."

"How *is* Sir Havelock these days?"

"Fine, fine."

"Perhaps *he's* the one who really ought to consult Heming Wentworth?"

They exchanged a smile, as at a particularly subtle joke which they alone could share.

The talk with Blainey did much for Charles, but Gerald did most of all. Charles took time off from the Office and went to Cheshire to see the boy, who knew nothing of what had happened and was supremely happy in his aunt's home. It was the spectacle of this happiness that helped Charles far more than Gerald ever afterward knew. Charles kept putting off the job of telling him the truth, as much for his own sake as for Gerald's; and when this reluctance became revealed as part of a state of mind, Jane's sister thought of an ingenious alternative. Gerald was five – an age when the loss of his mother, if he learned about it, might overtax his emotional resources, though he had quite easily accustomed himself to seeing her only at long intervals. Aunt Birdie's idea was that if the boy were sent to some American relatives who had already pressingly invited him, the blow might be deferred till it was much less of a blow. Such a plan was all the simpler because there had been frequent talk of sending him to America, and he had come to think of the trip as a desirable event even at the price of separation from his parents. It was leaving Aunt Birdie that bothered him most, for during his stay at her house he had developed a great attachment to her. Birdie, therefore, with a husband abroad and not much else to do, suggested that she should make the trip with him and stay till he had settled down and made new friends. Charles was in entire agreement. He went back to London to work on the practical details, and to such effect that within a month of the incident in Marlow Terrace Gerald and his aunt were aboard the trans-Atlantic clipper.

Charles saw them off and then, sick at heart but in better control of himself than for some time, faced the fact of his own future. Of course he would not need to see Heming Wentworth. There was really nothing the matter with him. Blainey had been right. Just rest — and he had had it. Now he had better get back to work. There were things to do, arrangements to make, matters he had neglected during his — whatever one called it — would *breakdown* be the proper word? And the first thing was to see Havelock again. He hadn't done so since the incident in Marlow Terrace. He hadn't felt it possible to do more than keep in touch with Cobb about him. But now he decided the nettle must be grasped, and in the same mood he would stop saying "the incident in Marlow Terrace," either to himself or to others, when what he really meant was "Jane's death."

He had moved out of the flat in Chelsea and had managed to get a room at his club. After dining there alone one evening, he made the journey to Kensington and rang the bell of his father's flat as casually as if there had been no interval since his former regular visits. Cobb admitted him, tactfully without surprise, but told him in the hallway that Havelock had not yet fully recovered from the shock of the whole thing; it had taken away the fun he got from air raids, so that he was still rather moody and cantankerous. Charles found that this was so, except for the cantankerousness, which was rather in himself as he realized that the old man was now all he had left in the Eastern Hemisphere. Havelock did his best to be amiable, but the visit was a short one. "I'll come back soon," Charles promised, still casually. He had given no explanations and none had been asked for. In the hallway again, as Cobb helped him on with his coat, Charles remarked: "Certainly keeps well physically, doesn't he?"

Cobb agreed that he did. "He's been writing a letter again, sir, but nothing to worry about."

"Oh? . . . Who is it this time – General Rommel or the Pope?"

"President Roosevelt."

Charles gave a low whistle. "You read it, of course?"

"Yes, and it seemed all right, so I let it go. I thought it would cheer him up – Sir Havelock, I mean. I don't suppose the President'll ever see it."

"But what's it about?"

"A statue of Columbus in London. Sir Havelock thinks there ought to be one."

"Isn't there?"

"Apparently not, sir."

"Why, no, I can't think of any. Not a bad idea, Cobb, but a little awkward just now, since Columbus was an Italian. Mustn't glorify the ancestors of our enemies, must we? . . . However, I don't think His Majesty's Government, in the circumstances, will consider the suggestion treasonous."

It eased Charles to find this sort of wry humor in most of his concerns, and he was beginning to be known for it. Some people said he was witty, others that he joked about matters that weren't funny; a few guessed that he was desperately unhappy and had found a way to come to terms with both the desperation and the unhappiness.

Charles did not ask for a longer leave, as some of his friends urged; he said truthfully that he found his work a help, or at least a time-occupier, and even his night duties were useful in solving the problem of sleep. He was well liked and his friends rallied round with as much hospitality as conditions permitted them to offer; but he really did not mind being alone when he was also, as so often happened, exhausted.

One day it fell to him, as a representative of the Foreign Office, to escort a Middle-Eastern potentate and his entourage to an airport whence a military plane would fly them carefully home. Charles had had something to do with his visit to what was usually on such occasions referred to as the war-torn island; it had been a visit staged with psychological shrewdness and not without a likely effect in terms of oil concessions. Accompanying the small party was a British Military Attaché who would travel back with the potentate and keep him happy during the trip. (For what better reason, after all, did one learn those obscure and difficult languages?) The Attaché's name was Venner, and he persisted in calling Charles "Allenson"; Charles did not correct him. But he found the young fellow congenial company during the short time they had together at the airport. They were granted this respite because their illustrious charge had asked to be left alone for a period of prayer and meditation, and after harassed consultations with airport officials a small room not very suitable for the purpose had been discovered and commandeered. It was the room (so an official said) where incoming suspects were searched for smuggled drugs or diamonds.

Charles, thinking of the last time he had seen anyone off at an airport (his own son and sister-in-law), paced up and down a plywood corridor with the Attaché; thought also of the potentate on his knees a few yards away, after the fashion of his ancestors for a thousand years; thought also of the great engines warming up nearby, ready to carry him to Biblical lands in a matter of hours; thought also of the millions of Londoners waiting in their own homes for the probable nightly dose of death and destruction. Truly a moment to take refuge in some deep philosophy, if one had any.

The pilot, fidgeting to be off before a raid could start, approached them with the question, hushed yet matter-of-fact: "How long d'you think his nibs is going to be in there?"

"Few minutes — five — ten, possibly," answered the Attaché. "Not more as a rule."

The pilot shrugged and went off.

Charles then said: "I suppose you know his nibs pretty well?"

"Oh yes. I've been with him several years."

"What sort of a fellow is he?"

"Not bad, as they go. Crafty. Suspicious of his family. Loves practical jokes. Generous when he's in the mood. Extravagant. Greedy. What impressed him most, I think, during his stay here was that in the midst of our own crisis we're building him two beautiful Rolls-Royces with satinwood panels and solid gold ash trays. He figures we wouldn't do that if we weren't going to win the war. But, of course, we wouldn't do that if we didn't need his oil to win the war. So I guess we're craftier in the long run. . . . He's a hard bargainer, though."

"And of course fabulously rich."

"So rich he's worried stiff. He's secretly afraid that someday somebody will ruin the oil trade by finding a synthetic substitute — like they did to Chilean nitrates. We planted a rumor once that a scientist had invented something . . . just to explore a weak spot."

"And what happened?"

"He got rid of half a dozen wives immediately — as an economy measure. Didn't miss them either, so far as I could see."

Charles said, whimsically: "I suppose you don't when you have so many. . . . But I miss mine — she was killed a few weeks ago in a raid."

The Attaché was naturally startled and considerably embarrassed. "Oh . . . er . . . I'm sorry to hear that, Allenson. . . . That's really bad."

"Yes, it does rather hit one." And then Charles continued, as he could only have done with someone who had missed his real name and whom he would probably never meet again: "I was very fond of my wife. She was a damned good sort. She'd be better at this than I am — handling his nibs, I mean. 'Manhandler' I called her once and she said it was a compliment.

So it was, by God. I wonder why the F.O. never has women to do these jobs — everyone knows how useful a wife can be in an Embassy. . . . Are you married, by any chance?"

The Attaché said he was.

"Well, hang on to her then. Don't let her run into danger." Having offered this advice without undue emphasis Charles added: "I'm talking a lot of nonsense, you must forgive me."

"Oh no, not at all. . . ." A small commotion was shaping up toward the end of the corridor. "I guess he's finished — now we can start, thank goodness. . . . You'll be all right going back into town, Allenson?"

"Oh yes, of course . . . thank you."

After Charles had performed the ceremonies of the occasion and had heard the plane take off at some distant end of a darkened runway, he walked to the government car whose chauffeur was waiting with the same kind of fidgetiness the pilot had had, and for the same reason. "So far so good, sir," he said, starting up. "We live in 'opes."

In the car Charles felt, not for the first time in his life, that he had made something of a fool of himself. Or rather, of some other fellow named Allenson. He must remember to look up the List tomorrow to see if there was an Allenson anywhere. He hoped he did not exist.

At the beginning of May he spent a week end in Suffolk at the house of an undersecretary who was ill and wanted him to help to draft a reply to Turkey about Moslem Irredentists in Cyprus. Charles took his car, which he now rarely drove, and enjoyed the journey through country previously unknown to him. On the way back on Sunday afternoon he chose to wander off the main roads in the general direction of London, not caring how he would eventually arrive there. The drastic curtailment of private motoring had given these East Anglian byways back to the nineteenth century, and with trees and hedges freshening to green along the twisting lanes, the drive was one of pure enchantment. As he reluctantly covered the miles the thought of London's dark streets and a possible air raid that night added a tragic beauty to sights and sounds — children in gay dresses romping through a churchyard, a gnarled old man leaning on the gate of a field, two soldiers on bicycles whistling as if there were not a war in the world.

The sun was down by the time he stopped for tea at a café where he was the only customer. When he left, the streets were dark caverns under the searchlit sky. He drove on a half-dozen miles or so, guideless except by a rough sense of convergement and increasing urbanization and by a curious awareness of London ahead like some great breathing animal, downed but not cowed, waiting for more blows and ready to take them. It would be a good night for a raid, though lately there had been a falling-off in the intensity and frequency of them. At one corner he had to stop for traffic long enough to read the name on a lamp-post, *Chilford Road.* The name stirred a memory; Chilford was the next station beyond Linstead on that railway whose trains ran every hour throughout the night. He felt the impulse of a whim; if the road he was on led through Linstead it would be interesting to have a glimpse of the place; if not, it didn't matter. But after a few minutes memory stirred again; he was passing Linstead Station, and how easy, indeed inevitable, to take the turn beyond the secondary school and the Carnegie Library.

It was a night of scudding cloud, but a full moon shone behind, half breaking through in patches of pallor. Wind scoured between the long rows of suburban houses till the pavements looked like bones picked clean. Charles could see gaps in the rows; he knew that the whole district had been heavily bombed. Presently he came to a corner he did not recognize because of an open space littered with rubble and flanked by shored-up sides of houses; but this, he knew, must be the corner of Ladysmith Road. He made the turn and drove slowly along . . . for the first time in twenty years.

He was surprised how faint and gradual was the approach of memory about it. He could not recall, offhand, what the exact number of the house had been – in the teens of the two hundreds, he thought, but had it been 214 or 215 or 216? Soon 215 disengaged itself as on the wrong side of the road – no mistake about that. Then it came to him that as one had walked from the street to the front door, the bay window had been on the right-hand side; this threw out 216. So it must be 214. He slowed the car to walking pace and drew immediate partial confirmation from some twinge of inner memory – the laburnum trees; yes, the laburnum trees, they were in flower, they had grown, they nearly touched. Ladysmith Road was at last the leafy avenue that had been dreamed of. But the house itself he would not have known from a hundred others. There was a brass plate on the gate, reading when he came close – *Miss Lydia Chancellor,* L.R.A.M. – *Pianoforte Lessons.* He wondered if Miss Chancellor were young or middle-aged or old – whether she had moved into 214 after the Mansfields, or had ever heard of them. He began to picture Miss Lydia Chancellor, L.R.A.M., and in no time at all she became a heroine, of whatever age – giving her sedate pianoforte lessons come raid or shine.

And then, while he stopped his car at the curb, he heard a sound that for all its plausibility in the context of his thoughts, nevertheless startled him like a touch of ice. It was the tinkle of a piano behind the darkened bay window. Miss Chancellor was at work. He heard the fumbling play of the pupil, then a colloquy of muffled voices, then the piano again – the same tune accurately, authoritatively. It was Brahms's "Lullaby," and Miss Chancellor played it as if she were marching soldiers round a barracks square. Not a note was out of step. Charles listened in fascination, but soon heard footsteps approaching, and with need of some excuse for having stopped, could think of nothing but to half open the car door and pretend to be tying his shoelace. It was the local policeman on his beat. "Quiet tonight," said Charles.

"Yes, sir, we're all right so far." And then, as if the shoelace were not wholly convincing: "Looking for somewhere, sir?"

Charles had to find an answer, and it came as familiarly as

the feel of a switch in a room one thought one had forgotten. "The Prince Rupert . . . isn't there a pub of that name near here?"

Suspicion vanished; anyone looking for the Prince Rupert clearly had a right to stop his car wherever he liked to tie his shoelace or anything else. "First on the right, second on the left, sir."

"Thanks," said Charles. He closed the door and drove off. . . . And why not to the Prince Rupert, after all?

Two minutes later he was pushing through the swing doors into a vestibule that had been built to ensure obedience to the blackout regulations. The interior was pleasantly warm, hazy with smoke and shaded lights, companionably buzzing with talk, but not noisy. Charles went to the bar and asked for a bitter. It was rarely his drink, but the word had framed itself for speech before he could think of anything else.

Except for the dimness and the improvised vestibule, he did not think the Prince Rupert had changed since his last visit. It had then, he recollected, been recently modernized in a style which some architect had imagined to be "Old English"; there had been a rash of dark-stained planks laid on plaster, and beams that were not beams. But now, after such a decent interval, the sham had acquired a half reality of its own. The bar counter, for instance, originally polished to look ancient, had lost its polish and taken on an attractive patina of plain usage.

Memories now were assembling so fast that Charles took cautious inventory of them, as with an old trunk in an attic that may have things in it one doesn't expect and might not want to find. The framed picture of a pretty girl holding up a glass of beer reminded him of something . . . or perhaps nothing. Another picture, of a khaki-clad soldier posing with a large Union Jack, harked back to that period, so alien, so distant, of the phony war. Abuptly, amid these musings, he felt a touch on his arm. It was an old man whom he did not recognize. "Mr. Anderson. . . . Am I right, sir? You'll remember me . . . *Fred Mansfield.*"

Charles stared, and a whole flock of memories broke through, so that his voice was hard to control as he shook the bony hand. "Of course I remember . . . of course. . . ."

But he hadn't, at first, and if he had met the man in the street he knew he would have passed him by. He remembered the voice, though – the high-pitched gentle Cockney. And soon, of course, the features fitted in, so that he could judge Mr. Mansfield hadn't changed much either, except to look older and frailer, especially in the throes of his excusable excitement.

"*Charlie*. . . . Well, of all the . . . and 'ere again – 'ow many years is it?"

Charles had to think, and in thinking remembered how, during those early years in European capitals, he had sometimes imagined meeting Fred Mansfield again – a meeting in which, out of his own deep hurt and humiliation, he would tell the fellow exactly what he thought of him. But now, it seemed, even the hurt and humiliation could be remembered only with an effort; and perhaps for this reason he didn't actually know what he thought of him, or of himself either, except that they had both been victims.

So all he answered was: "Yes, it was a long time ago. . . . What are you drinking?"

"No, Charlie – this is on me when I get me breath. . . . Gorlummy, wot a surprise! . . . Mrs. Appleby, two bitters for me an' this gentleman. 'E's an old friend of mine. . . . Mr. Anderson – Mrs. Appleby." Charles shook hands with the landlady, and something else occurred to him. "It was Mrs. Webber, wasn't it, Fred, the last time I was here?" It seemed quite easy and natural now to call him Fred.

"That's right! Now fancy you rememberin' Mrs. Webber. . . . Mrs. Appleby, Mr. Anderson remembers Mrs. Webber!" But Mrs. Appleby did not seem specially interested. "Poor Mrs. Webber died of a stroke, and then there was the Johnsons, and then the Brackleys – nobody liked *them* – they let the 'ouse down, they did. . . . But now we're all 'appy again, ain't we, Mrs. Appleby?"

"Maybe some of us are," said Mrs. Appleby as she turned to other customers.

"The fact is," whispered Mr. Mansfield confidentially, "she ain't 'ad it too easy litely. That larst raid shook 'er up. Two bombs just rahnd the corner, but only a few winders broke in 'ere. Ain't that luck?"

Charles agreed that it was. "You're looking very well, Fred – very well indeed."

"Can't complain. Not so bad for seventy-eight. Your dad still alive an' well, I 'ope?"

"Yes. He's eighty-one."

"Good for 'im. I remember Sir 'Avelock. . . . I ses to 'im, when 'e left 'ere that time, Sir 'Avelock, I ses, it's bin a honner and a pleasure. Same 'ere, Mr. Mansfield, 'e ses, or words to that effect. I daresay 'e remembers me too."

"I'm certain he does."

Mr. Mansfield gripped Charles's arm in a still rising abandonment of delight. "You know, Charlie, it's 'ard to believe, seein' you again like this. I can't say you don't look older, because you was only a boy in those days, but you certainly ain't changed your drinks, 'ave you? Bitter it was an' bitter it is, an' 'ere you are at the Prince Rupert like you was at 'ome." But he added, suddenly curious: "You rahnd 'ere on business?"

"No . . . just chance. I was driving back from Suffolk and found myself so close I thought I'd see what the old place looked like." As soon as he said it he knew it rang false; it sounded like some sentimental Old Boy revisiting his alma mater. But to Mr. Mansfield the explanation seemed perfectly satisfactory.

"You'll find some changes, Charlie. That is, if you was 'ere in the daytime and could see. Lots of bombs in the 'Igh Road."

"And at the corner of Ladysmith Road too."

"You saw that? Ah, that was a narsty one. Land mine, they said."

"No damage at Number 214, I noticed."

"So you came by an' 'ad a look? Well, well, to think of you rememberin'. . . . I don't live there no more. When the wife died I moved in with Evelyn an' 'er 'usband – in Roberts Road. Just the next turnin' from 'ere. Convenient."

"I'm sorry to hear about Mrs. Mansfield."

"Poor old soul, she missed a lot o' trouble, that's one thing. Bert 'ad to 'ave an operation an' ain't bin the same since. Maud's married and got two boys – lives at Chatham – 'er 'usband's in the Navy."

"And Lily?" said Charles, with sudden breathlessness.

Mr. Mansfield beamed, "Lily? Why, she done the best of any of 'em. She's married an' in Orsetrilia – got quite a family." He laid his glass on the counter and began searching his pockets. "Look. . . . She sent me some snaps only a month or two back – taken outside the 'ouse – seaside place near Sydney." He found a photograph and held it for Charles to inspect. "See the 'ouse – pretty, ain't it? Their own, too. . . . Garden all rahnd – not like the 'ouses 'ere. And that's the car they 'ave. . . . 'E's got a good job out there."

Charles was transfixed by an emotion he could only control by being facetious. "Very nice – very nice, indeed – and Mr. Robinson seems to have put on a little weight."

Mr. Mansfield looked puzzled. "*Robinson?*" Then he swung a cordial hand to Charles's back. "Gorlummy, that ain't Reg Robinson! . . . Is *that* wot you thought? The name's Murdoch – Tom Murdoch. Orsetrilian Scotsman, that's wot 'e calls 'imself. . . . But fancy you thinkin' it was Reg. . . . Dunno wot ever 'appened to Reg. They was sort of engaged for a time, but it didn't larst. Ain't 'eard of 'im now for years."

"You were saying Lily had a family. . . ."

"You bet she 'as, an' I got a picture of them too, if I can find it." He found it. "See. . . . Count 'em. . . . An' this is another one of Lily by 'erself. You can't see the 'ouse in this." He handed them both to Charles.

Charles looked at the one of Lily first. She too had put on weight, not enough to make her stout, but to give her a look of ripeness that of course he could not remember; and yet it was so much like her, so much a fulfillment, that he felt he recognized her as clearly as if he had known her like that in his own life. She was smiling and the little gap between the two teeth at the upper left-hand side was still there. She looked gay and cozy and richly alive, and his heart missed a beat in its rejoicing.

The other photograph showed a row of attractive-looking children ranging in age from thirteen or fourteen to perhaps two.

Mr. Mansfield was gloating over his shoulder. "See? I said you'd 'ave to count 'em. . . . *Six* – an' another on the way since then. I wrote back to 'er when she wrote an' told me that – Lily, I wrote – just a joke, of course – even if it ain't your fault, you really are makin' a 'abit of it. But she likes kids and she 'as 'em so easy, I suppose she don't mind." And with a wink Mr. Mansfield added: "I tell you, Charlie boy, you was lucky that time."

"*Was I? I wonder.*" Charles hardly whispered the words and was glad they were not heard. He handed back the photographs, forcing himself to catch Mrs. Appleby's eye and order two more bitters. "She looks fine. When did she meet this Mr. Murdoch?"

"That's wot I never can remember – the year, I mean, but it was the Wembley Exhibition that done it. Tom was in the Orsetrilian Pavilion – that was 'is job, you understand. Lily and me went there one day, we was lookin' at a stuffed kangaroo and a man come up and ses to me – 'You interested?' Well, I wasn't, not special, not in kangaroos, but it turned out 'e was interested in Lily – that's why 'e come up to me and started the conversation. All a matter of chawnce, ain't it? Like you droppin' in 'ere tonight. They was married within three months."

"And happily too, I can see."

"Well now, you know Lily – or at least you remember 'er. She always was wot you might call a 'appy girl." Mr. Mansfield put the photographs carefully back in his pocket. "I saw in the papers when you was married, Charlie."

"Yes. I have a little boy of five who's now in America." The thought of all the children in Ladysmith Road and Roberts Road made him feel apologetic about this. "We had relatives over there and they wanted to take him."

"Natchrally," said Mr. Mansfield, unaware of any need for

apology. "Just like Lily wants me to go to Orsetrilia and live with 'er and Tom, and I would too if I was a kid. Gorlummy, if I was a kid I wouldn't want to stay in England. But at my age it's different. You get yer roots in a plice, Charlie, that's the way it is."

The drinks arrived and Charles lifted his glass. His voice shook a little, but not noticeably to the old man. He said: "Well, Fred, let *me* say it this time. . . . Here's to us and our dear ones. . . ." That had come back to him too.

They talked on till closing time; then Charles took Mr. Mansfield back to his house in Roberts Road. They shook hands at the gate, and Charles meant it when he said he hoped they would meet again. During the very short walk (not worth while to get in and out of the car), he had noticed that Mr. Mansfield was a little unsteady on his feet – hardly from the few drinks, but more likely a sign of age that had not been apparent in the Prince Rupert. Another and perhaps a sadder sign was that Charles had been introduced in the bar to no one except Mrs. Appleby, who had not been too cordial. It rather looked as if the old fellow had outlived his cronies and that younger patrons found him a bore. Charles's sympathy was acute because he himself had a morbid fear of being a bore, a fear that sometimes made him awkward and speechless, or else foolish and facetious, in the presence of people who were perfectly satisfied for him to be himself. But Fred Mansfield *was* himself at all times, and always had been; and if others found him a bore he would bore them more by not realizing it, or else (as he had with Mrs. Appleby) find some charitable reason for having been snubbed. And to Charles this seemed the saddest thing of all.

He drove back to London and was in bed before midnight. There was no raid, but he could not sleep. He wished he were in a house or flat where he could go to the kitchen and make himself a cup of tea, but his club bedroom had no such facilities; and after an hour or two of lying awake he got up and looked in desperation for some job to do. It was too late to dress and go out again, and he had little to read except the penciled notes he had made at the undersecretary's house; these, with their deep concern for Cypriotes and Turks, did not easily engage his attention in the mood he was in. Lacking any better idea to pass the time, he turned to the suitcases he had brought with him from the Chelsea flat; he hadn't unpacked, since his stay at the club could only be temporary, but he had stuffed them so hastily with personal things that he thought it might be worth while to sort out the contents. Several were full of papers grabbed from desks and bureau drawers – old letters and miscellaneous documents he hadn't looked at for years, but which, from the fact that he had ever preserved them at all, might be considered of some importance. But of course, as always happens with such accumulations, many seemed at this later date quite valueless, so he began to tear them up. There was a certain pleasure in doing this, though to be on the safe side he would take the fragments to the office in the morning and burn them in the fireplace – notes on the Tacna-Arica boundary dispute, for instance, flimsies about forgotten visits of forgotten foreign officials, a copy of a preposterous letter from a duchess to Ramsay MacDonald complaining that she had been insulted by a customs inspector at Pontarlier (this, Charles remembered, had been handed round the Office for laughs). And there were also more personal oddments – ancient menu cards and concert programs with names and addresses scribbled on them of people he had met and had wished to remember at least for a time; worthless paper money of countries that had devalued their currencies; clippings from newspapers and magazines; reports of company meetings; a dossier of correspondence with the P.L.M. about a lost trunk; old lists of dinner guests in Jane's handwriting with places at table arranged according to protocol (what a job that had sometimes been!). And then – suddenly – a foolscap envelope full of snapshots and letters from Lily. . . . Lily standing by the Serpentine Bridge, eating a bun from a paper bag; Lily leaning out of a train window waving her hand; Lily against the background of the turnstile entrance to the Zoo; Lily in a mackintosh and sou'wester, facing the wind and rain on the slopes of Box Hill; Lily feeding the squirrels in Regent's Park; Lily in the doorway of a cottage that had a home-painted inscription "*Teas,*" with the "*s*" turned the wrong way. . . . So many places, so many scenes, and in nearly all of them Lily was smiling – not with the fixed grin of a pose, but as if she had always had something to smile about . . . which perhaps she had. The letters, too, were lighthearted, though usually not much more than fixings or confirmations of appointments. She had hardly been a good letter writer, though nothing she ever wrote was stiff or self-conscious. She simply could not be bothered to write when she was to meet someone soon; which was why, doubtless, the longest of all her letters to Charles was the last – the one when she was not to meet him soon, or indeed again.

When Charles unfolded this letter after an interval of a good many years, the memory it gave him was predominantly of the Rhineland village where he had first read it – a cold twilight with snow in the air and Brunon handing him a batch of mail picked up at the post office. He remembered his own distress with something of the sad contentment that time always brings; so that he even paused to light a cigarette, as if to savor the rereading.

DEAREST CHARLIE,

I don't know how to write this, but I must, and I hope you won't be hurt. Perhaps you won't be after all this time, it seems years and years to me. Reg and I are engaged. Oh Charlie, please don't be upset. It's for the best, like your dad and my dad both told me, and especially now you've done so well in all the examinations and are going to have such a wonderful future. I was so happy when I heard about that, really I was. You know it was the one thing that had been worrying me all along, that you'd spent too much time with me when you ought to have been studying. But now that's all right. I'll bet you were pleased when you heard the news. My dad told me about it and I wanted to write then to congratulate you, but he said No, he'd given his word. But he said I could write this. Oh Charlie, I can't say much more. I'll always remember you and hope you'll go on having great success, I'm sure you will. I can't say all I would like to in a letter, perhaps it wouldn't reach you if I did, so better not, eh? I know you never liked Reg, but he really is all right when you get to know him. Charlie, I did love that visit to Cambridge. Dear Charlie, this is all I can say.

Yours affectionately— LILY

Charles put the letter back in the envelope, and of all the emotions revived and reviving in his heart the only one he could express in the words of thought was a rueful: Poor old Reg, so you didn't get her after all, did you?

A week or so later Charles gave up the Chelsea flat for good and, since he could not stay at his club indefinitely, found a house in Westminster, near the river and within walking distance of the Foreign Office. It was a larger establishment than he needed for himself alone, and after much speculation as to how such a plan would work, he invited his father and Cobb to share it with him. One of his reasons was that Cobb, though too old for much personal activity, would excellently supervise and supplement any other domestic staff that Charles might be lucky enough to get; he hoped at least for a woman to cook and clean. But the chief reason was Havelock who, at last in his eighties, was beginning to experience that slight diminution of the life-force which often visits men as early as their forties. Also, according to the doctor, he had had an almost imperceptible stroke; it made him cut down his daily walking from five or six miles to two or three. Even more importantly, it clouded his mind to a merely dull inertia at times when formerly he would have been zestfully foolish; it stilled the riot in his veins to a mere fracas. All of this Charles considered, without cynicism, to be a great improvement. Certainly a household arrangement that had many other advantages was thus made possible.

There was an added consideration in the likelihood that Charles himself would be away a good deal in the foreseeable future. He had been told, informally, that a delegation to America was in the cards and that he would be a member of it.

Charles went to America in the autumn of the year. Most of his time was spent in Washington, but he had the chance of a week end at Parson's Corner, Connecticut, where Gerald was living with the Fuesslis. The leaves were turning, and the country round Parson's Corner was very beautiful. Aunt Birdie had already returned to England and before doing so had told the boy about his mother; as everyone had hoped, he had taken it well. Almost too well, indeed, for Charles's equanimity; it made him realize that Jane, like himself, had had little chance to enjoy parenthood during the rootless years imposed by his career, and that losing her forever had been easier for Gerald than separation from Aunt Birdie when the latter left Parson's Corner – for then, Mrs. Fuessli said, had occurred the real privation. But even that had only been temporary; Gerald had soon recovered. Throughout the week end with the Fuesslis his son's innocent happiness made Charles both sad and glad. It also made him act, perversely, the role of the Galsworthian English gentleman that the Fuesslis expected him to be even while they laughed at him for it – as if this laughter was the only return he could give for their kindness and generosity. They would never guess it, he knew, but the social freedom of America was something he passionately envied – or rather, it was something he wished he could have been involved in from his own early youth; as it was, there were all the conditioned reflexes of his upbringing hard at work to point out the flaws – one of which was the mood in which the local paper reported his arrival under the headline: BRITISH BLUE BLOOD VISITS PARSON'S CORNER. It took him ten minutes to explain to Mrs. Fuessli that he had no blue blood, that his family was rather boastful of not having any, that blue blood was all nonsense anyhow, and that his father's title was the equivalent of Woolworth rather than Tiffany. But it took him the same ten minutes to realize that she would always continue to think of him as an English aristocrat, that she thought of all aristocrats as idlers and fortune hunters even though they might appear to be rich themselves or to have jobs, and that her warm affection for Gerald was invincibly joined with a relish in sending Fauntleroy to the local nursery school, where he mixed with all the other children of the town and was (everyone fortunately could agree on this) having a rare good time.

So Charles left Parson's Corner in deep gratitude and slight dismay, thinking alternately that Gerald's life in America would not matter much when the war was over and he could return to England, and the next moment hoping that it *would* matter, very much indeed, and that the boy would get something out of it of lasting value. Of course there was nothing for him, Charles, to do but wait. That joke he had had with the Fuesslis about taking Gerald to dinner on his seventeenth birthday was really a symbol of a father as well as a son growing up.

Charles reached London a few days before Pearl Harbor. It was another turning point of the war, and the second that year. He kept thinking of Parson's Corner and how the news must have reached the Fuesslis – how they would doubtless be trying to explain to Gerald what had happened. He wrote them a long letter immediately, a letter so warmly personal and intimate he hoped it would finally convince them that blue blood or not, he was a human being. He didn't know (until years later, when he didn't mind) that they had proudly sent it to the local paper in which, printed verbatim and with editorial endorsement, it had convinced the whole neighborhood that he was a great English statesman and patriot.

Now that Hitler's chief embroilment was with Russia, air raids on London had almost ceased, though no one could forecast the duration of the respite and it was clearly impossible to relax any precautions. There was, however, an immediate burgeoning of social life – a pale but defiant shadow of what it had been before the war, yet in many ways pleasanter than those last sepulchral dinner parties of 1939, the tables then loaded with food and the conversation heavy with foreboding. Now, at the close of 1941, the tables were lighter, but the talk was at least that of people who had proved something, if only the nature of themselves.

Even the disasters of 1942 did not bring back the mood of that dismal year after Munich.

Charles still took his turn at fire watching but the absence of raids gave him more time off, and he was frequently invited out. Jane had made him a good talker, often by knowing when and how to talk to him; but now, he must presume, it was for his own sake and for his own unaided efforts he was sought after — which surprised him at first. Perhaps, he reasoned, it was because his work placed him near the center of events, and people hoped he would spill secrets (it amused him to pretend to be doing this while actually avoiding it with great care). Or else it was because he was alone and easy to fit in. The real reason was one so simple that he hardly considered it — people liked him. His manners were rather prewar, they admitted, and the things he said were sometimes a bit too clever in an older-fashioned way, but he was a decent fellow, always ready to do you a favor, and really, some of the things he said were sound enough, if only they had been put less elegantly. He was also, people thought, quite tolerably happy after a tragedy that might well have broken him; but in this they were wrong. Charles was not tolerably happy; he was tolerably unhappy. That is to say, he was unhappy, but he had found or made it tolerable.

When his name was in the New Year Honors List there was much professional raillery. "Oh God, look who's down for a C.B.E. . . . *Stuffy Anderson!*" But then, as an afterthought: "Well, it was about time he got something."

Havelock had another stroke in the summer of 1944; this one was more disabling, affecting his left side and preventing him from taking more than a stumbling walk around the neighboring streets. Gradually his world contracted to the room in which he spent most of his time, and from which he could see Big Ben and the twin towers of the Abbey. His mind had achieved a level of tranquillity that had not much impaired the quality of the brain, and it was odd to speculate on the difference in his fortunes if this mental change could have been inflicted in early life, and without the physical. Charles formed the habit of visiting his father for an hour or so before going to bed, no matter how late he returned from work or a social engagement; the old man enjoyed it, being fairly sleepless and fairly sleepy at all hours of the day and night. He liked to hear Charles's comments on the events of the evening, and Charles would repeat any special titbits of conversation he could remember. Charles found that he often enjoyed these post-mortems himself — so one-sided compared with those that he and Jane had shared, yet an agreeable way to sort out one's own impressions aloud and over a final drink.

The buzz bombs and V–2s arrived, several within noisy distance of the house, but Havelock, though they failed to excite him in the old way, did not dislike them nearly as much as Charles did, and was able to rationalize the situation in terms that Charles had to admit were very rational indeed. "At eighty-four you haven't got a life to lose. You have only a fraction of a life — and nobody would bet on it being more than a very small and vulgar fraction. So why should I worry?"

"Or I," said Charles, "if I could look at it your way. My own fraction's climbing down. Couldn't possibly be much more than a half — and not the better half."

"Why not?"

Charles laughed and parried the question, but when he was alone it was one he put to himself. *Why not?* He thought of his life up to date; it wasn't hard to imagine a future that might be luckier. On the other hand, with buzz bombs putt-putting overhead, it sometimes wasn't easy to imagine a future at all. Perhaps only old people and youths were always ready to indulge such a luxury.

Havelock grew weaker gradually, and with the weakness came passionlessness, so that he could talk over old days and old issues without rancor. He told Charles once, quite calmly, that he had always been doubtful whether he were really his father at all, because the dates of his wife's return to him after their separation and of Charles's birth permitted the suspicion. Charles was not as shocked, or even as concerned, as he might have expected to be, but he was interested — and mainly because the idea seemed to offer a possible clue to many hitherto puzzling facets of Havelock's behavior. He found also that the idea brought him closer to his father in sympathy, as if the spiritual tie of a revealed neurosis could be stronger than that of the body. He was almost disappointed when, on mentioning the matter to Cobb, the latter discounted it. The dates, Cobb said, made it nearly (though not quite) impossible, and besides that, there had been no whisper at the time, as would certainly have happened if any other man had been involved in the separation.

"Then why *did* she leave him?" Charles asked.

"She couldn't stand him," Cobb answered.

They were both unwilling to discuss the matter further, except that Cobb brought up the matter of the family likeness. "It's not just looks, sir — as it was with Mr. Lindsay — it's something hard to explain, but it's there, and I notice it more as you grow older. Of course you're nothing like your father in tastes and disposition, and yet . . . well, I wouldn't have any doubts if I were you, sir." Cobb added, perhaps as an implied compliment (or else the reverse, Charles could not be certain): "He was very handsome at your age."

"He still is."

"Yes — and there's a look about him now — sometimes when he's dozing in a chair with the sun on his face — he looks — well, sir, he looks just like a *saint*."

Cobb smiled at the notion, and Charles also smiled. *Sir* Havelock, yes — but *Saint* Havelock was a bit too much.

When he next saw his father Charles gave him what he hoped was the good news, expecting him to take more comfort from it than Charles could himself, for he knew by now that if he had been supplied with irrefutable proof that Havelock was not his father, his chief feeling would have been curiosity about who had been. He often wondered why his relationship with the old man had entered a phase of such warm indifference, such affectionately cynical toleration. He supposed it was largely because it was too late for anything else, yet still in time to realize that if you forgive people enough you belong to them, and they to you, whether either person likes it or not . . . the squatter's rights of the heart.

❧

There came the days of the German collapse, when a future—personal, national, and world-wide—seemed to emerge from the clouds of doubt that had hung heavily for a decade. Presently Japan surrendered also; the war was totally over. It was the second such occasion in Charles's life, as in that of millions of others, and completely different from the first. There were no wild scenes, no bonfires to scorch the lions in Trafalgar Square, no celebrations that became riots. To Charles the big personal event was Gerald's return—a boy of nine with a decided American accent and a tendency to find fault with the way things were done in England. Charles knew no easy cure for this, but could not regard it as too deplorable, remembering as he did that England (and for that matter America too) had been made great by people who had found fault with the way things were done in England. But he felt there was some need to lessen a child's disappointment with a country whose cars and trains and ice cream sodas were so small, so he took Gerald for a seaside holiday and hoped it made him feel happier. He could not be sure; the boy was not one for showing his emotions. Charles also talked to the headmaster of the prep school where Gerald would begin his first term in September. The head told him there would be several other new boys who had spent recent years across the Atlantic. "They'll probably be ragged a bit at first." (But later he wrote to Charles that it hadn't happened like that at all. "So far from being at any disadvantage, the boys who have lived in the Great Democracy seem to have made themselves a sort of aristocracy that the other boys look up to. Remarkable." Charles agreed that it was, but he was also much relieved.)

One other thing he had been slightly concerned about was how Gerald would get along with Havelock. Of course there would only be the school holidays to present any problem, and even these would not be spent entirely at the house; nevertheless there was just the doubt in his mind that always existed in any human affairs connected even remotely with his father. But again to Charles's relief, everything happened as he could have wished – indeed, more so, for Havelock captivated the boy to a degree that almost presented a problem of its own. Charles could take sardonic comfort from thinking how like Havelock it was to show that as a grandfather he could succeed where Charles as a father seemed to have failed. But at any rate, Charles had to admit it eased the transition from American to English life by giving Gerald a personal excitement.

Though still clear in mind, Havelock was weakening physically, and there came a time when he could put words on paper with less trouble than he could speak. This meant that one of his favorite pastimes was still available, and Charles often found him busy with the anthologies, composing new parodies of chosen poems. Some of his efforts were obscene or scatological in an earlier manner, but an increasing number were respectable, and a few were rather charming. On a September evening soon after Gerald had gone to school, Charles came home late from a meeting and found Havelock bent sleepily over some penciled pages. One, to his surprise, was in Gerald's handwriting – it was a poem the boy had learned at school in America, Joyce Kilmer's "Trees." Apparently he had told his grandfather about this and had obligingly copied it out for him, and now Havelock had been at work on it. Charles would not have disturbed him for conversation, but the old man opened his eyes and pointed to his effort. "Just imagine," he muttered, slurring over the words with difficulty, "they made him learn it by heart over there. It's not a bad poem, but it's not as good as all that. . . . Now read what I've made of it."

Charles read:

> I think however well you know 'em
> Trees aren't as lovely as a poem;
> No majesty of palm or pine

Can rival Shakespeare's mighty line,
Or grandeur of the sylvan glade
Equal the spell that Wordsworth laid;
Nor even in the Yosemite
Where tops of trees are out of sight
Can you find fairer things or finer
Than in the verse of Heinrich Heine:
Trees have been here since earth began,
But poems only came with man.

"Very pretty," Charles commented, and might have left it at that had he thought twice. But it had been so long his habit to deflate Havelock gently, whenever the occasion offered, that even now he could not forbear to add: "I'm afraid trees haven't been here since earth began, but they came earlier than mankind, so perhaps your point holds. Another flaw is that the last word of your seventh line isn't pronounced 'Yosemite' to rhyme with 'sight,' but 'Yosemmity,' with the accent on the 'sem.' "

Havelock looked considerably put out. "Oh? How do *you* know?"

"I've been there." (He and Jane, en route to South America, had once traveled from New York to San Francisco and visited Yosemite on the way.)

"You have, eh? You've really been all over the place, haven't you?" Havelock went on, with a touch of irritation: "So it's Yosemmity? Well, we'll just have to change lines seven and eight, that's all. But not now – I'm too tired. . . . You might give it a thought yourself, Charles, if you have time – you're a clever fellow. . . . I want to send it to Gerald with my Sunday letter."

Havelock was already half dozing and Cobb waiting to put him to bed. Charles said good night and went to bed himself. An hour later, while he was reading a detective story, an alternative couplet occurred to him:

Nor even in Yosemite
Where trees are in extremity. . . .

He didn't think much of this, but as there seemed no possible rhyme except "extremity" it might well be as good as could be got. On the kind of impulse to please his father which came most often when they were not together, he tiptoed into the adjacent room, found him already asleep, and also the penciled poem on the table beside his bed. Charles inserted the change, then went back to his own bed. But now he was wide awake himself, and vagrantly, with the theme of trees still on his mind, he thought of the trees so far from Yosemite and so much smaller, the little trees in Linstead, all planted by hand, the trees in Ladysmith Road that Mr. Mansfield had chosen, loved, and watched as they grew, and Mr. Mansfield himself, who would doubtless, given a choice of poems as well as trees, have preferred Joyce Kilmer's idea to Havelock's. . . . Oh, the laburnum trees. . . . He could not sleep for thinking of them, and of faces under their yellow blooms, and of the days and nights of his youth. . . .

In the morning Havelock was weaker and stayed in bed, but he had already seen the new lines and approved them. "That's fine, Charles, that really does the trick. Now I can send it off to Gerald. . . . Thank you, Charles. Thank you very much." His eyes began to moisten, but this happened frequently now, with or without an emotion. "Thank you, Charles," he said again. "You're not only a clever fellow, you're a *good* fellow."

It was not quite the last conversation they had, but it was the last of the parodies, and Havelock's letter to Gerald enclosing it was the last of his letters to anybody. He did not get up again, and after falling asleep as usual one November night he was found by Cobb in the morning, half smiling in death, with no signs of distress or of a final struggle. "One of the things you rarely see," the doctor commented.

Charles visited Gerald at school to tell him what had happened, and the boy burst into tears with more display of feeling than Charles had yet observed in him — and much more (from what Aunt Birdie had said) than when he had learned about his mother. Perhaps it was because he was now older and the loss was more recent. Or perhaps, Charles had to admit, Gerald had been Havelock's last conquest – the last and by all odds the most innocent. Proudly the boy showed his father the poem and the letter – a really delightful letter, warm and lively and humorous. It also contained a postscript to which Gerald naturally paid attention – a promise to give the boy "the gold watch that the Shah of Persia gave me."

Neither Charles nor Cobb had ever heard of such a thing, but when Havelock's safe-deposit box was opened, there it was, gaudy but undoubtedly gold – *presented to Havelock Anderson – September 10, 1910.* Charles was still curious, and after some research discovered that Havelock had successfully represented the Shah in a claim against a London insurance company for jewels stolen from a Biarritz hotel.

Besides the watch the deposit box yielded other discoveries, including the most varied collection of worthless stock and share certificates Charles had ever seen. He had long known that his father dabbled in the market, but he had always assumed the existence of a solid preponderance of sound investments. Now it became apparent that Havelock had lacked financial judgment as he had lacked many other kinds; but what dreams he must have had, Charles reflected, riffling through the scrip of long-defunct enterprises concerned with everything from no-sag spring mattresses to unbreakable gramophone records. Even the cash obtained from the sale of Beeching had been thrown away in Japanese bonds on the gamble that Japan would stay out of the war. (And yet, Charles remembered, it was Havelock who had had the premonition that Beeching would one day burn to the ground, and earlier still, just after the First World War, it was Havelock who had scouted Charles's easy assumption of a lifetime of peace. . . . Perhaps Blainey's verdict applied as well, or at least as charitably, as any: all his life Havelock had been a rum fellow.)

After paying debts and taxes the estate was worth a few hundred pounds, no more. To Charles, who had enough of his own, this came as no personal blow or even disappointment, but it saddened him as a final symbol of his father's worldly failure.

Of the spiritual failure that mattered so much more, he hated to think at all, because at times he wondered if this were an inheritance that had passed to him in part already. He was in a lost and lonely mood as he settled up Havelock's affairs. He had never been certain that his feeling for his father amounted to love, but he missed him far more than he would ever have thought possible.

Household changes followed inevitably. Cobb, now over seventy, had a handsome bequest in Havelock's will, if only there had been money to pay it. Charles arranged for him to retire on a comfortable pension, since a widowed sister in Scotland was ready to share a home with him. Charles then gave up the Westminster house and was looking for something smaller, when he was suddenly offered another diplomatic post. It was still only a First Secretaryship and in one of the less-important European capitals, but he knew how few such jobs were available, with a whole crop of new men coming up on the heels of the older ones. Seniority was no longer the overriding factor, and bright youngsters were sometimes drawn now from other fields and pushed high on the ladder without ever having had to climb it. Charles did not think this bad, but he did feel (modestly) that it made the profession of diplomacy less attractive for a man like himself, and if he had been young again perhaps he would have tried something else. But he was not young, and here was a perfectly good First Secretaryship to say Yes or No to. He said Yes, even though it meant an immediate departure from London and missing Christmas with Gerald in Cheshire, where Aunt Birdie had invited them.

The years passed. Charles did pretty well, he thought, and heard privately that some of the sly ironies he inserted into his briefs and memoranda were passed round the highest circles for amusement if not edification. But he had better be careful. Wit was apt to be dangerous in English life; nine times out of ten the Gladstones prevailed against the Disraelis – and he was only a duodecimo Disraeli.

During this period the façade grew over the structure of his life in a thin crust of mannerism. He was aware of it, ruefully but with resignation, while memory reminded him of the danger. That memory was of the elderly professor who had taken him out for a breath of fresh air when he had collapsed over the desk on the last day of his Cambridge Tripos examinations. Why, he had speculated then, did university dons grow up like that – finnicky, desiccated, tee-heeish? Now he knew, or could guess; and the understanding was a warning. He found a corrective in thinking (as he could now without too much distress) of Jane, imagining her comments on this and that, hearing her voice exclaim, if he went too far in the dangerous direction: "Oh now, Andy, come off it!" Or she had said, as they went to a dinner party: "If the Langlons are there, don't tell that story about the Dragoman and the Archbishop – you told it at the Nungesser's last year and the Langlons were there then." (And it was a very amusing but long story which he told very well indeed.) Such things, among so many others, had made her a treasure; and he felt this absence every time he put on or took off his dress shirt. For those had been the moments, not the most important or profound in their lives, but the ones at which Jane had been most of all Jane – before or after a party.

He did not get transferred to a more important post, and this made the prospect of an eventual Legation so dim that he quenched his hopes about it. It was not so much that he was past the age, meaning his own age, as that the age, meaning the postwar age, had in some sense passed him. It was hard but interesting to reckon why this was so, and he had a number of theories. Perhaps it was because in some frozen corner of the hierarchic mind there still lingered a breath of prejudice against him on account of that old misbehavior of Havelock's. Perhaps it was because he did not know the correct people who were new, or the new people who were correct. Perhaps it was because at some dinner party there had been no Jane to stop him from being just too amusing about something or somebody. Perhaps it was because he dined out too often and knew too many people altogether. Perhaps it was because of the nickname, or the handwriting — which for some reason had tended to become even smaller with the years. Perhaps it was because he had been to Brookfield instead of Eton, or (in this new era of topsy-turviness) because he had been to Brookfield at all instead of starting out with proletarian virtue from a state elementary school. Or perhaps it was simply because the world was changing. He had begun his career in an age when it was still an asset to a diplomat to be suave and witty and impeccably dressed; and he had lived into an age when the striped trousers and morning coat had become a symbol to many of all that was blameworthy for human ills, and when, perhaps because of this, generals and politicians and journalists were apt to take over from professional diplomats at every crisis. But the *ignorance* of some of the supplanters — politicians especially! How often Charles had had to explain to elected representatives in the privacy of the Foreign Office facts of history and geography that were more appropriate to the lower fourth! And he had once had contact with an M.P. of much volubility on foreign affairs who mixed up Colombia with the District of Columbia and British Columbia; and of this man, when he became also a director of a large industrial combine, a lady admirer exclaimed: "Don't you think, Mr. Anderson, he's a splendid example of how far a man can get nowadays without any of the advantages of upbringing or education?" To which Charles was unable to resist the reply: "Yes, indeed — except that you should perhaps have said '*dis*advantages.' " It was possibly incidents like this that did not help Charles to become an ambassador.

He sometimes recalled what his old friend Weigall had said at Cambridge: "You and I, Andy, are stuck in between — we weren't born at Chatsworth or Blenheim, nor did we starve in tenements or pick crusts out of gutters — we just come from country homes with bits of land and families that go back a couple of centuries or so. . . ." But when he reached as far as that in diagnosing his own case, a sense of proportion as well as of humor came to the rescue. For what if he had found, at the time when the matter cropped up, that Havelock had *not* been his father? Would he have cared much? He knew he wouldn't. Then where was his pride of ancestry, apart from his pride in what he could claim as ancestry? As for the bit of land, it was now a disused airfield, and as for the country home, it had been bombed and burned, and a score of young Englishmen (so he had been told) had met death in those old rooms with cards and glasses and billiard cues in their hands. To believe that blood mattered, in any sense that did not include theirs, was surely to be bloodguilty.

During one of his leaves in London his boss at the Foreign Office invited him to a small bachelor dinner at which the other guests were a Minister of the Crown, a famous historian, a millionaire motor manufacturer, and a soldier who had held a position in the Middle East that enabled him to refer to Pontius Pilate as "one of my predecessors." Conversation was at times brilliantine if not brilliant; it was also more pessimistic about the future than Charles found pleasant to hear — his own favorite pessimisms being of a much gayer kind. The Minister of the Crown complained of a lack of potential leaders among the younger men in government, the motor manufacturer said Coventry could not seriously compete in world markets with Detroit, the soldier said the Russians would reach the Atlantic in three weeks if they set their army moving, and the historian offered comfort in the reminder that both Greece and Rome were much more powerful in the inheritance they left to succeeding ages than ever in their own actual heyday. Charles said next to nothing. Over the port the Minister further remarked that one of the most popular of all errors was to confuse prophecy with advocacy, so that a wise man often refrained from saying publicly what he thought would happen lest he be widely supposed to wish it to happen. The historian agreed, and said it would be interesting to collect a few prophecies from persons who could feel, as they made them, completely unhampered by such a consideration — if, for instance, a man could set down honestly on a single sheet of paper what he forecast for the next century, the paper to be signed, put away, and guaranteed hidden till the year 2050. The Minister replied that by a curious coincidence he would be laying the foundation stone of an atomic research plant the following week, and it had already been arranged to seal under the stone such miscellaneous articles as current copies of *The Times*, ration books, coins, theater programs, and bus tickets. If those present that evening cared to write a few lines as the historian had suggested (devoting not more than, say, ten minutes to the task), he personally would undertake to place them along with the other items. . . . The idea was taken up with an alacrity that soon became an absorption; rarely could an after-dinner argument have been so effectively launched and stifled. The butler brought paper, pens, and ink, the time was noted, and the six men began to write. As the least distinguished of the group, Charles knew his inclusion was only by courtesy, but this seemed to free him for a special kind of inspiration. He began as follows:

> My name is Charles Anderson. I belong to a somewhat out-of-date profession called diplomacy. This is a relic of the days when even wars were polite, so I'm naturally polite myself and also a bit of a relic. I'm supposed to have certain "immunities" under international law, which means that in a foreign country I can drive a car to the common danger without being prosecuted. If, however, that country gets into a war, then I must share the common danger, since a neutral flag painted on a roof can't be seen at night from four miles high. And if my own country gets into a war and loses, I might be hanged as a criminal if I were important enough — so thank goodness I'm not. The whole thing would have been so unforeseeable a century ago that I doubt whether my own guesses about the coming century can be much better. Anyhow, one of them (fathered by the wish, of course) is that England will survive — and not only as an inheritance like Greece and Rome. We're such a damned peculiar people, such a mixed bag of stout fellahs and decent idiots, with a smattering of high-minded hypocrites and brainy saints. We don't quite fit the theories — Spengler's

or Toynbee's or Marx's or anybody's. So we can't be counted on by the theorists — or counted out either. Perhaps God isn't bored with us yet (Victor Hugo's phrase, not mine). Perhaps we shall solve the trick of all tricks for this millennium — how to step down without falling over backwards, and then how to build the new must-be on the foundations of the old has-been. I won't see it happen, but my son may.

Another guess is that what I'm writing now won't stay under a stone till 2050. (Funny how the other fellows here seem to be taking that for granted.) But there's another kind of stone my father once came across in the churchyard at Pumphrey Basset — an ancient gravestone of a female dwarf with the inscription on it — *Parva sed apta Domino.* Somehow I wouldn't mind betting that will outlast an atomic research plant, and perhaps in the long run mean more. . . .

In his minute script, and writing fast because he did not take the occasion too seriously, Charles was having an easier time (he surmised) than the other five, on whom posterity and the ticking clock seemed to impose a grueling test. When the ten minutes were up and he had almost filled both sides of the paper, he passed it over without rereading, and reached for the port while the others were begging an extra minute to make corrections.

Musing thus on the future had set him thinking about Gerald, whom he would send in due course to Brookfield and Cambridge if only because he could not, in England at the middle of the twentieth century, think of anything better to do with the boy. Just as he preferred a dinner to be "black tie," not because he was a snob, but because it avoided the problem of what else.

It was about this time that he took up painting again with full knowledge not only that his work would never be of consequence, but that even his talent was less than it had been thirty years before. His pleasure, though, was nearly as great, and perhaps enhanced by the small amateur reputation he acquired among people who really did not know much about art at all. Once, on a wet Sunday in a Mediterranean city, he painted — from memory and in his bedroom at the Legation — a curiously attractive portrait of his father, as he remembered him during the old man's last years. Havelock was sitting by the window of the Westminster house, staring out over wet pavements and the tops of umbrellas, with Big Ben and the Abbey towers in the misty twilight. "I made it rain for him" — Charles later explained to friends who had known Havelock and admired the portrait — "just as I'd put a Sicilian peasant in the sun. His life was like a day that starts well, but then the clouds come up and it begins to pour and all the things you'd rather do have to be canceled, but by the time evening comes you'll have found something else to do and you won't even look to see if the sky has stars in it. But it may have."

Later that year (1950) Charles again half expected promotion. He was beguiled by a rumor that proved false, and in the dispassionate mood that followed he began to think of retirement. But then he was offered the chance of another switch to the Foreign Office, which suited him because he liked to live in London; so he put off the retirement and found the prospect of it an increasing comfort and even a mental stimulus. He felt mildly ambitious to do something, within the nearer reach, that would bring back the feeling of innocent schoolboy credit; on this, perhaps, he could make his bow at the Prizegiving of life and receive a smattering of applause from those who did not expect to see him again.

And yet the very mildness of the ambition made it hard to accomplish. The feeling of near-success, which is also near-failure, followed him to Paris, where, as member of the British delegation to a somewhat second-string international conference, he could believe that his career had reached a peak — perhaps not its highest, perhaps not even high, but still a peak of sorts, and very likely the last.

These things were on his mind during dinner at the Cheval Noir on Gerald's seventeenth birthday; they were on his mind as he followed the boy in a taxi across the city; they were on his mind as he sat in Rocher's ice-cream dispensary, facing his son and the girl his son had gone there to meet. "He thinks it's wonderful," she had said, "that you should be representing England at the Conference." How could he live up to or down to such an image in his son's eyes? It was just another thing to please and plague him, and suddenly he saw the gulf between father and son far wider than he had imagined, part of some structural rift of humanity.

It might have bothered him further had he not just then received a second shock of a far more peremptory kind. For outside, only a few inches beyond the plate-glass windows, and peering in upon their little group with riveted attention, was the face of a man whom Charles least of all wanted to think about, much less encounter in the flesh. And the apparition, having seen that he was seen, began immediately to wave the kind of greeting Charles could not possibly ignore.

So Charles waved back and was only able to explain that the intruder was one of the Conference delegates by the time that Palan, plump and clumsy, yet curiously notable as always, came threading his way among the tables toward them. "This *would* happen," Charles muttered to himself.

Paris IV

It was not only that Charles did not want to see Palan; he would have been embarrassed to be discovered at a place like Rocher's by anybody. At the Cheval Noir a surprise of such a kind would have been barely tolerable, little as he wished to spread the news of that restaurant to outsiders; and at any ordinary Parisian pavement café, however proletarian, he could have summoned enough aplomb to meet even Sir Malcolm Bingay's eye. But to be spotted in an ice-cream parlor sucking a pink concoction through a straw . . . it simply did not add up to anything he could take in stride; it was like those dreams he sometimes had in which he realized, at the moment of being presented to a *chef de cabinet* at a garden party, that he was completely nude from the waist down.

Nor did he expect that Palan would miss the ludicrousness of the situation. Doubtless it would stand him in good stead at the Conference in the morning – would acidify his attitude, revitalize his sarcasms. He had already found so much in Charles to poke fun at; from now on there would be more. Charles braced himself for an effort of courtesy as the fellow waited; clearly there was no alternative but to introduce him. He did so. Palan then bowed and stooped to kiss Miss Raynor's hand in a way that would please her all the more (Charles reflected) if she were unaware that in correct European circles one did not kiss the hands of unmarried women. And it was like Palan, who must certainly know that himself, to take the impertinent liberty or else to have sized her up as a susceptible American who would feel such gallantry to be one of the perquisites of foreign travel. Meanwhile Palan's eyes were roving over the scene with a certain ironic detachment. "It looks very good, what you all have got in the glasses. What do they call it?" To Charles's regret Miss Raynor smiled and told him. "Just a raspberry frappé."

"So?" answered Palan, regarding it judicially. "But I think not for me." His loud and bad French was already drawing attention from nearby tables. "I shall have Banane Split." He sat down and shouted the order to the nearest waitress. Then he pulled out a handkerchief and began mopping his forehead. "I must explain that this is just *bonne chance.* I am walking along and I see M'sieur Anderson through the window. He looks so happy, eating his ice cream. It is a sign of the times, is it not, that the French are acquiring so many of your American habits. . . . It used to be English — the rosbif — the afternoon tea . . . but now it is all American — ice cream, soda fountain, jukebox. But you, M'sieur Anderson — somehow I did not think of you as an addict — yet why not, after all? It is doubtless a treat for you too." He turned again to Miss Raynor. "I am a great admirer of things American!"

The girl looked as if much of this had escaped her, but she caught its complimentary flavor and responded with a second smile that gave Charles a twinge of jealousy. It was not that he thought himself less physically attractive than Palan — on the contrary; but he could not help feeling that Palan's style of success with women should somehow be picketed as unfair to gentlemen.

"It's Gerald's seventeenth birthday," he said in French, relieved to have found an opening for a personal alibi. "We were just celebrating."

"But of course." Palan now turned his attention to Gerald. "Seventeen! Ah, a wonderful age! And how long are you to be in Paris, Gerald?"

(He called him Gerald already — and as easily as that! To Charles this was something else to be jealous of, yet confusingly to be appreciated as well.) Charles answered: "He's leaving for England tonight." He added: "And Miss Raynor has to leave for

America — also tonight." He felt as if he were quietly closing doors in Palan's face.

Palan then transferred his attention to Charles. "Leaving us two old fogies here in Paris," he commented; and Charles did not like the phrase, for he was sure Palan was nearer sixty than fifty.

"But *seventeen!*" Palan was continuing. "Can you guess where *I* was at seventeen? . . . In a military hospital — already I was wounded in battle. That was the Balkan War." (Charles did the mental arithmetic — 1911 — it would make him fifty-six.) "I was what they called a hothead in those days — at sixteen I ran away from home to enlist — I lied about my age. I have told many lies since, but never one as crazy as that." He suddenly rolled up his sleeve. "You see? I have it still." Along the whole length of a hairy forearm there ran a scar like a highway between forests. "You think I was a great patriot, eh? But no, I ran away because I thought I would prefer war to being at home. But I found war was even worse. My father used to beat us when we were young. He was very rich and loved to beat people. One day at last I beat him — and that was why I had to run away. . . . They killed him after the Revolution. So you have trains to catch tonight, both of you? If my father had caught his train he would not have been killed. But he was late at the station and the train had gone. There were no more trains. That time comes in all our lives someday — when there are no more trains. But I hated him. And now — just to make things equal — my son hates me."

"You have a son?" Charles said, with so little reason to be astonished that he wondered why he was even interested.

"I have five — and seven daughters — but the son who hates me is the only one who has anything to do with me. Life is like that."

"Why does he hate you?"

"Because he is a hothead too — though not the kind I was. He is a cold hothead. He is in charge of soil conservation in the province of Alma Valchinia, but already he is talked of as a coming man. And at twenty-four! What a career! Why, when I was that age I was wrecking trains with dynamite — I was *activist!* You could not have made me spend my life examining dirt!"

Charles wished that Palan would not shout; it was unseemly that such a conversation should be overheard, though he supposed that Palan cared as little for that as for his other eccentricities. Charles was glad when the Banana Split arrived. He noticed that Palan attacked it with a zest that was either childlike or wolfish — depending, Charles mused, on how far one had gone in finding excuses for the fellow.

"You like it?" Miss Raynor said, watching Palan quite tranquilly. She spoke in English, though she had no reason to suppose he understood. Then, however, he answered in English with a definite American accent: "Do *you? I* think they make them far better at Schrafft's."

Miss Raynor laughed incredulously. "*Schrafft's?* That's where I often have lunch. There's one next to my office."

"You have an office, Anne?" (And even "Anne" already!)

"I work in one. . . . So you know New York, Mr. Palan?"

"For three years I lived there. Central Park West. I know the Stork Club and also the Automat. I have stayed at Ellis Island and also at the Waldorf-Astoria. I have eaten hot dogs and caviar."

"But not together? Or perhaps that's no worse than cheese and apple pie."

Palan laughed loudly and patted the girl's hand. But Charles was reddening. He could not enjoy the joke because he was thinking that after all those Conference sittings during which he had suffered Palan's bad French, it now turned out that the man could just as well have spared him such an ordeal — or at least have substituted the lesser one of his English! But it was not the memory of the French that bothered Charles most, but the possibility that on several occasions Palan might have caught a few words of English that Charles had whispered to Sir Malcolm — a few witty but tart asides, prompted by some specially irritating attitude of Palan's, but not wholly excusable, not really sanctioned by the codebook of good manners. The thought that Palan might have heard and understood made Charles feel slightly ashamed, and the conclusion that, even if so, Palan had clearly not minded a bit, made Charles feel also annoyed. Perhaps, after all, the fellow was as thick-skinned as those who opposed him needed to be.

Palan was still continuing, in English: "But I was telling you about my son. He is a model. He does not smoke or drink or have women. You cannot bribe him – or plead with him – you cannot even make him laugh. When *I* laugh he probably reports it to the secret police."

Charles moved uncomfortably. This was definitely not the sort of talk to be indulged in loudly by any diplomat of any nation in any language in a public place. He wondered if Palan were slightly drunk, or perhaps exceedingly drunk in some unique way of his own. This gave Charles a solicitude that was entirely professional – in the freemasonry of diplomacy, if it still existed to any degree at all, one could surely pass a hint of warning even to an adversary. Charles said therefore, to change the subject: "I agree that stuff isn't as good as it could be, though you certainly seem to be getting through it."

Palan refused or was unaware of the hint. "My son is not like me," he continued. "He speaks carefully, he works carefully, he does everything carefully. And correctly. And quietly. He would not raise his voice in sending you to the firing squad. But it is worse when he lectures on soil conservation. Then you are so bored you *wish* to be sent to the firing squad."

Charles turned abruptly to Miss Raynor. "I'm sorry about dinner. It's too bad you weren't with Gerald and me."

"Thanks, Mr. Anderson, but I knew it was a special occasion – I expect you had a good time on your own."

"Oh. . . So he *did* mention it?"

"Yes, he said you'd had this date for years – to take him to dinner when he was seventeen. I think that's charming."

"It really began as a joke," said Charles, and he told of the incident with Mrs. Fuessli when Gerald was six.

"*Fuessli,* did you say?"

Charles nodded and spelled it.

"It's such an unusual name I wonder if they're the same people I know. They live in Connecticut — "

"Yes — a small place. Parson's Corner."

"That's it — they *must* be the same — Mr. Fuessli has a hardware business — "

" — and Mrs. Fuessli's very pretty."

"I'll tell her you said so."

"They're both well, I hope. Charming people. I haven't heard from them lately."

"They're fine and they'll be so thrilled to know I've met you here like this."

Palan suddenly banged his spoon on the table top, like a child to whom enough attention has not been paid. "So you two both know the same people in America! Is that not wonderful? You will tell me now that it is a small world. But it is not. It is a big world. . . . But I can pretend it is small too. *Look*. . . . Do you see that man out there — standing against the lamppost pretending to read a newspaper?" He pointed through the windows. "That man also is thrilled to know that I am meeting you here."

This would never do; Charles was now convinced that Palan was drunk. He looked at his watch; thank goodness it was already past eleven. He said, calling for the bill: "We really mustn't make you cut it too fine, Gerald — I'll leave you to take care of Miss Raynor. . . . Palan, if you're going my way. . . ."

To his relief Palan seemed ready enough to leave, though only after ceremonious farewells. Charles shook hands with Gerald and the girl; while he was doing this Palan grabbed the bill and tipped the waitress extravagantly and ostentatiously. Charles frowned at this climax of bad manners, but somehow, remembering his own on those several occasions at the Conference, he found that with barely a gesture of protest he could take Palan's arm and marshal him into the street.

At the curbside Palan said in French: "That ice cream is bad for the stomach. Let us go to my hotel and get some cognac."

"No, if you want a drink come to mine. And since you speak English why don't we stick to that language?"

"All right, but you come to *my* hotel. It cannot be your everything — *your* language, *your* son's birthday. . . . How much more do you want? You come to *my* hotel."

Whatever reason Palan had for demanding this was a reason why Charles should not consent to it, so he said merely: "I think perhaps it's too late for a drink anyhow. We both have work tomorrow." He hailed a taxi and gave the address of Palan's hotel; he would drop him there on the way to the Crillon. Palan made no further mention of the drink, and from this Charles concluded that his earlier insistence on having it at his hotel had been merely a whim. But of course one could never be sure. To such a level had social intercourse between accredited diplomats reached by the middle of the twentieth century.

Inside the taxi, as they began the journey back to the more fashionable boulevards, Palan remarked: "A very fine boy, M'sieur Anderson. I congratulate you."

"Thanks."

"And the girl too. She is *his* girl?"

"Oh no — just someone he met in Switzerland. They played tennis together."

"But he is in love."

"I doubt that. Probably just a holiday acquaintance — "

"The perfect structure for a love affair. A few days only, with good-by at the end! It is in countless dramas, in epic poetry, in grand opera — "

"I daresay, and most of them Gerald wouldn't care for at all. He's rather realistic, and so's Miss Raynor, as far as I could judge."

"You like her?"

"She seemed very nice."

"So that if your son really wanted to marry her — "

"At *seventeen*?"

"At seventeen, my friend, I was already a father. . . . You find that hard to believe?"

"By no means. You had also, so you say, fought in your first war. In England we try not to do things quite so early."

"And to balance that, you do many things late – perhaps too late."

"Possibly. And I'm glad to say that a great many things we don't do at all." Charles shot that back as if to say: I too can bandy words, if you insist.

Palan continued: "I suppose you wish Gerald eventually to make *un beau mariage dans le monde?*"

"I hope he'll make a happy marriage, that's all."

"You mean you would not object to an office girl as a daughter-in-law?"

"Good heavens, no. What do you take me for – a snob?"

"Of course – because it is one of the coefficients of power. Your country's power is now in decline, so you are trying hard to diminish the snobbery. It will make you a very attractive people provided you do not succeed too well. I would like to discuss this further with you some day."

"If we had more time. I don't recall how we got on to the subject, but – "

"We were talking about Gerald and Miss Raynor."

"Since they'll soon be catching their trains in different directions, there really isn't much to talk about."

"If they *do* catch those trains. My father did not catch his. He delayed too long, trying to persuade his mistress to leave the country with him – my mother, of course, had gone on ahead with the family jewels. She died at Monte Carlo twenty years later, whereas my father missed his train and – "

"I know – you told us. But I assure you Gerald won't miss his."

"How can you be sure?"

"Well, for one reason, he has an appointment with his dentist in London tomorrow morning."

Palan seized Charles's hand and shook it amidst his loud guffaws. "My friend, it is the most perfect of all reasons. *Credo quia impossibile est.*"

"Or because he said so – that'll do for me." (But would it,

after the lie about the boat train?) Charles added, with extra conviction to mask his growing uncertainty: "They'll catch their trains, don't worry."

"And what will it prove?"

"Does it have to prove anything?"

Palan guffawed again. "Anatole France put it well. '*De toutes les aberrations sexuelles, la plus singulière, c'est la chasteté!*'"

Charles was amused in spite of himself. "You seem to have quite a range — Tertullian, Anatole France. . . . What next, I wonder?"

"An epigram of my own. . . . Tennis among the Alps, ice cream in Paris — bless their innocent little hearts . . . the *Incorruptibles*. . . . Whereas you and I — in our far different ways — we are the *Incorrigibles*."

"I'm not sure I know exactly what you mean."

"That is what makes it so funny — that in your own way you also should be so innocent. What has protected you? Are you a deeply religious man?"

Charles found this question too baffling either to be answered or resented. He said: "I wouldn't say so, but if I were, I wouldn't say so either."

"Then you are very rich?"

That was easy. "No . . . far from it. But I don't see what all this has to do — "

"Do you think the capitalist system will survive?"

"*What?* . . . Well, what a question!"

"Yes, is it not? I should have thought you would have had your answer ready — as we would on our side. But perhaps you are not so confident."

"Perhaps also we're not so interested. It's you people who've made it the only question to be asked. We believe it's only one — and not the most important — that has to be answered."

"That also I would like to discuss with you if there were time."

Thank goodness there isn't, Charles reflected, as the taxi came to a halt outside Palan's hotel. "Here you are," he said, helping Palan to the pavement. "We shall meet again in a few hours and meanwhile I think we both need some sleep. . . . Good night."

"Good night, my friend." Palan pressed Charles's hand with a boozy but not effeminate tenderness. "I have enjoyed talking with you. It is very funny today to be an English gentleman. It is almost as funny as to be an anarchist. Both are out of style. . . . Au 'voir, m'sieur."

Charles waited to see him safely through the revolving doors, then continued his own journey to the Crillon. What a day, he summarized, as he mixed himself a drink in his room and made another jotting for the book he was going to write. "It is very funny today to be an English gentleman – almost as funny as to be an anarchist." Not bad, not bad. He also put down the quotation from Anatole France.

But he lay awake thinking mainly about Gerald. It was a different sort of concern from the one he had had earlier; milder but more persistent, just a small private regret – not that the boy should have preferred Miss Raynor's company to his (how natural that was), but that he should have chosen not to mention her during the dinner. And evidently, but for the way things had happened, Charles would still have been in ignorance of her existence. It showed how little a son could wish to confide in a father . . . but then Charles had to add to himself – "as if I didn't know that already." Which brought him back to old thoughts, and the extent to which he had tried (and perhaps failed) to come closer to Gerald than Havelock had to him, and the extent to which his failure (if any) had been an inheritance as lasting as the gold watch that had belonged to the Shah. Well, he had tried at least, and whether he had so far failed or not, he knew he must go on trying. He decided that when he got back to England he would take Gerald on some holiday of their own – the Lake District or North Wales, perhaps; and to clinch the idea in his mind he made the amazing concession: "Why, I'll even watch him play tennis, if that's what he'd like." This, surely was *il gran rifiuto* of some kind or other, and having made it, he fell asleep.

When he walked through the hotel lobby the next morning he saw Miss Raynor sitting on a couch reading a newspaper. He was more than surprised; he remembered Palan's remark about not catching trains and was perturbed. Was it *possible* . . . ? He walked over, greeting her with a smile only.

"You're staying here too?" she exclaimed, showing some surprise and perturbation of her own.

"Why yes . . . but shouldn't I have said it first?"

"I know – or rather, I didn't know – I mean, I didn't know you were staying here. I just came here because I – I'd booked here weeks ago."

"Very sensible – they're often full up unless you do that."

He regarded her with kindly shrewdness, as if to say: Are you going to tell me or do I have to ask you? Evidently the latter, for after a pause he continued: "I thought you were leaving for Cherbourg last night?"

"Yes, I – I intended to at first, but – but after I saw Gerald off on his train – "

"So he left?" Even unaccented the question seemed clumsy; he added hastily: "I daresay I got things muddled. . . . Have you had breakfast?" And to forestall an answer: "Perhaps another cup of coffee?"

"But aren't you on your way – "

"The Conference starts at eleven. I usually walk over for exercise – it's not far. But this morning I'll ride."

They found a corner table in the restaurant. She seemed preoccupied, and while he chattered fluently about Paris and Switzerland and as much about the Conference as she could read in the papers, he too was preoccupied. When the coffee arrived she said abruptly: "I'll have to tell you the truth. I've been trying to invent something for the past few minutes but it just won't work – because I expect you'll tell Gerald you met me again here."

"I daresay I might have, but not unless you wish."

"He thinks I'm on my way to America."

"So did I." Charles smiled encouragingly.

"I'd like him to go on thinking so."

Charles waited for her to continue. Being of a professionally suspicious nature he was reflecting how easy it would be (though perhaps unnecessary) to telephone his London flat to find if Gerald had already arrived there.

She went on: "I don't know how I can explain it without seeming either – priggish or – or boastful – or something I hope I'm not."

"I don't think there's much fear of you seeming that."

"So I'd better just tell you the truth? Well . . . the fact is . . . Gerald has an idea he's in love with me."

He waited again, remembering that this too was what Palan had said.

She went on: "I don't suppose he told you."

"No."

"Probably he was afraid you'd think it too silly."

Charles said gently: "I hope he wasn't afraid of that. I never think any kind of love is silly. And I'm not sure what the difference is between being in love and having an idea you are – especially when you're young."

"But seventeen's perhaps *too* young – for thirty-three."

"Thirty-three?"

"Yes. Quite a problem if we were *both* in love." She flushed a little. "And rather embarrassing to have to explain all this to his father."

"It needn't be embarrassing. It could all very easily have happened. . . . But tell me how it did happen."

"We met a couple of weeks ago – at Mürren. Of course I liked him immediately – perhaps I encouraged him at first, without intending to. We talked and argued."

"What about?"

"Oh, politics, religion, economics, the state of the world – life in general. He's at the age for argument, and I can always enjoy one."

"So can I – though – for him – perhaps I seem to have passed the age." That sounded rather sad, so he went on gallantly: "It's quite possible you know my son better than I do."

"Oh no, of course not."

"Tell me about him, anyway. What do you think of him?"

"You really want my opinion?"

"Very much."

"Well, to begin with, he's first-rate company – clever – serious and yet gay about it – full of enthusiasms and idealisms. He's less inhibited than most English boys, I should guess. And all-round in his interests – games as well as studies. Dances well, for instance. He asked me to a dance at the hotel."

"And to play tennis?"

"No, I suggested that."

"He said you were good."

"I wasn't bad, considering I hadn't played for years. He's quite good. We won against some people who were very bad indeed."

Charles nodded. It was not unlike certain occasions that in his own professional career had ranked as successes. He was thinking of this when she added: "That's really the whole story."

"Is it?" He smiled. "Well . . . so much for *l'affaire suisse*."

"Don't joke about it."

"I'm sorry. You play tennis – I make jokes – each of us, it seems, has a way of dealing with a delicate situation."

She laughed then, for the first time. "But you like making jokes – far more than I like playing tennis."

"I should hope so. . . . But seriously, how did the scene change to Paris?"

"Because I left Switzerland when my stay there was finished – I've been in Germany since – so he wanted to meet me here – just once – before I finally go home. I told him there wouldn't be time, as I was only just passing through, but he said it so happened he'd be in Paris anyway – because he was having dinner with you."

"Plausible."

"I still tried to put him off, but he said he was sure his dinner with you would end in time to give us an hour or so. He seemed to think you'd want to go to bed early during the Conference."

"He just thought of everything, eh?"

"He put me in a spot where I couldn't refuse."

"Well, I don't really blame him."

"I hope you don't blame me either. If I hadn't kept up the pretense of leaving I think he'd have changed all his own plans and canceled his appointments in London today. Of course I didn't want him to do that."

"So there really *are* appointments?"

"Oh yes. One of them's this morning – with his dentist. He told me all about it. He's very punctilious about such things. Almost ascetic in some ways – doesn't drink or smoke –"

"He did both – a little – at dinner with me last night."

"Then he loves you," she said softly. "The oddest things can prove love, can't they? And since you asked me, I must tell you what a delightful son you have . . . the uninhibited ascetic. All those early formative years in America and then an English school – really, you couldn't have devised anything more ingenious. . . . I hated to lie to him, especially when I was seeing him off and he thought I was just going to another platform to catch *my* train."

"You were lucky – and clever – to have managed it so well. When *are* you leaving?"

"Next Tuesday. By air."

Charles looked at his watch. "I – I can't put into words – quite all – that I feel . . . and how grateful I am to you for – for being so kind to him. I'm fond of that boy, though he probably doesn't realize it – why should he? – we've had so little chance to get to know each other." He turned the slight tremor of his voice into the beginnings of a laugh. "Just one more question – sheer curiosity – before I have to go. . . . Why Rocher's?"

"I know – of all places. But even that was sweet of him. He thought because I'm American it was what I'd enjoy most."

"Then you've given me the right cue – will you dine with me one evening at a place I know you will enjoy?"

"Yes – if you won't be disappointed."

"Why should I be?"

"Gerald told me you're a great authority on food and wine. I'm not. I just love good eating and talking."

"One of which I promise and the other you're bound to supply yourself."

"Oh now, *please*. . . . Is that the kind of thing diplomats have to say at conferences?"

"If only it were. . . . What about tonight?"

"Fine . . . and by the way, why did *you* come to Rocher's?"

"That's one of the embarrassing things *I* might have to confess – during dinner."

And so it was arranged. Before he finally left she said "Good luck," and as he rode to the Conference he felt both in need of and fortified by it.

Sir Malcolm Bingay was still indisposed and Charles had to carry the ball – to use an athletic metaphor which seemed to him singularly inappropriate. Most of the day he was embroiled with Palan, who gave no sign of any effects of the previous evening's dissipation – or indeed, of having had any social intercourse with his opponent at all. Charles was puzzled but not altogether surprised. His own strategy in such circumstances was to ease himself into a situation like a key into a lock, to see first if it fitted before one tried even the slightest turn. All morning he performed this fitment, matching Palan's performance by one of his own that was perhaps equally baffling; but in the afternoon he gave the first sharp twist by interjecting a phrase of English into his French and adding (in French): "I will not translate for the benefit of M'sieur Palan, because I have a feeling I shall be understood." Palan did not bat an eyelid.

The whole day was a nerve-exhausting stalemate, a laborious exploration of deadlock.

In the evening Charles took Anne Raynor to a small restaurant near Les Halles. He put on a black tie and was interested to note that her dress would have been suitable whether he had or not.

He also noted that she knew more about food and wine than might have been expected from her disclaimer. All these matters, however, were secondary to the fact that he liked her and that their shared affection for Gerald seemed to bring them into a warm contact. During the day he had had to telephone his London flat on some business matter, and his housekeeper had mentioned that Gerald had arrived there in time for breakfast (not that Charles had really had doubts). He told Anne that Gerald must have had a tiresome day. "I can't imagine anything worse than going to a dentist after an all night train-and-boat journey – except perhaps the kind of day I've just had myself, arguing with that fellow who joined us last night at Rocher's. The odd thing is that personally I don't dislike him. He fascinates me slightly. He has a peculiar trick – I'm sure it's a trick – of making you feel he's always just about to see your point of view. Of course he never does. He can't let himself. He has his line to follow and daren't deviate by a hairbreadth. Only you don't always know what the line is till you've wasted hours in futile debate. That's another trick they have – physical exhaustion as a weapon."

"Don't you also have to follow a line?"

"Oh yes, but not so slavishly. We allow ourselves a little leeway. If I might make a parallel, Palan's side are the trams, but we're the trolley buses. . . . What was your impression of him, by the way?"

"I'd say he's an interesting character. . . . No, I don't dislike him either."

"He's a braggart, and I'm sure half the things he says about his past are lies."

"But if the other half are true it would still be remarkable. Do you really think he was being watched as he said last night?"

"By his own men, possibly. Nobody's ever trusted completely on their side."

"I wonder why he joined us then. Couldn't it get him into trouble?"

"I thought of that too. He wanted me to go back to his hotel afterward for a drink. I fancy he'd drunk a little too much himself. He was talking in a rather wild way. Of course I didn't go."

"In case he might be trying to trap you?"

"Into what? . . . No, it's hard to give a reason, except one's general suspicion of those fellows. Their code's different, therefore you have to be on your guard all the time. A strange thing, diplomacy, nowadays – full of novelties." He felt he had better turn the subject a little. "Television, for example, in your country. I understand Gladwyn Jebb made a great hit that way recently. How would Metternich or Castlereagh or Disraeli have taken to it, I wonder?"

"I think Disraeli would have been fine if he'd remembered to be like George Arliss."

"Then Abraham Lincoln should really have sounded like Charles Laughton, but I'm quite sure he didn't."

She laughed. "I don't think *you* need worry, television or not. You're rather like most Americans' idea of an English diplomat."

"That alarms me. Perhaps it also explains why I haven't climbed any higher in my profession. . . . You know what they call me?" Some faintly masochistic urge propelled him to the disclosure. "*Stuffy Anderson.*" There—he had said it. It was always a barrier that had to be crossed, and in any friendship whose progress pleased him he always wanted to mention it first, rather than have it later discovered.

She said casually: "Yes, I know. Gerald told me."

"What? *He* knew? Now how would . . . Oh well, I suppose there are all sorts of ways."

"He said it showed how popular you were."

Charles was somewhat consoled. "Nice of him to think so – or to pretend that he did. But I don't believe he's altogether right. Not that I'm *un*popular – far from it. But many of my colleagues probably think the nickname suits, and I daresay it does – I'm a bit of a back number in some ways. . . . For instance – my reason for coming to Rocher's last night, I said I might have to confess it to you." He then explained about Gerald's fidgetiness during dinner and the excuse of the fictitious boat train for an early departure. "Of course it was just because he wanted to meet you – I don't really blame him at all. But I was curious, and also, well, being the old-fashioned person I am, I thought he might have plans that would land him in some less desirable company. . . . So I followed him. What an ignoble suspicion to have had, and what an out-of-date thing to do! But you see, it's the old world that I remember – old in history as well as in geography."

"I've sometimes found the new world not so young."

"It would be a comfort to think so. And back numbers *are* – occasionally – more readable than the latest. As an editor, hasn't that ever worried you?"

"Why are you talking to me like this?"

"I really haven't the slightest idea – unless it's because I'm tired after bickering with Palan all day. To him I've got to appear always alert and combative – whereas with you I can relax and be myself."

"But you're not yourself when you're too modest."

"Yes, I am – and also when I'm conceited. I'm both."

She turned to him with a slow serene scrutiny, then asked: "What sort of life have you had?"

"*Life? My* life?"

"Has it been happy – or – or rather unhappy?"

But this was going too far; he woke abruptly from the trance of self-revelation into which his tiredness and her comfort had made him slip. He answered, talking fast while he pulled himself into control: "You Americans – it's the *pursuit* of happiness, isn't it, not the happiness itself, that's laid down as one of the aims of your republic? My father used to point that out. . . . So to you it might seem that I haven't pursued happiness very successfully. You might even say, if you knew, that once or twice it's pursued me and I've run away from it. That, of course, is unforgivable, and I think had I been born in America I should at least have stood my ground. . . . But as for calling my life – as a whole – *un*happy, I'd certainly say no to that. Oh, definitely no – at least nothing to complain of, mainly run of the mill. . . .

A little more wine? Good. . . . Things kept happening — the usual mixed bag of events — and they still are. This evening, for instance — how delightful! Such a long time, Anne, since I enjoyed myself so — er — so *unspeakably*. Meeting you last night was quite an event — for which, to be fair, I have to thank my son, haven't I, and the fact that he was so willing to deceive his father! Unscrupulous but — in the circumstances — very fortunate. And not silly. Oh no. Love can be many things, but that isn't one of them. People who say so have never known it — or else have forgotten it. I was a few years older than Gerald when I first had the experience, and the girl — she was actually younger than he is now. There were people then who said it was silly. I didn't think so, and I've never thought so since."

"What became of her?"

"She married somebody else — and happily, I believe."

"You also married somebody else?"

"Yes. And that was happy too — until — "

"I know."

"Gerald again the informer?"

"Yes, if you put it that way."

"I hope, then, he also told you — though he could hardly have remembered — what a remarkable woman my wife was. She was great fun and she had courage and loyalty and she knew how to get her own way with people. She helped me tremendously in my work. She . . ." The waiter came and took his order for another bottle of wine. He had drunk very little. He went on smoothly, but as if it were not what he had been going to say: "She usually stopped me from making a fool of myself. . . . Now it's your turn. . . . I mean, to talk."

"All right." She smiled. "What shall I talk about?"

"Yourself. I know so little about you. For all I know you're . . ." He tried to think of a way to finish the sentence. ". . . you're engaged to a Texas oil millionaire."

"No. . . . But how did you know I was an editor?"

"I asked at the hotel desk. I found out all I could about you."

"I wouldn't like you to get a wrong impression. It's a children's magazine and I'm really a teacher. . . ."

He got back to his room about one o'clock, which was much later than usual during the period of the Conference. But he felt refreshed and did not plan to hurry the ritual of the last drink alone and the half hour of pottering over his diary and letters. As always after an evening out in good company he missed Jane. "Now there's the kind of girl you ought to have married," she had said, in joking self-disparagement on a very few occasions; but the peculiar thing was that she had had a rare knack of saying it about the right – or at least not the utterly wrong – women. There had been Clara Delagny at Santiago, and the German baroness at the Gismondi party at Villefranche. . . . It had been fun, evaluating them with Jane, who knew so much and could make such good guesses even about what she didn't know. . . . So he mused now upon what Jane might have said about Anne Raynor, and was still musing a moment later when the telephone rang. It was exceptional to be called at such an hour and he hoped Bingay didn't want him for anything; he didn't feel like discussing business. But the thought that he might have to made him brace himself for the professional and official manner, so that when he heard and recognized the voice he was less taken aback than he might have been.

"M'sieur Anderson, a thousand apologies for disturbing you. . . . It is I, Palan. . . ."

"Yes?"

"I would like, if I may, to see you for a few minutes."

"You mean – *now?*"

"If you please."

"But I – I'm just about to go to bed."

"I am here, in the lobby downstairs."

"Well, I'll come down if it's really important, but – "

"No, no, I will come up. It will be easier that way. What is the number of your room?"

"It really *is* important?"

"Yes. May I come up now?"

There was a note in Palan's voice that intrigued Charles at least as much as it warned him; it sounded like a child's eagerness until one pictured Palan standing at the open desk within earshot of the hotel clerks, as he would be, presumably; and Charles found such lack of concealment far more puzzling than any amount of deviousness. That, he reflected, was the besetting neurosis of his profession; when a man did anything straightforwardly one was always suspicious. An obscure distaste for the neurosis made Charles answer: "All right. Come up. Three-three-four."

A measure of excitement gained on him during the short interval of waiting. It was, he knew, the result of his evening with Anne; it had infected him with a curious sense of new adventure, of desire to step boldly where normally he would have been circumspect. He warned himself, but even the warning only added to the inward excitement. Presently he heard footsteps along the corridor. Assorted wisps of memory from a hundred spy and detective novels came to him as he went to the door. Bingay would certainly think he was doing a foolish thing. Suppose Palan were not alone? One heard fantastic stories of what those people were capable of. . . . Anyhow, he opened the door, and Palan *was* alone, looking no more fearsome than he always would at that hour, for he was one of those men whose beards grow fast and dark.

"*Merci, mon ami. J'espère que vous n'êtes pas fatigué.*"

"Not too much, but I shall need some sleep soon. . . . Come in – and please speak in English."

"*Si vous voulez.*" Palan walked across the room and pulled the blinds slightly aside at one of the windows overlooking the Place de la Concorde. Charles did not like this. "What are you looking for?" he asked rather sharply.

"To verify what I already guessed. One cannot go anywhere without someone watching."

"You mean *you* cannot. *I* can, I hope."

"Not always. You were watched tonight." Palan laughed. "*I* watched you, my friend. I saw you take the American girl to dinner at Rousellin's – the American girl who was supposed to have returned to America. You were there for four hours. Then you brought her back here, where she is staying also. Am I not right?"

Charles was on the point of becoming angry. "Look . . . you said you had something important to say. The way I spend my evenings is of no importance – except to me."

"She is a very charming girl." Palan slumped into an easy chair and stretched his legs. "Do you remember, M'sieur Anderson, last night you invited me here for a drink, but I permitted myself to take a rain check."

"A *what?*"

"I beg your pardon – an American word, meaning that one expects on a later occasion the pleasure one has previously declined."

"All right, but I have only whisky."

"Excellent."

As he was pouring it Charles could not repress the instincts of the host. "I hope you don't mind Irish. The flavor is perhaps an acquired taste."

Palan took it, sniffed, swallowed, and nodded. "It has my full approval." He swallowed again. "I must explain that I did not follow you tonight with any sinister intent. I merely wished to see you as soon as possible without interfering with any other engagement you had."

"That's all right. Anybody can follow me who wants to."

"You are, I am sure, quite proud of that. It is like your English boast that your policemen do not carry guns, and that your speakers in Hyde Park are allowed to say what they like. It is all so very true – up to a point. But where *is* that point?"

"Yes, indeed, since it's getting on for two o'clock and we resume our official discussions at eleven."

"M'sieur Anderson, you have come to the point yourself with

great accuracy. I do not think that I shall be resuming any official discussions."

Palan pulled out a case and chose a cigar, offering one to Charles.

"No, thanks. . . . What do you mean?"

Palan lit his cigar with deliberate slowness, but Charles was now tolerant, for he could detect emotion behind the movement and knew that everyone is entitled to some such technique of delay and self-control.

Palan said: "You who have made so many small jokes about me at the Conference – and of course I know you have – must now learn that the biggest joke of all is not *about* me, but *on* me. Simply this – that I have been recalled to my country."

Charles was silent, asking the question merely by the way he placed an ash tray at Palan's elbow.

Palan continued: "They are not satisfied with the way I have conducted its affairs at the Conference. They think I have not been strong enough."

"*What?*" In his utter surprise Charles was aware of a pleased puzzlement that anybody should think his own side had had even any degree of success, and an equally puzzled and sudden sympathy with Palan which, as he diagnosed it, he knew to be absurd. He exclaimed: "But that hardly makes sense! It's *my* country that should complain, not *yours!* Why, dammit, you've had your own way nine times out of ten in everything so far!"

"But you do not realize, M'sieur Anderson, that nine times is not enough for my country. It must be *all* the times. Anything less than that is failure. Of course you cannot understand that. You cannot understand the methods of the cold young men who are rising to the top. So I will tell you what will happen now that I have been recalled. They will send you one of them to take my place, and he will not give way even that tenth time. He will be like my son."

"Then the Conference will fail."

"It has already failed. Though it may continue for some time after my successor arrives."

"But how about your chief in all this? Surely he must back you up — you're under his direction — he can hardly let a subordinate be blamed — "

"You think he cannot?" Remember, M'sieur Anderson, that as a nation of innovators we are *capables de tout.*"

"But what's the evidence against you? If you'll accept a left-handed compliment, I think you've handled your side of things deplorably well."

"It is charming of you to say so. Such a testimonial at my trial might be of great help."

"You're not serious?"

"Or perhaps no, there may be no trial. I shall be liquidated without any."

"Oh, come now — It can't be so — so — "

"So *serious,* eh? You are now seeing the joke?"

"I must admit I — I mean, it's hard for me to — "

"Because naturally you are not afraid of being liquidated yourself?"

"*Me?* Good God, no."

"Your people do not do that sort of thing, as I am so well aware."

"Even if we did, I don't think Sir Malcolm and I would be in much danger. Responsibility for the failure of the Conference is so obviously not ours."

Palan considered this for a moment, then said half whimsically: "M'sieur Anderson, will you forget you are a diplomat for a moment and answer truthfully a very simple question?"

"I can't promise, but you can ask."

"All right. . . . Just this: If, by pressing a button, you could set off an earthquake to destroy my country, what would you do?"

Charles smiled grimly. "I wouldn't want to destroy your country, but if by pressing a button I could destroy your government I'd not only press it, I'd lean on it for an hour to make quite sure."

"So when you forget you are a diplomat, you become a schoolboy?"

"It was a schoolboy's question."

"Would you have answered it differently when you were one? Our Revolution took place when you were at school – how did you feel about it then?"

"So far as I can remember, everybody was most enthusiastic. We all hoped your country was going to become more like our own."

"And, of course, you could not set for us a higher standard."

"I daresay. We were very naïve. We still are. We're a naïve country."

"It is your rightful boast. Nothing else could have saved you in 1940. . . . But I wonder if our personal positions had been reversed – yours and mine, at that early age – I wonder if I should have been more like you, or you more like me?"

"I doubt the latter. I can't imagine myself dynamiting trains."

"Oh, but I can. Very easily. . . . Surely you will not admit that there is anything an Englishman cannot bring himself to do in an emergency? Why, you have even beheaded your king – a somewhat more barbarous regicide, would you not say, than the one you condemned us for recently? In our country yours has always had many admirers, including those who – returning the compliment, as it were – hoped that yours was going to become more like ours. Or does the idea of that shock you?"

"If you mean going Communist it doesn't shock me at all. I personally would be against it, but if it had to happen we might do a better job than your people have. Of course it wouldn't be the same job, and we shouldn't give it the same name. Your own melancholy example would guide us a lot in what to avoid, but besides that we have certain advantages – our civil service, for instance – reasonably efficient and free from corruption. Then too our traditions, which we should keep as intact as possible – and our constitution that so happily has no existence in any written document. After all, a thousand years' experience of making changes *is* rather a help in disguising them – next to the Papacy

I daresay we know more of the tricks of successful survival than any other institution in history."

"And all *this* . . . from *Stuffy Anderson!*"

After the initial shock Charles was neither so startled nor so affronted as he would have expected. He merely replied: "I suppose you overheard that somewhere."

"A few of your younger colleagues – speaking of you entirely without malice."

"I'm quite sure of that. Anyhow, it doesn't matter."

"Of course not. It was just their way of liquidating you."

"*What?* . . . Oh, nonsense – why, I've had that nickname for God knows how many years."

"Then God must also know how long ago you began to be liquidated, my friend. But as you say, it does not matter. Successful survival is what counts – more than victory."

"Successful survival, in this world, *is* victory."

"You are doubtless right – and that is another reason why the real joke is on me. . . . May I?" He put his hand to the whisky bottle, adding: "You said it is an acquired taste. I have already acquired it."

Charles smiled, but watched with some dismay while Palan poured himself a very generous amount. Palan then raised his glass with ceremony. "A toast. . . . Will you permit one?"

"If you like."

"A toast, then, M'sieur Anderson, to your country – where they liquidate you alive and imperceptibly, so that you can remain so useful as well as ornamental for such a long time."

"Palan, that's all very amusing, I'm sure, but I'm still in the dark about the real purpose of your visit at this time of night." Charles then realized he had dropped the prefix to Palan's name – with him a rather significant stage of intimacy. What he really wanted to convey, as a fellow professional, was that he was sorry for Palan's personal predicament; but as a diplomat he was much more skilled in expressing regrets he did not feel than those he sincerely did. He compromised, therefore, on a remark that could have any meaning Palan chose to give it. He said quietly: "It's very late – but don't let that discourage you."

Palan stirred restlessly, as if probed by one or other of the possible meanings, then put his hands to his temples in a sudden access of emotion. "M'sieur Anderson, have you ever – in your life – been *afraid* – of anything?"

"Why, of course."

"When? Of what?"

"During the war – in some of the air raids. And other times too."

"Did you ever – do you ever – have dreams in which you are afraid – and when you wake up you are afraid even to remember them?"

"I don't know about that, but I sometimes dream I'm at some important function without the right clothes. Embarrassing enough."

"Without the right clothes? And that is all?"

"Sometimes without any clothes. I think the psychiatrists would call it a recurrent anxiety dream. Most people have one kind or another – actors, I understand, dream of forgetting their lines – "

"And what kind do you suppose is mine?" Charles noticed that Palan's breathing had become heavy, as if he were under increasing stress – or else, perhaps, the half tumbler of whisky was beginning to take effect. "I will tell you, my friend. I will tell you of the dream I have had lately, time and time again." Palan leaned forward with hands clenching and unclenching. "I have dreamed that I am back in my own country, in the city of Gorki where I was born – Nizhni Novgorod it was in those days – but I am there again and it is today in my dream – No, it is not a dream, it is already a nightmare – I am there, and yet I cannot remember how I made the journey or what possessed me to do it – and I keep saying to myself in my nightmare: Why did you do it? Are you *mad?* Why are you here? There is no chance now that you will ever leave again – why did you come back? Why?

— Why? — *Why?*" Globes of perspiration swelled out on Palan's forehead as he repeated the word.

"But then you wake up and find yourself in Paris."

"For the time. But there is not much more time."

"When are you supposed to leave?"

"My replacement is due to arrive by air tomorrow. I am expected to return by a plane that leaves tomorrow also."

"Expected to?"

"You said 'supposed to.' I said 'expected to.' What we both mean is 'ordered to.' . . . After tomorrow, if I am still in Paris, I shall have burned my boats. Perhaps I have already begun to do that. There were men in the street just now . . . and after all, it would not be surprising. . . . I have been careless at times — I have the old kind of brain, the European kind, the brain that slips its leash and scampers off for adventure and the fun of things. . . . I have perhaps laughed too much . . . and you may have noticed, M'sieur Anderson, that in your excellent company I am still able to laugh. So if they have followed me here there can be little doubt in their minds."

"But there are still some doubts in mine."

"I know. It has been rather sudden — I mean, my decision what to do. I did not reach it, finally, till I walked past Rocher's by chance last night. By chance. Utterly by chance. My body was wandering with my mind — not far, but suddenly too far ever to return. I was under a considerable strain, you understand, and to see you there so comfortable, so *gemütlich,* eating your ice cream like a good bourgeois — to see you there so — so *en famille* . . . for I took the lady to be attached to you and not to your son till you explained. But perhaps I was right after all. If so, I congratulate you. Only in America could anyone so charming be still unmarried. It is a great country and they are a great people. Just think — they call this city Paris, France, in order to avoid any possible confusion with Paris, Texas, and Paris, Illinois."

Charles smiled. "I think your mind's still wandering. Let's get back to the point. Where were we?"

"In the Paris streets. You cannot imagine what my emotions were. I had walked for hours — and miles."

Charles said quietly, as to himself: " 'It is not many miles to Mantua, no further than the end of this mad world.' "

"Pardon?"

"A quotation . . . nothing . . . *my* mind was doing it then. . . . Go on."

"There is no more to say. I am just waiting . . . for courage . . . to destroy by a single act the work and faith of a lifetime."

"Perhaps the faith, at least, is already destroyed."

"Yes . . . dissolved in fear."

"And disappointment. I don't think, Palan, fear alone would have brought you."

"You are kind to say that. It is why I have come to you instead of Sir Malcolm — a whim, I admit — just as the condemned man in one of your English prisons is allowed to choose what he wants for his last breakfast — how truly civilized that is! . . . Forgive me — I am overwrought, near the breaking point, and at such a time I cannot help seeming to take these matters lightly."

"I understand. I'm a little bit like that myself."

"I have noticed it, and it makes you *simpatico* — whereas I do not find Sir Malcolm *simpatico*."

Charles could not repress a sharp twinge of pleasure, for he too had never found Sir Malcolm *simpatico*. He said: "Sir Malcolm's indisposed, anyway, so perhaps — "

"Perhaps it is even *en règle* then, as well as a whim, that I should put myself in your hands?"

"In *my* hands?"

Palan bowed slightly. "If you do not object, m'sieur."

"Oh, not at all, not at all." Charles muttered the formula with which an Englishman sloughs off anything that causes him too little concern — or too much. As he did so he returned Palan's glance levelly and with a good deal of shrewdness. The situation was clearly of a kind he had read about lately, in newspapers and books and also in official reports; it had not happened to him before, but it had to a few others, though perhaps never so disconcertingly as to that Scottish nobleman when Rudolf Hess suddenly dropped into his back garden. . . . Charles said, as casually as he could to cover the flurry of his thoughts: "Very well, Palan . . . but, of course, you know I can't promise anything officially – I'll have to talk to Sir Malcolm tomorrow, and he'll no doubt refer the matter to London. . . . Though, naturally, if there's anything on your mind I'm at your service for as long as you want – all night if necessary."

"So now at last you are willing to lose your sleep?"

"In a good cause – always. Do you mind if I jot down a few things as you talk?"

"You evidently take it for granted that I have much to say."

"I would assume so, yes. You'd hardly expect us to accept your *bona fides* without some more – or perhaps I should say – some *less* tangible evidence than yourself in person."

"Not only *simpatico* but a smart cookie."

"*What?*"

"American for clever chap. You should learn American – might be useful someday." And then, as if a breaking point had actually been reached, Palan's mouth became shapeless and speechless for a moment, while his eyes could only stare strickenly. Charles said, with sudden compassion: "I've no authority to say this, but if I were you I wouldn't worry about catching that plane tomorrow."

"Or about *not* catching it?"

"Perhaps that's what I really meant. Because surely there comes a time when counting the cost and paying the price aren't things to think about any more. All that matters is value – the ultimate value of what one does."

"That has been your philosophy?"

"I've tried to make it so."

Palan mopped his forehead and Charles waited, feeling he had said all he could to convey those of his emotions that were both expressible and permissible. After a long pause, Palan said: "I beg your pardon. I am in control now." He moved his hand again to the bottle. "May I – once more?"

"Certainly." But Charles took it and began to fix the drink this time – a much less potent one. While he was so engaged he said quietly: "So you were born at Nizhni Novgorod."

"You know the city?"

"I've never been there. It used to have a big fair every year, didn't it?"

"Oh yes. The Nizhni Novgorod fair was famous all over the world. In those days. But not any more. Nothing is the same any more."

"No, I suppose not." Charles handed him the glass. "Don't gulp it now. It's whisky, you know – not ice cream."

Perhaps because this was the feeblest of all the jokes that had passed between them, they both laughed immoderately, seeking to relieve the tension that had gripped them and was also drawing them together. Then Palan said: "Before I begin to talk seriously . . . one more toast – to *ourselves* – to the stuffy shirt and to the old hothead. . . . The one not so hot, as they say in America, and the other – perhaps – not always so stuffy. . . ." He raised his glass. "I take it that the nickname is from the phrase 'stuffy shirt,' is it not?"

"You mean *stuffed,*" Charles corrected. "No, nothing to do with it at all – at least, not in origin. But never mind . . . let's get to work." He raised his own glass and muttered "Cheers" or something that remotely sounded like it, then drew a notebook and pencil from a drawer of the desk.

Late one night a week later Charles wrote from his room at the Crillon:

My dear Anne,

I daresay you'll have seen from your *Times* and *Herald-Tribune* that *l'affaire* Palan has become public. It's pretty big news in the English and European papers, and my name has been given some prominence – more, in fact, than a minor diplomat could expect or desire. I must say it seems odd that after a lifetime of doing my job with fair success and no publicity at all I should suddenly achieve headline fame (or is it notoriety?) because an allegedly reformed character calls me *simpatico* and gives me the kind of eulogy generally reserved for obituaries. Of course the situation, as well as being politically gratifying, has caused some private amusement among our own people, but I shall hope to live it down if only Palan will stop giving interviews. However, the whole thing is probably no more than a nine days' wonder, though it will give me something extra to put in my book – which, by the way (and doubtless as a result), Macmillan has tentatively agreed to publish. So I really must begin work on the thing soon.

The new man they sent over to take Palan's place is just what he forecast – glum, grim, youngish, bald, and pink-cheeked, like a rather nightmarish baby. We have had our first clash already. Somehow, though, I don't think our people will waste much more time here – everything since the Palan defection has been really anticlimax. I shan't be sorry to get back to London again, especially now you are back in America. In a rather complicated way (which I shall perhaps have the chance of explaining to you some time) you yourself are at least partly responsible for the outcome of the Palan thing, though of course neither of us could have been even remotely aware of any such chain of cause and effect – any more than (I will also explain this to you some time) the monkey that bit the King of Greece in 1920 could ever have supposed he was changing the history of the world. On consideration the parallel does not seem too flattering, but I will let it stand since (after so much that Palan has said about me) my reputation as a *farceur* is well established. . . .

And now to more personal matters. . . .

Several months later Charles wrote from his flat in Knightsbridge:

My dear Anne,

Thanks for your congratulations. Of course it's just a routine thing they give you more or less automatically when you've been a certain amount of time in the Service. I'm rather surprised the American papers made any mention of it — it was only in small print even over here. No, it doesn't carry a handle, thank goodness. Like my father, who was Sir Havelock for forty years, I'm snobbish enough to feel that a knighthood would put one on a level with many people one wouldn't care about — though of course if I were ever offered it (which isn't, I think, any longer a good bet) I should probably rejoice in secret. Anyhow, the C.M.G. leaves me very happily plain mister — it's really nothing but a small enamel cross hanging on a red and blue ribbon just below the white tie when one wears tails — and nowadays, even in London, there are few such occasions. . . .

. . . Gerald has just gone back to school after a fine Christmas we had together in the Lake District, doing some of the easier climbs — easier for him, that is, with his six-foot reach. He's very well and happy and has got to know a girl of about his own age to whom I can only apply the adjective "strapping" in revenge for the one which, he reported, she bestowed on me — "spry." Now how do you like that? Am I spry? Gerald met her halfway up a mountain, or halfway down, whichever way you look at it, but the way he looks at it is that fate engineered the whole thing. Perhaps it did. She's a nice girl, anyhow. . . .

. . . and Palan continues to enjoy the favor that so often in this world seems to be granted to the one rather than to the ninety-and-nine. I understand he's already negotiating with Korda for the motion picture rights of his life story. . . .

. . . and I have the interesting news, which I hope will please you, that I shall soon be crossing the ocean for a short spell in Washington — nothing uniquely important except to me personally, since there'll be a chance to see you. I shall arrive in New York about the tenth of next month. . . .

. . . and now, before I send this off, may I add how much I . . .

When he had sealed and addressed the envelope Charles pottered about for a while, looking for that last little thing he would do before going to bed. He took out his notes for the book, but could think of nothing to add to them; then he pulled aside the curtains and looked down on the cars and buses cruising under the lights of a second postwar London in his lifetime. He felt that so many things had happened before, even though far differently, and the thing to do was perhaps just to sit by the window for a few minutes and remember how.